# A Falcon's Aerie

## Book Three of the Evaria Series

**Angèle Mort**

# The Tides
## *Kerell – Sea of the Goddess*

elene shifted cautiously towards the end of the bed, easing her body out from between the two sleeping men. The gentle rocking of the waves, which Selene had come to find most comforting, did not serve to lull her to sleep this night. Once free she placed one foot carefully in front of the other, expertly timing each step with the shifting of the boat. She removed her nightdress and pulled on her clothes in silence.

Xaiden shifted in what seemed the most spacious of hammocks, due to the fact that he shared it with no one. She held her breath. He merely groaned and turned sides, rather than waking as she had expected. Selene exhaled a gentle sigh with the turn of the water. She had insisted that they each take their night in the hammock in turn despite Xaiden's protests. Sharing the bed with two others was no worse than what she would endure at most inns. It was better perhaps, since there she would be forced to sleep between strangers every night.

Selene glanced back towards the bed to find that Cael had rolled over to fill the vacant space in her wake. She resisted the urge to laugh as his arm draped around Felan, for it was no secret that the two shared some small amount of hatred for each other. Before the next tilting of the floor, she was out the door and into the hall beyond.

The deck was quiet above. No clouds sullied the sky, leaving it bright with a full moon surrounded by unrecognizable patterns of stars. A lone sailor sat upon a barrel near the central mast, a burly fellow with a close-cut beard. She knew him only as Sky, for that was what the others called him. No true names were used on this voyage due to its nature. He offered no more than a nod as she passed him. It was a better greeting than most of his brethren would offer a Rakaii. If they found it odd the way Cael treated his marked ones, then they said nothing of it. She did her best to keep to her role when any of them were near enough to witness. Sky turned to stare out towards the horizon, paying her little heed. These nights she lay awake more often than not, so most of the sailors were well used to her presence.

Selene leaned over the railing. The wind blew warm here, even at night. It was scented, as always, of salty seaweed and the woodsy oils used upon the ship's deck. She had heard the captain say yesterday evening that they were nearing their destination; perhaps even so close as to be there by early this morning. Nervous excitement kindled within her at the thought.

The water below was as dark as cartographer's ink, yet was also peppered with small, glowing jellyfish that formed patterns as if to mirror the language of the stars. The wind whispered its song against the planks of the boat. It sounded much like voices, though perhaps it was a whimsy of her fatigued mind. Selene stepped lightly towards the bow of the ship, running her hand along the railing. There she stilled her breathing and listened. The wind did indeed seem to carry voices from the darkness beyond. They melded together in a strange, eerie song as she focused her hearing upon them.

She focused on the horizon. There was nothing to be seen in the distance, nor most suddenly in the waves below when she turned back to them. The jellyfish had moved on, perhaps into the depths for fear of morning's approach. Just then, movement drew Selene's attention. Something wet crept onto the railing several feet from where she lingered. It was no longer than a loaf of bread from a baker's shop, and it writhed like a captured snake. She pulled an oil lamp from a nearby barrel and inched forward to get a better look, but before she could come near enough to determine what the creature could be it slipped back from whence it had come. Curiosity begged her to search for it, for she had always held some interest in creatures of the sea.

Cael's consciousness blossomed within her mind only seconds before she caught sight of him. Wavy, brown hair shifted in an ever-present breeze of the ship's creation. She swept it away from his dark eyes as he drew near, though only after checking to be sure she was not within any of the sailors' view.

"What are you looking for?" He followed her gaze down the side of the ship.

"I'm not sure," she replied.

"That will make it difficult to find," he quipped.

"Here," Selene said, leading him to the place where the creature had been. The railing was wet, and a puddle of water larger than the spray of the calm sea would allow lay on the planks beneath. The reflection of her lamp's flame danced within it.

"What do you think it could have been?" she asked.

"All manner of strange things make their home in the sea. Simply because it hasn't been cataloged doesn't mean that it's dangerous."

"I never said that it looked dangerous," she corrected.

"Not aloud." He gestured to the twist of metal upon her forehead. "But your circlet betrays you."

"Perhaps it is mistaken."

"Unlikely," he said. "Lest you forget, I have access to all of your feelings, including that of trepidation."

"Not trepidation," she corrected. "Curiosity."

"Is that so?" A grin twisted his lips as he spoke.

"It is. Reading feelings through a circlet is an art, at least according to the most recent edition of *The Keeping and Husbandry of Rakaii*."

"There are days when I wish I had not disenchanted those books."

"If you hadn't, then how could I use their contents to irritate you?"

"My point exactly," he replied. "Speaking of which, they're coming."

With the sigh that followed his words both Xaiden and Felan appeared from below deck.

"Can you hear that?" Felan asked as he attempted to straighten his mass of blonde hair by running his fingers through it. He was dressed, but obviously hadn't bothered to take the additional time to search for a comb. "Sounds like singing."

"Oh good," Selene answered. "I thought I was losing my sanity from so many weeks at sea. Hearing voices on the wind."

"I hear nothing of the sort," Xaiden said with a furrow of his brow.

"Well, you are fairly old," Felan offered. "Perhaps your hearing is starting to fade."

Additional strands of grey had recently crept into Xaiden's otherwise dark beard and head of hair to join those few which were already present. To someone who did not know him as marked he could well be approaching his fiftieth year. To this day Selene had not been able to pry out of him how old he truly was.

A flash of Xaiden's irritation barreled through her. He quieted it almost immediately.

"I am not too old to best you in a duel, Felan."

If not for the brief sense of levity that touched her through the circlet, she would have thought him to be serious.

"It's a bit early in the day for a duel." Felan swept the offer aside with a laugh.

They all seemed in a fine mood, at least for the moment. It was for that reason that Selene swallowed her anxiety before it could turn on her. This moment was so like those of old, before betrayals and complications, and so she greedily desired to keep it for as long as she could. The long weeks at sea had done much to bring them together, though true forgiveness, if it was ever to materialize, would take a sight longer.

"What do you think, Cael? Too early for a duel?" Selene turned to find that he was no longer with the group, but rather a good way toward the bow of the ship, levering the top portion of his body over the edge to look into the water below. There could not be much to see, for although the fading of the stars told her that the sun would soon rise, the water still appeared dark from where she stood.

Cael waved them closer. "There was something here."

"That's what I was trying to tell you," Selene informed him. "And look, there's the puddle beneath just like the last one."

"Over there," Felan pointed to the railing on the other side of the ship, where something slimy glinted in the growing light.

Cael sprinted towards it.

"You two stay here," Xaiden ordered as he followed.

"Some things never change," Felan grumbled.

"I suppose not," Selene agreed.

"It's at the front now," Cael called as he slipped around the far side of the cabin and out of her view.

Selene leaned over the railing. Light was just beginning to touch the surface of the sea, coloring it from midnight to silver-blue. She watched the water splash against the sides of the ship as it sliced through the waves. Sea birds began to call as the light of the sun crested the horizon. It was only a few days ago that the birds had returned, for in the middle of the deep ocean there seemed to be none.

"The singing is getting louder," Felan remarked.

"Perhaps," she replied absently.

A slippery looking object several feet in width crested the water below her. It emitted a flash of speckled lights in shades of red as it disappeared beneath the waves.

"What kind of fish was that?" Felan asked. "It's odd that something so big would be so close to shore."

"It must still be fairly deep here for a ship of this size to sail without scraping the bottom," she reasoned.

"I suppose so." He was now uncertain, and anxious.

From where the first creature disappeared a new one emerged. It was long and moved like a snake. It came slowly from the depths, moving impossibly; straight up from the sea to reach above the railing with no effort. Its body was easily the girth of a water barrel, and no eyes lay where the head of the creature should rightfully be. The underside of its body was clad in bright red skin with row upon row of round, white disks like porcelain plates from a child's tea set. Selene spied over the railing, not daring to move too much for fear that the creature would strike her. The back end of it disappeared into the sea beneath.

"Should we run, or not move at all?" Felan whispered. Fear poured from him with as much strength as the wind that carried the sails above.

The creature pulled back into the water with terrifying speed.

She and Felan stepped away from the railing as one.

"Has it gone?" she asked.

"For the moment, at least," Felan replied as he calmed. "Do sea snakes get that large? Please tell me that they don't."

"It is something very odd indeed," she murmured. "It was shaped a bit like a snake, but I don't think it was one. It didn't seem to have eyes, or a mouth."

"At least with no mouth it can't bite us," Felan said as his eyes scanned the slowly brightening waters. "Not sure that means less danger, unfortunately. There are plenty of ways to die without being bitten."

"Thank you ever so much for reminding me," she replied. "Xaiden is just around the corner. Perhaps he'll know what it could be."

"What's he up to?" Felan pondered.

She thought at first that he spoke of Xaiden, but upon following Felan's gaze she realized that he was speaking of one of the crew. He was older, with tidy rows of black and gray braids lining his head. Selene had grown to like the man somewhat, although he never had much to say. He had released the ship's wheel and was headed down the stairs towards them. Had they done something wrong? They were not so close to the edge as to be in danger. Perhaps they had simply piqued his curiosity with their gathering.

Felan pressed his hands to his ears. "The song. It's so loud."

Selene could hear it; a myriad of voices pulsing, whispering, like putting one's ear to a seashell and hearing the song of the depths. At first it was nowhere near as loud as Felan pretended, but then all at once the volume increased. It felt as if her ears might rupture.

The crewman stopped near the edge of the boat, just next to where Selene stood. His usually expressive eyes betrayed nothing, and his pupils were so wide that the earthy brown layer outside of them could barely be seen. The singing ceased as he pressed his face close to Selene's ear. "You will be safe," he whispered.

Without warning, he climbed the railing and jumped overboard.

A brief moment of confusion gave way to panic as the man plummeted into the water below. Selene summoned her levitation ability. She pulled at the water where she had last seen him. He was nowhere to be found. "Why isn't he swimming to the surface?" The ship's crew were all excellent swimmers. It made no sense.

"Something is dragging him down," Felan said in a panic. "He's confused. He thinks that he's still on the ship but he's breathing in water." Felan's skin was pale in the growing light. "That's all I can hear."

"But where is he?" If she could get just a glimpse of him, she could pull him to safety.

"His mind has gone silent. You can't save him, Selene. He's gone."

At the far end of the ship a bell began to toll. It was a warning that she had only heard once before on their voyage, at a time when a storm rolled in the distance. This time there was no storm to be seen.

The crew. Felan's voice echoed through her mind. They're all thinking the same word. Sirens.

What does it mean? she asked.

Sailors poured from every hatch, bleary eyed and wobbly with sleep, but moving with increasing speed as their minds turned to waking. They began ripping short pieces of cloth from their shirts and stuffing them into their ears.

Something new caught Selene's attention. Creatures coated in pink and green algae took hold of the railing near where she stood. Not creatures, she corrected. Hands. They gripped tightly, pulling up the attached body. Pale, smooth skin was peppered here and there with scattered clumps of seaweed. Its face resembled a human, perhaps from afar. Its eyes and mouth were in the correct place, at least. There was no nose to speak of, nor ears upon its narrow face. A layer of scallops and barnacles coated the top of its head where hair should be. Several more creatures followed the first.

Felan pressed something into her hand. Two wads of twisted cloth. *For your ears.*

*But I don't hear anything,* she protested. The song had faded from her ears as the creatures pulled themselves aboard the ship.

One of the sirens wriggled smoothly towards her, leaving a pool of sea water in its wake. Algae crusted skin covered a human shaped torso, which transitioned smoothly to an eel-like fin beneath its belly. It had the appearance of a human in the way that the scales of a venomous snake resembled the ground beneath it. The sheen of its tattered tail took on the pink and yellow colors of the rising sun. Near human eyes considered her; pools of silver-blue cresting waves. Barnacles clustered in a line between them; their feather-like tentacles tasting the air.

They enthrall you with their song, Felan warned. We hear it through you. Selene, please!

"Sacred one," the Siren hissed. "One blessed by Tritan's kin." Its teeth were those of a predator, rows of jagged points.

By her circlet she knew that Cael and Xaiden were closing in on her position. They wanted her to flee, but she had no desire to do so. It was important, what this creature meant to say to her. It was all that mattered.

Nails of broken seashells reached for her. The familiar odor of salt and seaweed embraced her as the creature touched her face. "We release you from your bond."

It pulled the circlet from her head. Emptiness found her. A scream pierced her as she grasped for the emotions of the others and found nothing. She was alone.

"A slave no more," the siren whispered. "Worry not, for the kraken will not harm you. We bind her through our song."

The siren twisted around with the grace of a striking snake. It bit through a sailor's arm as he moved to pierce it with a jagged metal spear.

Selene tumbled over as the boat tilted. One of the eyeless serpents she had witnessed earlier was twisted around the railing. Its skin now flickered with spots like faerie light, shifting between patches of deep red and midnight blue. Another much larger one twisted towards the mast at the center of the ship. A man screamed as a third plucked him from the deck in mid-stride and pulled him into the water.

Selene scrambled for something to hold on to, but there was nothing to be found. The largest of the serpents had reached the mast. It wrapped itself around the structure and pulled. Selene slid as the boat tilted, gaining speed until her back met the railing with a thump. Barrels rolled past her and tumbled into the water. She turned and took hold of the railing. Beneath her lay not waves, but a behemoth monster which stole her breath. She realized at once that what she had thought to be individual serpentine creatures were actually part of a much larger animal. An eye, the yellow of sunflower petals, held a black pupil so large that she feared if she let go, she might fall through it and never return. The beast was larger than an elder dragon by far. Its body pulsed with waves of colored light as it struggled to pull the ship down.

A burst of cannon fire deprived her of her hearing, leaving a faint ringing sound in its wake. The ship righted itself without warning. She tumbled across the deck. Pain lanced through her leg as she struck the railing on the opposite side. Selene lay in wait as the ship ceased its rocking. After a moment she struggled to her feet. A massive knot of rope had wound its way around her arm as she fell. Selene fought to slip her fingers between the sections. If she could loosen it enough, then perhaps she could free herself. The beast was gone for the moment, but she had no doubt that it would return soon.

*Where are you?* Felan's voice found her mind through the clamor of screaming sailors and cracking wood.

Near the center of the ship, she replied. Against the railing. I can't get loose.

I'll come to you.

He appeared from somewhere behind her, as did several tentacles, which slithered onto the deck. They were much closer to her legs than she would have preferred.

"My arm is trapped," she explained. "I don't suppose you have a knife?"

"No, unfortunately," Felan said as he pulled at the rope. "We have to get off of the ship before they sink it. Cael says that sirens don't often leave survivors."

"Is that supposed to be helpful?"

"Our best chance is to get into the water. We can swim for shore."

"It's a long way," Selene noted as she gazed towards the only land she could see. It was but a line near the horizon. She was a decent swimmer, as she had grown up in a fishing village, but she had never attempted such a distance.

"I loosened it a little," Felan informed her. "Try and slide your arm out."

Selene twisted her arm back and forth, inching it slowly from the rope's grasp. "I think I'm nearly free," she said at last. With those words the ship leaned suddenly towards the waves. The rope snapped tightly, trapping her once again. Wood splintered beneath her feet. Felan disappeared from view. Tepid water invaded her lungs as she tumbled into the sea.

# The Forgotten
## *Kerell – Sea of the Goddess*

*Where are you?* Felan's voice echoed through her head as she descended slowly through the water.

She found that she could not form a reply as her lungs begged for air.

It was quiet in the depths. The only sound that breached the water was the quickening of her heart. She continued to tug at the rope, but it refused to release. A flash of movement caught her vision on the left. She turned, but it was gone. Then came another, on her right. The rope loosened its grasp upon her flesh, pulled apart by some ghostly thing that refused to remain locked in her vision.

Something slick brushed against her skin. It wrapped itself around her chest. She struggled against it, but her efforts proved futile. Her body ached for air. Without warning she was lifted from the water. She gasped as she crested the surface.

Selene gazed down as she coughed. The creature's tentacles encompassed her. They wrenched her aside, only to release her. She tumbled down through the waves once again. The tide pulled at her. Which way was the surface? Panic compressed her lungs.

Rough hands took hold of her, one on each arm. Barnacles scraped against her skin as the Sirens dragged her away from the light. *Open your lungs*, her body begged, as if a breath of water would be as useful as one of air.

*Do not, lest you wish to drown*, a voice in her head replied. It was as light and high in pitch as the screech of a hawk.

Selene's vision began to darken. *Air!* her body begged one last time as the pressure around her grew.

*Take the left path to safety*, the unknown voice in her head instructed.

Something was pulling on her legs. *Please, no!*

You owe us no debt.

The sirens released her. Fear pierced her chest once more, so strong as to overwhelm the pain in her lungs. She was dragged downward, and then suddenly back up. She struggled to swim but could go only where the current swept her. Then, with a sudden burst, she met air. She pulled it desperately into her lungs. Her hands passed over rock slick with algae until at last one of them met something solid. With great effort she heaved herself from the water. She could do no more than lay gasping upon the rocks while the world circled around her.

After a few minutes she was able to sit up without fear of passing out. A few more slid by and she could stand. It was so dark that her eyes struggled to adjust. Once they finally obeyed, she was greeted with two paths. *Take the left path to safety*, the sirens had advised. But her mind told her otherwise. The one on the right looked like it went upward, while the left path tilted back down to the depths.

Perhaps it is a trick, her mind offered. Many creatures of the sea enjoyed toying with their prey before consuming it. Sirens should be no different. After a moment's thought, she started along the path that led upward.

The tunnels of the cave held as much water as tidal pools lingering near the shore. Thick strands of seaweed coated every surface, and strange creatures with fronds like the downy feathers of a goose were peppered here and there amongst it. They waved as if caught in a current and emitted a faint purple light, which was barely enough to see by. Their movement gave Selene the uneasy feeling that she had never left the water. Perhaps this cave flooded with the shifting of the tides? She shivered with cold and went to wrap her arms around her chest. As she stepped down her foot found something slicker than algae. She tumbled backward and stuck out a hand to catch herself. There was nothing to hold. Her rear hit the ground. The seaweed did nothing to cushion her fall, spongy though it seemed.

Selene pressed one hand to the ground in order to stand. She gasped as pain, sharp and piercing, lanced her palm. Her eyes caught movement as she lifted her hand to examine the wound. A cluster of the purple, downy creatures emerged from the twisted tubes in which they dwelt. It was one of the few groups that lay upon the floor rather than the wall above, and she had placed her hand directly upon it. Her palm now burned as if she had put it to flame.

Exhausted though she was, Selene pulled at her healing ability. What she sensed was not seared flesh but rather hundreds of holes, so miniscule as to seem of little consequence. It was doubtful that she would have been able to see them, even in a brightly lit room. She healed them anyway. Her hand continued to burn. *Poison*, her mind warned. The thought echoed, alone in her head. How strange it seemed that she had been alone in her mind for years and thought nothing of it. Stranger still that now she was free of the circlet and yet so desperately yearned for the thoughts of her companions. *They are alive*, she assured herself. *Keep going. You'll surely find them.*

Selene looked first this time before putting her hand against the ground. Her eyes must have finally adjusted to the darkness, for she noticed that coin sized creatures like rounded slugs darted through the strands of seaweed. An eel, speckled like a sparrow's egg and the length of an arrow, struck out from between the strands to grab one and swallow it whole.

"With my luck you're poisonous too," she said aloud.

The creature paused to consider her. It did not seem afraid in the least despite their difference in size.

"No need to bite me, if that's what you're thinking," she assured it. "I've enough toxins in my flesh as it stands."

Selene watched the eel slip into a puddle of water behind her. It was water that had not been there a moment ago. *Better move with more speed*, she thought as she stood. Her hand now throbbed like freshly burned flesh and a strong, stinging pain extended up her arm. Her healing ability did nothing to soothe it.

The water rose silently; eating the narrow tunnel almost as quickly as she could put it behind her. Her feet pulled up with much greater effort than was usual, as if she was trekking through deep mud rather than strands of seaweed with rock beneath.

Water now pooled above Selene's ankles. Perhaps the Sirens' advice was a trick of another sort altogether. Perhaps there was no way out of this place regardless of which path she chose.

The walls, which thus far had been within arm's reach, fell suddenly from view as the tunnel she had been traversing widened into a room. The sound of spindly feet clicked through the darkness. Crabs, she reasoned, though her mind conjured images of cave dwelling spiders and refused to let go of it no matter how earnestly she begged.

Selene turned to go back, with hopes of avoiding the creatures from which the sounds came, but there was no longer a path to be found. She struggled to slow her breathing and pressed forward. The ground was flat and smooth here, though still covered in seaweed. The walls were pale and oddly rounded, like the inside of a bowl. No venomous feather-creatures lurked here, at least not that she could see, but rather the seaweed itself glowed a pale green, providing light in their stead.

Selene moved forward cautiously. The floor was becoming rounded as well, and she had no desire to fall once again. Green light swayed against the ceiling as seaweed thick with a coating of slime sloshed against her feet. Her toe struck something hard. She cursed and wished she had thought to put on her boots before leaving the ship's cabin. Though perhaps it did not matter. In her struggle they would have likely been lost to the sea.

She looked down to find a rock, perfectly round and a bit larger than a fully-grown chicken. Gazing upon it brought a strange sense of familiarity. "Of course it looks familiar," she chided herself aloud. After all, she had seen plenty of rocks in her time. Fatigue could cause odd effects of the mind, and it was certainly no ally of clear thinking.

A strange hissing sound met her ears. She squinted into the darkness. There was nothing but seaweed and water, the latter of which now pooled to reach halfway between her ankle and knee. The hissing noise sounded again, closer this time. Something tickled her ear. She raised her hand instinctively to wipe it away but found nothing there. A wisp of air chilled her left arm and the side of her face. Perhaps the path to the surface could be found in that direction.

Selene turned, stepping carefully, for she had certainly learned her lesson about touching unknown objects in this realm. More rocks lay ahead, troubling obstacles upon a slick and poorly lit floor. She successfully stepped over one, and then the next. She could now see what must be an opening in the wall, marked by a short strip of cavern where no luminous seaweed grew. It was gone the moment she caught sight of it, replaced by an odd sheet of silver coins. *Not coins*, her mind corrected. *Scales*.

The creature turned on her with speed impossible for its size. Its gaping mouth rushed at her head. Selene stumbled backward, more by accident than instinct. The water now seemed warm as it enveloped her skin. She pulled a ragged breath and sunk beneath it. Her head bumped painfully against what she now realized must be an egg in a clutch of its brethren. The creature flowed above her. Its body moved as a silk flag would in the wind, if flags were prone to anger and known to have any particular purpose in mind.

Can this be how dragons look in Kerell?

The green glow of the seaweed that now surrounded her head flashed across the monster's scales as it drifted above her. It rounded to turn and strike again.

Water pulled heavily upon Selene as she stood. Her attempt to run was far from successful. The dragon turned with the speed of a saltsnake. It grabbed her arm with its upturned mouth and lifted her from her feet. The creature flung her to the far side of the cavern. Pain lanced through her side as she struck the wall. She landed roughly in the water beneath.

Selene gasped as she broke through the surface. After what seemed an eternity, she managed to regain her footing and stand. The water now came up past her hips. Her eyes passed over the walls of the cavern, searching desperately for the opening she had seen. At last, she spotted it. Unfortunately, the dragon had also spotted her. It lunged at her as she lunged at the opening in the wall. The creature struck her back, sending her surging forward. She landed hard on the upward tilt of rock at the mouth of the tunnel.

Selene scrambled upward, crawling frantically until she felt she must be out of the creature's sight. She squeezed against the wall, trying desperately to catch her breath. Her lungs still ached from the water that had invaded them. The dragon pressed its mouth through the opening. Two feelers, like that of a catfish, swept the sides of the tunnel around her, nearly touching her feet. By the grace of the Spirits, it then turned away. As suddenly as it had appeared, the dragon was gone.

*It was only protecting its eggs*. The thought was of little comfort when also considering that she had nearly been killed.

There was no time to rest. The water pushed steadily upward. Selene wobbled to her feet and continued on.

There was no way to tell how long she had walked, for no clues to the passing of time breached the cave. The spot of light that flashed against her vision was as unexpected as the warm breeze that accompanied it. Was it true, or a figment of her exhaustion? It spurred her legs to movement regardless. The light grew larger as she walked, and the air warmer. Seaweed gave way to rough, clean stone, then to soft sand. It was so bright outside the cavern that her vision was blurred. Her eyes stung with pain. She blinked to clear them and was rewarded with a view of turquoise waves tipped in white, which washed onto a bed of pristine, golden sand. There were no living creatures within sight. No sign of any ship marred the perfect ripples of ocean water.

Selene dropped to the ground. She lay atop the sand for a moment, enjoying the warmth upon her skin.

I shouldn't stay here. Not out in the open.

Her clothing was heavy with water and coated in sand. Every small sound and feeling, every large ache and pain, came rushing to greet her now that her heart had slowed. The mere thought of healing anything with her latent ability caused her head to throb. Scarlet lines of raw skin crossed her left hand where she had grabbed the rope. The right was swollen such that her fingers resembled boiled sausages. Pain pierced her skin as she brought some ocean water up to rinse the oddly bright, rippling marks upon her palm. With a thought, clean flesh consumed them. The marks returned before the next wave could lap against her feet.

*And now?* her mind asked as if it expected an answer.

Although the sun had barely risen a quarter of the way across the sky it was already hot enough to cause discomfort. She had learned from listening to the conversations of the sailors that the land of the Kerell was always warm in nature, with temperatures year-round to match those of mid-summer in Evaria. She should concentrate on finding fresh water and shade, in that case, if she wished to survive.

To each side of her stretched a long yet narrow beach of sand that nearly glowed beneath the rays of the sun. The end of the beach was met by a forest; dark and filled with a variety of broad-leafed plants. Voices of unfamiliar birds and the occasional growl of what might be some larger creature echoed from the foliage. She kept to the area of damp sand just beyond the waves as she walked. It was easier walking there than upon the dry portion beyond it, which sucked at her feet and attempted to burn them all at once. Light footprints in the sand were erased as the waves flowed over them. The movement helped her believe that she was accomplishing something, although in truth she had no idea where she was heading.

Selene?

The word startled her so much that she nearly tripped. She glanced up ahead and caught sight of him. She was relieved, but then panic caught her once again. He was alone.

"You survived." It was a ridiculous thing to say, yet she could think of nothing else in the moment.

"So did you," he replied. The man looked as disheveled as she felt, although no looking glass lay within grasp to confirm such a fact.

"The others?" she asked.

"I'm happy to see you alive as well," Felan replied with a scowl. "You find me and that's all you think to ask?"

It caused her to want to start an argument, though perhaps it was the stress of the day rather than his selfish words. "You know full well that's not how I meant it," she said instead.

From behind his ear trickled a thin line of blood.

"Your circlet," she whispered. "Did the sirens remove it?"

"No," he replied. "It just fell out a moment ago."

"It fell out," she echoed in dismay.

"Where did you come from?" he asked before she could say anything more. "I've been up and down this beach so many times and found nothing."

"There's a cave a little way back. There was one, I mean. I suppose it's flooded until low tide at this point." She bit at her lower lip. It tasted mildly of sea salt. "Perhaps Cael released you?"

"Is there another option?" Felan asked as he brushed sand from his arm.

Selene's stomach turned. "There is one, yes."

"What is it?"

The words left her mouth with great difficulty. "That he's dead."

Felan's expression was unreadable. "What happened to your hand?"

"Doesn't matter."

"Yes, it does," he countered. "Why haven't you healed it?"

"It's some sort of toxin," she replied. "I can't. Did you feel anything when your circlet dropped?"

"No, I don't think so. I was busy attempting not to drown, so you'll have to forgive me for not paying better attention."

"I'm simply trying to get some more information," she huffed.

He pulled an irritated breath. "What sort of thing should I have felt?"

"Islyr told me that when a circlet holder dies it feels like you're dying with them."

"Well," he asked cautiously. "What did you feel when Damaeus died?"

"Nothing," she replied. "But he was already a bloodsoul when he placed my circlet. He was technically already dead."

Sand sprayed from Felan's hair as he scratched the top of his head. "To be honest, I was in and out of consciousness for a little while. I'm not sure."

"Can't you call out for them?"

"What makes you think that I haven't been doing so since I woke?" he said shortly. "Selene, I'm exhausted."

"You're right," she admitted after what might have been too much silence. "I'm sorry, Felan."

"Can we focus on us for a moment? Xaiden and Cael can fend for themselves."

It was then that she noticed that one side of his face was beginning to form layers of bruised color. She healed it, which elicited a startled yelp from him.

"Apologies," she said as she watched him clutch the previously injured area. "I should have asked you first."

"It's ok," he replied. "I just wasn't prepared for it."

"Have you found any signs of civilization?" She found it difficult to change the subject but did so anyway as it seemed to be needed.

He was silent a moment. "No," he replied finally. "What should we do?"

Her mind was struggling to catch up with all that had recently occurred. "We should try to find a source of fresh water first. The weather is already hot, and by the sun it's only late morning."

"Sounds reasonable enough." Felan pointed in the direction from which he had come. "I saw some cliffs back there. Maybe there's a waterfall or a river that feeds into the sea."

It was better than anything she could come up with. "Alright. But let's stay on the beach for now if we can. I don't know much about the creatures in these sorts of woods."

"The forest doesn't look easy to walk through, anyway." Felan looked down at her feet. "And you don't have any boots."

"I wasn't planning on doing much walking when the day began." She made a mildly successful attempt at keeping the bite from her tone.

The sea water that drenched Selene's clothes dried quickly as they walked, leaving an itchy film of salt and sand upon her skin. They reached the cliffs that Felan had seen but found no fresh water flowing from them. The cliff's edge ended farther out into the water than she cared to swim, blocking them from continuing along the shore. They sat in the shade of a cluster of trees to rest, for she found that she still felt dizzy and weak. The respite was short lived. The day grew rapidly warmer as she had surmised it would. What little shade was present disappeared, devoured by the movement of the sun, and then what skin was exposed to it began to burn.

"Look," Felan said, putting a hand up to his eyes. "A ship."

Indeed, a rather large ship sailed in the distance. It was much too far away to catch anyone's attention upon it, which seemed for the best as it was likely to be filled with Kerell mages. They watched it until it disappeared from sight behind what had to be the most inconveniently placed cliff she had ever encountered.

"Probably a port over there," Felan guessed. "Could you fly up and see?"

"Not with those," Selene replied, pointing to a colony of squabbling sea birds at the edge of the cliff. They were twice again the size of a raven and possessed hooked, predatory beaks. She watched as one snatched a smaller bird from the air.

"We might be able to walk there," he suggested. "Not sure what we'll do once we arrive, though."

"I suppose that's our best chance, but I don't fancy walking into an entire town of Kerell. We haven't got our circlets now. We're no better than stray dogs to them."

"I'm no better than a cur," he corrected. "You're probably more like a prized hunting dog loosed from its master. I'd bet that female marked ones are as rare here as they are in Evaria. They'll drown me and put you up for sale to the highest bidder."

"I think I'd rather be drowned," she replied.

"Let's try for neither."

"We should get off of the beach and find some more shade," Selene suggested. "I feel as if I'm being roasted over a spit."

They glanced into the depths of the forest as one.

"I do remember a few things from the books Cael gave me," Selene offered as she made her first cautious steps into the woods. Sticks and leaves crunched uncomfortably beneath her bare feet. It was slightly cooler than the beach, but perhaps only due to the lack of direct sunlight.

"I might be able to recognize some edible plants upon seeing them." She hoped that the plants here were not like those at home, in that there were many poisonous ones which looked similar to their edible counterparts.

"That's not very reassuring," Felan said in a sour tone.

She realized then that the books were a bit of a sore subject for Felan, due to what had happened when he'd delivered them.

"About that, Felan," she began. "Whatever you thought was happening with Cael and I when-"

"I don't really care to know," he interrupted.

"You don't?" she asked without thinking.

"No," he shoved the stem of a nearby plant aside with such force that it issued an audible snap. "Most of the things that happened in the past are of little consequence. You learn that when your memory is taken from you."

Selene stopped the conversation then, for it caused an uncomfortable pain to form in her stomach when thinking of Cael. She was tired and hungry besides, which was making her more irritable than she should rightfully be.

Moisture danced in the air here, swirling thickly around all manner of strange looking plants in garish colors. Purple, spiky ones clung in every available crevice like sea urchins in a tidal pool. They were highly toxic if eaten, that much she could remember, as were the bright pink 'faerie cups' which clustered around them. The latter held what looked like tiny droplets of water, which were actually sticky traps to lure insects as prey.

"They're appropriately named, I guess," Felan noted.

"Felan," she began.

"I know, I'll stay out of your mind. I'm sorry. It was too quiet. Your mind is so unusual. It's entertaining."

She stopped briefly to scowl at him.

"Poor phrasing," he said. "I only meant that your mind rarely stills. One idea springs to another in an endless chain of thoughts that most would not dream to connect to each other. It's interesting, to say the least."

"You've not convinced me that's a compliment," she said. "That aside, I suppose I don't mind you rummaging around in there as much as I did before." She could not help but think it odd that he would find her thoughts entertaining. "When I was disconnected from Damaeus I felt relief, but this time I just feel empty, like I've been abandoned. It's like I'm not whole without the three of you."

"I feel the same," Felan admitted. "Though if we do find Cael and you relay that to him then I will never forgive you."

Selene managed a weak laugh, and her stomach joined it, grumbling from lack of food. "My stomach feels as if it might consume itself soon," Selene said.

"Mine too," Felan commiserated. "Do you remember what any of the edible plants in Xaiden's book looked like? If you picture the drawing in your mind, I could help you spot them."

She pictured the few she could remember.

"Are you certain that brown one is edible?" he asked. "It looks as if it's coated in hair."

"Xaiden said that you're only supposed to eat the inside," she informed him. "And that it tastes much better than it looks."

"Don't think I've seen any of those around," he said. "Any edible creatures? I might be able to catch something in animal form."

"Nothing like what we have at home. Mostly birds and reptiles here. Snakes and the like." The few creatures she had caught a glimpse of so far had disappeared too quickly for her to get a proper look.

"What about that thing?" Felan pointed to a furry creature who hung upside down by its tail from the branches above. The animal's body, including its oddly long arms and legs, were coated in gray fur which faded to white near its extremities. It regarded her with a bald face and intelligent eyes that were much too human for her liking.

"Doesn't look like something I'd want to eat," Selene informed him as the creature swung back and forth on its branch. "We'd never catch it anyway. Wolves can't climb trees last I checked."

"That's not what I meant," Felan huffed. "Look at what it holds in its paws."

The animal took a bite from the round, yellow item as Felan spoke. Juice dripped from its chin as it tilted its head to one side.

"Some kind of fruit?" she asked.

"I hope it is," Felan replied.

"Doesn't seem very afraid of us," Selene remarked. "Every other animal I've seen so far has vanished as soon as I spot it."

The animal swung up to perch upon the branch. It watched Selene and Felan with curiosity as it finished its lunch.

"I don't see any more fruit around here. Maybe if we follow him, he'll lead us to wherever he got it."

"I suppose he might," she replied doubtfully. "Unless he's no longer hungry."

"It's a better plan than wandering aimlessly through the forest until we die."

Selene found that she could not disagree, so they waited. After throwing the pit of the fruit aside the creature licked its paws clean, then began leaping through the treetops. Although it was agile enough in nature that it could easily have lost them, the animal never strayed too far, nor did it move any more quickly than they could manage through the underbrush.

"Almost seems as if it's waiting for us," Felan noted as the creature stared at them from above.

They walked until Selene feared that her feet would carry her no more. It did not help that most of the journey seemed to be uphill, though only slightly. The birds of the forest were much louder here than at home, and so brightly colored that they seemed like something pulled from a faerie story.

Selene did not hear the rush of water until they were nearly upon it. She had spent so much time looking either down at her aching feet or up at the strange animal that when they finally came upon a clearing it took her mind a moment to register this new space. The full force of the sun hit her, overwhelming her eyes. As they adjusted, she found a lake which could easily have fit a half-dozen horses end to end. The edge was ringed with thick foliage, leaving an area of rock and sand of perhaps five feet between woods and water most of the way around. The source of the rushing sound was revealed to be a small waterfall, which poured from a cliff at the opposite side of the lake.

"Where did he go?" Felan asked.

Selene could no longer catch sight of the animal that had led them there. Not that it mattered to her overly much. Her need for water was far stronger than her hunger at the moment. Sweat drenched her clothing after the walk, and she so desperately wished for something to drink that her tongue felt like a strip of cured meat. Yet despite all that had occurred, her mind still was not addled. Predators often waited near water sources in the hopes of trapping prey. She stepped cautiously out of the forest and onto the lakeshore. She could not imagine how any of the animals here managed to survive, given the amount of noise they made. The chorus of howls and squawks rendered it impossible to hear if any large predators might be approaching.

A bird with feathers of red and yellow as bright as the tunic of a minor lord landed near the lake less than a few feet from where she stood. It sidled cautiously over and took a few sips of water. Perhaps it was safe after all.

"That one doesn't seem afraid of us either," Felan remarked.

"You're right," she agreed. "Perhaps so few people come here that it doesn't perceive us as dangerous."

"Or it senses your affinity," he suggested.

"What about your affinity? Shouldn't it be frightened? Wolves aren't often a friend to birds, ravens aside."

Felan shrugged as if it was of no consequence and focused his attention on the lake.

The water was clear, save for the few ripples that strayed from the waterfall at the opposite side. Minnows the size and shape of sewing needles chased each other throughout the shallows. They darted away as Felan scooped up some water in his hands.

"It's not saltwater," he exclaimed happily before giving up formalities altogether and pushing his mouth straight into the lake to drink.

Selene followed suit. The water held a sweet taste as it hit her tongue and it was brilliantly cold. She waded in until it met her waist, then plunged beneath. It was not long before Felan joined her, running through the shallows with as much speed as he could manage before breaking into a swim.

"Do you think that the air is always so hot here?" Felan asked as he half-heartedly tread water beside her.

Selene struggled to pull herself up onto a nearby boulder, a portion of which protruded from the surface of the lake. It was difficult with her hand, which was now so swollen as to render her fingers useless. "Spirits, I hope not." Her belly was full of water. It felt wonderful, yet as she had learned far too many times in the past it was not a substitute for food.

"Your arm." Felan reached out as if to touch the swollen flesh.

She had been avoiding looking at it too closely, truth be told, for it gave her stomach a queasy feeling which was amplified all the more with the thought that she could do nothing to heal it. The swelling had moved up her arm to the elbow, and the flesh was now a light purple in color.

"We'll have to do something about it soon." He looked far more concerned than she felt.

"There's naught to be done," she replied. "Not here in the wilderness."

"I suppose you're right," Felan conceded as he moved from treading water to floating upon the surface. "We'll have to find something to eat, eventually."

Selene could not help but be grateful that he had decided to change the subject.

"After this we could sit a while," Selene suggested. "Once we're rested, we could head out again and try to find some type of civilization. I still think it's our best chance of survival."

Felan scowled. "And when they sell us into slavery?"

"There isn't another option," Selene informed him. "We can't live out here. And they might have something for my arm. If we locate a town, then perhaps we can sneak in and take some food.

With the luck of the Tides, we might find someone who would help us. There must be some few Kerell who would be sympathetic to our cause. I find it difficult to believe that they're all heartless slavers."

"I don't understand how we could possibly find someone to help us when we barely know the language. And even if we did, are you just going to walk up to the nearest friendly looking person and ask them to kindly refrain from enslaving us?"

Selene sighed. "Ok, then maybe we could sneak onto a ship to get home."

"Yes, because sneaking onto a ship worked out so well for me last time."

Selene said nothing more, for she had the feeling that again it was hunger rather than Felan's attitude which was eating away at her patience. It was when she turned away from him that she noticed the creature that had led them here had returned.

*"He's back,"* she said in her mind so as not to startle it. It was a good bet that Felan continued to listen to her thoughts.

Felan turned to look with her. The animal's fur matted against its skin as it waded into the far side of the lake. It excelled at swimming, and paddled much as a person would. As it reached the waterfall it disappeared beneath it. Seconds turned to minutes as they waited for the creature to reappear.

"Perhaps we should take a closer look," she suggested.

"Or perhaps not," Felan countered. "What if it drowned over there, or something ate it from beneath the water?"

"I don't think that's the case. It was definitely swimming in that direction on purpose. And there would have been more of a disturbance in the water if it had been eaten."

Felan looked uncertain.

"Well, I'm going even if you aren't," Selene said. She stripped off her shirt and set it upon the small portion of the rock that crested the water. It was more tattered cloth than garment anyway after traversing the forest, and her smallclothes were mostly intact.

"Selene," he began.

"You should take yours off too," she informed him. "It will drag you down once we reach the waterfall."

Felan removed his shirt and tossed it next to hers on the rock.

"So, you've summoned some bravery, then?" she teased.

"I can't very well let you go by yourself," he replied as he tread water next to her. "You won't be able to swim very well with your arm in such a state."

"I grew up in a fishing village," she countered. "I can likely swim better with a swollen arm than you can with two good ones."

Selene paddled as close to the waterfall as she could before splashing water obscured her vision. It was much louder up close, and so she was forced to speak solely in her mind and hope that he was listening. "*I'm going under,*" she warned him. "*Ready?*"

"*Not really,*" Felan protested.

Before he could complain any further, she held her breath and dove beneath the wall of water. The pain that traveled up her arm in waves eased somewhat as frigid water engulfed it. She came up easily on the other side and took a moment to draw a breath as her eyes adjusted. Before her was a slab of stone, and beyond that the mouth of a cave disappeared into the darkness. She pulled herself up, and before long Felan was beside her.

"We're being watched," he noted.

The human-like creature was just ahead, busily grooming water from the fur at the end of its tail. It turned and moved farther into the darkness. Light blossomed in the cavern as it did so, emanating from lines of glowing stones that followed the walls of the passage on both sides.

"They're much like the stones we found in Ranur's storage room," Selene noted. She wandered over and picked one up. It was just the right size to fit comfortably in her hand and was mildly warm to the touch. Felan's face was framed in the unearthly blue glow of the stone as he approached. "You should take one too," she suggested.

"I suppose it couldn't hurt," he replied. "There may not be any more farther in. I have nothing against caves, but I'd rather not be walking in total darkness."

They traveled the cave in silence. After a few minutes of hearing only the sound of their footsteps and the receding rush of water, Selene could bear the silence no longer. "Have you remembered anything else?"

"Not very much," he replied. "A few scattered memories here and there, but for the most part the circlet did nothing to help me regain the memories you and Cael stole from me."

She was not sure why she had asked, for she knew what his answer would be. "I'm truly sorry."

"You've told me that over and over again, and I'll tell you again that there's no need. I understand why you did it."

"We've told you everything that we can remember."

"And yet to me it's like hearing a tale of someone else's life. My past isn't hidden somewhere in a forgotten part of my mind. It's just gone."

"You don't know that," she began.

Felan slowed his pace and turned to face her. "I've had time to think," he said. "And I've decided that it doesn't matter."

She found it difficult to believe.

"I'll make new memories to replace the old. There are plenty of people who would be happy for such an opportunity."

The statement at first struck her as odd, but with thought she rounded up a few memories whose absence she certainly would not weep for.

It grew colder as they walked, so much so that she began to shiver. Ahead the passage narrowed, and above them lay a slab of stone. Faded words were carved within. Although they looked to be composed of letters of the common tongue, she found that she did not know their meaning.


ARRETE

C'EST ICI L'EMPIRE DE LA MORT


"Can you read it?" she asked.

"No," he replied. "I know the letters, but not the language."

"What else can we do but move on?" It seemed a better option than going back into the forest, at least.

"Shall we, then?" He swept one hand outwards as if offering for her to go first.

"At least you admit that I'm the braver of us," she said as she started ahead.

"Never said that." He matched her pace.

It was darker beyond, and as she came near the wall something bit into the side of her leg. She brushed her hand against it, and her fingers came away wet.

"You're bleeding," Felan remarked as he caught up with her.

As she brought her hand close to the glow of the stone, she found that he was right.  Dark blood coated her fingertips. She healed it with a thought despite the pain in her head and looked down to see what had pierced her skin. Levering the light towards the wall of the cave revealed naught more than stone.

"Something bit me," she muttered.

"No, you stumbled into the wall," he corrected.

"I'm fine." She couldn't recall stumbling, which was odd.

"You look pale," he noted.

"It was a moment of dizziness. I haven't eaten." It was a decent attempt at ignorance, by her account, but apparently not decent enough to fool Felan.

"I haven't eaten anything in quite some time either and I'm not falling into walls. The poison in your arm is spreading. It could be affecting your balance."

"If that's true then there's nothing to be done about it. And you're not a healer, last I checked."

"I don't need to be a healer to tell when someone is about to lose consciousness."

"I can keep walking."

"Until you're not able to."

Selene released a heavy sigh. "Then you'll go on without me."

"Doubtful," he replied stubbornly.

Selene's body began to ache as she walked. She wrapped her good arm, along with the stone, around her chest in a futile attempt to cease shivering. At once she wished to be back beneath the relentless sun, if only long enough to grab the tattered remains of her shirt.

"At least you've got a layer of smallclothes on your torso," Felan noted. "I've got nothing."

"It's not doing me much good, I assure you," she countered through chattering teeth. Her legs began to throb. A fresh bubble of pain erupted in the area where the feather creature had struck her, and as they walked and time wore on it spread, claiming her chest. A light touch of her healing ability was met once again with what she had feared. The slithering feel of poison.

"Selene," he began. Concern lay plainly upon his face.

She found that she had no desire to discuss it. Going forward was just as risky as turning back. "Speak of something to get my mind off of the cold, will you?"

"Alright." He paused to rub his hands back and forth along the outside of his arms. Tell me what I was like before all of this. I mean, when we became friends, back before the Aranth truly began to fall apart."

She thought for a moment. "Somewhat carefree. And more than a bit mischievous."

A grin inched onto his face within the dim blue light. "You liked me that way."

"Yes," she replied. "I did."

His grin quickly faded as he caught sight of what lay ahead. Selene's mouth gaped as groupings of stones caught to light in succession; up the walls to the ceiling above.

"I'm all for a bit of adventure," Felan said breathlessly. "But with this I believe it's time to turn back."

Selene caught sight of the columns first. Shaped like portly barrels of ale, they were layered with rows of ivory stones. These met a domed ceiling of rounded tiles, similarly colored. It was not until she found the chandelier, however, that she truly realized what the room was composed of, for where candles would normally reside sat human skulls with glowing stones set within.

"Amazing, isn't it?"

Selene became startled at the sound, for the question had not come from Felan. On instinct she reached for her sword, but of course she did not find it. The movement was rewarded with a new bout of pain that leapt from her fingertips through her shoulder.

"The empire of the dead. A graveyard of the ancients. Created by necessity in the aftermath of a terrible plague, or so the stories tell."

"Who are you?" she asked in a panic, though it was probably the least important of a hundred questions she should have started with.

"My name is Solutus," the man answered from the shadows of a corner. "Be calm, for I mean you no harm."

"If that is so, then step into the light," Felan countered.

"Of course," Solutus replied.

A face weathered by scars emerged. Without question he would seem fearsome to most, with a muscular torso, and hair cropped so short as to be indeterminate in color. But none of those things were what made Selene's breath catch in her lungs.

"*The Aranth brand.*" Felan had found it too.

"I don't see many from our land," Solutus said as he moved closer.

"He's on the list," Selene said. "He must be."

"And what list is that?" Solutus asked as his body tightened.

"The king gave us a list of Aranth who went missing and were likely sold to the Kerell," Selene explained.

"Perhaps I would be on such a list." The man's posture relaxed. "In the past I was known as Arlen. Solutus is a name I chose for myself after I made my escape from the city. But why would the king send you here?"

"We've been sent here to rescue you."

Solutus laughed with such force that he was made to brace himself against a nearby wall. Selene glanced at Felan, whose face echoed the look of confusion upon her own.

"A fine job you've done of it," Solutus said at last. "Two pups like you sent into the heart of Kerell territory? Graelen must have lost what little intellect he once had about him."

Selene could not help but take insult, even though he was likely right.

"It's not wise to speak ill of the dead," Felan warned him.

Solutus sobered immediately at the words. "So, he's dead? Did he drown in his guilt for those of us lost? And thus, in those final moments he decreed that two young Aranth should be sacrificed in a misguided attempt to bring us home."

"There were more of us," she explained. "We were shipwrecked and lost the rest of our party."

"Even a whole ship of Aranth could not hope to conquer this place," Solutus informed her. "The Aranth force must have grown considerably in my absence. Tell me, how many are there?"

"We are in the midst of rebuilding," Felan explained in a vague manner that he usually reserved for Xaiden.

Solutus' expression grew dark. "I asked how many."

Selene shifted from one foot to her other. "Discounting the younglings in training, there are six of us."

"I see." Solutus stepped back into the shadows.

"Wait," Selene called out. "Where are you going?"

"You'll need to have something done about that arm." His voice echoed from the cavernous walls. "You've got less than a day by the looks of it. I also thought you might want something to eat."

Selene glanced at Felan for reassurance and found him scowling at her arm. She followed his gaze. The swelling had doubled, and her skin was now marred with the purples and yellows of deep bruising despite her repeated attempts to heal it.

"I don't see that we have any other choice, do you?"

She nodded and they followed Solutus into the shadows. Hall upon hall they traversed, all built of human remains just like the first. The ancients had become more creative as time passed, for the bones formed patterns more frequently as they travelled. A whirlpool of skulls was accented by spiraling masses of leg bones, and mosaics of smaller bones had been artfully placed to create landscape scenes. As they moved on, whole skeletons had been propped up with narrow pillars of stone as if for show, recreating the scenes of the living in rounded alcoves constructed from the bones of their brethren. One skeleton rested his jaw on his hand, posed as if bored by the unending passage of time. Two more were seated across from each other at a table of bone, as if about to play an unseen game of forces.

The most impressive and unsettling display was a skeleton king who sat proudly upon his throne, complete with a crown and scepter of leg bones lashed together. It was while meeting his unearthly gaze that Selene realized she could no longer feel her arm, which was both somewhat of a relief and disconcerting all at once. She busied herself with marveling at how big the city of the ancients must have been for so many to have died with some still left to bury them, and at once wondered how many were buried here, for the neatly stacked walls of bone did not seem to have an end.

"Must be thousands," Felan muttered.

"These caverns stretch beyond measure," Solutus explained. "They are regarded as a cursed place by those in the city, which works perfectly to our advantage."

They entered another room as he spoke. As she breached the threshold Selene reveled in the heat that washed across her skin. This room seemed to be occupied by living people, much to her surprise, and was large enough to fit several carriages within. Here the bones met in waves and circles. At the center, a pile of the glowing stones had been set, though these gave off an orange light rather than the blue of those before. Several men sat around the pile; their expressions unreadable in the meager light. They stood, one after another, and Selene counted eight within sight. The room wobbled as she stared.

Solutus grabbed her good arm, causing her to drop the glowing stone held within it. She shook him away and took a step back.

"Only attempting to help," he said. The words warped strangely within her ears.

She pulled at her healing ability, intending to use it upon her arm once again, but could not find it through the fog of vertigo that enveloped her. Solutus caught her before she could strike the floor.

Selene could do naught but stare as she was carried through the room, in and out of shadow and onto a pile of blankets. Above was a likeness of the sun, with arm and leg bones composing its rays, and a skull for the center.

"I'm fine," she attempted to tell them.

"You must be able to do something for her," came Felan's panicked voice.

"She'll require a medic," Solutus replied calmly. "Though of course life is difficult here. We will need something in exchange for our hospitality. Feeding you both, and caring for her, is no small matter."

"I have little to offer," Felan replied. "Perhaps I could hunt for you, or help to bring in supplies?"

"I'm certain we can arrange something," Solutus replied. "Come, have some food. She will be safe here."

"I would rather not leave her," Felan replied, much to Selene's relief.

"As you wish," Solutus replied. "Pliny," he called out.

From somewhere outside her vision a man replied hastily in Kerell. Footsteps approached, and shortly thereafter her arm was shifted and prodded uncomfortably. An argument erupted. It had the tones of one, at least. They spoke quickly and the words were in Kerell. Most of the meaning remained lost to her. Selene's mind rolled as if she was still at the mercy of the sea, yet there was one word that caught her attention, for it was used repeatedly within the conversation. *Attonitus*. The strangeness of it sloshed around in her head.

"What does attonitus mean?" she heard Felan ask.

"It's somewhere between an animal and a plant. A venomous, feather-like thing that roots in the cracks of damp caves. Most who touch it fall unconscious within a day, and death comes within a week. We have only a small amount of antidote here. Maybe not enough. It must be stolen from Kerell city, you see."

Selene's vision was beginning to darken. The blackness pulled in from the edges until all that could be seen was the skull that composed the center of the false sun above. Her legs began to tremor, and there was naught she could do to make the movement cease. She was pulled up to sit. She thought for a moment that her head might burst from the pressure as she moved. Her mouth was forced open, and some warm, bitter liquid drizzled down her throat. After that, time passed in a most odd manner. She could hear the comings and goings of the men at times when she woke, and on occasion they would sit her up to pour more of the bitter liquid or perhaps some broth into her mouth.

There was no way to tell day from night here, though when she woke fully she assumed it must be night, for several men lay snoring nearby. Bitter air nipped at her flesh as she slid from beneath the woolen blanket. Her arm and leg both ached fiercely, yet a touch of her healing ability was enough to remedy the situation. The stone of the floor was frigid against her bare feet. She silently thanked the Spirits that it was not composed of bones like the walls and ceiling.

*"Felan?"* she called out only in her mind. For some reason it felt prudent not to wake those who were sleeping. Upon receiving no reply she took a few steps, testing to make sure that she would not collapse. *Steady enough.* Her bed had been fashioned within an alcove to one side of the main area, and upon stepping back she was unhappy to find a skeleton looming above. With its jaw slightly agape and two bony hands set against its belly it looked most disconcertingly as if it was laughing. At the same time, it put her in mind of forty-two. Likely they did not have issues with bloodsoul here as they did at home, for she had not seen any thus far. The odd notion of the artfully placed bones sliding out to grab her filled her mind. She deftly shook it aside and took that as her cue to move along all the same. Perhaps when Solutus returned she would ask him for a bed somewhere less ominous, assuming that such a place existed down here.

Upon scouting the open area, she found neither Felan nor Solutus but rather a group of sleeping men around a pile of stones glowing with low auburn light. She tiptoed carefully around bundled layers of blankets, which moved up and down in time with their occupants' sleeping breaths. It was warmer here, for heat emanated from the stones into the room beyond as if from a campfire's flame.

Upon the far side of the room was an archway, and beyond that a smaller room with a few crates upon the floor. Selene levered the top of one open, and inside found some medicines and haphazardly folded blankets. In the next she found what she had been searching for. Two thick wheels of cheese encased in wax. She felt weak with hunger. Certainly, they would not mind if she had a small piece. Selene plucked a knife from a nearby shelf with intent to procure some. As she turned, she met an unfamiliar face. The man was so thin that his cheekbones showed, and she could see that his hair was thick and oily even in the darkness. He grinned and grabbed her wrist. The knife dropped from her hand to clatter upon the floor.

Selene had brushed against an eel in the river once as a child. The feeling as the man's skin touched hers was much the same, though combined with the burn of a marked one's touch. Her muscles seized as one and she found that she could not move.

He held her wrist aloft so that she would not strike the floor, and then called to one of his companions for aid. Together they dragged her back out through the common room, past a set of iron bars, and into a small room on the side. *A cell*, she realized. She could not move her mouth. Repeated calls to Felan in her mind elicited no reply.

One of the men who had dragged her leered above, blocking her view. She could see naught but a mess of dark hair that swept down past his shoulders and narrow, squinting eyes. Spittle sprayed from his lips to land upon her face as he whispered to his companion in the language of the Kerell. The man pulled at her breeches. She wanted to scream, to strike at him, but she found that she could do nothing. He removed her smallclothes with the help of his companion, then they both stood back a pace to stare. The first one spoke again, giving the other a slap on his back as he did so. Whatever he said brought them both to laughter. She caught only two words of their conversation: *wife* and *forgotten*. Selene could make no sense of them and feared the worst as they drew close to examine her. Her attempts to struggle earned her no more than the subtle movement of one finger. Her mind swung when she attempted to find her latent ability. With only a touch she could take one of them down as she had with Ranur. The man's hair cascaded around his face, obscuring her vision as he leaned over her. His foul breath invaded her. She could now move the rest of her fingers, yet her latent ability remained out of grasp. His tongue was warm against the side of her face, and then her lips.

Selene's eyes caught movement in the shadows. The man who was standing guard collapsed suddenly. His head struck the floor with a satisfying thump. Some hard object clattered against the floor nearby. It came to rest, warm against the bare skin of her torso. The man above her turned at the sound. His eyes grew wide. He toppled over, gasping as if struggling to breathe. With difficulty she levered herself onto one side. There she was met with the face of her savior, if indeed saving her was his plan. The paralysis faded quickly, now that the man responsible for it was unconscious. After only a few seconds she was able to sit.

"Will you be able to walk?" the man asked.

"Yes." Her mind was slow to clear.

"My name is Jev," the man said, as if that meant everything. He had a pleasant face, though that little was all she could tell in the darkness.

"I think I should go," she managed to say with some effort.

"Where are you planning on going?" Jev asked.

"Anywhere but here," she replied as she struggled to leave the floor. Both her arm and her legs throbbed terribly once again, which was disconcerting.

"That sounds fine." The man looped his arm around her for support, and she found that she was in no state to protest. "I shall accompany you."

"I have someone to accompany me already," she replied as she struggled to control the spinning of the room.

"You would simply leave me here after I've saved you from those brutes?" She could hear a measure of amusement in his voice, and it irritated her greatly.

"It's not that I don't appreciate your efforts," she began. A wave of nausea hit her with the strength of a winter storm. What little was in her stomach was lost upon the floor. It barely missed the man's boots. "But I can go on my own," she finished weakly.

"Not by the look of you," Jev countered. "They had little antivenin in this place to begin with. Not enough to fully cure you. It takes a mage to put that stuff together. It's alchemy and magic combined, and there are no mages here."

"That's perhaps the only good thing about this place." Her words were slurred and difficult to form.

"I'm one of the few markèd ones who has made it in and out of the city without being seen," he continued. "Besides, you've come to rescue me, the way Arlen told it. You'd be a fool to leave without me. What would your king have to say about it?"

Her thoughts finally managed to connect the past to the present. "Jev is short for Jevelir," she guessed. "You're Aranth."

"I was Aranth," he corrected. "But yes. Not many speak the common tongue in this place. That should have been your first clue."

The fact had not crossed her addled mind, in all honesty. "Did Felan ask you to find me?"

"No," Jev replied. "He knows full well where you are."

"Then why isn't he here? Why did he send you and not come himself?"

"That would be due to Arlen."

"You mean Solutus," she remembered. "His affinity is a strange, tiny bear with abnormally long limbs."

"It's a gibbon," Jev corrected. "And I refuse to call him by that ridiculous name."

"If you say so," Selene replied distantly. Why in the name of the Spirits would the floor not hold still? "Is Solutus keeping Felan here?"

"In a way he keeps all of us here," Jev replied.

"I won't leave without him," she said stubbornly.

"These caves run underneath the entire city," Jev countered. "I don't know where he is. I would have enough time to search for him, but you certainly don't. Come, let's get out of here while you can still walk."

"Just tell me," she said as they made their way ever so slowly away from the cell. "Is he well?"

"As well as he can be, I suppose. Hush for a moment."

She was about to protest, but then noticed the mass of sleeping bodies in the room beyond. There were so many that a chorus of snoring echoed from the ceiling above. She moved silently through the room with Jev to guide her. Once far enough away, she tried yet again to obtain answers.

"How does Arlen keep them here?" she asked. "By brute force?" She could not see how unless his latent ability was something spectacular, for he was only one man amongst what seemed to be just shy of one hundred.

"His latent ability protects us from being detected. It's like a curtain around the catacombs which makes it so that the mages can't sense us down here. It's the only reason we've survived in this place for so long."

"Solutus said that this place was forbidden to the mages."

"It is forbidden for the Kerell to come here, yes, but you must know that not all pay heed to such warnings."

"I suppose that makes sense," she admitted.

"For the sake of the Goddess," Jevelir swore beneath his breath.

Solutus stepped out from within a shadowy alcove a short distance away.

"Hello Arlen," Jevelir called out as the man drew closer.

"I no longer use that name," Arlen snapped. "Why is that so difficult for you to remember?"

"Apologies," Jevelir said without offering an explanation.

"And where are you off to so early in the day?"

"I was giving Selene a bit of a tour," he said. "She should know her way around given the circumstances; don't you think?"

Solutus' lip twitched in the slightest as he considered. "I suppose that would be useful, yes."

"So, we'll just continue, if it pleases you."

"It does not," Solutus replied.

Selene's stomach twisted into an uncomfortable knot upon hearing the words.

"I will take her from here, thank you."

The burn of Solutus' mark struck her, soft and dizzying, as he took her hand. Jevelir opened his mouth as if to protest, but instead closed it once again without uttering a word. He turned and headed back the way they had come.

"Jevelir is correct, if just this once," Solutus said as they walked. "You should certainly know your way around what will be your new home."

"I can't stay here," she replied. Time was impossible to grasp in this place. Only the Spirits knew how long she had lingered.

Solutus frowned. "You act as if you were offered a choice in the matter."

Selene drew a quick breath. She pulled away from him to lean against a nearby wall. It did not matter how long ago she had arrived here, in truth, for any amount of time was too long. "I've had quite enough of this place, thank you." With that she summoned what little was left of her strength and kicked him, striking the most delicate place squarely between his legs as hard as she could. She was still weak, but with luck it would bring enough pain to give her an advantage.

Solutus cried out and doubled over. Selene ran, though it seemed as if the floor twisted beneath her feet with each step. She could hear the man issuing orders as she sprinted through the cave's shadowed passages. Then came the sound of so many footsteps behind her; tapping like drops in a summer rainstorm. She turned corners at random as she ran, giving no thought to where she went. It didn't matter, after all, for she had no idea where she was to begin with.

Selene turned the next corner and slid to a halt. Solutus was there, no more than a few feet before her. She turned to run, but in what seemed an instant his arm was around her throat. He dragged her with little effort and said nothing as her heels scraped against the rough stone of the floor. The sprint had drained what little energy was left to her, and each time she struggled his arm tightened around her neck. Patterns of bones swept past her vision and then, iron bars. He laid her down upon the ground more gently than expected, upon a pile of woolen blankets.

"We'll have no more of that," he said.

Selene pulled herself weakly up to sit.

"I shall return when my anger has subsided," he added.

The door of metal bars rattled as he latched it. He slid the key into the pocket of his breeches.

# Hidden Forces
## *Evaria – Capital City*

Islyr paced the small area of carpet in front of Evaria's throne. In the distance the bell tower sang. He paced his steps to match its chime. *One, two, three.* Time had mattered little during the years he had lived at the base of the Crimson Abyss. *Four, five, six.* In this civilized world it meant everything. *Seven.* Devren had requested his presence at the hour of seven. The young king was now late. On the heel of the final chime emanated a tapping noise, so slight as to barely be heard. It was no more than a few feet behind him. Islyr gripped his staff and spun. He would crack the fiend's skull before they could strike. But as he turned his mind recognized the face. He stopped short, not more than an inch from the man's temple.

"You tread on dangerous ground," he warned with a glare.

"Hardly," the thief replied. "The throne room's pretty solid, now that it's been properly repaired from that pesky dragon incident, that is to say."

"I meant figuratively, Viverr, not literally."

"I know you did. And I imagine that you're not so happy about me sneaking up on you," he added with glee. "That'll be because I almost made it, eh?"

Islyr smiled despite his irritation. He could not deny that the rogue was a master of his trade. "Something like that," he replied.

"So, where's our boy king, then?"

"You would call him that within his hearing?" Islyr asked.

"Of course not. It's suicide to purposely anger a king, especially one so young."

Islyr was not inclined to disagree.

"Have you heard from your sister, then?"

"No," Islyr replied.

"Ah, it's a bit of a sore subject, I'd imagine," the rogue continued, perhaps upon noticing Islyr's expression.

Selene was headed straight into the jaws of Kerell territory, to a land Islyr wished above all else that she would never be forced to set foot upon. "She is a grown woman," he said. "And as such is entitled to make her own decisions."

"True," Viverr replied. "Say, do you think Felan went with them?"

"No marked one with any sense would purposely sneak onto a Kerell-bound ship."

"So you say, but that man does have a great love of making terrible decisions."

"That's true. Perhaps he did after all." Islyr was trying his best to be cordial with the rogue, but on the whole he found conversations difficult to endure, especially those which concerned his sister. "Perhaps you could ask Devren, if he ever decides to show himself."

"So where is the lad, anyway?" Viverr asked as he shifted a bundle of wet cloth from one arm to the other.

Islyr knew that beneath the fabric lay a mottled egg. It was now of such a size as to be unwieldy, and he knew from experience that it was terribly fragile. "You're likely to drop that," he warned. "It would be safer in your room."

"Not a chance," the rogue countered as he clutched the egg to his chest. The skin of his fingers was so wet as to be wrinkled. "Can't risk that it might hatch while I'm gone."

Islyr glanced at the water dripping from the man's shirt to form a puddle upon the otherwise pristine marble of the floor. "Then why not leave it with Cyanna? You trust her, do you not?"

"As much as I trust anyone other than myself, which is to say not at all. Don't take that the wrong way, mind. It's not to say that I dislike the girl. She's like a daughter to me, or as close as I'll ever come to having one."

Islyr raised a brow at the man.

"Don't need one of your looks, thanks so much. Let's just say that only over my corpse will this dragon be bonded to anyone other than myself and leave it at that."

"Are you certain it's a dragon?" Islyr asked as innocently as he could muster. He knew it was cruel to toy with the man but found that he could not help but do so.

"Are you certain it's not?" Viverr replied smoothly.

"Do you really want me to tell you?"

The man's laughter echoed from the room's cavernous ceiling. "I wouldn't believe you anyway. Let's just wait until it hatches and see, shall we?"

"Certainly," Islyr replied. It would not be so long, by the look of it.

"Greetings, friends." Devren's voice carried easily across the throne room as he entered. "Apologies for my untimeliness."

"Since when do kings apologize?" Viverr muttered.

"I heard that," Devren informed him.

"You were meant to," Viverr countered. "Otherwise, you wouldn't have."

It was odd, for no ruler of any sort had ever apologized within Islyr's hearing. He could not decide whether it was for good or ill.

The boy offered Viverr his sternest look, which was comical rather than frightening due to the youth of the face it presented upon.

"At your service, Majesty," Islyr offered. He bent at the waist, solely for the purposes of formality.

After a few seconds Viverr mimicked the gesture, but not before carefully rearranging the egg.

"We'd better start right away, I suppose," the boy said as he lowered himself awkwardly onto the throne. He looked towards the pairs of guardsmen who stood at each door. "Step out," he ordered. "I will call for you when we are finished."

The men offered a salute before stepping beyond their respective doors and closing them behind.

"I've called you both here to offer a proposal of employment," Devren continued when the room was clear.

Islyr sighed. He had already declined the offer of joining the Aranth presented by the lad's father. In fact, his sister had used a boon owed to her by the former king to free him of that obligation.

"Well, I already work for you," Viverr quipped. "So, there's that finished, eh?"

"I know that you're already under my employ," Devren replied with a scowl. "I would like to propose a new league of Aranth. A subset that is unknown to anyone but the inner circle."

Islyr felt a flutter of curiosity rise through his usual fog of wariness. He was not yet willing to give in to it.

"Would this new breed of Aranth happen to come with a raise in pay?" the rogue asked. "Because if it does, then I graciously accept your offer. Now, if you would be so kind as to excuse me, I've a few important things to attend to."

"I haven't even finished telling you about the job," Devren said, echoing Islyr's thoughts on the matter. "And as you pointed out only a moment ago, you are already in my employ, so the only place you need to be is right here, listening to your king. Do you disagree?"

Viverr's mouth gaped for a few seconds. "Of course not, Majesty," he muttered. "Apologies."

"Very well," Devren continued, though it looked as if he had not expected Viverr to bend to his will so easily. "I have heard tell of hunters from overseas invading our shores; sneaking off with what marked ones they can find and spiriting them back to the land of the Kerell. They've been spotted more in the last month than in the past few years."

"Aren't those the men you've been hunting, Islyr?" Viverr asked.

Islyr had ended the lives of a great many Kerell mages, it was true.

"You know something of these men?" Devren asked.

"Yes, Majesty," Islyr replied. "They are called Tenere-Rakaii. In the land of the Kerell they are used to catch wild marked ones and those who have gone feral." Even during Islyr's time as Rakaii, which was now a fair number of years ago, the supply of Rakaii could not meet the demand for them. It was not surprising that they traveled here in greater numbers in recent days.

"I am in need of a force to specialize in dealing with these monsters. I thought that you and Viverr could be the core. You could then recruit others as needed."

The sound of getting paid for something he was already doing did sound appealing. "Would we be confined to the city?" Islyr asked. He had no desire to ask for permission every time he crossed a border.

"No," the young king replied. "In fact, you would be expected to roam wherever the work takes you. No restrictions. And you would have the backing of the crown to further your pursuits."

"And can I do as I wish with the mages when we find them?"

"Unless I require something specific from them. Other than that, I don't care what you do with them so long as they're gone."

Perhaps having Devren in charge would work out to Islyr's advantage after all.

"I will agree to a trial of said service, to begin," Islyr said. "On the condition that I am free to leave at will if it is not to my liking."

"Yes, I accept your terms." Devren held out his hand.

The light, misty warmth of the boy's mark washed over Islyr as he shook it.

"I would offer you the Aranth brand," the boy said. "But we have no mage at the moment, and it requires a ritual of magic."

"I am not offended," Islyr replied. He did not want it, truth be told.

"I suppose I'm in as well, officially," Viverr said. "But two members doesn't seem like near enough to take on even one mage. Tell me, would someone have to be marked for us to recruit them?"

"You can recruit anyone you see fit," Devren replied. "They just need to be capable of doing the job."

"You have someone in mind?" Islyr could not help but ask.

"Maybe I do," Viverr replied cryptically.

"Excellent," Devren said. "You start now."

"Now?" Viverr's eyes widened at the revelation. "As in, right this moment?"

"Do you know of another definition for the word?" Islyr asked.

"I've been told of a mage who is much too close," Devren explained before the rogue could continue to whine. "He has been staying at the Wavefront Inn, near the center of town."

"I know that place," Viverr said. He shifted the egg to his opposite arm. Drops of water pattered against the floor as the wet rags surrounding it swung back and forth. "That's a right fancy inn. Gold inlay on the chair rails and real bone-porcelain cups. Aurin and I made off with a spectacular haul last time we were there."

Devren offered the Rogue a disapproving look.

"That was long before we became Aranth," he added, as if that improved the situation.

"I haven't heard tell of him," Islyr mused. "Did your informant provide you with a name?"

"No," Devren replied. "But he did say that the man had a companion with him."

"A captured Rakaii?" Islyr guessed.

"It sounded like it, though the shop keeper didn't see any sort of circlet upon him."

"I've noticed that the new ones are small," Islyr informed him. "They can easily be mistaken for jewelry." He fought against reliving the memories of the last few Rakaii he had attempted to free. Their Tenere had met violent ends, so not all had been lost.

"Other mages have merely stopped here," Devren continued. "They arrive at the port and move on. But this one has been lingering in town for several days now."

"So close to the castle?" Islyr said. "They are becoming bolder."

"Try to avoid killing him if it's convenient," the young king said.

"Only if it's convenient?" Viverr quipped.

A scowl crossed Devren's face. "Just stop him however you're able. If you can avoid killing him it would be best, as I would very much like to question him."

"That makes sense," Viverr admitted.

"We'll do our best, Majesty," Islyr added formally. It appeared that the boy was capable of learning from his errors. It was a promising sign. "Come along, Viverr," he said as he made his retreat.

"We're partners in this," the rogue huffed as they climbed the stairs to the upper floor of the castle.

Islyr purposely offered no reply.

"That means you don't get to order me around," Viverr clarified.

Islyr remained silent still, for he knew that the rogue would continue to speak regardless of whether or not he participated in the conversation.

"And it means that you have to respect my opinions." He glanced at Islyr as if expecting him to say something.

Islyr knocked upon the door that they were now facing. "It doesn't mean that at all," he replied.

"Come in," Cyanna replied from within the room beyond.

"What are we doing up here, anyway?" the rogue asked much too late.

"Wait here," Islyr ordered as he opened the door.

One could describe the princess' room as cluttered, if the things within were not so artfully arranged. She had a penchant for sculptures, though he could not be certain if it was recent or had always been so. Hanging from the typical stone walls that graced every room of this floor were multiple shelves of planed wood, and upon these shelves sat a myriad of tiny creatures carved from all manner of materials; everything from seashells to precious gems.

"Greetings Princess," Islyr said, bending at the waist.

"Hello Islyr," Cyanna replied. She was sitting at her desk, penning what seemed to be a letter. She looked very much the warrior these days, for she had cut her hair short and had built up the requisite physique in what seemed like a short span of time. The only thing to ruin the illusion was the loving way she stroked the little scrub pig on her desk with one hand while writing with her other. Islyr looked the small, furry animal over. He had not seen the creatures in detail before Cyanna took up the care of them. Viverr referred to them as potatoes with fur. It was as accurate a description as any. Islyr started in with the point of the visit before the rogue could discover it and protest. "Viverr is too proud to ask you himself, but he wanted to know if you would be so kind as to watch his dragon egg for a short while."

Cyanna brought her face close to the scrub pig and whispered something to it. The creature chattered as if in reply.

"He would trust no one else with the task," Islyr continued.

The rogue appeared in the doorway as expected.

"You would trust me with your dragon?" Cyanna said happily. She leaped from the chair and captured Viverr in an embrace.

"Of course, I would," Viverr said smoothly as he pried himself away. "You're the only one."

Cyanna glanced around the room as if searching for something. It provided Viverr with the opportunity to offer Islyr an irritated glare.

"Ah, here." Cyanna pulled her washbasin from its stand. "I just poured clean water in a few moments ago," she explained as she pried the egg from Viverr's fingers and placed it gingerly in the basin.

Islyr considered it to be the perfect plan, for Cyanna was good with creatures and Viverr would be of no assistance fighting Tenere while attempting to haul an egg the size of a melon around the city.

"Come, Viverr. We must go now."

"We should be back in no more than a few hours," Viverr said as he backed from the room. "If it starts to hatch, you'll come and find me, won't you? We'll just be down in the city proper."

"Do you think it will hatch today?" Cyanna asked excitedly. "I've always wanted to see a baby dragon."

"No," Viverr replied. "I do not."

"All right." A puzzled expression crossed the girl's face. "If it starts to hatch, I'll send for you right away."

"Time to go, Viverr." Islyr dragged the man out the room by the cuff of his shirt. "Thank you, Princess," he added, remembering his graces.

"I've already told you once that you're not in charge of our little company," Viverr mumbled irately as they descended the stairs.

Islyr did not feel the need to point out that by default he was in charge, for he was the first to officially sign up for the task, and the rogue had been doing as he was told for the entirety of this venture thus far, brief as it was. "I do know more about Tenere," he stated instead.

"Perhaps," Viverr replied. "But I know more about finding people. And about not being seen while doing it."

"That might be true," Islyr agreed.

"That was a clever trick you pulled," the rogue grumbled. "Getting me to hand my egg over to the girl."

"Thank you."

"It won't be as easy next time."

Islyr was well aware of that particular fact. "Once was enough," he replied with satisfaction.

With a few moments of walking in silence they reached the main doors of the castle, and then the end of the castle grounds without bothering to stop at the stables to procure horses.

"I've no love of riding," the rogue informed him.

"That's one thing we both agree on." It was true, though he had not found much else in common with Viverr in the time they'd spent together.

"Smart man," the rogue added. "Giant, unruly beasts, horses are."

"What are your thoughts on a friendly wager?" Islyr asked as they descended the steps to the city below. He knew well that the man would be unable to resist. "If it turns out that the beast in your egg isn't a dragon, then I'll lead our new group."

The rogue's eyes lit with glee. "I'll take that wager. And if it is a dragon, then I'm in charge." Viverr pulled a short-bladed hunting knife from his pocket and drew it lightly across the palm of his hand while he walked.

"Done." Islyr said after doing the same. He held out his hand and the rogue shook it eagerly to seal the wager. He tensed as their blood met and the strange burning sensation of Viverr's mark swept across his own. The feeling was as slick as cooking oil.

They reached the city in little time despite the lack of horses.

"Let's start at the shops surrounding the inn," Viverr suggested. "See if anyone unusual has stopped in. I know the owner of the shop next door pretty well."

"Which shop?" Islyr asked.

"The one that sells glass floats for fishing. Perhaps you're familiar? It's called Samuel's."

Islyr stepped deftly around a woman carting several buckets of oysters in each hand. She paid him no attention despite the fact that they had nearly collided.

"They're decently sized glass orbs that keep fishing lines afloat in the sea," Viverr explained.

"I grew up in a fishing village before the Kerell took me. I know what a fishing float is."

"We'll, I didn't," the rogue replied. "At least not until Samuel told me."

"He's your friend, is he?" Islyr asked skeptically. "You don't seem to be much in need of fishing floats."

"Just because I've no need of his wares doesn't mean we can't be acquainted, does it? Who are you to criticize my choice of friends?"

"None of my business, I suppose." Islyr inhaled the delightful, doughy smell of the bakery as they passed it. Sadly, he could not hold it long enough to fend off the chamber pot scent of the alley as they slipped down it to avoid being seen. "But if you've no need of floats then how did you meet the man?"

"Friend of a friend." Viverr paused as they rounded the corner into the back alleyway. "Maybe you could wait here?"

"No," Islyr replied.

Viverr did not try to convince him any further, much to Islyr's surprise, but rather led him to a dead-end where three squat, oven-like structures resided. The temperature increased significantly as they approached. The flames within the ovens turned scattered shards of broken glass to a display of dancing faerie lights in the near-dark of the alleyway.

"He's usually back here," Viverr muttered. "He can't be far if the ovens are alight."

"We should try in the shop." Islyr recommended. "Perhaps he's helping a customer." He went to grasp the handle of the back entrance. The door pushed open much too easily in his hand. He turned to Viverr and put a finger to his lips. The rogue seemed to understand, and pointed upwards, to indicate that he would climb the ladder to investigate the second floor.

It was probably better for them to split up, just in case the Tenere was still inside. Islyr pushed the door open just enough so that he could enter. The small squeal it made seemed loud enough to wake the Spirits. Weathered boards of wood squeaked beneath his feet as he made his way through a narrow hallway.

Glass floats nestled in boxes filled with straw occupied the first of two closet-sized rooms he entered. The second contained components of rope netting for wrapping around them. Islyr then came upon the main sales floor. All seemed well there. A rainbow of fishing floats hung from the ceiling and walls, scattering pinpoints of light here and there upon the floor where the sun struck through them. Nothing seemed broken, nor did anything seem out of place.

Viverr poked his head down from the loft above.

"Up here," he said.

Islyr climbed the ladder hurriedly. At the top was what might have been a bedroom, though the general chaos of its contents made it difficult to tell. Every piece of furniture had been overturned and most were in pieces. Feathers and straw from what had likely been a mattress coated the floor like snowfall.

Islyr resisted the urge to plug his nose. "It smells terrible up here." Indeed, the scent of urine was stronger here than it had been in the nearby alleyway, which had no doubt been coated in it.

"That'll be some of Samuel's magic," Viverr said.

Islyr briefly pondered what sort of magic could have anything to do with urine.

"Gnomes have very powerful magic," Viverr explained as if able to hear Islyr's thoughts. "Though I'm sure you already knew that."

"What possible reason could I have for knowing that?" Islyr replied. He did know it, in truth, though the memories that accompanied the fact were not ones he enjoyed pulling to mind.

"Samuel has this spell he often uses," the rogue continued, heedless of Islyr's annoyance. "It's his favorite. It increases the volume of liquids."

"What has that to do with the way it smells up here?" Islyr asked.

"Well, a bladder can only hold so much liquid, you see."

He did see, unfortunately. "I've never seen a gnome," he lied, changing the subject.

"You've likely seen one and simply not known it," Viverr said. "Most of them just look like diminutive people, after all."

"Diminutive people who express their bladders to avoid getting caught?" Islyr noted a spot of blood upon the floor. He pressed his finger against it to see how recently it had fallen. It was the size of a bronze coin but had not dried yet. They must have been here fairly recently.

"No, of course not," Viverr replied, as if the most ridiculous nonsense had just come out of Islyr's mouth. "Samuel increases the volume of urine in other people's bladders to avoid getting caught."

"That's one of the oddest methods of defense I've heard of," Islyr informed him.

"It's usually quite effective," Viverr continued. "Although it seems that it didn't help him escape this time."

"This time?"

"We'd better head over to the inn. I'd like to find Samuel before they ship him to Kerell."

"As would I," Islyr agreed. It didn't seem as if the Tenere was in much of a hurry given what Devren had said, yet Islyr was not willing to take any chance that they might lose him.

"I didn't realize that Tenere were interested in anyone other than marked ones," Viverr said as he followed Islyr down the ladder and out into the alley where they had entered.

"Tenere are interested in any magical creature who can be sold for profit," Islyr replied.

"I'm all for making a profit, but not from the sales of other people."

"Only mages are people in the eyes of the Kerell. You and I are no more than animals."

"Just to clarify," Viverr said as they reached the street proper. "You're not interested in finding Samuel. You're only interested in catching the Tenere."

"I am interested in both, to some extent," Islyr replied. "I think that's why Devren placed us together. I'm motivated to put an end to the Tenere."

"And what about me?" the rogue asked with a knowing grin.

"I'm not quite certain what your motivation is, to be honest, but I'm certain he thought it would be helpful somehow."

"Let's just keep it as a surprise then, shall we?"

"I assumed you might say that."

"Devren wants him alive, if possible," the rogue reminded him quite unnecessarily.

"Yes," Islyr replied. "But he said nothing about what we should do with him after we question him."

Viverr grinned. "Right you are, my friend. Let's go find him then, shall we?"

The inn was close, and they arrived at its gilded doors in little time. Beyond those doors was a spacious lobby which was just as grandiose as Viverr had suggested. A man in a delicately stitched vest of lavender fabric and matching breeches turned to Islyr and Viverr. He looked them over with ill-disguised disdain.

"Hello good sir," the rogue began. "My name is Viverr, and you are?"

"Alain," the man replied curtly. "And you, sir, are not welcome here."

The man pointed to the wall behind the reception counter. A charcoal drawing depicting Viverr's face hung there, between a few scattered others. Above the grouping was a sign which read *Banned*, in scrolling letters.

"What's this now?" Viverr said with mock dismay. "I paid for those damages quite a few moons ago."

"And yet you are still banned," Alain said.

"I'm quite respectable these days, I'll have you know."

"Banned for life," the man added, as if clarification was needed.

"You wouldn't ban a member of the king's guard?" Viverr tilted the back of his hand towards the man's face so that his Aranth brand was visible.

If Alain was surprised, he managed to hide it well. "What is it that you want?"

"Alain is a fine name," Viverr continued, heedless of the man's disgruntled stare. "It is my pleasure to meet you, sir. I was hoping to gain some information concerning a patron of yours."

"We pride ourselves on our guests' privacy at this establishment."

"I'd believe nothing less." Viverr pushed his finger against the man's chest. "But I also know what sort of man you truly are."

"Perhaps we should go," Islyr suggested, for the gentleman looked in no mood to offer them information of any kind, and his irritation was clearly growing with each passing second.

Viverr seemed not to hear Islyr in the slightest, and instead continued. "You sir, are a man who is loyal to his king."

Alain's eyes narrowed. "Most obviously I am."

Viverr lowered his voice as he ushered the reluctant man to a quiet corner of the lobby behind some potted plants. "It just so happens that we are on a secretive mission for said king. You wouldn't want to stand in the way of justice, would you?"

"Perhaps not." Alain retained his look of irritation.

"Every man should want to provide a service for their king. Especially a service that is well compensated." A gold coin appeared between Viverr's fingers.

Want of the coin flashed in the man's eyes. "I may have some information that would be of use to you. If you have another of those coins on hand."

Viverr did not hesitate. "A man of breeding," he said. "Alas, this is the only gold coin I have, but perhaps this other would serve better to loosen your tongue." The gold coin disappeared to be replaced by one of platinum.

The man reached for the coin, but Viverr pulled it deftly from his grasp. "We're looking for a man from the land of the Kerell. Arrived here recently. You'd know him if you saw him. Likely wearing mages' robes of some garish color. Partially shaved head. Should have two rings on his index finger."

"I know him," Alain admitted at last. "He was staying here. Just returned briefly to change his clothing, then he checked out. Can't say I'm sorry for it. He smelled awful."

"I'm certain he did," Viverr replied with a laugh. "And might you know where he was headed?"

"Out of town," Alain replied. "He asked what paths there were south from here. That's the only reason I know of it."

"Was anyone with him?" Islyr asked.

Alain's eyes grew distant. He did not reply.

"Oi!" Viverr waved a hand in front of the man's face.

"No," Alain said at last. "He was alone."

Viverr flipped the coin to Alain. The man caught it with little difficulty despite the silken gloves he was wearing. After checking to see that no one was watching, he slipped the coin into his pocket.

Viverr patted the man on the shoulder. "Thank you kindly, good sir."

"Still, you are not welcome here," he reminded Viverr before heading back to his clientele.

"You could have let him keep the coin," Islyr chided once they were again out on the street and a good way from the inn.

"How'd you know that I took it back?" Viverr asked.

"Observation," Islyr replied. "But honestly, you must have little need for coin now that the kingdom is paying you, not to mention the free food and housing."

"You have no idea what I've a need for."

"I suppose that's true," Islyr conceded.

"He's lucky I only took the one that I gave him," Viverr replied. "Besides, I heard tell that he's a terrible sort. Kicked a kitten last week and refused food to some poor orphan children."

Islyr offered him an incredulous look. "Oh, really?"

"No, of course not," the rogue replied with a grin. "It made you feel a bit better about me pilfering that coin though, didn't it?"

Islyr rolled his eyes at the man.

"Always prepare for the unexpected." Viverr smiled as he brandished the coin. "Aranth today, pariah tomorrow." It disappeared from his fingers as if by a mages' spell. "That fellow is a braying ass, regardless of his treatment of cats and orphans."

"Seemed to me he was just doing what the owners of the inn required of him," Islyr said.

"Yes, well you don't know him very well, do you?"

"Neither do you," Islyr countered.

"Well, he should consider our encounter a valuable lesson, in that event."

Islyr resigned to let the matter die, for in truth it did not matter to him enough for an argument. They walked in silence for a moment. "To clarify, you're still willing to help me catch the Tenere, even though Samuel isn't with him?" he asked as storefronts and cobblestone homes passed beside them.

"Of course," Viverr said. "I committed to this new little faction of the Aranth, didn't I? He's got him, anyway."

"Alain said he was alone."

"I know what he said," Viverr replied. "It's that foggy look he gave when he talked about it that matters. The mage put some sort of spell on him. I could feel it."

"What did you do at that inn in the past, if I may ask?"

"We stayed there a time," Viverr said after a moment.

"We?" he asked as they reached the few small buildings at the edge of town.

"Yeah, me and Aurin."

"Ah yes, Aurin." The rogue's well-muscled companion made up the other half of the famous Sleeping Bandits. Or he had, before they had both been hired by the Aranth and so were bandits no more. "Where is Aurin these days, anyway? I haven't seen him since returning to Evaria city."

Viverr seemed suddenly puzzled. "You know," he said. "I actually have no idea."

"Seems as if you did more than stay at the inn, for all the trouble Alain gave you," Islyr added, for he sensed that the rogue might not want to speak of his missing companion.

"We may have borrowed a few things."

"Borrowed implies that you intended to give them back." Islyr raised a brow at the man.

"Perhaps it's more of a trade, then? A few valuables in exchange for an encounter with the famous Sleeping Bandits. It's more than fair on their end, as I see it.

"Just as I expected you to say," Islyr replied.

The path ahead twisted around a little home composed of beach stones held with clay. On the other side lay a narrow iron gate set into a rock wall. It was there that Islyr spotted him; a tall man with a partially shaved head, dressed in a mages' robe of blinding violet. Viverr disappeared behind a nearby row of hedges. Islyr ducked down beside him just before the mage turned to check the path in their direction.

"Little slow on the hiding, my friend," Viverr whispered. "You almost got us caught."

Islyr did not bother to reply, but rather issued a sigh born of frustration.

"What sort of magic do they typically use?" the rogue asked.

"Does it matter much? It's not as if you're in any danger from it."

"Yes, it matters," Viverr replied testily.

"Most that I've met tend to favor fire magic. Any damage to those imprisoned can be easily healed by way of a *tractatori*."

"Keep to the common tongue," the rogue chided.

"I don't know the word for it in the common tongue," Islyr shot back. "Otherwise, I'd have used it."

"We should go after him now, before he gets into the woods. Not sure what Devren would have to say if we burned down a forest trying to get this mage, but I doubt it'd be anything complimentary."

"I agree," Islyr said. "We'll set upon him while he's distracted and still within the city proper. This area is fairly clear. We should be able to capture him with little difficulty."

"And what of Samuel?" Viverr asked.

"We can find him later," Islyr replied. "It's better to capture the Tenere alone, so there's no chance of your friend being harmed." Islyr glanced through a hole between the leaves of the hedge. Metal squealed as the Tenere snapped the bolt from the gate with a crook of his finger. The latch thumped to the ground beneath. "If you can get close enough to touch him the battle will be won."

"Right. You distract him."

"Not yet. We need some sort of plan. Just give me a second to think."

A low, cracking noise, like the breaking of fine branches, was the only warning Islyr had as Viverr snapped into his animal form. A furry, triangular head with a dark mask burrowed out from Viverr's clothing. The ferret disappeared beneath the hedge faster than a shadeslight into the fog of the abyss.

"Goddess and Spirits almighty," Islyr swore as quietly as he could manage. He clutched his staff, stood, and stepped out onto the path directly across from the mage.

"Tenere," Islyr called out in the language of the Kerell. "If you're searching for a prize worthy of the Empress then you have found one."

The Tenere stepped away from the broken gate to look Islyr over. Only when his eyes met the inking that mapped Islyr's face did the light of recognition flood into them.

"Ferir," the man replied in kind. "Grand champion of the death match."

"You have learned your history," Islyr readied his staff.

"There were rumors that you hovered in this place like a lost spirit."

"Most rumors have little truth to them." Islyr watched the man closely.

"That is so. Not many believed the tales, but they will when I bring you home."

"Kerell is not my home," Islyr replied. "You'll bring me there dead or not at all."

The rogue was certainly taking his time. Mages were not to be trusted, and he had already talked for far too long.

"No one will purchase a dead Rakaii," the mage said. "And I know that you have no desire to walk the steps to the Beyond."

"You know nothing of my desires."

"Any Rakaii who has won as many death-matches as you have, Ferir, cannot have any great love for meeting his demise."

The man was right. He had spent countless years in the arena. It would have taken no more than a shadow's breath of hesitation to allow his opponent to win. He could have ended his reign at any time, but each time he had chosen to kill rather than resign his fate to the Spirits.

The mage's hand twitched. A sphere of blue light appeared between his palm and fingertips. It shot towards Islyr without warning. He threw himself to the ground. It passed above him, narrowly missing his head. If he had delayed by a second more it would have struck him. He was back on his feet in an instant. The wall of the house behind him shimmered with crystalline light. Not fire magic, but something new.

A twist of one corner of the mage's lips was all the warning Islyr was given. He was struck in the back, as if by a massive club. He tumbled forward to strike the ground in front of him. The beach stones that had made up the wall of the house tumbled to the ground around him, striking his arms, legs, and chest.

*Cold*, his thoughts echoed as he shielded his head. Ice magic. But how had the mage caused it to explode? The man was standing over him now. His dark irises were offset with odd streaks of violet which glowed as sunlight would through a stained-glass window. He rolled Islyr over.

*So cold.* Islyr wished so to strike the man, but his muscles refused to obey.

*"Did you think I would come to this savage place unprepared?"* The mage reached into his satchel to pull out a piece of silver metal no larger than a sewing needle. He crouched down next to Islyr.

"The circlet of a new era," the mage explained as he held it to the light. "They are sleeker and hold more beauty than those of old."

Islyr struggled to move. His hand inched towards the man.

*"None of that,"* the mage said.

A painful chill swept across Islyr's forearm, causing all movement to cease.

"Now, this will be painful, but only because you've managed to irritate me," the mage explained. "I trust you will keep that in mind for the future. The ride to Kerell by boat is lengthy, as you well know." The man paused. He opened his mouth as if to say more, but rather tumbled forward instead, straight onto Islyr's chest.

Viverr, still in ferret form, climbed atop the man to look down at Islyr. There were many choice words Islyr would have liked to use in that moment. Unfortunately, his lips were as unwilling to move as the rest of him. His predicament was remedied as Viverr moved forward and pressed a paw to his cheek. The rogue then scurried back onto the grass.

Islyr shoved the mage from atop his chest. The man rolled limply. He found it painful to stand. He would be heavily bruised, come morning.

"Did you kill him?" Islyr asked.

"I don't think so," Viverr replied as he dusted grass from his freshly human form. "It's a bit of a shock for mages; having all of their magic taken from them at once. He's merely passed out is all."

Disappointment tightened Islyr's chest despite the fact they had been ordered to bring the mage back alive if possible. "How long do we have to get him back to the castle?"

"Nearly an hour, I would say. We'll make it well before he wakes."

"And you're planning on going just as you are?" Islyr asked, looking the man over.

"Are you bothered by a bit of nudity?" the rogue replied with a laugh. "I didn't take you for the type."

"No one who has lived in the land of the Kerell for any length of time is bothered by nudity," Islyr informed him. "I was speaking more on their behalf." He gestured towards the crowd of townspeople who had gathered nearby.

"Move along now," the rogue announced, turning his back away from them so that his mark could not easily be seen. "Go back to whatever you were doing. There's nothing of interest happening here."

"I feel as if they might disagree," Islyr noted. He watched as a few people in the crowd shifted and whispered to each other. No one looked ready to leave as instructed.

"Alright, then." Viverr held the back of his hand aloft. "Official Aranth business," he shouted to the crowd. "Leave now, or risk being in contempt of the throne."

The crowd reluctantly dispersed. This would likely be the most entertaining thing they saw today.

"They won't remember any of this, as it is," the rogue said as he hastily gathered his clothing.

"As it's been explained to me, the only thing the magic of Evaria will alter is anything having to do with your mark. But a man running around nude in broad daylight? That, they'll certainly remember."

"Just keep your opinions to yourself," Viverr muttered as he looked the mage over. "He's not a light man, that I'll say. How do you suppose we get him back to the castle?"

"Are you saying that you'd like me to carry him?"

"Well, you can't very well expect me to do it."

"You might pretend that he's a rather large bag of coins," Islyr offered. "Would that be sufficient motivation?"

"It's not a matter of motivation so much as ability," Viverr said. "I don't think I could even if I wanted to. I'm not much for exercise, in case you failed to notice. You, on the other hand, seem in excellent shape."

"Yes, that's fine," Islyr injected before the rogue could prattle on any longer. "But if I carry him then you must remain silent until we get back to the castle."

"An excellent deal," Viverr agreed. "But I feel I must say one last thing before we depart."

Islyr suppressed a sigh. "And that is?"

"We may both hate riding, but in this instance it would have been convenient to have a horse."

Islyr found once again that he could not disagree.

# Solutus
## *Kerell – Caves of the Dead*

Hours slipped endlessly by as Selene waited. She could hear the others speaking, yet just as before, the speed of their speech left little time for interpretation. She had tried all of her latent abilities, as well as her affinity. None of them seemed to work here. Time was counted now by the meals that the men slid through the gap beneath the bars; two per day. When she was tired, she slept, as there was no firm way to tell night from day in the darkness of the catacombs. She watched those outside the bars, for there was naught else to do. One thing was certain, there were more men here than she could hope to fight alone.

They took turns bringing her food and emptying her chamber pot, and at times others walked by to offer glances that made the fine hairs on her skin rise. Every few days they brought a small vial of shimmering liquid. She assumed that the vials must filled with antidote, and always drank them as instructed. Before long she had an approximate count of no less than twenty-five individuals. How long could Solutus possibly remain angry with her? She began to make scratches upon the bones that decorated the back of her cell; one for each plate of food that was brought to her, as an attempt to mark the passage of time. If only she had thought of it at the beginning, she might now have a better idea of how much time had passed. After ten scratches, or what might be five days, she had gained much of her strength back. She made up her mind that this day would not go as planned for them.

*"Ientaculum,"* the man said. *"Comedo."* He shoved a plate containing a handful of dried fruit and some cooked meat into her cell.

Selene shoved the plate right back out towards him. It was foolish to refuse food, as she had received so little, yet she found that she could no longer hold her frustration at bay.

"Let me out," she demanded. "I must speak with Solutus."

The man laughed. He shoved the plate back beneath the bars.

"Please," she added. Perhaps a change of tactic would appease them. "It was a misunderstanding," she lied. "Let me speak with him. I only wish to apologize."

The man shook his head. Frustrated, Selene rammed her foot against the bucket that served as her chamber pot. It clattered against the bars, splattering her captor in the process. He jumped back, yelling something that she could only assume was a curse to the Spirits themselves, then called a few words back into the darkness of the room. With that he turned and disappeared from sight.

*That certainly didn't help*, she thought as she braced her back against the wall. She would need to come up with another plan. *A better one next time*, she chided herself.

When the man returned, Solutus was with him. Her outburst had not been in vain. He had finally returned to claim her. Relief swirled with the anger that tightened her chest.

"Apologies, my dear," he began. "It was not my intention to leave you in there for such a length of time." His accent, she now realized, was an odd mixture of southern Evarian and Kerell. He stepped deftly around the spilled contents of her chamber pot and drew close to the bars.

Selene was not certain what to make of the man's demeanor after the treatment she had previously received. Embarrassment slipped through her fatigue and frustration like a saltsnake from between rocks as she looked at the mess that her anger had so recently caused.

"Not to worry," Solutus replied, following her gaze. "Someone will come out to clean it presently." He hesitated with a key near the latch. "Now, if I am to let you out you must promise that you will not attempt to flee. You are still weak, and I am concerned that your health will not hold if you exert yourself like that again."

"Of course," she replied. She would have promised him the Spirits' allegiance had she thought she could procure it, so much did her desire to be freed from the cage overwhelm her good senses.

He held the key up to the latch, but hesitated. "I must have your word."

"You have my word that I will not attempt to flee," she lied.

The latch clicked as he turned the key within it. The door groaned open. Solutus offered a hand, which she accepted more out of fear of angering him than any need of it. The burn of his mark served to calm her, oddly, for she still could not touch any of her latent abilities and it was of some comfort to know that they were still there. From a nearby shelf, which she happily noted was made of leveled rock rather than bones, Solutus pulled a blanket. She had not realized until then that she was shivering. The wool of the blanket scratched in the slightest, but it was so beautifully warm that she pulled it tight against her shoulders.

"Tell me of this place," she said as they walked, for perhaps some knowledge of it would aid in her escape.

"This is my sanctuary," he replied. "The only place in Kerell where Marked Ones are safe from the mages who rule the land above."

"But how do you accomplish it?" she ventured.

"It is not of any consequence," Solutus replied. "You need only know that you are safe here."

They came to a stop before an arched doorway, across which a length of fabric had been hung as a curtain. It was thick, and in good condition compared to much of the cloth she had seen here. Solutus pushed it aside and ushered her though. Inside was a bedchamber. At the center was a pile of sheets and blankets in various shades of red. Surrounding this was a makeshift wardrobe and table, both composed of found items, for the slabs of wood were of varying colors and thickness. Solutus opened the wardrobe, and from it he pulled a folded shirt and breeches. He handed it to her.

"They're not likely to fit you properly," he explained. "There are no females here, yourself aside."

"Thank you," she replied. Her mind still spun from the rush of recent events, and she wobbled in the slightest in her attempt to sit gracefully upon the bed.

"I could hardly refuse aid to a fellow Aranth," he said with an oddly crooked smile.

"Was it very long ago that you served Evaria?" she asked.

He thought for a few seconds in silence. "Years. I could not tell you exactly how many. And then I was Rakaii for more years than any marked one should have to endure. After I managed to escape, I found myself here, in the land of the dead. Time passes oddly here." He stopped then, as if lost within his memories.

Selene felt as if she should say something but did not wish to incite his anger, for it seemed highly unpredictable. "It is good that you were able to escape," she attempted at last.

"There is a bowl of fresh water on the table," he said, returning from wherever her question had taken him "Come out when you are washed and dressed, and I will accompany you to the common area for dinner."

Selene wanted no more than to flee, yet she dared not attempt it lest it end as it had before. She nodded in consent as he parted the curtain and stepped out of the room. She washed and dressed with as much haste as possible, for the promise of proper food was nearly too much for her stomach to bear. The clothes were not overly large, but they sagged a bit in odd places. They were fairly clean, in any event, and far better than traversing the frigid cavern in her underclothes.

Once she was fully clothed, she followed Solutus quietly to what he had named as the common area, which turned out to be the large, circular room in which most of the men slept. The bedrolls had been moved aside, and in their place men sat upon the floor, neatly circling the central plie of glowing stones. They rose as one upon noticing Solutus' presence.

A survey of the room allowed her to pick Felan out amongst the others. She started to call out to him, but as she met his gaze his eyes widened. He shook his head, though the gesture was nearly imperceptible. Something was wrong here.

Solutus gestured for her to sit, strangely not upon the floor but on a raised area of rock above the others. A woolen blanket had been set upon the seat to keep the cold from beneath at bay, and heat rose from the glowing stones at the center of the room to warm her. As she touched the blanket to sit, the others copied the movement. The number of men was close to one hundred, as she had first thought, assuming they were all present. It was far more than she had caught sight of while in her cell. The thought caused her stomach to form an uncomfortable knot. She was handed a bowl of what looked like chunks of meat and chopped vegetables in sauce. A medley of unfamiliar spices invaded her nostrils.

It became obvious when Solutus began to speak that his first language was that of the Kerell. How he had ended up with the Aranth so long ago she might never know. Three of his men walked up and down the circular rows of their brethren handing out bowls of food. Solutus said a great many things while they did so. Selene could understand little more than a few words of what was spoken, which she found to be greatly irritating. It seemed that she did not have much of a mind for new languages, at least not as Cael or Xaiden did. She attempted to meet Felan's gaze once again while Solutus spoke, but he did not look up from his food. An attempt to call out to him in her mind fared no better.

After the speech Solutus took a seat beside her. He settled himself a bit too close for her liking, with their knees lightly touching, yet she did have to admit that the stone platform was more of a size for one, and her situation seemed a great deal more comfortable than the plight of those upon the floor.

"What did you tell them?" she risked as he ate.

"Every day I remind them of what I provide for them here," Solutus explained. I keep them safe from the Tenere, feed them, and provide basic necessities. In return I expect order, obedience and contribution to our society."

They did seem most orderly in his presence, so unlike the behavior of those who had thrown her in the cell. Most especially unlike the one who had licked her and attempted to mount her. She could not help but shudder as the memory returned to her.

"I do intend to remedy that."

Selene choked back a piece of meat that had been attempting to make its way down her throat. The taste of the spices was as strong as the scent, and wholly unfamiliar.

"I beg your pardon?" The words escaped rudely between fits of coughing.

Solutus waited patiently for her to recover. "Nepos, the man who treated you so poorly. He will receive punishment, I assure you."

"Your latent ability," she wagered. "It has to do with listening to other people's minds, like Felan's?"

When he laughed it was a hollow sound which filled her with unease. "No, nothing so base as that."

"*Felan et Nepos*," he ordered aloud in Kerell. "*Veni ad me.*"

Both Felan and Nepos stood and stepped forward. They stood beneath him, as if patiently awaiting instruction. Solutus issued a few rapid directions in Kerell, after which Nepos walked to the pile of stones at the center of the room and plucked one from the edge. Holding it cupped in his hand he returned to stand before Solutus. It was not until he drew close that Selene noticed the set of his jaw, and the tears that leaked from the corners of his eyes. The smell of burning flesh invaded her nostrils. Upon reaching Solutus' position Nepos dropped the stone into a shallow depression that lay in the ground beneath him. He then returned to the pit and collected another.

"How many would you say, my dear?" Solutus asked, turning to her. "Nepos came to us fairly recently. It appears that he has not yet acclimated to the rules of my city, so he must learn."

Disgust twisted the meager amount of food in her stomach. What amount of pain could make up for Nepos' attempt to take her by force? Back home men were frequently strung up for such, albeit mostly those who had found success in their unconscionable acts.

Solutus waved his hand towards her, as if using the gesture to brush her concerns away. "Let us settle on ten. That sounds reasonable to me."

Nepos paled at the decision but did not contest it. Minutes passed painfully slowly, until finally with a nod from his leader Nepos finished moving the final stone. By his stance it was plain that the man was nearing the end of his endurance.

"Well enough," Solutus allowed at last. "Offer a proper apology to the lady and you may return to your seat."

Selene found that she did not care much whether he apologized at this point, for she could barely stand to look upon his face. That, and the smell of burning flesh now thoroughly permeated the room, causing her dinner to threaten an untimely return. She offered a gracious nod at Nepos' words, even though she understood none of them as they were in Kerell.

"Now, Felan."

Selene's chest tightened as Solutus spoke her friend's name.

"Explain to your companion what I've told you."

"I would be happy to, your majesty," Felan replied with a bow.

Solutus smiled. "Such titles of respect are not necessary. I know that I hold the allegiance of my men, yet I am no sovereign. My chosen name will do."

"Apologies, Solutus."

"Accepted. Continue, please."

Felan looked up to where Selene sat above him. "I have come as your companion to bear witness. Is it acceptable that I take this role?"

She began to ask him what he meant, but the look of terror in his eyes told her that she would be foolish to do so. Nearly invisible in the dim light, he mouthed the word 'yes'.

"Yes," she replied.

"Excellent," Solutus proclaimed as he stood. He next called out for Jevelir. The man appeared presently, though from where Selene could not tell.

"And as we are long-time friends you shall be my witness. Do you accept?"

"I do," the man replied.

Solutus stood and motioned for her to do the same. Selene could not determine the source of the unease that was growing within her, yet each word that emanated from Solutus' mouth served only to amplify it. He placed a hand upon her shoulder. His words came in rhythm, like a chant.

"Two come to bear witness to the exchange of power," Solutus said in the common tongue, between lines of the chant. "She has agreed that it is mine to be taken."

"What is this?" Selene asked when she could stand it no longer.

"It is a ritual that creates a bond of magic," he answered.

"Marked ones cannot cast spells," she protested.

Her words were buried by one hundred voices vibrating in unison. Solutus' chanting had ceased, yet it was echoed by the others in the room in the language of the mages. The tone resonated through her chest. It was a sound to call the Spirits, like that of the Sending Hymn. One hundred voices rose to echo from the walls of hollow bone.

She grabbed Solutus' shoulder. "A bond of what sort?"

"Of our latent abilities," he explained in a whisper, as if noise might break the magic of the chant. "Only by taking some power from each of those hiding here can I create the shielding that keeps this place safe, amplified by the bones of the old ones. They allow me to use your abilities in your stead."

Her expression must have betrayed her, for he added. "Your power will be taken little by little over time, until it becomes only mine. Most claim that they barely notice the shift."

Selene lowered herself clumsily to the bench. He pulled her back up to stand.

"You'll stay here. Thus, you will have no need of your powers. I shall protect you."

"No," she said. "Solutus, please, I must leave to find my friends."

"Your abilities will regenerate with time," he said, as if that was meant to be reassuring. "Within a few weeks of separation from this place you'll be nearly back to your full power."

"I said no." Even one week was far too long. She needed to find Cael and Xaiden. Selene reached for her healing ability. She touched it for an instant, but then it drained from her.

"Unfortunately for you, the ritual is merely a formality," Solutus whispered. He grabbed her arm. "It is so much easier to maintain compliance with the illusion of choice. Now stand with me, or I will force you to do so."

"I won't." Selene pulled from his grasp and stumbled backwards. Her latent ability flowed through her without warning, like warm water that spread outward from her veins. With instinct rather than thought she gathered it and shoved it towards Solutus. The man flew back as if struck by some large, unseen creature. A sharp crack, like that of wood split by an axe, rang out as he struck a nearby wall, then landed on the floor beneath it.

Selene looked across the cavern. All was silent. Movement began in the far corner of the room, where a lone man rose to stand. Others followed suit, popping up like barnacles opening with the rising tide. They did nothing but stare at first, perhaps as much in shock as she, but then, ever so slowly, they began to move towards her.

Selene took a step back as if compelled by the Spirits. Something wrapped around her wrist. The faint burn of a mark, a slow trickle, rushed through her as she looked down to meet Solutus' gaze. Irises the color of river mud encircled dark pupils, one large enough to fill the eye's center, and the other barely perceptible in the darkness. A rivulet of blood leaked from one side of Solutus' head. It had created a short trail across the floor where he had struggled to crawl to her.

"They're coming," he said in Evarian. "How will it feel to be responsible for the enslavement of so many of your people?"

Selene yanked her hand from his grasp. "What does that mean?"

"They will find them now. They circle this jungle like birds of prey on the hunt."

"I didn't mean for this to happen," she breathed.

Solutus struggled to speak. "What you meant to do is of no consequence. They will not care to hear of your intentions while struggling against their chains."

His body went limp and slumped to the floor before she could form a reply. She watched as he continued to take shallow breaths. Pressure set upon each of her shoulders. Hands pulled her aside and down the stairs.

"They're close," Jevelir said. "There's little time left."

Selene stumbled down the last step. She glanced around the room as she righted herself. Solutus' men were no longer advancing, but rather scattering like birds flushed from the hedges.

"They're running," she replied foggily. "We're not in any danger."

"Yes, we are," Jevelir replied. "More running and less questions would be ideal."

"Selene, we have to go," Felan agreed, appearing from her left.

Her body protested this idea heavily, for fatigue encompassed it, slowing her as if she was walking through the deep mud of a riverbank in spring.

"Pull her if you have to," Jevelir ordered as they traversed the seemingly eternal hall outside the common room.

A roar rumbled across the shadows of the cave, and a few loose pebbles at her feet rattled against the floor. A scream pierced her hearing as she ran.

"Turn," Jevelir said. "There's a tunnel to your right."

The glowing stones were spaced no less than twenty feet apart here. It was nearly impossible to see through the shadows, but she could hear enough to know that their situation was dire. Screams of terror echoed from the cavernous walls in all directions, laced between roaring screeches and what sounded like the flapping of many flags in the wind.

There are no flags here, her mind informed her. And there is no wind.

"Turn again, here." There was panic in Jevelir's voice. "We're almost out."

*Wings*, she realized. It was the flapping of wings.

A startled yelp was the only warning she was given as Felan was yanked from her side and dragged away. Jevelir released her other arm, and she tumbled to the rocky floor. He plucked something from the ground. The stone glowed for a second as he held it in cupped hands. He threw it in the direction that Felan had been taken and shoved Selene's upper body against the floor.

The force of the explosion caused her ears to ring.

"I'm alive," Felan moaned weakly from the shadows.

The cavern had collapsed in part, shielding him from view.

"I can't fit through," he cried. "Keep running. I'll find you."

Jevelir dragged Selene forward, stumbling around lumps of rock and the odd bone broken from the cavern walls, but strangely no bodies of those who had fallen. *Focus,* she chided herself. Meager light appeared in the distance. It grew in strength as they drew closer.

"We'll have to crawl," Jevelir panted. "The opening is only large enough for one, and it's tight."

Selene pressed her body to the floor. Once fully upon it she wanted no more than to lie there for eternity.

"Quickly," Jevelir said, prodding her in the side. "They're close."

"You go first," Selene offered. "You can help pull me out."

Jevelir surged ahead of her. She supposed there was no time to argue, in any event. He struggled but managed to push himself through the narrow opening. For a few seconds she entertained the thought that he had left her, but then his hand extended through the crack, shattering the illusion. She levered her head through first and managed to free herself as far as her shoulders.

The songs of animals rang out around her. They were in the jungle, somewhere. Something cold clamped down on her ankle. She kicked with what strength she had left, but it refused to release. She was dragged backward. Jevelir took hold of her other wrist with his free hand. He held steady, but whatever it was that gripped her was strong; more so than any human she knew. Her bones ached as it squeezed upon her flesh.

"Let go, Jevelir," she pleaded. She felt as if it would pull her to pieces.

"I won't," he replied. "If they get ahold of you, you're done for."

Selene could see nothing of what held her, for it was impossible to turn back with a stretch of rock pressed against her middle. *Bloodsoul?* she wondered as thoughts of the millions of bones which decorated the catacombs flashed through her mind. Through her exhaustion she summoned their language; a rumbling growl containing an order to release her. It traveled farther than she intended, shaking a few leaves from nearby trees, and causing the cries of all animals in the vicinity to cease. She knew at once that the creature was not a bloodsoul, though by the luck of the Tides her order had the desired effect on the creature and on Jevelir, for they both let go of her at once.

In seconds the thing gripped her again, yet this time it barely touched her foot and released. This touch was slick and wet, unlike before. Her latent abilities drained from her like ale from a broken barrel, leaving a terrible, empty feeling in their wake. She summoned the rest of her strength and dragged the lower half of her body through the opening and out into the night.

Selene lay upon the ground, breathing heavily as she surveyed the small portion of sky that was visible through the layers of leaves. She had expected daylight upon freeing herself from the cavern. What she found was a full moon with companion stars dotting a clear sky. To her eyes, now so accustomed to darkness, it was the strength of the sun in the heat of the day. She looked down at her foot. It was not blood that lay there, as she had assumed, but rather a familiar looking silver liquid that shimmered like molten metal. It seemed that Ranur had sold at least some of it to the Kerell before she had ended his troubled existence.

"Spirits' sake," Selene swore. She wobbled as she stood. They were in a clearing with forest surrounding. She made a pact with herself never to enter another cave in this land, for they all seemed to be filled with danger and misery.

"They've locked on to us for certain now." Jevelir's voice held an edge of panic.

"I can keep running," Selene said, though the way the world seemed to shift without warning beneath her feet told her otherwise. "We can still escape them."

"I might alone, but you can't," Jevelir informed her.

"Run then, and leave me," she said, fully prepared that he might.

Jevelir was silent a few seconds, as if considering. "I might be able to hide us, at least for a while," he said at last. "There's a small chance they might not find us." He looked around. "There's nothing here I can use, but the beach is nearby. Follow me."

"Wouldn't it be better to stay in the forest, where there's sufficient cover?"

"They certainly know you're here now due to whatever it is you just did. That's powerful magic. Even I can tell. They'll know you're valuable, even not knowing you're female, and they now know what direction we're in as well. They'll send all of them for us unless something better comes along, which is doubtful."

"Send all of what?" Selene asked as he helped her up from the ground.

"Creatures of stone," Jevelir replied. "Some mages create them to help with the capture of feral Rakaii."

"But what are they?"

"Rakaii call them the Spiritless. I don't know what they're called by the Kerell. Doesn't really matter."

Perhaps there was truth in that. "How will we get free from them?"

"We won't," he snapped. "They always find you. The only thing keeping them from us was Solutus, and now he's gone."

"But you must have a plan."

He laughed. "A plan, yes. My plan is to try to kill as many of them as I can before they take us. Will that do?"

Selene gripped the trunk of a nearby tree as the world once again spiraled unexpectedly around her. The bark was rough and damp beneath her fingers. "Let's go, then," she managed.

She focused on placing one foot down, and then the other. It was all she could do to stand, yet by the luck of the Tides the world cooperated and remained steady around her as she followed Jevelir through the thick underbrush.

The sound of waves struck her as they drew close. The give of the sand was a welcome respite from the branches and thorns of the forest. Her feet felt torn and were likely bleeding, for they were still bare, as they had been since the shipwreck. She still could not feel any of her abilities, sadly, so healing would have to wait. Perhaps she was too exhausted for it, in any event.

As Selene and Jevelir navigated the last of the leafy branches the ocean finally came into view. The deep, ink blue of waves at night reflected the light of the full moon above. There was no time to admire its beauty, for she was dragged by Jevelir to a nearby rocky outcropping. Once there he plucked a pile of stones from the ground, each about the size of her closed fist.

"I'm weak." He handed the stones to Selene before taking as many more as he could carry. "He left me some of my power, enough to be of use to him, but most of it he siphoned out, just like the others. You'd think it would have mattered that we'd been friends."

Selene followed him, struggling under the weight of the stones, until finally they came to a clear spot in the center of the sand where she was instructed to release them. Nothing moved upon the length of the beach, nor in the distant forest beyond.

"We'll make our stand here," Jevelir explained as he sorted the pile of stones into varying sizes. "Not that it will save us in the end, but at least we can say we made an attempt, for whatever that's worth."

The area was far too open to mount any sort of defense. She prepared to tell him so but was stopped as he plucked a stone from the pile and spoke.

"We're making a circle," he ordered. The rock he held began to glow. He handed it to her. For the most part it remained much like a regular stone in appearance, though etched lines now swirled across its surface, glowing briefly with low green light. "Doesn't have to be perfectly round, but we'll both need to be able to fit in the center."

Selene didn't protest. She simply took the stones as he handed them to her and placed them on the ground. They finished placing them with little time to spare, for the leaves of the forest rustled near where they had left it for the beach.

"That'll be those stone bastards," Jevelir said. "Last one, thankfully. Sit down, now."

Selene gratefully did so. Jevelir briefly held one final stone, this one with a glow of white, in contrast to the green of the rest. The air flashed around them as he placed the stone into the circle, completing it. "They won't be able to see much through it. Like gazing through cloudy water, though we'll be able to see them just fine."

And with that, two of the Spiritless erupted from the forest and landed on the beach. They looked equal to a large person in size and had wings much like that of a bat or dragon, though any more detail was lost to the dark of night. Even at this distance she was certain that they were not creatures she would wish to do battle with, although if Jevelir's opinion on their chances of staying hidden was to be believed, then she was not likely to be given a choice in the matter.

The Spiritless did not appear to be able to see through the strange shield that Jevelir had created, though from the inside it was as clear as fine glass. She witnessed no more than the occasional shimmer of light to note that it was still in place. It was unnerving, having the creatures so close without any visible barrier between them. They searched the beach, their eyes glowing with dull, red light as they hunted. Each time one of their faces turned in her direction a knife point of fear lanced her chest.

"This is unfortunate." Jevelir's whispered words pulled her to attention.

"They haven't seen us yet," she replied. "Perhaps they won't find us at all."

"Not them," Jevelir clarified. He pointed to the circle of stones. Water now washed around the bottom of each, rising and falling with each wave.

"The tide is coming in," she realized. "Is the barrier not solid?"

"I couldn't make it completely so," he informed her. "Or we wouldn't be able to breathe."

"You're the one who insisted on creating this on the beach," she said.

"Yes, because rocks are difficult to find in the jungle," he countered. "Spirits keep me."

Selene followed Jevelir's gaze. Four Spiritless hovered in various places upon the beach. All of them were now looking directly towards where she and Jevelir were hiding. The creatures wasted no time in flying up to the barrier. As they drew closer, she finally got a proper view of them, though in truth it was much too close a view for her liking. They were well-muscled, with faces that lingered somewhere between human and animal. Their eyes put her in mind of clouded rubies. It was as if an expert sculptor had somehow offered his creations the spirit of life. Upon the neck of each one, tied with a narrow strip of leather, was a corked, glass vial filled with silver liquid.

Fingers of rock coated in green moss scratched against the unseen barrier, causing a ripple of movement within it. Selene looked up to find a flattened face with rough skin. Deep holes where eyes should reside instead glowed like the stones in the pit at the center of the catacombs. The eyes of the closest Spiritless brightened like kindled flame. As if beckoned by the first, several more emerged from the woods. They landed and folded their wings, forming a circle that mirrored that of the stones of protection.

"How long will the barrier last?" she asked as one of the creatures growled at another. Pointed teeth like jagged rocks dotted the inside of its mouth.

"I don't know," he replied. "This is the first time I've tried this."

"You don't know how your own latent ability works?" She was exhausted and frustrated, and once again it was gnawing at her mood.

"I'd climb right down from that high and mighty pedestal if I were you," he snapped. "I guarantee you aren't aware of everything yours does either. Latent abilities have some subtleties. They aren't always what they seem at first to be."

Selene huffed with frustration. She wanted nothing more than to lay upon the sand and close her eyes, despite the fact that it was cold and damp. The water now lapped just above her crossed legs with every wave.

"Just what does your latent ability do?" she asked in an attempt to distract herself from the Spiritless that hovered much too close to her face.

"I can imbue stone with temporary abilities."

"What sort of abilities?"

"Most anything I can think of. Sometimes things work, and sometimes they don't." He plucked a rock from the small pile of those that remained. A swirl of pale, blue light encircled it. He handed it to Selene. As it touched her palm little pinpoints of light like stars appeared above the stone, along with a tiny version of the moon. It stayed for a moment before dissipating with a pop into a shower of glittering light.

A shadowed grin touched her lips despite her fatigue.

"A great many are like this," he explained. "More festive than practical. But my master's daughter used to love them."

It was difficult to imagine that he had once been Rakaii, though it made sense with how long he must have been trapped in the land of the Kerell.

"Solutus helped me escape," he whispered.

"I'm sorry," Selene began.

"He's not the man he used to be," Jevelir added before she could continue. "He wasn't, I mean. It's for the best." He picked up another stone. Lines with the glow of firelight swept over it as he handed it to her. "Explodes when it hits something, so don't throw it until the barrier comes down."

The stone was warm against Selene's skin, yet not hot enough to burn. Behind the line of Spiritless she witnessed several figures emerge from the forest. These were human.

"Try to hit the mages if you can," Jevelir said. "They're the only ones you can do any damage to, assuming they don't have their shields up. The skin on the Spiritless can't be harmed, at least not by anything I'm able to make." The sharp burn of his mark penetrated Selene's cheeks as he put his hands upon them and levered her head to meet his gaze. "The most important thing to remember is that they want you alive at any cost."

"What about you?" she asked.

"Disposable."

The mages approached but kept a safe distance. It was difficult to get a decent view of them with only the light of the moon. She could at least see that they did not wear what she would consider to be mages' robes, but rather light armor, perhaps of leather, and that one was female and the other male. They quarreled amongst themselves.

"Can you hear what they're saying?" she asked.

"No." Jevelir gripped the stone in his hand tightly. "But they'll find a way though the barrier shortly, of that I have no doubt."

With a wave of the female's hand the stone creatures scattered, only to land in small groups nearby. There were now at least ten in number, and more trickled out of the woods with every passing moment. The male mage spotted Selene and his eyes grew wide. He approached the circle of stones together with his companion. The pair drew so close that either one could have easily grabbed hold of her had the barrier not been in place. He said something unintelligible to the female, which caused her to lean in close. She gazed at Selene with dark, almond-shaped eyes rimmed expertly with coal. As the woman stepped back, her mouth opened to gape in the slightest.

"What's wrong with her?" Selene whispered.

"Just realized she's going to be exceedingly wealthy in a few moments, if I had to wager on it."

"But we don't have anything of value," Selene reminded him.

"It's you," he said with a look that made her feel idiotic. "You're the only thing of value here."

"I'm not a possession," she countered.

He laughed. "You'll be one shortly."

Jevelir shot a look at the mage and Selene followed it. The woman was now standing, having found her composure. She pointed here and there, directing the Spiritless to where she wanted them to be. After that was completed to her liking she began chanting, her mouth opening with words that Selene still could not hear. The mage's hands turned upward, readying what could only be a spell to bring the barrier down.

"It has been wonderful getting to know you, Selene," Jevelir said with resignation.

She had no chance to reply, for the barrier wobbled, throwing ripples through the air surrounding them. The sound of it dissipating reminded her of cracking ice, but the rush of air that followed was hot rather than cold. She had no more than a second before the Spiritless dove at her. She threw the stone that Jevelir had given her at the mage with as much strength as she could muster, but one of the creatures dove between them. The rock exploded as it hit the beast. It catapulted the creature back, but Selene was too close. It threw her backwards as well. She landed in the water. It was not so cold as the waters of home but was shocking all the same. She drifted for no more than a few seconds before what felt like a handful of stones encompassed the length of her arms and legs. The creatures lifted her from the water to stand. She glimpsed Jevelir as they pulled her up. He was sprinting towards the woods. A futile attempt, it seemed, for several of the creatures trailed closely behind. Selene's bare feet pulled roughly through the sand as they dragged her closer to where the mages stood. It seemed they were taking no chances, for one creature held each of her arms and at least five more stood guard nearby.

The female mage stared at Selene, lost in thought for the moment. She looked her over. The most perfect set of teeth Selene had encountered flashed within the woman's bright smile. The mage grabbed her companion's hands. The two then jumped into a giddy embrace, the likes of which Selene had last seen when Viverr had come across a particularly costly piece of treasure. Xaiden had not cared much for the gesture, nor for rogue's invasion of his personal space, as she recalled.

Her mind fought to focus; to make sense of the mage's actions through her fatigue. She could escape. There had to be a way out that she hadn't thought of. *There isn't,* her mind replied. *It's done.*

The male waved the creatures forward with a crook of his finger. Selene's legs lifted beneath her as two more of them took hold. Their wings flapped, breezing alternating currents of air against her wet skin. Would they take her to the city? Stars danced within a sky of Evaria's midnight blue as they lifted her away.

# Into the City
## *Kerell – Capital City*

Advancing daylight passed as slowly as the night which had preceded it. Selene could barely move in her tiny enclosure, and rows of sticks did not make a bed conducive for sleep. She had hoped that her captors would stop to make camp at some point after capturing her, and that perhaps she might be let out of her cage for a time, which might present an opportunity to escape. It was not to be. The cart at the front of the queue apparently held enough room for sleeping within, and rather than stop, the two mages had simply switched out between them; one rested while the other kept watch. It did seem that she was precious to them, as Jevelir had implied. They checked on her three times as much as they did the others, riding next to her on strangely lithe and agile horses that she had not seen the likes of at home. As the sun rose so did the heat of the day, and she was suddenly thankful for the veil of cloth that lay draped across to the top of her enclosure.

A familiar looking cliff now towered above her, complete with the same sharp-beaked birds squabbling above it. How long had it been since the poorly placed cliff ended their progress towards the city? Struggle as she might, she could not recall.

They came at last to a clearing in the forest. A series of arches had been carved through the bottom of the cliff at this end, with a road leading beneath. Although she could hear the waves of the ocean, she could not see it due to the thickness of the foliage. She held tight to the bars of her cage as well as she could with bound wrists. Her swollen arm sent lightning strikes of pain through her as the carriage bumped along a path of clay and stone. The best she could do was to kneel. The height of the cage would not allow her to stand. She was still weak, and thus the world swung dangerously around her at times. Even still, something within begged her to gain better purchase; to see the city that likely would likely be her home for some length of time. *But not forever.* Her mind countered. Perhaps she did not quite believe it, even so.

As they passed under a grand arch the sun glinted off the sand that stretched from the side of the road to the beach beyond. At last, she could see the city, and with the sight of it came a quick intake of breath. It was beautiful. Evaria's buildings seemed haphazardly built in comparison. Kerell city must have been carved from the most pristine mountain in existence, for its residences and shops were composed of perfect, bright stone to match the beach below. It was easily three times the size of Evaria city, though it traveled upward rather than across the land. Selene craned her neck to spy through a hole in the fabric which covered the roof of her cage. At the top of the city was what could only be the residence of Kerell's Empress; a building of gleaming stone which spiraled up to a central tower decorated with massive flags of maroon and gold.

The city gates lay open. They were larger than any from the cities at home and were composed of metal complete with imposing spikes. There the caravan stopped to exchange a few words and some coin with one of several guardsmen. Upon gazing upward, she found two stone horses rearing across the top of the gate, their front hooves touching at the center. The stallions were expertly sculpted and of such a size as to dwarf those found in life. Atop them sat stone riders, one male and one female, nude and carved in surprising detail. Selene was so entranced with them that she was a moment late in noticing the guardsman who now stood directly next to her cage. He looked her over with interest, and she could do naught but stare in return.

She had come to learn her captor's names during the journey, by way of listening to the words most repeated and their intonation when they spoke. The woman in charge was named Aster, and the muscular man with the oddly flat nose who hovered around her was Phaedrus. No telling whether the information would be of any benefit, but there had been little else to do during the long hours of travel but listen. The guardsman offered what seemed like a congratulatory handshake to Aster and Phaedrus both and ushered them inside.

The roadways were much smoother inside the city, and so wide across that two carriages would have no difficulty passing each other. Despite their oddly pristine condition she was not overly fond of the roads here, for some rose at more of an angle than she was comfortable with, at least while trapped in a cage of sticks. She attempted to see farther back as they traveled, hoping to catch a glimpse of Jevelir, or perhaps Felan. She had not seen either of them, nor had she heard their voices since being taken by the mages. There was no way to know for certain whether they had been captured. The additional silver liquid that they had splashed upon her through the bars of the cage during the night kept her from so much as a whisper of any of her latent abilities. She had to assume that the others received similar treatment.

Selene distracted herself with watching the people of the city as the carriage worked its way higher. They interacted much as the people of Evaria did, and although she could not understand their words, their actions were wholly familiar. There were stalls where food and amenities were being sold, people carrying baskets of goods, families with children of all ages, and the odd stray mongrel or cat. It was decidedly more like home than she had imagined, and at the same time oddly different. Clothing was light here, for one. Most of the men wore a skirt-like length of gauzy cloth draped around their lower half, and the women had little more. All were dyed in the brightest of colors. It was much as she had seen in the book of Kerell fashion that she had studied, yet in practice it still caused a fair amount of shock to see so many people walking about almost as nude as the statues that graced the city gates.

At last, they reached what must be their destination. The procession halted before a grand looking building decorated with a row of carved pillars. Her cart separated from the others, driving through one of the carriage-sized arched doorways at the front of the home. *Not a home.* She corrected. *A shop.*

Upon a wooden sign the word Rakaii had been carved between several others that she could not translate. The words did not shift within her sight, as those in books of magic often did, so perhaps not all writings of the Kerell were enchanted as she had assumed. Aster shouted orders at her Spiritless as she dismounted. The creatures jumped down from their places and ventured inside, leaving only Phaedrus, who lingered long enough for an embrace and a kiss from Aster.

Selene had no more than a moment to daydream of escape before the Spiritless returned. She noted that several of the monsters now carried thick wooden poles between them. Aster directed them with a gesture towards Selene. They pulled the fabric from the bars above her, but rather than open the door to the cage as she had hoped, they shoved both poles through the spaces at the top, one to her right and one to the left. With a creature at each of the four corners of the cage they used these poles to lift it, and thus she was carried forward.

The front hall was unusual, at least by Evarian standards. More rows of narrow pillars flanked each side of the long, spacious room. Oddly, there was no desk for a shopkeeper to tend to. Instead, piles of pillows in gold and deep purple, to match the tone of the walls above them, lay about the floor. The Spiritless held her enclosure there just long enough for her to peruse the paintings of men and unrecognizable animals that graced the walls before moving onward.

They continued to a central courtyard. It was square in shape, with doors on all sides. There was no roof here, yet more of the gauzy material the Kerell seemed so fond of had been hung across the opening above, perhaps to keep out the full strength of the sun. In the middle of the courtyard an enclosure of fencing had been built. It was composed of metal rather than wood and was large enough to fit at least five or six horses inside. It put her in mind of the pens that were used to train yearlings at home. As they set her crate gently down at its center, she realized that she was correct. This was a training pen, not for beasts, but for Rakaii. Doors closed and latched with a click on every side of her as the Spiritless disappeared into the building beyond. This left her with only Aster and her companion.

With a few muttered words from Aster the door to Selene's cage opened. Selene glanced from one captor to the other, unsure of what to do next. The walls were much too high to climb, and she doubted that she would get far in her current state, not least with Aster and Phaedrus so close by. Phaedrus was barely shorter than Aurin in size, though slender in nature. She had learned during the trip through the woods that he was surprisingly swift when necessary. Aster waved her companion back and away from the center of the pen. At the gesture Selene realized that she had been staring at the man. The female mage then crouched down to Selene's level. She spread her palms out towards her and approached slowly.

"*Placidus,*" Aster said softly.

Selene did not understand the word, but she caught the meaning well enough. She was naught more than a wild animal to them, perhaps a dangerous one at that.

"*Placidus,*" Aster repeated as she inched closer. Double rings of white stone graced the index finger of the woman's left hand.

Selene furrowed her brow. It was obvious that Aster wanted her to come out of the cage. She found that she had no desire to leave the imagined safety of it, despite the fact that it was uncomfortable at best. Phaedrus made several comments which sounded much like suggestions, each of which Aster dismissed with a wave of her fingers. Phaedrus at last produced a biscuit and handed it to his companion. Aster accepted it with a grumble. She held it out towards Selene then, and upon not receiving the desired response, pretended to eat, perhaps to show what it was, and held it out once more. Selene sighed. It was true that she was hungry, as there had not been much food in the cave and none had been provided on her journey from the beach to Kerell city. Her pride fought with her stomach for a moment. She would have to come out sometime, after all, and more than likely their tactics would change to something harsher if these first attempts did not succeed. Selene crawled from the cage with great effort, for her wrists were still bound together and her arm was still painfully swollen. The sand was warm and dry against the fingers of her good hand, yet unyielding against both the one that was injured and her painfully bruised knees. She stood with a grunt. Hours of riding in a cramped cage had not done her body fair service. Everything ached.

She approached Aster slowly, from pain rather than fear, and took the biscuit she offered. This elicited a smile from the woman at last. Her next movement was so swift that Selene had no time to react to it. A light stab of pain struck above her right ear, no more than the bite of a horsefly. Selene's hands flew to the site on instinct, and she received a larger amount of pain in reply.

"Spirits' sake," she swore without thought.

This caused a change in Aster's expression. She rattled off something in Kerell to Phaedrus.

"I told you that she could speak, didn't I?" the man said in return.

"How could you possibly know that? She hasn't said a word since we took her."

It was true. Selene had been listening, but had not uttered a single word, mostly due to the fact that she thought they would not be able to understand her.

"Have a look in her eyes," Phaedrus said. "You can see the intelligence there."

"Can you understand me, then?" Aster asked, turning her attention to Selene.

"Yes," she replied.

"You're a genius, Phaedrus," Aster said, glancing back at the man with glee. "You're right, she does have that look about her. We'll have to keep her reigned in tight at first."

"Thank the Spirits you speak the common tongue," Selene breathed.

Aster laughed. "I'm not sure what language you speak, but Kerell is the only tongue I know. I've simply set your circlet to translate for you."

"My circlet?" She could not feel any presence, at least not as she had when she'd worn one previously, for no sense of consciousness mingled with her own.

"The translation isn't perfect," Aster continued, ignoring Selene's confusion. "If you have a question about something I've said, just ask."

Selene pressed her bound hands once again to the space above her ear where Aster had touched her to find that a small, hard object now protruded there. She was rewarded with a sharp sting of pain. Her fingers came away with a small amount of blood.

"Don't touch it," Aster said, taking Selene's hand. "And don't try to pull it out. It could kill you. Do you understand?"

Selene nodded. "Yes, but,"

"Good," she interrupted.

Phaedrus placed the handle of a hunting knife into Aster's outstretched hand. The mage took it and pulled the blade through the binding around Selene's hands, releasing them. She then uttered a few words of magic. The places where they had splattered the sliver liquid upon Selene warmed, and then faded.

Selene flinched as Aster took hold of her swollen arm. An attempt to draw back only caused the mage's grip to tighten. She turned Selene's wrist to expose the spot on her arm where the creature had stung her, what now felt like ages ago.

"Phaedrus, fetch some antivenin," Aster ordered. "And get Naevus and Datio to the bath house, will you? Now that she's properly contained, I'll let them clean her up."

Selene was too much in shock to protest as Aster led her beneath one of the strangely arched doorways and back into the building. Down at the end of a hall they came to another roofless room, although this one held two pools of water separated by a low wall of stone. Each had a set of steps going down into it on three sides. At the bottom was a patterned mosaic of gray and white tiles. Near the closest side of the pool stood two men wearing the common clothing of the realm, which was to say not much clothing at all. They were nearly identical in feature, with kind eyes set in oblong faces, although one had a prominent birthmark upon his cheek that the other lacked. The same dark, curly hair topped both of their heads.

"Get her washed," Aster ordered. "Then set her up in twelve. I'll meet you there shortly."

"Yes Mistress," they replied in unison.

"Watch her arm. It's in bad shape. And don't let her out of your sight or let any of the intact near her."

"Of course, Mistress."

Aster took Selene's head between her hands and leveled it so that their eyes met. "I'll be back shortly. Behave and do as they say, yes?"

Selene said nothing, for her mind was still reeling from all that had occurred. A bit of pain spiked through her head, tossing her thoughts aside.

"Yes?" Aster said again.

"Yes," Selene replied automatically.

"Yes, Mistress," Aster corrected with another snap of pain.

"Yes, Mistress." As Selene spoke the words a bizarrely pleasant feeling slithered through her body. It was gone within a breath.

Aster grinned. "Good. We've much to accomplish in the next two weeks, but we'll make it."

With that she sprinted off, leaving Selene to stare at the two men in confusion.

"My name is Naevus, the man with the birthmark said, and this is my brother Datio."

"My name is Selene," she answered.

"Selene." Datio moved his mouth as if tasting the word. "Exotic sounding."

"It is," Naevus agreed as he pulled the uneaten biscuit from Selene's hand and set it upon a nearby table. "Maybe they'll let you keep it. Now, let's get those clothes off, shall we?"

Selene's foot took a step backward, much of its own accord.

"Look, you're frightening her," Datio informed him. "You can't talk to a feral that way. We'll both be punished if Mistress has to come back in here to straighten her out."

"I'm not feral," Selene informed them irately, though in truth she was not certain why she took such offense to the comment.

"No?" Naevus asked with a smirk. "They found you living out in the jungle, didn't they?"

"The jungle?"

"Yes, the jungle. That terrible place with a lot of trees and wild animals?"

"Oh, you mean the woods?" Selene began as her courage slowly returned, "Not living there so much as lost. And it was only temporary."

"Well, you weren't captive raised, that's for certain," Naevus continued. "You don't even speak the common tongue."

"Perhaps I don't speak *your* common tongue," she countered. "That hardly makes me a wild animal."

Naevus gestured to the wall behind Selene, and with that she turned to find a body's length of mirrored glass set within a silver frame. The creature that stared back at her was something pulled from the campfire stories she had been told during her time as a Rider. Her hair was matted against her head on one side, with bits of twig and leaves stuck within. Her body was coated with dirt and dried salt, including her face. Her clothing lay in shreds, and her arm presented much as if someone had taken a club to it, for it was twice its normal size and bruised in shades of purple and yellow. To best it all, a rivulet of smeared blood decorated her cheek from where Aster had placed her circlet.

"So, if you're not feral then get in the bath like a good girl and we'll wash you," Datio said.

She could not rightfully dispute that she needed a wash. "I don't need any help," she replied stubbornly, reaching for the bar of soap in Datio's hand. "You can go."

He retracted it with a swift movement. "Mistress said we had to stay and wash you, and that we shall."

Selene's brow creased. Her patience was waning. "I'm not sure how you manage baths around here, but where I come from females don't simply run about naked in front of men."

"Not ever?" Datio asked incredulously.

"Not frequently," she amended. "Excepting those of thorough acquaintance."

The two men shared an amused look. "They have very strict rules about nudity in the wilds of the jungle, do they?" Naevus asked.

"I've told you I'm not from the jungle," she said.

"Then where exactly are you from?" Datio asked.

"Never mind that," she snapped. "Just hand me the soap and brush and be on your way."

"No," Naevus replied firmly. "Now strip, or I'll dump you in clothes and all."

"We're not permitted to leave you," Datio explained, somewhat more patiently than his brother. "Mistress Aster has tasked us with guarding you. At least one of us has to keep you within our sight at all times."

"At all times?" Selene repeated in exasperation. The thought of what would happen if she had to use the privy brought color to her cheeks, though in truth it could not possibly be any worse than what she suffered while crated.

"That's why she set both of us on you. New ferals have just arrived and she doesn't want any mishaps."

Selene paused. "What sort of mishaps?"

"Ferals are quick," Naevus said with a wink. "Most of the new ones are locked up until they're trained, but sometimes even the well-trained ones will find a female too much to resist."

"Most especially if you're in heat," Datio added. "You're not in heat, are you?"

Selene scowled in place of a reply.

"A few minutes unguarded could find you mated," Naevus continued. "You're worth less at auction if you're already with child. Buyers want to be able to find the right match, you know, to help with social status and to form alliances and such."

Selene struggled to keep her anger in check. "But what if I -"

"I believe we've had enough of a chat," Naevus interrupted. "Mistress is waiting."

Selene's feet lifted from the floor, and before she could do so much as squeak in complaint she was lying on her back, floating several feet above the ground.

"Let me down!" she exclaimed.

"We gave you a chance," Naevus said as he pulled at her breeches.

Within a few seconds the tattered remains of her clothing had been removed. She was then righted, and her feet were placed back upon warm stone. As soon as she was set free, she swiftly moved her hands to cover the most sensitive areas of her body as well as she could.

"Now, you're not getting these nasty rags back, so it's either stand here naked until you get bored of it, or get in the water," Naevus informed her.

Selene stepped to the side of the pool. She gasped and retracted her toe as it touched the surface of the water. It was hot, rather than cold. She frowned at her reflection.

"Go on," Datio urged. "It won't burn you. You wait too long, and Naevus will dunk you in with his ability."

"It's true," Naevus confirmed with a smile.

She attempted it again. It was much the temperature of tea that had been recently poured. She lowered herself in slowly. As Datio had promised, it did not burn her skin. Once the water had reached her neck she found that her body relaxed, despite all attempts otherwise.

"Is this accomplished with magic?" She hoped that the question didn't sound quite as daft to them as it did to her own ears.

"No, of course not," Datio replied. "A hot spring runs beneath the city. Most places here have built pools to contain it as it flows up, and an exit where it drains out into the sewers."

"Sewers?" she asked in confusion.

"The pipes where the dirty water drains out of the city," he explained.

"And she claims she's not feral," Naevus quipped as he pulled the scrub brush from Datio's hand and rubbed a cake of soap against it.

Selene sank down lower into the pool, until her chin barely touched the surface of the water.

"That's better," Datio cooed. "Just be calm. We won't harm you."

She did feel calm, oddly enough. It was as if the heat of the water was pulling her anxiety from her.

"How can I be sure you won't harm me?" she asked as the last of her anger seeped away into the warmth of the water. "Aster said that I'm not safe around the other males. Why would she trust you?"

"We're just so very well trained," Naevus said with a laugh as he began to scrub her back.

Selene found that she no longer had the will, nor the strength, to resist the calming effect of the water.

"That's his idea of a joke," Datio chimed in. "We can't mate with you because we're eunuchs."

"You're what?" she asked, lifting somewhat from her daze.

"We've been castrated," Naevus explained, perhaps mistaking her shock for confusion.

"Is that common?" She resisted the urge to look at the affected area, for she now noticed that they had both shed their clothes before wading into the pool.

"Only with house Rakaii. Those better suited for the arena are left intact." Datio pulled his soapy fingers through the tangle of her hair.

"All house Rakaii, or only some?" She tried not to think of what might now be happening to her friends, assuming that they still lived.

"Nearly all of us," Datio replied calmly, as if he was speaking of the latest trend in clothing rather than bodily mutilation. "How does the law go, Naevus?"

"The whole of it is fairly complicated," Naevus replied as he continued to scrub her. "But in short, no more than one month after the day one is found to be a Rakaii he must be castrated unless deemed suitable for use in the colosseum, for breeding, or as Iucundum. If it's an adult feral you have one month after capture."

"Iucundum?"

"Pleasure Rakaii," Datio explained.

"And there are no exceptions?" Selene asked curiously.

"Oh, there are a few," he replied. "Only a city official would know them all, and I'm certainly not that. Come on out now and we'll get you dried off."

Selene allowed them to help her up the steps. The air was cool against her skin as she pulled herself from the water, and her body felt heavy and drained upon finally leaving the pool behind. Her feet dragged so that she nearly tripped. Datio rubbed a soft towel over her skin to pull the remaining water from it, and together the two men pulled her arms gently through the wide sleeves of a gown and fastened it at her waist with a silver clasp, the shape of which put her in mind of a swan in flight. Despite the fact that the garment was so long as to reach her ankles, the gown covered nothing, for the fabric was more transparent than cheesecloth. A triangular opening was left at the front, starting between her breasts and ending at the center of her belly.

Naevus poured some oil from a glass bottle into the palm of one hand. He rubbed it briefly between his fingers before spreading it through Selene's hair. The scent was light and pleasantly floral, though not in any way familiar.

"You clean up nicely," he said as he looked her over. "A bit bruised in places, but no doubt they'll bring a healer to work on you tomorrow. Come along, then. We'll show you your enclosure."

A glance in the mirrored glass revealed just how little her new garment covered. If the Spirits required clothing, then this fabric would likely be their first choice. The thought of walking the halls in it brought color to her cheeks. That aside, Selene had no desire to sleep in an enclosure of any kind, for it sounded much like another word for a cage. She planted both feet firmly against the floor. "Can I wear something else?" she asked in dismay.

"If you're thinking of what you came in with, then the answer is no," Naevus said firmly. "That will be going straight to the midden heap, where it belongs."

"No," she replied with all the poise she could muster. "I don't care to have that back, thank you."

"That's an expensive gown you're wearing," Datio informed her. "The Mistress wore it herself not so long ago."

"She gave me her dress?" Selene asked in confusion.

"We don't have any women's clothing here," Datio explained.

"Mistress makes a living from capturing feral Rakaii, and the jungle isn't teeming with females, in case you hadn't noticed," Naevus added. "You should be pleased that she allowed you to have it."

"I'm just not sure it's suitable."

"From feral to empress in only a few moments." Naevus rolled his eyes. "May I ask what you find wrong with it?"

"It's indecent," she insisted.

"Nonsense." Naevus lifted her from the ground once again, this time floating her through the doorway and down a previously unvisited hallway. "Clothing is only decorative, after all."

"Not where I come from," Selene countered. "It's for warmth. And you're not meant to see any of a person's body through it."

"That sounds terrible," Naevus said. "I hope you never have to go back there."

"Absolutely prudish," Datio agreed.

Selene sighed. "You can put me down. I'll walk." If she was going to be caged again then she would at least gain a few moments of dignity beforehand.

Her feet lowered to touch the floor. The stone was cold here, unlike the air surrounding. "Do you wear shoes in this place, at least?" she asked as they resumed walking.

"Yes," Datio replied. "Though not indoors of course, that would be rude. You do ask a lot of questions. Best to keep your thoughts to yourself around the Mistress."

"Why would I do that? Aster said that I could ask questions."

"She didn't mean that you should just ask whatever comes into your head," Naevus explained. "She meant that if you don't understand an order she's given, then you should ask for clarification."

"Oh, I see."

"And never use just her given name," Datio warned. "It must always be Mistress, or Mistress Aster. Unless you enjoy pain, and I assume that you don't."

Perhaps it was best not to ask any more questions after all, for she had not been overly fond of the answers thus far. They stopped at last before an alcove filled with a pile of colorful pillows similar to the few she had seen on the way in. The floor was no wider than the inside of a carriage, yet the ceiling extended at least an arm's length above her head as she stood.

"Here we are," Datio said with a grin. "Climb in. You can sit for a few minutes before the Mistress comes to fetch you."

She could barely stand as she entered the room, for the mound of pillows left no sight of the floor beneath. A breath of cool air caressed Selene's skin as she passed beneath the arched doorway of the enclosure, causing her to shiver. A barrier to keep her in, no doubt.

"They'll want to see what you can do when they come for you," Naevus explained.

"Haven't I been tortured enough for one day?" Selene asked. She would be happy to fall upon the pillows and drift to sleep, regardless of whether or not they lay at the bottom of a cage.

"By tortured, do you mean cleaned up and brought to civilization?" Datio asked.

"Seeing as you like having things explained to you," Naevus said as he watched her plop down upon the pillows with a sigh. "I'll tell you how this works. The barrier senses your circlet, and the mistress can set it up any way she chooses. Currently, you can enter your enclosure anytime you wish, but if you'd like to come back out through the barrier then you're required to have either the Mistress or one of us escort you."

"It'll be like walking into a wall, otherwise," Datio added. "Don't try it. You'll only injure yourself."

The barrier which blocked the holding room at home and the pain of her nose smashing against it came briefly to mind. "I'm familiar with barriers, thank you," Selene responded as politely as she could manage. There was no use in being rude to them, after all. They were not the cause of her predicament and had been mostly civil towards her so far.

"There's a plate of food and a pitcher of water with a cup on the shelf up there," Naevus continued. "I'll be just out here." He settled himself on a pillow outside the door.

Selene stood upon the pillows with difficulty, wobbling this way and that as she found the shelf set into the wall and poured herself a cup of water. Next to the cup was a plate with some rounded cakes that looked to be made of grain and dried fruit. She lifted one from the plate and took an experimental bite. It was softer than expected and mildly sweet. The water was cool, which surprised her given the heat of the room. It held a mild aftertaste of what might be mint. In too little time Aster appeared at her doorway. She extended a hand through the barrier. Selene readily accepted it.

"Excellent," Aster said. She looked Selene over as she stepped into the hall. "Did you have any difficulty?"

"Not much, Mistress," Naevus replied.

"Well done." With Aster's words both men shivered and wobbled in the slightest as if momentarily inebriated. "Toss some food to the other new ferals," she continued as if nothing was amiss. "Come back here when you're finished."

"Yes, Mistress," both men said in unison.

"Drink this." Aster held out a miniature glass vial. The liquid within looked much like ink.

"What is it?" Selene asked.

A now familiar spike of pain lanced her head.

"Such insolence," Aster muttered. "I told you to drink it. Now do so before I lose my temper." She held out the vial once again.

Selene took it. She upended the contents into her mouth and swallowed. The liquid was bitter and laced with unfamiliar spices that clung to her tongue. Her injured arm grew warm, and the pain faded somewhat. She handed the now empty vial back to Aster, who slipped it somewhere beneath her robes. The woman then began to walk. She motioned for Selene to follow. Selene did so, as no other choice was given to her.

They arrived shortly at a somewhat familiar place. Selene had seen enough training courtyards in her day to recognize it upon sight. There were racks of swords, bows, and shields. At one end sat a covered viewing area complete with benches, which faced towards the freshly raked dirt of the sparring pit.

"She's prettier than many I've seen," Phaedrus noted as he rounded a corner to meet them at the center of the courtyard.

"Save for those owned by the Empress," Aster agreed. "Submissive enough to work with, so far. Let's see what she can do, shall we?" She opened a wooden chest, which sat beneath the roof in a nearby alcove. From it she pulled a rolled scrap of paper, which she handed to Selene.

The words upon the wax seal writhed like worms in a puddle of rain.

"Open and unroll it," Aster ordered.

"I can't read words of magic," Selene protested. "I'm not a mage." She knew what the paper was, for she had found something like it in Damaeus' room. It was meant to ferret out her latent abilities, and Cael had long ago warned her not to reveal her ability to control the dead.

Pain emanated from her circlet, along with the mild rolling of her stomach. It was not severe, much like the feeling one gained in the morning following a night of too much drink. It quickly slipped away to nothing.

"No need to waste a scroll, Mistress," Selene bargained. "I assume they must cost a fair amount."

Aster laughed. "So very giving, aren't you. Worry not. The cost of the scroll is nothing compared to what we will get for you at auction."

Selene was not fond of her tone, for it bordered on mocking. "My ability has already been opened," she said as evenly as possible. "I can tell you what it is."

"Fine then." Aster folded her arms across her chest. "What is it?"

"Levitation," Selene replied. "Like Naevus."

"Fairly useful." A smirk crossed Aster's face. "And the other?"

"Why would you think that I have two?" Selene asked. "Don't most marked ones only have one ability?"

"Quite an attitude," Phaedrus muttered. "I thought you said she was submissive."

"I said submissive enough." Aster sighed. "All females have two abilities. Now, read the scroll before I lose the last of my patience."

"The other is healing," she added quickly.

One of Aster's brows made a slow ascent, and her mouth dropped open in the slightest as it had when she had first spotted Selene on the beach. "Healing," she muttered.

Selene at first thought that she might have said something to upset the woman, although no pain yet coursed through her head.

"Healing?" Aster's voice cracked as she repeated the word, this time with volume.

"Yes, Mistress," Selene replied cautiously. Aster's moods seemed dangerously unstable at times and it seemed best not to upset her.

"Healing and levitation. You're a manipulator."

"I don't think I am," Selene replied hesitantly.

"Phaedrus," Aster ushered her companion towards them with a frantic wave of one hand.

"I want you to fix his nose," she commanded.

Upon closer inspection she could see that as well as being unusually flat, the bridge of Phaedrus' nose was bent to one side, perhaps from having been broken. The injury had healed long ago, however, and thus she could not simply put it back without breaking it once more. Selene relayed this to Aster, but the woman waved the objections briskly aside. "You can," she insisted. "Your abilities are linked, and you use them together for better effect. Healing is naught but forcing flesh to grow and multiply. You can order it to do your bidding, just as I order you. Now do as I say and repair his nose."

Selene focused on Phaedrus' nose. Her chest tightened at the thought of Aster's command, for in truth she had no idea how to go about such a thing. Both abilities hovered within her reach now, for she could feel them. They begged for her to take them. She awakened her healing ability and centered it on the crooked portion of the cartilage, then called forth her levitation ability as well. At first one slipped away as soon as she caught hold of the other, but with a few moments of practice she had a delicate hold on both. Holding such a vast amount of power was exhilarating. Could she use it to escape? The immediate narrowing of Aster's eyes provided the answer, and a spear of pain through her temple grounded her. She was the one using the power, but Aster could separate her from it with no more than a thought. There was a barrier around the woman as well, for where Selene's abilities were concerned it was as if she did not exist. And what would killing Phaedrus accomplish, aside from angering Aster?

Aster offered Selene a crooked smile as another spike of pain struck her temple. "Do you think this is the first time I've trained a Rakaii? We are both thoroughly shielded. No Rakaii magic will affect us aside from that which we ask of you."

Selene forced the flesh and cartilage of Phaedrus' nose to move where she wanted, and it obeyed. With a bit of maneuvering, and a lot of concentration, the task was complete. It was straight.

Aster cupped Selene's cheeks between her hands once again. She pulled her forward. A thick odor of spices lingered about the woman like an aura. At so little distance she could see that tears had begun to pool within the corners of her eyes. Perhaps she had not done as well with the repair as she had thought. It seemed straight enough, though she had no notion of how it had looked before it had been broken. Selene opened her mouth to tell Aster that it was her own fault if it looked terrible because she had forced her to do it, but she was interrupted by the woman before she could speak.

"What have I done to deserve you?" Aster inquired through tears.

Selene attempted to back away but found that she could not.

"A gift from the Goddess," Phaedrus whispered as he rubbed his newly repaired nose. He also looked as if he might cry.

Selene struggled from Aster's grip. These people were not of a right mind. Most alarmingly of all, they owned her. The first few lines of an old folk song her father used to sing ran through her head.

A dog has no choice of his master. He relies on the luck of the Tides.

And whether a kind or a cruel one, a dog by his master abides.

Her latent abilities snapped out of reach, leaving naught but a lost, empty feeling behind. Aster now had Phaedrus wrapped within her arms. The two were muttering non-sensical phrases through their tears. Selene lowered herself to the ground. She did not bother to sit in a dignified manner, but rather crossed her legs so as to be comfortable. The cheesecloth dress rendered her nude anyways, so these two had already seen all that there was to see. A different angle for the nudity could not matter overly much.

Selene set one elbow upon her knee and rested her head in her palm. With the other she began to draw swirling patterns in the sand. She had to believe that eventually they would stop muttering to each other and explain in some manner what was going on.

"The one at the top of the hill," Aster suggested, "Near the arena."

"Too much noise," Phaedrus complained. "Besides, I want land with enough room for a properly sized training ring."

"Just as a hobby?"

"Of course. And I'd like a fountain. With a statue in the middle. We could commission one from Erato."

As Selene listened, she noted that what at first seemed to be nonsensical ramblings actually had some form to them. They were speaking of expensive things they wished to buy, of travel, and of social hierarchies. At last, she had heard enough that she could do naught but ask for the sake of her sanity.

"A manipulator is worth a lot of coin, I suppose?"

Aster turned her attention back to Selene. "Get up. You'll soil your gown."

Selene dusted sand from the back of her clothing as she stood, though in truth her backside held more sand than the garment due to the way the fabric flowed.

"The gown doesn't matter," Phaedrus said as he took Selene by the arm. "We don't have to worry about those sorts of things anymore."

"I suppose you're right," Aster agreed with a grin.

Selene's mind churned with thoughts of how irritating it was to be ignored as they escorted her back to her enclosure and ushered her inside.

"If anything happens to her, I'll sell both you and your brother for use as bait in the arena," Aster said to Naevus, who had most suddenly rounded the corner at the woman's approach. "She's worth more than most people make in their lifetimes. Do you understand?"

Selene did not hear Naevus' reply, for with the comprehension of her worth came a terrible realization; that her value would make escape nigh impossible.

# Fair Trade
## *Evaria - Capital City*

The Mages' Quarter was the cleanest dungeon Islyr had ever encountered. The thought crossed his mind every time he ventured down its stairs, which until recently was not often.

"Are you certain he's secure here?" Viverr asked nervously.

"I thought you took all of his magic," Islyr said.

"They're not like us. I can feel it when I use my ability. They don't have magic within them as most creatures do. They pull forces from their environment for use with words. Then they hoard it like a dragon would its treasure, keeping it available for future use. As soon as the touch of my latent ability wears off, he'll be gathering it up again. I could keep taking it away, but I've no way to know how long my ability lasts on him. I've not had the opportunity to use it on a great many mages, you see."

"He's more secure here than anywhere else in the castle," Islyr replied. "Wasn't it you who told me that Cael repaired the magic of this place?"

"I did, but the spell books Cael used were old, and who knows what this fellow is capable of. All of the magic here is ancient stuff, and he seems rather up to date on the latest of spells, don't you agree?"

"I wouldn't know," Islyr lied. Magic was not his favorite topic of conversation. He knew what he had been shown during the years he had been enslaved with the Kerell, which was more than most citizens of Evaria would learn in a lifetime. That knowledge made him certain that a regular dungeon would never hold a mage, and thus one constructed specifically to hold creatures of magic, however old the spells might be, was the best they could accomplish.

The mage stood as they entered. "*Have you come to release me?*" he asked in the language of the Kerell.

"What did he say?" Viverr asked.

"Just nonsense," Islyr replied. He slid a tray with an apple and a bowl of stewed oats beneath the bars.

The man scowled at the apple. He plucked it from the tray and sniffed it.

"That is food," Viverr explained much too loudly. "Fruit. It grows on a tree. You eat it," he added, with an accompanying pantomime.

"He doesn't have any difficulty hearing," Islyr said with as much patience as he could muster. "He simply doesn't know much of the common tongue. And he tried to enslave us. Why should you care if he doesn't eat?"

"Because if he dies of starvation then we can't get any information out of him, can we?"

"Perhaps we could," Islyr said. "I could bring him back as a bloodsoul, but we wouldn't be able to speak to him unless you happen to be fluent in bloodsoul. Do you know anyone with a skill for necromantic languages?"

"That was a jest," Viverr realized after a few seconds too many. "They so rarely come out of your mouth that I couldn't be certain."

Islyr pulled Viverr a short distance down the hall and around a corner, to a little room on the side meant for use by the guardsmen. It held no decoration and was just big enough for a table for eating, two chairs, and an empty bucket for use as a chamber pot.

"What's the point of leading me all the way out here?" Viverr complained. "He can barely put together two words of the common tongue. He doesn't understand what we're saying."

"I disagree," Islyr replied. "The best way to get someone to speak freely in front of you is to pretend that you can't understand them."

Viverr pulled both hands across his face. "Time is running short. We need him to tell us where Samuel is."

"I've asked him in every way I can think of," Islyr replied.

"I know you can be more persuasive than that," Viverr offered with a pointed glance at Islyr's staff.

"Devren said that we're not to torture him."

"Look, I'm simply going to say aloud what everyone has been thinking. Devren's not really a king. He's only a child."

"Being young doesn't make him any less of a king," Islyr countered. "He could order you hanged for insubordination just as easily as an adult in the same position. If we want to maintain our position as Aranth we should do as Devren says."

"You don't give a horse's ass about being a member of the Aranth," Viverr said.

"So you say," Islyr replied vaguely.

"And torture would add so much ease to this process."

"I agree that it would."

"And you know he deserves it. I've done a few terrible things in my life, but I could never conscience keeping another person as a slave."

"I said I agree with you," Islyr snapped.

"Then get him to talk."

It was a tempting thought, yet for some reason unknown to anyone but the Spirits themselves Islyr loathed the possibility of losing his new position and the many resources that came with it.

"We require some information to leverage against him, or some privilege," Islyr mused. "At this time, we have nothing, and of this he is well aware."

"His freedom," Viverr suggested. "That would be something of value to me, were I trapped in a cage in a foreign land."

"He's too clever for that," Islyr replied. "He knows that we can never let him have it."

"There must be something we can offer. It's been days now. Who knows what he's done with Samuel."

It did look grim, though he was not about to let Viverr know of it.

"How about I do the talking this round," the rogue offered. "You can translate for me."

"Fine," Islyr agreed. Every time he spoke to the mage the urge to shatter the man's skull became more difficult to resist. He had long ago run out of things to say to him, in any event.

A strange squealing noise, much like that of a rusted gate, emanated from somewhere ahead. It was followed shortly by a loud crunching sound, and the clattering of what could only be stones from the wall. Islyr looked at Viverr. They both quickened their pace.

"Right," Viverr said. "First, we just need to get him talking in general, anything will do, and then we'll -" His voice faltered.

It took Islyr a moment to make sense of what lay before him. It was as if they had stepped outdoors, although this was surely the hallway that they had traversed only a moment ago. Something crunched beneath his boot at his next step. His eyes traveled downward. *Leaves.* His chest tightened as they traveled back up. The trunk of a massive tree was twisted around the bars of what had been the door to the mage's cell, pushing it aside to leave just enough room for the man to slide through. Islyr's foot struck something hard. It rolled, only to stop upon hitting the side of Viverr's boot.

"Apples," Viverr said in amazement as he plucked the mottled red object from the ground near his feet. "That bastard grew a tree from the seeds."

"You're the one who told him that apples grow on trees," Islyr huffed.

"I feel like that's fairly common knowledge," Viverr replied. "And you can't blame this on me. You said the Mages' Quarter would hold him."

"I warned you that he could understand the common tongue." Islyr squeezed between the wall and the trunk of the tree. It was a tight fit. Rough bark tore at the fabric of his shirt. "Come on, Viverr. We have to find him."

"I'll never fit through there," Viverr said. "Not in human form. Go on. I'll catch up."

Islyr readily accepted the offer. The stairs were a blur beneath his feet as he ran. Mages were a narcissistic lot. The man would not think to flee now that he was within the castle. He had come here for something specific, and he would not leave without it. *The list.* He had found one on nearly every mage he had killed. It had contained the names of all the marked ones in the royal family. And the most valuable? *Cyanna.*

The journey to the Royal Wing seemed longer than usual. One hall after another disappeared with speed as he ran. Islyr reached Cyanna's room expecting her to be gone. He breathed a sigh of relief as he heard her speak.

"No, you can't eat that. It's not food," the girl chided.

Islyr stepped into the open doorway to find her sitting at her desk, alone.

"Hello, Islyr," she said cheerily. "No, I told, you it's not food, it's for reading."

"I beg your pardon?" Islyr replied curiously.

"Not you Islyr, sorry. I was talking to Avery," the princess explained as she plucked a small furry creature from where it sat upon the desk and placed it into a little, wooden box filled with hay. "Look, there's ink on there and everything, you'll make yourself ill."

"Avery?"

"One of my scrub pigs," she said, as if that explained everything.

"You can speak to scrub pigs?" Islyr asked.

"My second latent ability," the girl explained. "I discovered it just a few days ago. I can speak to most animals, not only scrub pigs. Isn't that grand?"

"It is," he agreed. "In Kerell your second ability is called The Blessing of the Goddess." Islyr had often wished that he had a second latent ability. Something a bit more useful in battle would be ideal. Sadly, that was a boon given only to female marked ones.

"Is everything all right?" Cyanna asked, perhaps upon noting his expression.

A squeal like that of a rusted hinge emanated from the little scrub pig which sat upon Cyanna's desk. Its patchwork of calico fur shook as it chattered and dove out of its box and behind a stack of books. Cyanna's eyes grew wide with alarm.

It was not until he felt the cold of the mage's fingers upon his neck that Islyr realized what a terrible mistake he had made. Ice spread from his neck to the rest of his chest, paralyzing him before he could utter a word.

"What an honor it is to meet you, my dear princess," the mage said in the Evarian tongue. He slid past Islyr and entered Cyanna's room.

In one smooth movement the girl stood and reached for her sword, yet the mage had more experience, and thus was far quicker. She stood frozen with her fingers barely upon it and could do nothing as he deftly slid the pointed tine of an earring-like circlet into her skull near her left ear.

Islyr felt very little pain as the mage fitted him with a circlet similar to Cyanna's. Hatred was another matter, for it filled him, burning through his mind. He would kill the mage. It did not matter if the circlet put an end to him for it.

"I have no doubt that you would use the last of your strength to kill me," the mage said in Kerell. "This is why I shall keep you frozen until we reach our destination."

*Yet you cannot do so forever,* Islyr thought, knowing that he would hear.

"Perhaps not," the mage replied. "But I can for long enough. Now come along. You and the female combined are a bounty worthy of the empress herself. We will depart without delay."

The mage drew a battered metal ring from the pocket of his robe and lay it upon the ground at his feet. He uttered many words beneath his breath and the air before him wavered as it would over stone on the hottest day. Islyr was dragged towards the anomaly. The air was as warm as the mage's touch had been frigid. Islyr found himself at once in a small room whose ceiling, walls and floor were all composed of wood. The world rocked beneath him.

*A ship.* He would be taken back to Kerell. Panic rose within him like a fast-returning tide, drowning the anger he had so recently held. The mage pushed him into one corner of the cabin, beside several neatly packed crates of clay urns whose etchings danced within his vision.

Cyanna was next to be pulled through the opening in the air. As the Mage stepped into the cabin, movement in the room beyond caught Islyr's eye. There was no way to keep his thoughts to himself due to the circlet. Islyr vanquished the image from his mind a few seconds too late. A shard of ice erupted from the mage's hand as he turned to face his attacker. It struck the wall on the other side of the hall and shattered, leaving a haze of flakes in its wake. The rogue was quick, thank the Goddess and the Spirits alike.

The mage grumbled in frustration. It appeared that he did not consider Viverr to be worth the effort of capture, for he simply turned and stepped into the cabin. He had found something else of value, however, for in his arms he carried Viverr's prized egg. After a last sweeping glance around Cyanna's now empty room, the mage reached back into the opening and pulled the voyage ring through. A warm breeze rushed past Islyr's face as the gap in the air caved in upon itself.

# The Misty Maiden
## *Evaria – Capital City*

Viverr brushed flakes of ice from his shirt sleeve as he stood. While it was true that magic could not harm him, it was possible that real ice drawn together by magic could. Islyr and Cyanna were gone. Islyr could hold his own, of that he had no doubts. The man had escaped from the Kerell once before, had he not? Cyanna was another matter. She was much like a daughter to him, or as close as any was likely to come. The foul, salty odor of seaweed wafted past Viverr's face as he entered the girl's room. They must be at the docks, for if portals could cross the seas, then mages would have no need to travel by ship to get to Evaria.

"This is a fine mess," Viverr complained to the empty room. "Now that magical jackass has got my friends and my dragon egg."

The stack of books on Cyanna's desk squealed and chattered as if in reply. Viverr jumped back.

"Apparently I'm an idiot," he said as one of Cyanna's scrub pigs waddled into view. "To be startled by the likes of you is somewhat of an embarrassment, I'll admit. And what do you want?"

The creature chattered again.

"I don't speak the language of scrub pigs," he informed it. "And your type doesn't much like me, so you're aware. I'll get your mistress and bring her to you. Will that do? So long now, pig."

In what should have been an impossible feat considering its stubby legs, the creature lifted its front end a few inches into the air, as if begging to be plucked from the desk.

"Gah," Viverr huffed. "You want to go with me that badly? You win, wee, furry potato. Come along, then."

The creature's fur was as soft as fine silk. It chattered contentedly as Viverr placed it into his belt pouch.

The main dock in the city was the nearest into which large ships could sail without fear of bottoming out. He would head there straight away. With the luck of the Tides, he could catch them before they set sail.

Viverr headed down the stairs and through the castle as fast as his legs would allow. He managed to get to the front gate in only a few minutes, and down the passage to the edge of town in only a few more. At the side of a small fountain, he stopped for a few seconds to catch his breath. Scattered groups wandered about around the area, drawing buckets of water from the fountain or chatting much too loudly. He made his best effort to avoid notice.

Viverr sat upon the wall of bricks at the edge of the fountain. The scrub pig squealed in complaint.

"Easy for you to say when you're being carried," Viverr countered.

The man closest to him offered a confused look from beneath a wide-brimmed straw hat.

Viverr raised the back of his hand to show his Aranth brand. "Just consulting with my animal companion. Mind your business."

"Apologies, Sir Aranth," the man said as he turned away.

The pig chattered happily. The brand was useful at times. Viverr had removed the magic from it the night after they'd placed it, so it was more a symbol of his allegiance to the king than a cage of magic, like the brands on the others.

The pig squealed once again.

"Yes, alright," Viverr said. "We'll go. I just had to breathe a minute, that's all."

It was true that they were losing time. Viverr lifted himself reluctantly from the wall and headed out. He shortened the route by weaving through a few familiar alleyways. The creaking of wood and the smell of salty air accosted him as he crept between the stacks of crated goods and caged animals that sat upon Evaria's docks. A few people milled about, piling crates or sorting fishing nets, yet it was not as crowded as he had hoped it would be. If he was to remain anonymous, he would need to stay hidden, and a large group of strangers would have been ideal for the task.

In order to rescue his friends, he would first need to figure out which boats were headed to Kerell, and also which one of those held his companions. It would have to be done quickly. It took some time to ready a boat to set sail for such a journey, yet that allowance could undoubtedly be adjusted at the request of a wealthy mage, or in this case a disgruntled one. The shipmaster's office would be the place to start.

"Discretion is the name of today's adventure," he said to the scrub pig. "We haven't the time to search every ship."

The pig poked its head out from beneath the flap of his belt-pouch.

"I feel as if I should give you a name," he continued. "I'll call you Potato, seeing as you look like one. No offense intended. I am rather a fan of potatoes."

The scrub pig chattered happily in reply.

"Now, we'll need the docking record book if we're to figure out which ship your mistress is on. Luckily, the shipmaster's office is just nearby."

The building had been artfully painted to look as if it was encrusted with barnacles and sea stars, and thus was difficult to miss.

"Time for a little show, Potato," Viverr whispered as he stepped up to the entrance. "We'll cause a bit of a distraction and slip out with the book before they've the chance to miss it." He waved a finger at the pig. "You be quiet now. We don't want to draw attention to ourselves until we're ready."

The little bell tied to the door rang out as Viverr opened it. The sound of an argument met his ears before he set so much as one toe into the doorway.

"Are you in charge here or aren't you?" asked a man in a loose shirt and breeches stiff from salt water. He had the odd mix of accents that often sprung from sailor's mouths, and a crooked nose that said he had seen his fair share of brawls. A strip of dark blue cloth was tied around the man's forehead, to denote that he was the captain's first mate. Whatever this matter was, it must be important.

Viverr slid around the door and into the room, making an effort not to draw attention to himself while doing so. No need to cause a distraction here, for one had already been provided for him. Now, where was that book?

"I'm in charge," a man with weathered skin and a graying beard assured him. "Did the sign on the door slip your notice?"

"Spirits keep you." The sailor slammed his hand against the desk which sat between them. "Then you make it right."

"It's as right as I can make it," the shipmaster replied. "Now go back to your ship and wait for my order for release."

"My captain paid ten silver for the right to pull the Paricia from port on the hour, and we mean to take it."

Viverr spotted the docking record. The thick tome lay on the table directly between the two men, which was not ideal. It was surrounded by stacks of maps and letters.

"You can take it," the shipmaster replied. "But only after the Misty Maiden is on her way out to sea."

The scrub pig squealed. Both men scowled at Viverr.

"Pay me no mind, gentlemen," he said sheepishly. "I'll wait my turn."

"You'll let that bastard set sail on demand when you know what cargo he carries?" the sailor yelled with another pounding of his fist. The desk rattled. The shipmaster's attention traveled downward as several items from atop it cascaded to the floor. The sound of breaking glass met Viverr's ears.

The docking log was not amongst the things that had fallen, unfortunately.

"That was my hourglass, you bastard," the shipmaster growled.

"I'll break more than your hourglass if you don't keep our arrangement," the sailor replied.

"You break just one more of my belongings and I'll break your jaw," the shipmaster barked. "Ship's cargo is no matter to me. And it's not technically against the law. The Misty Maiden goes first."

Potato let out another clipped squeal, although this time neither man paid it any heed. The sailor lifted a barometer from where it hung on the wall near his head. He released it to shatter on the tile floor below.

The shipmaster was true to his word, for his only reply was to strike the man's jaw with his fist. He was an older man, but still spry enough, for the cracking of bones could be heard. The two men backed into the corner of the room, swinging punches at each other. They seemed most evenly matched, for very few of the strikes connected. Viverr took the opportunity he was given, and as the sailor landed a strike across the shipmaster's left eye he grabbed the logbook and bolted from the room.

Once out of the shipmaster's office he slowed to a walk. The noise of the brawl was now noticeable outside as well. A small crowd had gathered to look through the front window, and he could see two of the king's standard guardsmen rounding the far end of the docks.

The volume of the argument reduced to no more than the buzzing of flies as Viverr made his way onward. He slipped between stacks of crates on the closest dock and settled on one to sit. He opened the sizable book. "Spirits keep me," he swore as he looked over page upon page of shipping information. "How am I supposed to find anything in this mess?"

Potato poked his head out from beneath the flap of his belt-pouch. He watched as Viverr turned the pages, looking for anything that might be of use.

"You're no help at all," Viverr complained.

The little pig crawled out to sit on the book as Viverr grabbed the corner of one page in preparation to move to the next.

"I can't turn the pages if you're sitting on them, and the minutes are passing more quickly than I'd like."

Potato chattered. He pressed his nose near the middle of the page.

"Whatever is your plan? I don't suppose you can read."

The pig eyed him. He pressed his nose to the paper once again, in just the same spot as before.

"The Misty Maiden?" Viverr read aloud.

Potato let out an excited squeal.

"I don't suppose you're truly a marked one in disguise."

The pig offered him a blank look.

"Yeah, that's a bit of a stretch. You could be right though. Those two idiots in the shipmaster's office mentioned it. Said it had unusual cargo. Maybe that's our ship."

The little pig dove back into his belt-pouch.

"Guess it's as good an idea as any," Viverr said as he stood. "Perhaps you're cleverer than you look." He placed the tome on a nearby crate. "This book is far too cluttered to be of any use. Whoever heard of a Shipmaster brawling and taking bribes? And that man has no organizational skills whatsoever. When we get back to the castle, I'm recommending that he should be dropped in the depths of the sea and replaced by someone competent. You're more fit to be shipmaster than he is."

Potato chattered in agreement.

They came upon the Misty Maiden in little time. The ship was certainly large enough to make the journey across rough seas to the land of the Kerell, yet it was unassuming in decoration. In fact, it was much too unassuming. The only reason not to boldly decorate a ship of that size was to make it difficult to remember. They surely meant to hide something.

Viverr snuck around the dock side, slipping behind some crates which were labeled as perishable goods. He crouched down and observed the crew for a moment. Only three were visible. Two of them were taking the opportunity to nap in sunny spots on the deck like cats on a windowsill. The third stood as a lookout, likely in case some scoundrel had the idea to sneak aboard. As it turned out, he was that very scoundrel.

Viverr placed his feet carefully in the spots of weathered wood which seemed least likely to creak beneath his weight. He recalled that the Shipmaster had said the cargo wasn't technically illegal, which could indeed mean marked ones. Slavery of people wasn't permitted, but by Evarian law those with a mark weren't technically people, but rather closer to animals. Anger rose in his chest as he thought of it. *And this with a marked one on the throne. Disgusting.* The sound of footsteps roused him from his thoughts of anger. The one who he had decided to name Lookout was headed towards him. Viverr wedged himself behind a stack of barrels and old piles of rope just in time. But the man wasn't coming for him. He was up to something much more troublesome. He was waking the others and readying the ship to sail.

*This could be problematic,* Viverr thought as he slipped behind a group of men and eased the ladder down into the ship's hold. Far too much light emanated from the many sconces set into the walls. Upon closer inspection they did not hold torches, but rather those glowing stones that the Kerell held in such high regard. More cause to believe that this was the ship he sought.

The light within each stone flickered as if it held a flame. He cautiously pressed his fingers near the edge of one to be certain it wouldn't burn him. Then, with a touch of his latent ability he severed the stones from their magic, leaving only a few of them to see by. He had better vision in the dark than most, and he would need every advantage against the mage. Ahead was a hall with seven doors. Three on each side and one at the end. There were no numbers or markings upon them, and there were no glass windows in any of them to spy through. *Nothing more to do than to try them one at a time,* he thought.

Viverr did have a great love of exploring unknown places. It wasn't the fastest method of finding someone, however, and he had little time before the boat set sail. He pressed his ear to the first door. The wood had been sanded smooth and was cool against his flesh. No sound could be heard within. He reached for the doorknob but found none, nor was there any button or lever to be seen.

*Spirits keep every mage that touches Evarian soil*, Viverr thought bitterly. He reached out with his latent ability and found the door thick with layers of magic. *Perhaps my luck isn't so terrible after all.* This much warding could only mean that something valuable was kept within. Viverr pulled the spells apart thread by thread, like a loose corner on an old tapestry. The magic faded back to whence it had come with a satisfying hiss. He pushed the door open and was happy to find no further spells within.

In an unfortunate turn of events, his companions were not within the room either. It was a storage room which held several large chests, a stack of barrels held up by a rope net, and a pile of bagged dry goods, most likely food. He turned to leave, but then one of the chests caught his eye. It was the only one with a padlock upon it. *Why lock only one of the three?* he asked himself. *Because there's something valuable inside*, his mind replied. He picked the lock with ease and threw open the lid. Potato popped his head out to have a look. A strange mix of things lay inside. His dragon egg was not amongst them, sadly. Viverr glanced over the variety of items. There was always time for a little thievery, was there not? And one could make the argument that anyone who would keep another person in servitude most assuredly deserved to be robbed. He lifted a tomato-sized velvet bag filled with coins. Platinum, by the feel of it. Whomever owned this chest was well off indeed. He slipped the bag into one of his empty belt pouches, along with a couple of miniscule scrolls that likely contained spells, and several bits of well-crafted jewelry set with stones of opal. *That ought to be enough to anger them*, he thought. He had best continue on if he was to find Islyr and Cyanna. He turned to leave but stopped short when Potato leapt out of his pouch and into the chest.

"Quit causing trouble," he whispered as he reached for the pig. "We haven't the time for shenanigans."

The little pig scurried to the corner. He tugged at a square of patterned fabric that lay there. Viverr lifted it up to find a stone jar beneath, perhaps twice the size of the bag of coins he had taken. Something was etched upon the side in gold lettering. The words did not dance within his vision as he had expected, yet still it was in a language he could not read. He went to replace it, for it was oddly heavy and would take up much needed space that could otherwise be used for loot, yet once it was in his hand, he found he had no desire to let it go. He tossed some of the jewelry back into the chest and squeezed the jar next to the coins, then retrieved Potato.

"More trouble than you're worth," he grumbled lightly as he placed the pig into his other pouch.

Once again in the hall, he opened the next door. It was a sleeping quarters filled with linens and hammocks, all of which, thankfully, were empty. The room beside it was similar to the last, as was the next. He supposed it did take a large number of people to run a ship of this size, but this was nigh ridiculous. How would he ever find Cyanna and Islyr in this place? *If they're even here,* he thought. Potato chattered quietly and poked his head out.

"Let's simply carry on then, shall we?" he whispered.

The next room contained nothing more than crates of cargo which, if they were marked correctly, contained ordinary shipments of fabric and preserved foods. At the far end of the hall was a room that had been prepared for shipping livestock. He eased the door open far enough to enter, and it quickly became apparent that no livestock was contained within. But there, in the corner of the room, lay his precious dragon egg. It sat in a wooden bucket which was filled to the brim with water. Viverr stepped carefully, cringing with every obnoxiously loud crunch of hay beneath his feet.

The bucket lay nestled between two empty cages, each large enough to contain a fully grown mule. One door lay open. The other, oddly, was sealed with a large iron padlock similar to the one that had been on the chest. *Quite a large amount of security for an empty cage*, he thought as he leaned down to collect the dragon's egg.

The hay at the bottom of the cage shifted unexpectedly and hot breath blew against the side of his neck. He turned, ever so slightly, but still could see nothing. It was not an empty cage after all. Potato poked his nose out to sniff the air. He chattered a little. The creature snorted. The hay on the bottom of the cage moved as if something was pawing at it.

"Just what sort of thing is your new friend?" he asked.

The little pig offered no reply.

"This land has such wonderful creatures, does it not?" said a thickly accented voice.

Viverr could not help but jump at the sound. "I dislike being startled very much," he said as he turned to face the scoundrel. It was the mage.

Viverr retreated until his back touched the cage. "At least I'm on the right boat," he said casually. "I'll take my friends back, please."

"You are very brave," the mage replied, again in the common tongue.

"So, you do speak Evarian," Viverr said as steadily as he could manage. On a regular occasion he would be running and looking for a place to hide. Instead, he forced himself to consider the fate of his friends.

"Only when I want to be understood by the beasts that inhabit this place," the mage replied. "It is beneath one of my status."

"I didn't realize there was much beneath the status of a filthy slaver," Viverr said as he moved both hands to rest behind his back.

"Perhaps I'll keep you and market you for the arena. Your attitude could make for excellent entertainment before you die terribly."

"I realize that I'm much too handsome to resist." Viverr slid one of the lockpicks he kept tied to his arm carefully outward, moving it from his sleeve into his hand. "But unfortunately, I'm not for sale at the moment."

"Livestock does not get to choose whether it is bought or sold," the mage informed him. "That is for its master to decide."

Viverr's fingers met the smooth metal of the padlock. A light touch of his latent ability ensured that no spell lay upon it. "Unhappily for you, I am not an animal. In fact, I'm a personal friend of the king."

"Your king is no more than vermin when compared to our empress. A rat king to rule the land of beasts."

It seemed that the empress was a bit of a delicate subject of conversation, which was perfect for his purposes. "She's no empress of mine," Viverr said callously as he slid the pick into the opening of the lock. "Anyone who forges an empire on the backs of an enslaved race isn't fit to wash our king's dirty smallclothes." The lock clicked and fell open. He caught it before it could tumble to the floor.

The mage's hand glowed as he gathered magic. Viverr readied himself to move. With luck whatever was in the cage hated mages as much as he did. The boat lurched unexpectedly forward, tossing both Viverr and the mage to one side, and toppling the bucket that held his dragon egg. Viverr rolled as he struck the floor. Potato tumbled out of his pouch and into the hay nearby. By the luck of the Tides, he seemed unharmed.

"Run and hide," he ordered.

The mage was already rising from where he had fallen. "Is that another Rakaii to add to my bounty?" he asked with curiosity. "How generous of you. I have not seen one in that form before."

"He's just a friend," Viverr replied vaguely.

"You say you are not an animal, yet you speak to them as if you are one. If it is not Rakaii then perhaps it will make a nice stew."

The mage aimed a shot of magic at Potato, who had neither run nor hidden as Viverr had implored. Viverr lunged at the man, catching him by surprise. The little pig squealed and slipped through the bars into the cage with the invisible creature. Viverr pushed the mage over and jumped on top of him. The man struggled beneath him, clawing to get a hold on Viverr's neck. Viverr pressed his palm over the mage's mouth. "Can't cast a spell if you can't talk," he muttered. He reached his free hand into his pouch to get his knife, but his fingers met only the bag of coins he had stolen earlier. The knife must have tumbled out during the fall. *The lock.* It was heavy enough. It would knock the mage out if he managed to hit him hard enough. It should still be nearby. Pain shot through his palm as the mage bit down upon it.

"Spirits keep you!" Viverr swore as blood welled up from the wound.

The mage shoved Viverr off of his chest and rolled out from beneath him. Seconds fled as Viverr gained his footing and stood. The mage muttered a few words of magic.

"Magic can't harm me, you horse's-" The intended expletive was cut short as something hard struck Viverr in the head. *The wooden bucket*, he realized as his vision blurred, and darkness threatened to move in from all sides. At least the hay was soft as he fell upon it.

The mage stood over him. The metal of what must be a circlet glinted from between his fingers. "You've lost," he gloated. "At this point in our game I feel I must sell you to the cruelest of masters, simply for spite."

The boat lurched once more. The mage struggled to gain his footing. The door to the invisible creature's cage squealed open. The mage's eyes grew wide. He scrambled back through the hay but was not quick enough. A whinny, similar to that of a horse, met Viverr's ears. The mage jolted backward ever so slightly as a hole appeared in his chest. He gasped and arched his chest forward. A long horn appeared as it pulled from him, coated in thick blood.

Viverr drew a breath. He inched backwards until he touched the wall between the two cages. He was trapped and could go no farther. Oddly, the creature did not come for him, but instead bolted through the door that the mage had left open behind him. Hoof beats echoed through the hall, becoming softer with distance.

Viverr pulled himself from his stupor. The mage had slumped to the floor and was no longer breathing, which Viverr could not help but think was for the best. With the mage no longer a threat, he scanned the room for Potato. His new little friend must not have been crushed by the angry creature, happily, for his body was not to be found in the now empty cage. It did seem to be more of a discerning angry creature than most.

After a moment, which was much too long by his estimation, Viverr found a jagged hole where some insects had eaten through the wood of the wall at the back of the cage. It was just large enough for the scrub pig to fit through. In the room beyond the hole was what looked to be a human foot, upon which a large iron shackle had been set. Of course, the mage would not leave his most precious cargo visible to others. He had hidden it in a secret chamber.

This was the farthest door in this hall, so therefore there must be some way to access the hidden area from this room. It so happened that Viverr had vast experience with these sorts of doors, for the best items to pilfer were not frequently left in plain sight. He found the latch behind a stack of crates that reeked with the smell of live chickens, though oddly none were contained within. With a single pull of the lever a panel in the wall slid aside. Inside was Potato, along with a treasure trove of other valuable things.

Viverr plucked the scrub pig from the floor and placed him back into his pouch. This room was a rogue's dream. Expertly crafted pottery and skillfully rendered paintings sat amongst precious oils and fine silks of rare colors. He wished at once that there was more room in his belt pouches. *You're a new man*, he chided himself. *An Aranth. Respectable.* The mage had apparently been sleeping here as well, for a hammock hung in the corner with blankets laid upon it. Viverr's companions had been set amongst the finery. They were still frozen and were shackled as well. The spell that kept them paralyzed was a strong one indeed, for despite the fact that the mage was deceased it still held. *He must have anchored it to something other than himself,* Viverr thought. The mage was clever, although the trick would in no way keep Viverr from destroying the magic. A heavy touch of his latent ability freed them both.

"We'll need to hurry," Viverr said. "The boat is on the move."

Islyr held steady as Viverr picked his way through the lock on his shackle. He then worked on freeing Cyanna, which took a fair sight longer than he wished, for she was held by shackles on both her hands and feet.

"Are you well enough to walk?" he asked once both of his companions had been fully released.

"I'm fine," Islyr said curtly.

Cyanna merely nodded. Viverr led them both out through the hidden door.

"What happened in here?" Islyr asked, noting the blood on the floor and the deceased mage from which it had come.

"Got himself killed, though not by my hand. Didn't you feel his death through your circlet before it dropped?"

"Happily, no," Islyr replied. "Perhaps the freezing spell had something to do with it?"

"Who knows," Viverr replied distantly. He knew little of Kerell spellcasting, in honesty, and did not much care to learn.

Something clattered across the main deck above their heads. The sound was followed by a scream of terror.

"Please tell me you didn't release whatever beast was in that cage," Islyr said with a scowl.

"I needed a bit of an advantage, and an angry creature seemed to be as good a bet as any. Why don't you try to kill a mage without assistance and see how well it goes?"

"I've done away with several on my own, thank you," Islyr replied smugly. "And I'll impart to you that every one of those instances went well, this particular adventure aside."

"Shall we get out of here, then?" Viverr suggested. "I've had my fill of both mages and boats for today."

"Not yet," Islyr replied firmly. "We can't question him since he's dead."

"We're not any worse off, I suppose," Viverr conceded. "He was never going to tell us anything."

"Probably not," Islyr agreed. "But now we should see if we can find anything that will tell us what he was planning. It will be in his room, if anywhere. We must go back."

"He was planning to go home with a few marked ones and strike it rich," Viverr explained. "What else is there to know?"

"Devren asked us to ferret out as much as we can about the empress and her plans for this land."

"She does seem to be sending a large number of mages to Evaria of late," Cyanna agreed.

Everything in Viverr's bones told him that they should be making their way off the boat with more speed. He choked the feeling down and followed Islyr back into the treasure trove that was the Mage's room.

"And then there's the matter of your friend, Samuel," Islyr added.

"I doubt he'll have written down where he put him," Viverr reasoned. "Samuel wasn't with you two and the rest of the mage's valuables, so he's likely not on the ship at all." He was beginning to give up hope of finding the man, though he would never admit it aloud. "Let's uncover his plan and head back."

"The mage mentioned the empress quite a bit," Cyanna said.

"Doesn't mean a thing." Viverr plucked a finely crafted knife with an embossed silver handle from a small table beside the mage's hammock. "I've heard that they're all extremely loyal to their empress."

"Yet they don't usually speak of her as if they know her personally," Islyr said as he pulled open a nearby chest. "Grab anything that looks like a letter. Her seal is a rolling ocean wave."

"This boat is already on the move," Viverr reminded them. "I don't know about you two, but I'm not much for swimming."

"We'll get out once we have what we need," Islyr insisted.

"By your word, sir." The rogue could not help but lace his words with sarcasm. "You're welcome for saving you both, by the way."

"Thank you," Islyr said, though it hardly sounded like the man meant it.

"Thank you, really," Cyanna said with more conviction.

"Let's be quick about it, then. We won't want this tub to get too far."

"Not a fan of the sea?" Islyr ran a finger across the small hole near his ear where the circlet had been, wiping the drizzle of blood that emanated from it.

"Never," Viverr replied. "Also, there's an angry, rampaging creature on the deck above," he added as hoof beats and the clipped screams of sailors reached his ears.

"She won't harm us," Cyanna said with more confidence than was warranted in the current situation.

"How could you possibly know that it won't harm us?" Viverr replied. "Or that it's female? Its magic bends light right around it. We don't even know what sort of animal it is."

"It's a unicorn," she said confidently.

"Spirits keep me. You can see it, then?" Viverr asked. It seemed unlikely, given her age.

"I'm not a child," she replied with a scowl. "Avery told me about it."

"Who in the name of the Spirits is Avery?"

"Her scrub pig," Islyr said.

"You call him Potato," Cyanna informed him as she searched the only drawer in the bedside table.

"I've never known a scrub pig to speak common," Viverr mused.

"Oh, he doesn't speak at all," Cyanna replied.

"But you just said-"

"Focus," Islyr interrupted. "Look underneath and behind the furniture. It won't be in plain sight."

"As you say, oh great commander," Viverr muttered.

There were so many items stacked around the place as to be overwhelming, even to a connoisseur of expensive things such as himself. Viverr stood at the center of the room and scanned the tidy piles of items.

"You're not searching," Islyr said.

"A moment, if you please." Viverr held up a finger to silence the man. "If you were attempting to hide something, and you wanted to be sure that no one would find it in a room full of expensive treasure, where would you place it?"

"Beneath the least expensive item," Cyanna said.

"That's my little mouse," Viverr said proudly.

"You gave her a rank in the thieves guild?" Islyr asked.

"I did no such thing. She earned the title herself."

"Obviously," Islyr replied.

Viverr spotted a small crate labeled as hard tack sitting in the shadows near a corner. "Ah, here we are."

With Islyr's assistance they pried it open. Beneath a layer of palm-sized spheres of hard bread nestled in hay was a black leather pouch embossed with a rolling ocean wave. There was magic upon it of some sort. Viverr moved to dispel it.

"It's only a water repelling spell," Cyanna informed him. "Probably should leave it, considering."

"Just in time, mouse, as usual."

"I know," she replied with a grin.

He handed the pouch to Islyr, magic untouched. "We can leave now, eh?"

"Yes," Islyr finally agreed. "Are you certain that you don't want to pilfer anything else before we go?"

"I would if I could carry anything more," he replied, choosing to ignore the cut of the statement. "Let's get off of this Spirits-forsaken boat while we still can."

Viverr plucked his precious dragon's egg from the corner where it had rolled. Luckily it hadn't dried out too much. "Can't win our bet if I don't have my egg," he said as he tucked it against his chest.

"I find it amusing that you still believe you'll win," Islyr replied.

They made their way with haste down the hall and climbed the ladder to emerge onto the main deck. Viverr surveyed the grisly scene before him. It seemed that unicorns had no love of sailors, aside from that of spreading their blood about the place.

"That's a right mess," Viverr noted as he stepped deftly over a puddle of blood rimmed in dainty hoof prints. The sails of the ship lay folded down against the mast, happily, so the boat now made only a slow journey out to sea.

"Let's look for a lifeboat," Cyanna suggested.

It was a solid plan, if indeed any lifeboats remained. The only one he could see was of no use to them as it carried two sailors floating halfway between the ship and the shore. One man paddled frantically, while the other lay limply across the bottom. The dock was not too far a distance, yet from what he could visually estimate it was farther than he would prefer to swim.

"Looks like most everyone is dead," Islyr noted. "Let's stay together as we search."

"And watch out for the unicorn," Viverr added. "Spirits, I feel like an idiot saying that aloud."

"You shouldn't," Islyr assured him. "I'm not much of a fan of unicorns. They're dangerous without a handler."

"Can't see how you'd have much experience with them, seeing as they won't show themselves to most living creatures."

"I have more experience than I'd like," Islyr informed him. "They only show themselves to those we would label as innocents, meaning anyone who they believe won't harm them."

"Nobody I'm well acquainted with, in other words."

"You could say that. They're intelligent too. They can recognize individuals and remember who has done them harm."

"Like ravens, but lethal," Viverr mused.

"Indeed," Islyr replied. "Thus, the carnage we see before us."

"I think that might be a lifeboat," Cyanna said, pointing to several knotted areas of rope that hung from the ship's railing.

Viverr had no experience with large ships, but it was possible she was right. They crept cautiously to the area in question and looked over the edge.

Beneath was indeed a lifeboat, though it was both higher above the water and lower from the deck than he would have liked. "How do you hoist these things up and down, then? Just brute strength?"

"How should I know?" Islyr replied. "Just because I've sailed on a couple of ships doesn't mean that I know how everything is done."

"It looks like they were starting to lift it when they were killed," Cyanna noted as she leaned over the side. "If we pull it back up and climb in then I think we can lower it from inside using the levers."

It was then that Viverr felt a soft, warm breath against his neck. His muscles stiffened as something that felt like the point of a knife pressed gently against his flesh. He had not realized until today how much he detested unicorns.

"Don't move," Islyr warned. "She could perceive it as a threat."

"I'm not an idiot," Viverr grumbled as quietly as he could while still being heard.

His eyes caught Cyanna's cautious approach. His heart tumbled into his stomach. "Don't go and get yourself killed Mouse. Not after I just rescued you."

"Don't worry," she said with far too much confidence. One hand reached out, no doubt towards the creature. She lingered at the edge of Viverr's vision.

"For the Goddess' sake, don't touch it," Islyr warned.

For once Viverr had to agree. Visions of Cyanna being gored by the horned beast snapped through his consciousness. Time moved as slowly as the tiny droplets of blood that he could feel slithering down the back of his neck.

"She demands to come with us, or Viverr dies," Cyanna said.

"You can't expect us to fit a unicorn and the rest of us into a lifeboat," Islyr reasoned.

"Sounds to me like the punchline of a very poor joke." The words rushed out of Viverr's mouth before he could stop them. The creature snorted against his neck. He hoped that unicorns did not understand common speech.

"The weight might well sink us," Islyr cautioned. "That's if she doesn't kill us."

Viverr couldn't decide how heavy a unicorn might be. He had seen them depicted in tapestries, but the real question was whether the people who had stitched those tapestries had actually seen one, or whether it was the product of some mead-induced flight of fancy.

"She's young," Cyanna said. "And probably not very heavy."

"Probably?" Viverr echoed. "That doesn't sound like a safe bet."

"It seems safer than you being skewered through the neck," Cyanna replied.

He could not help but be proud of the wit in the statement, despite the fact that it was directed at him.

"Why can't she just swim?"

Cyanna was silent for a moment, so long that Viverr thought she might not answer.

"She says for the same reason that you don't want to *just swim*," Cyanna finally replied, carefully punctuating the last few words.

Viverr huffed in frustration. For every moment they navigated this ridiculous situation the shore shrank in his vision. "You're the resident expert on unicorns, Islyr," he said at last. "How likely is it that loading a unicorn and three people into a lifeboat will sink it?"

"I am by no means an expert," Islyr countered. "They're nearly the size of a deer when grown, from what I've been told, though perhaps less than half the weight of one."

The horn pressed deeper into Viverr's neck. Pain, much like the sting of a wasp, erupted in the muscle thereof. Did unicorns have venom as well? He sincerely hoped not. "Yes," Viverr panted through the pain. "Just tell her yes."

After a few seconds of silence, the sting receded.

"Let's just get off this spirits-forsaken boat," Viverr grumbled as he wiped the blood from the back of his neck. He was of a mind to touch the flesh of the infernal creature and take the magic from her. He would be able to see his new enemy, at the least. In the end he decided against it, for no doubt it would intensify her anger.

Between the three of them they managed to pull the boat up to the railing.

"And how exactly are we supposed to lift the beast in there, eh?" Viverr asked.

The question answered itself as hooves clattered against the deck, much too close for his liking. The sound met his ears once again as the lifeboat rocked like something possessed by an angry spirit.

"This might be the most idiotic thing we've ever attempted," Islyr said as he climbed over the railing.

"We've only been traveling together a short while," Viverr replied as he followed. "Give it a bit longer."

Viverr handed the dragon's egg to Cyanna and climbed gingerly into the boat. It was a tight fit indeed, and he squeezed in near the back which, with a regular horse on board, would have been folly at best. They lowered the boat into the sea with more effort than he would have preferred. By the grace of the Tides the waves were calm, although as the boat touched the surface of the water it entered his mind that he had no great love of the sea, most especially the great and terrible creatures who lived within it.

"Can you also speak to creatures of the sea?" Viverr asked Cyanna as he took up a set of paddles to row. The craft had most obviously been made with a larger crew in mind, for he found it difficult to reach both of them at once.

"I'm not certain," she replied. "I've never tried."

"Might want to attempt it when we return," he said as Potato shifted nervously in his belt pouch. He chose to believe that they shared a dislike of the ocean. "Just in case it's needed," he added.

"How could that help us?" she said innocently. "You act as if the ocean is teeming with giant monsters with a taste for human flesh."

Islyr endeavored to stifle his laughter by feigning a cough. "Are you comfortable back there, Viverr?" he asked when the fit was complete.

The man kept a straight face, yet Viverr could tell it was a jest at his expense. "Perfect, thank you," he replied in kind.

Viverr could not fathom how long they rowed. He knew only that the docks crept towards them with no great speed, and that by the time they finally reached them he had suffered more exercise from rowing than any decent person should be made to endure.

"Oh, thank the Spirits above," he sighed as he finally crawled, slick with sweat, to lay upon the rough wood of the dock. The unicorn, which would have been long forgotten if not for the occasional smack of what could only be its tail against Viverr's forehead, seemed to have no difficulty at all removing itself from the boat. Hoof beats clattered much too close to his face. Without pause it trotted away, startling a group of sailors, and leaving dropped cargo and unwarranted arguments over clumsiness in its wake.

"Will you make it back to the castle without a horse?" Islyr asked.

"I do at times regret my dislike of riding, but yes." Viverr eased himself up to stand, being cautious of Potato, who chattered a bit as he moved.

"He's hungry," Cyanna commented.

"Well, so am I," Viverr replied. "We can both eat when we get back."

Islyr started off without further comment. Viverr followed, though his every muscle protested the feat. With a bit more effort than was usual they were through town and on the path back up to the castle.

"Are you going to tell me how you know what they're saying, then?" Viverr asked as they walked. "It's not as if animals have words as we do."

"They do have sounds, which combined with movement provide some level of communication," Islyr injected. "Can you not understand other ferrets when you're in your animal form?"

"Some, but that's different since it's due to my mark. And I haven't come across many other ferrets, truth be told." Viverr huffed with the continued effort of walking. "You've never said a thing about being able to speak with animals in the past."

"It's my second latent ability," the girl said. "You know that all female marked ones have two."

"With Selene being the odd exception," Islyr added.

"Not sure what a person would need three abilities for," Viverr said, though to say that he was not jealous of Selene at times would be a lie.

"I wouldn't mind it," Islyr said. "Mine isn't useful on a daily basis, unlike some others."

"I suppose," Cyanna replied. "But you can bring some back from the dead and make others into bloodsoul, so it's almost like you have two."

"I hadn't thought of it in that way," Islyr admitted. "I suppose you're right."

"Never told me you found your second ability, Mouse," Viverr said, making his best attempt not to be offended.

"I only discovered it recently," Cyanna explained, perhaps hearing the dismay in his voice. "My latent ability manifests oddly, so at first I wasn't certain what was happening. I thought it was more like Felan's ability; being able to hear the thoughts of other people.

"But it doesn't work on people?" Viverr did not much like the thought of others reading his mind, most especially those he thought of as family.

"No, but I can't hear the animals speak either, not really. It's more as if my mind absorbs their meaning. I thought at first that I was interpreting the thoughts of the castle staff, strange though they were."

"But it wasn't the staff at all?" Viverr asked.

"No. As it turns out we have quite a few rats in the castle's walls."

"Does your ability work with all animals?" Islyr asked before Viverr could express his dislike of rats and their invasion of his home and his food in particular.

"Mammals and birds, at least," she replied. "I can't hear insects, for some reason."

"That's probably for the best," Viverr said. "I don't think I'd want to hear anything a mosquito or maggot has to say."

"Yes," she agreed. "I was quite pleased about that, actually."

"I'm off to the kitchens," Viverr announced as they finally approached the side entrance to the castle. "And then for a rest." The muscles of his arms throbbed as if he was still rowing. "You'll look after my egg for a while?" he asked Cyanna.

"And if it hatches and imprints upon the princess?" Islyr asked.

"It won't," Viverr replied with as much confidence as he could muster. "I simply don't fancy the thought of carrying anything up all those stairs at this particular moment." The chances that the egg would hatch within the next few hours was slim, in his estimation.

"Of course," Cyanna agreed. "I would be happy to watch her."

He trusted the girl more than he trusted most everyone, yet still leaving the egg with her did leave a hollow in his stomach.

"If only Selene was here," Cyanna added. "She'd heal your sore muscles in a shadow's breath."

It was true. That is if Selene could be convinced to take pity on him. It was a shame she was off on an ill-conceived errand overseas, likely getting herself killed for nothing.

"Exercise can be a benefit to your health," Islyr noted.

"Or an irritating necessity," Viverr replied as he pulled open the thick iron door that led to the castle interior and started inside.

"Wait," Islyr commanded. He threw his hand across Viverr's chest.

"Is it too much to ask you to let me rest every so often?" Viverr asked. "I did just rescue you, in case you've forgotten. After that dragon hatches, and yes, it is a dragon, we'll be doing things my way, which will obviously be for the better."

"Silence," Islyr commanded. "Look."

Viverr prided himself on caution, and on noticing things that few others did, and so it was with great disappointment that he spotted the elongated marks of ash that spread across the ceiling and walls within his sight. He drew his latent ability to the surface. No mage would get the better of him today if he could manage it.

He motioned to Cyanna, who laid the egg gently in the shadows of some shrubbery near the door. By the luck of the Tides, it wouldn't dry too much before they could get it back into the water.

Islyr took the lead, which was fine by Viverr's estimation. The man did have more experience battling mages, though he would brave a cloud of pixies before he'd admit it aloud. They followed the trail of scorched stone with little difficulty. The hollow in his stomach grew as he realized where it led. *The throne room*, he thought.

Viverr watched with interest as Islyr twisted his hands into several primitive thieves' guild signals. *I go around.* Wherever had he picked those up? Viverr nodded his head in consent, and crept into the throne room.

All was silent in the cavernous room. The pungent scent of charred flesh was quick to invade his senses. Next was that of blood. He counted seven dead guardsmen upon the floor, and strangely, one other in servant's clothing. None drew so much as the smallest breath as he watched them. He froze in place as the door on the far side of the room slid open. Only as he realized that it was Islyr entering the room did he breathe once again.

*Safe this side*, Islyr signed.

*Seems empty*, he signed back.

"All of the king's guard here are dead," Viverr informed them as he watched Islyr wedge a lance from a dead guard's grasp. "And then there's this one. Just a servant caught in the way, I suppose."

"No." Cyanna's face was pale. "He's not a servant. Help me turn him over."

They flipped the man onto his back. His hazel eyes stared eerily into the realm beyond. The fellow did look mildly familiar, though Viverr could not recall where exactly they had met.

"This is Alvan," Cyanna said, as if that should explain it all.

"Who?" Viverr asked, wondering if it was someone for whom he should offer condolences to the girl.

"One of the men who tutors Barrik," she explained. "He was to watch him today."

The princess' younger brother was so often left in the care of others that Viverr was hard pressed to recall his existence most days, though he would never admit that to the girl.

"And Devren's not here either," Cyanna noted. Anxiety pierced her words despite her obvious attempt to conceal it.

"The escape passage, perhaps?" Viverr suggested as he lifted a sword from the floor and handed it to the girl.

"You're not supposed to know about that," Cyanna chided as she accepted the weapon. "Only the royal family."

"I know about all of the passages in this place," Viverr replied as he made his way towards the throne. "Even the ones humans can't fit through. And many of them could use a good dusting, while we're on the subject. I don't much like getting cobwebs in my fur." He leaned down to reach his hand behind the thick, gilded legs of the chair. The button set into the bottom pressed inward with a light clicking sound that was ever so satisfying. The stones on the floor beneath the throne slid aside to reveal a set of stairs which spiraled down into the darkness. Torches lit themselves as his foot touched the third step.

"To the Spirits with the element of surprise," he muttered.

The door slid closed of its own accord as Cyanna, who was last in the line, put her weight upon the tenth stair.

"The magic still works here," Islyr noted quietly. "Not that it's of much use to us."

"Better that the Mages' wing had worked as it should," Viverr agreed. "It might have saved us from our current predicament altogether."

Islyr took a torch from the wall and leaned down to examine a set of boot prints that marred the otherwise perfect layers of dust upon the floor. "Several people have been through here. One seems to have been dragged. Not the sign I was hoping for."

"Nor I," Viverr agreed as he watched motes of dust dance around the flame of Islyr's torch. "Dust is still settling from their passage, so they must have gone through here fairly recently. Perhaps we can catch up with them?"

"Perhaps it would be better not to catch up with so many at once," Islyr said with a deep intake of breath.

"If they have my brothers, then we need to follow them" Cyanna countered immediately.

"I count at least five separate sets of prints." Islyr's unease was visibly building.

"Six," Viverr corrected. "It would be insanity to take on six mages at once."

"Perhaps they're not all mages," Cyanna suggested. "We must at least try to get them back."

"That's like saying we should stick our hand in a barrel of snakes because only a few of them are likely to be venomous," Viverr countered. "It's a bad idea. We should head back."

"But they have Devren," Cyanna said. "Maybe Barrik too."

"They won't have any use for Barrik," Islyr said. "He's not yet been found to be Marked."

"That's hardly reassuring," Viverr chided. "We know what they do to people who aren't considered useful."

Despite the darkness of the hall and Cyanna's attempt to hide it, he could see tears welling in the girl's eyes.

"I'm certain they're fine," Viverr lied. "Look, in Devren's absence you're the one in charge. If you want us to go after them, we will. Isn't that right, Islyr?"

"Perhaps."

"It's dusty in here," Cyanna said as she wiped at the corners of her eyes.

"Aye, it is," Viverr replied. "No use in going back towards the castle, I suppose. The dust is already stirred up from us walking through."

"True," Islyr agreed, no doubt upon noticing the girl's tears. "Might as well keep moving forward. Towards some fresh air."

"Thank you," Cyanna uttered quietly as they began walking once again.

Viverr could hardly blame her. Brave as the girl was, she was still little more than a child. Her brothers Devren and Barrik were really all that was left of her family. It brought thoughts of Aurin to his head, for the man was as close as family to him. Where in the name of the Spirits had he gone off to? Now that Devren had been taken, he might never find out.

At last, they came to the end of the tunnel. Cobwebs had been cleared from the release button on the wall, and a long swath of dust was piled into one corner where the door had recently swung open.

"Stay behind me," Viverr instructed. "I have the best chance of coming through their spells unscathed."

"And when they learn that you're immune to magic and begin to hurl items at your person?" Islyr questioned.

"That's when I distract them while you do them in," Viverr informed him. "It's as much of a plan as I've got at a moment's notice."

The cold, metal button pressed in with a click. The door whipped open with more speed than anticipated. Viverr drove his latent ability forward, shielding the front of his body. A gust of air carrying salt and the odor of seaweed hit him. His mouth dropped open in dismay as his ability buried itself once again. Before him lay a cavern big enough to hold a sailing ship. Indeed, it recently had. Beyond that was the open sea and, so far in the distance as to be no more than a speck in his vision, the ship in question.

"We're too late," Cyanna cried out in dismay.

"We'll send ships after them," Viverr said. "The rest of Evaria's fleet if we have to."

"That's our fastest ship," Cyanna said between panicked breaths. "And it has a spell on it that prevents it from being followed. It's made specifically to be used in case our family needs to flee, so that no one can find us. They've stolen both the ship and my brothers."

The narrow strip of rock that served as a dock had once held crates of emergency supplies. Viverr knew it was so, for he had every so often stealthily helped himself to a jar of preserves or a strip of dried meat. All of it was gone as well, no doubt carried onto the ship before its departure.

"What will we do?" Cyanna asked. "What will we do without them?"

"That, I believe, is now up to you." Islyr replied. "What are your orders, my Queen?"

# Remdig
## *Kerell – Capital City*

"Get up," Aster ordered. The woman's face was stern, as was typical. It was far earlier in the morning than any decent person should be made to rise. This had been the way of things every day for the past week. Selene rose before the sun and was sent back to her enclosure to sleep long after it had set. She was thoroughly exhausted, and her mood was suffering for it.

"What difference should one less hour of training make?" she said as she attempted to roll towards the wall, and thus farther away from Aster.

It was a mistake, clearly, for a bitter spike of pain lanced through her head. After a few seconds a much stronger one followed, spreading downward to her limbs. The feeling was akin to shards of glass slicing her flesh, though no wounds nor bruises appeared there. There was never a physical trace of the woman's cruelty, though it seemed that she held endless amounts of it.

"You will apologize." Aster was inside the enclosure now, which left little room between them. She rolled Selene over so that she was once again facing towards her. The woman was apparently in no mood to compromise.

"I'm sorry, Mistress," Selene replied automatically.

"Now, get up as I commanded."

"Yes, Mistress." She levered herself reluctantly from the pile of pillows, which sadly was a poor substitute for a proper bed.

"Get her dressed and meet me at the carriage with Naevus," she said to Datio, whose night it had been to sleep by Selene's door. Aster tossed him a folded bundle of clothing before marching down the hall and rounding the corner.

"She should offer you a bed placed in the hall if you're going to continue to spend all night out there," Selene said as Datio escorted her though the barrier. The now familiar burn of his mark washed over her like a glint of sun between shadows. "Or at least a bigger pillow."

"A pillow of any size is far better than the bare floor," he replied as he plucked at the end of the string that tied the bundled dress to loosen it. "Our Mistress is most gracious, and I won't hear otherwise."

"I agree," Selene replied, for it was a bit too early to receive much more pain, and the range of Aster's hearing seemed greater than most.

Datio untied Selene's shift and pulled her from it. Shivers enveloped her momentarily as the cold of morning touched her bare skin. They slowly faded as he pulled the fresh garment over her head and ran a brush through her hair. Several days ago she had stopped attempting to do such things for herself, for the battle was always lost.

"Let's see what today will bring," Datio said as he applied a light dusting of powder to her face.

"More pain, if it's anything like yesterday," Naevus grumbled as he approached.

Selene could not help but sigh in annoyance. She shifted from one foot to the other.

"Hold still," Datio complained. "You'll make us late." In one hand he held a little brush, and in the other a cup of beeswax and oil dyed crimson, which he was attempting to apply to her lips.

"Is it necessary for my entire face to be coated in mixtures in order to step outside?"

"If you plan on stepping outside into polite society, then yes," Datio replied.

"They why isn't there any on your face?"

Datio's brows drew together in a scowl. "There is, a bit. Mistress finds that your appearance is of more importance than mine at the moment, so the lion's share has been allotted to you. It's her right."

Selene could tell that it was a subject of irritation for the man, so she decided not to pursue it. "What's a lion?" she asked instead. "Do they hoard things like rats do?"

Datio chuckled a little, though the question was not meant to be amusing. Perhaps he was not cross with her after all.

"Doesn't matter," Naevus informed her. "Expanding your knowledge of animals won't help the mistress fetch a good price for you."

The little brush was smooth and warm against her lips and the mixture was mildly sweet to taste.

"Stop licking it," Datio warned. "I haven't the time to do it over again.

"I haven't had any breakfast," she reminded him.

"Well neither have I," Datio countered. "And you won't hear a word of complaint from my mouth. The mistress will feed us when she deems it necessary."

"We need to go now," Naevus said before Selene could offer a reply. "Mistress Aster is waiting."

"It won't be the end of her to wait a few minutes," Selene snapped.

"Perhaps not the end of her, but it might well be the end of us," Naevus replied. "You do realize that every time you get punished under our watch we get punished as well?"

In truth she had not noticed. The realization wound a thread of guilt through her as they ushered her forward. Selene followed Datio through the strange, open halls of Aster and Phaedrus' compound at a quickened pace. Naevus, as usual, walked a few steps behind.

"You can walk ahead of me with Datio," she said, looking back at him. "I won't attempt to escape."

"I should hope not after what happened yesterday," Datio chided.

Selene had experienced great amounts of pain in her life, but none of it equaled the punishment she had received from Aster yesterday upon her attempt to flee. It was as if her skin had been set aflame. There was no way to tell how long it had lasted, though at the time it seemed no less than an eternity. In the end she could barely lift herself enough to stand. Strangely, she suffered no lingering pain today. It seemed to be the way of these new circlets.

"I won't be taking any chances with that," Naevus grumbled.

They arrived at the front of the compound. There they ordered her to sit while Datio slid what were likely supposed to be shoes onto her feet. They were composed of thin, tan fabric, and had no sole to speak of.

"Are these made for wearing outdoors?" She had worn socks that were thicker by far.

"Just be silent," Naevus chided. "You'll anger the mistress with your complaining."

She swallowed her irritation and busied herself with examining the many paintings that graced the walls of the oddly rounded room. There were more portraits of men battling strange animals here than she had noticed when she had first been brought through. Upon closer inspection they were all of Rakaii, for circlets in a myriad of styles adorned their heads.

A light breeze caressed Selene's skin, chilling it. She still found it strange that this place was so open to the air. What would happen when the season turned to winter's chill?

"If by winter you mean the cold season, we're in it at the moment," Datio said with a smirk.

By the Spirits, she wished the man would stay out of her mind.

"Where in the name of the Goddess did the mistress collect you from?" Naevus whispered.

"The jungle," Selene replied quickly. "It's much colder beneath the canopy than it is out here in the city." It sounded ridiculous even as the words left her mouth, but perhaps they would still believe it.

Naevus offered a quizzical look.

"Enough chatter," Aster snapped, and for once Selene was pleased about the interruption. "Get into the carriage."

Selene obeyed. She breezed past Datio, climbed into the carriage and sat, watching placidly as Datio and Naevus followed and seated themselves on the bench across from her.

"This day is going to be just as trying as the last," Naevus said as the carriage driver closed the door.

"Don't be so pessimistic," Datio chided as they lurched forward into the street.

"Aster isn't riding with us?" Selene glanced through one of the carriage's two tiny windows. The streets outside were mostly devoid of mages. The hour was still so early that the sun had barely crested the sky beyond the waves at the edge of the city. Kerell city might be filled with terrible people, but that did nothing to detract from its beauty.

"No, of course not," Naevus replied. "The mistress has her own carriage."

"You might get to ride with your new mistress or master in their carriage after the auction," Datio informed her.

"I'm to be auctioned?"

"If you can learn to mind yourself in time for it," Naevus added, seemingly ignoring the dismay in her voice. "Which at this juncture seems wildly unlikely."

"Where are we going?" she asked in place of a reply.

"Wherever the mistress wants to take us," Naevus said, quite unhelpfully. "You ask far too many questions."

Selene gave up on getting any information from the two at that point, for they had begun to ignore her. She resigned herself to looking out the bubbled glass of the window instead.

The trip was not a long one, and within perhaps a quarter of an hour they arrived at the front of a little building which was well kept, though gaudily decorated. The stone that composed it was the same blinding white that graced most of the walls in the city proper, yet here it was laced with iridescent veins of purple and blue that glittered in the rising light of the sun. An artistically painted sign crafted from driftwood hung above. Although Selene found that she could read the letters, the meaning of the single word upon it was lost to her. *Gnomery.* No matter how much she thought of it, the word still made no sense. Perhaps it was too complicated for the circlet's translation to manage.

"Oh no," Naevus sighed as the door of the carriage pulled open.

Selene could now see much more of the building than what she could glimpse through the tiny carriage windows. It was surrounded by leafy jungle plants on one side. On the other side lay a cliff down which a thin stretch of water trickled, ending in a shallow pool beneath.

Perhaps the reason Naevus had refused to tell her where they were going was that he had not known until they arrived. The fact did not serve to calm Selene's ire in the slightest.

"Remdig," Datio muttered nonsensically.

*Remdig.* She rolled the word around in her mind. *Perhaps it's some sort of Kerell curse?* she mused as she made her way across the strangely polished road towards the building. It certainly sounded like a curse, at that.

"Pick up your feet," Aster urged. It meant, somehow, that she wanted them to move faster, not that Selene should actually pick them up higher. The fact had been clarified to her using a physical strike to the face several days prior. Apparently, Aster had thought that Selene was being willful. Shortly thereafter she had allowed her a bit of her healing ability, just enough to fix the bruise.

Selene glanced up at Aster. The woman must have sprinted from her carriage, for she was already at the door of the building; her knuckles rapping eagerly upon the closest wooden pane.

"Watch her posture. It's still terrible," Aster added upon looking back at Selene as she approached.

"There's nothing wrong with my posture," Selene muttered.

Naevus placed one hand on Selene's shoulder and his other at the middle of her back. He pushed the two towards each other, straightening her spine into what was apparently a more desirable position. She maintained it as best she could, though it was in no way comfortable.

Aster leaned in so close that the spices which lingered on her breath, likely from breakfast, wafted into Selene's face. "Stay next to me and behave," the woman warned.

Aster stepped through the door. How closely did the woman want her to follow? There was no way to be certain. Selene settled for staying no more than a few paces behind her. The sound of metal chimes rang out as they entered a room hung with silks in shades of iridescent blue and purple to match the veins in the stone of the entrance. The structure was larger than it had looked from the outside, for where the building met up with the mountain they had hollowed through the stone to create additional rooms.

"Remdig," a deep male voice called from far within.

Perhaps it was not a curse word after all, for it would be a strange way to greet a customer.

"Yes master," another man replied from closer by. "I heard the chimes, and I am definitely going to see who it is. It is a bit early for customers, but no issues there. I am always ready to assist."

"Without the commentary, if you please," the first voice grumbled from afar.

"Yes, Master Warig, of course. You know that I always follow your command to the very letter. I'm reliable, you know, not like those others. In fact, I should have been named Remdig the reliable. That was obviously an error on my mother's part."

So, it was not a curse, but rather a name. Remdig appeared from between the swaths of hanging silk, still muttering to himself until he caught sight of Aster, at which point he leaned into a sweeping bow. It was upon his appearance that the name of the building became clear to Selene, for although she had seen very few of them in her time it was immediately evident that this man was indeed a gnome. Reddish hair was clipped short on the sides of his head, and what was left long at the top had been fashioned into a knot in the way of an Evarian mage. He was diminutive in height, and his flesh was an odd tone of sepia that she had seldom seen in other living creatures. The yellow of his clothing contrasted brightly against the tones of purple and blue that dominated the room.

"Where's your master, gnome?"

"Greetings, Guest Mistress Aster," Remdig said, straightening to a stand. "And greetings to your, uh, entourage." He looked up at Aster, though his dark eyes did not meet hers, perhaps in a show of deference. "It certainly is a pleasure to see you again, and on such a fine day. You must accept my deepest apologies, however, for Master Warig is currently indisposed."

It occurred to Selene as Remdig spoke that his accent was unlike any other she had heard in this place. In fact, it was somewhat Evarian in nature. Panic came with the thought, and she discreetly glanced at Datio to see if he had heard it. He did not seem to have, for Naevus was in the process of whispering something in the man's ear, which caused Datio to crinkle his nose in distaste. Perhaps they did not like gnomes, or just Remdig in particular.

"Go and fetch Warig now," Aster attempted. "I have a matter of importance which must be attended to immediately."

"Again, you must accept my deepest apologies, Mistress. The master is also working on something of importance, and has specifically asked not to be disturbed until the shop has officially opened, which is…" The gnome glanced in several directions until his gaze finally fell upon a tiny, gilded clock which sat upon a counter carved with flames painted in blue and gold. "One hour and a quarter from now," he announced at last.

"Oh?" Astrid said. "And what might this something of importance be?"

"You certainly wouldn't want the full details of his current endeavor. Master Warig would be unhappy indeed if you were to pass away from being forced to hear the dreadfully boring tale of what he's currently doing. It's ever so important, you see, yet ever so dreary as well."

"It would be in your best interest not to tell me what I want."

The gnome adjusted a pair of bronze goggles with odd green lenses, which rested upon his head. "Yes, well of course I would never dream of guessing what such an obviously intelligent woman as yourself might be thinking. Let me see here. How about this? I'll go and check in with master Warig and ask him to come out here."

Aster's brows knotted together at the center; the first sign of a gathering storm.

"I can't surmise why in all of these years he hasn't processed you."

"Process me? Ridiculous! Why, I'm loyal. I've been passed down in this family for generations. And I'm useful. My prowess for enchanting items is unmatched. It would be a waste to process me. A terrible waste."

Aster rolled up one sleeve of her garment, as if preparing to cast a spell. "Perhaps I'll save him the trouble and process you myself. He'll thank me, I'm certain."

Remdig's eyes grew wide. "I'll fetch him right now. Will that please you, Mistress? I won't be but a moment," he swallowed nervously. "You'll stay here and wait for my return?" He did not wait for an answer to the query, but rather with quickened steps swept the fabric aside and disappeared between its layers.

Astrid followed the man, muttering as she ducked through the layers of silk and around the wide, and oddly bare wooden counter. Selene tread carefully behind her, for the hanging fabric obscured her vision and she had learned that the penalty for accidentally touching the woman was harsh. After reaching the other side of the reception desk and slipping through a partially opened door she found herself in a wide room with shelves on all sides. Upon the shelves sat all manner of stone jars. The largest of the highly polished objects stretched from the floor to her waist, and the smallest could have easily fit into the palm of her closed hand. They were grouped by size and color, and each had a word carved into the front, the letters of which danced in her vision. The urge to touch one stretched her resolve. Datio appeared to her right, materializing much as a spirit would. He took hold of one of her wrists, while Naevus took the other.

"I wasn't going to touch them."

"Your mind said otherwise," Datio countered.

"You must think us incredible idiots," Naevus added bitterly.

*Not idiots, but irritating? Very much so.*

Datio gripped her wrist tighter at the thought.

With a sharp turn to the left she found herself in a strangely wide room with a ceiling that stretched three times her height. Shivers found her skin despite the heat that hung in the air. Flat, gray walls were interrupted in exact measurements with doors composed of iron bars. From a few of them faint scratching noises and muttering could be heard, though the interiors of such were so much darker than the rest of the room that despite squinting it remained impossible to see what dwelt within.

Upon the floor a few circles of white powder had been arranged in varying sizes, the largest of which could easily hold several men. At the center of one was what looked to be a pile of ash. The cavernous room held a lingering smell of charred hair and flesh. Selene kept to the shadows near the wall. She made certain to stay more than an arm's length from any of the cells just in case something should have a mind to reach out and grab her.

From the far side of the room a tall man in a smudged apron approached. Selene thought him to be a blacksmith at first, though the lack of tools or a forge would say otherwise. His hair was cropped short over the whole of his head, and his skin had the weathered tone of one whose profession gave cause for him to be around a great amount of heat and flame. He wore a pair of copper goggles much like Remdig's, though these had blue lenses rather than green.

"Remdig." The word left the man's mouth heavily laden with ire.

"I, oh," Remdig muttered as he noticed Aster. "I asked her, ever so politely mind you, to wait in the lobby, Master," the gnome explained. "But as you can see, well, she did not listen at all, which I can't possibly be blamed for. And then she had the audacity to say that you would thank her for processing me."

"Remdig," Master Warig began again.

"As if I'm just some common sort of gnome and not the smartest, most magically talented gnome you've ever come across in all of your years. Have I not been useful in my enchantments? Have I not been profitable, and loyal? Have I not been passed down for generations in your family? I'm an heirloom. A treasured family heirloom, that's what I am."

"Remdig!"

The gnome paused for a second, his mouth open, as if preparing to continue. It closed slowly as he perhaps thought better of the plan. Master Warig pointed to the pile of ashes upon the floor.

"Get this swept up into a container and put it with the rest of the Illienne order. When that's done, fetch the harpy from eighteen."

"Harpy? Ugh. Such filthy creatures. They're noisy too, and their claws are like knives. Just terrible."

"And two pixies," Warig added, seemingly oblivious to Remdig's distaste. "Immediately," he added when Remdig made no move to depart.

"Yes, of course, master. Your wish is my literal command." With that the gnome wandered away, grumbling to himself.

"What do you want, Aster? I'm in the middle of processing an order."

"Do you require a gnome for that order? I'd be so pleased to assist if that's the case."

"That's very amusing," Warig said in a tone that revealed otherwise. He pulled a strip of thick red cloth from one of the pouches on his apron and wiped the sweat from his brow. "There are days when I would consider it. If he wasn't so talented at enchanting, then I might have rendered him to ash years ago. Now, as I said I am quite busy. State your business so I can get back to mine. I've plenty of pre-sealed product if that's what you're after. Take what you need and leave a list at the counter. I'll send someone to collect payment later in the day."

"It's not as simple as that," Aster replied, motioning for Selene to step into the light.

"Ah, is that a female?" He pulled his goggles up to rest upon his forehead, revealing eyes that glowed white in the shadows. The odor of sweat and flame invaded Selene's nostrils as he drew close. "Rare, that. You're about to move up in the world, eh Astrid? You'll be top shelf before you know it."

"Yes, well, there is an issue with that, which is why I'm here asking for assistance. I've known you to be discreet when necessary. There's one miniscule problem I'll need to surmount before my glorious ascension to the upper caste."

Warig put his nose close to Selene and pulled a deep breath, as if taking in the scent of her. He pulled his goggles back over his eyes to examine her. His deep laughter echoed across the cavernous room.

"Rather a big problem, in my opinion."

"I didn't ask for your opinion. I asked for your help."

"I'm not the one who's been pulling Rakaii from the catacombs. You know it's forbidden?"

Aster glowered at the man.

"Ah, I'm only joking. Everyone knows. The magic of that place is strong, and unfortunately for you, very distinct. She positively reeks of it. Is she the only one you got this time?"

Aster sighed. "No. I managed to trap a few decent males. Three of them are top tier. The rest are practically useless. Poor conformation, or abilities. Might sell them as fodder for the ring in a batch, unless you've a use for them here?"

"I might. Could work that into today's cost if you don't annoy me more than you have already."

"Not that it's any of your business where I get my Rakaii."

"It's become my business, now that you've brought her here."

"I'm the only one in this backward city brave enough to go to the Catacombs. The curses of the Ancients are best left in stories, where they belong. It's a ripe garden of Rakaii waiting to be harvested, as you can see."

"That I do, though the law would say otherwise. It's old magic in that place. Seeps right into them."

"It's faded after a few days in all of the males I've trapped."

"Females are different."

"Yes, I know that now." Aster folded her arms across her chest.

"It's made so that no human mage can touch it."

"Can you get rid of it or not?"

"Remdig can do it. But it's forbidden magic," the man grinned. "Which means it's expensive."

"I can pay you once she's sold."

Warig adjusted the lenses on his goggles, turning them ever so slightly this way and that as he looked Selene over, considering.

"A manipulator," he said. "You should have started with that. Top tier, indeed. Yes, I'll help."

"And for your percentage?"

"Just five, and that batch of inferior males you mentioned."

"Is that all? Done."

"And introductions to all of your new, upper caste friends once she's sold," he added with a grin.

"A fair deal." Aster held out her hand. Warig eagerly shook it.

"Remdig!" the burly man called out.

The patter of feet against stone grew louder as Remdig ran back towards them. He arrived very much out of breath. A long gash on the right side of his face dripped blood onto his bright yellow shirt.

"My deepest apologies, master," Remdig panted. "I was attempting to get the harpy from her cell, but as you can see, well, she is in a particularly bad mood, even for a harpy."

"Aster, do you mind?" Warig waved a hand towards the gnome.

"Not at all, considering what you're doing for me." Aster snapped her fingers and pointed to the ground next to her feet.

Selene stomped down the anger that was steadily rising in her chest and stepped forward obediently. A trickle of her healing ability opened to her. It felt like the flood of a swollen river in spring after having been denied it for so long. In truth it was so little compared to her full ability. But a trickle of magic was all she had needed to send Ranur to his time with the Spirits. Her ability was gone suddenly, replaced by pain; a feeling as if someone had driven a wooden stake through her head. She clutched her face in agony.

"No," Aster said. "Absolutely not."

The pain subsided, leaving no trace aside from a small amount of blood, which she could feel as it dripped from her nose. On the edge of her vision, she could see that Datio and Naevus had suffered the same fate.

"That was a warning. You won't get another."

The trickle of healing ability found her once again. She took it and healed Remdig's wound, forcing the flesh to mend itself. A feeling of euphoria found her, however brief.

"My apologies, Warig. She still has some training to go through, as you can see."

"That I can." The man was rummaging through a nearby chest, and seemed undisturbed by the incident, to say the least.

"Well, you have my thanks." Remdig aimed the comment towards Aster, but he was looking at Selene. He did talk perhaps more than was necessary but did not seem to deserve the contempt that Datio and Naevus offered him. Remdig took a rag from a nearby pile and wiped the blood from his cheek.

"Don't bother to thank me," Aster replied. "I would much rather have burnt you to ash."

"Bring the staff," Warig commanded. "And some chalk."

Remdig gathered the items as requested, pulling them from strange drawers carved into the walls. The openings seemed like solid rock until with a touch of his finger they separated, revealing various contents within. The staff was a short length of polished wood, copper in color and set with a clear crystal at the top. The gnome held it as if it was well known to him. His fingers settled perfectly into impressions in the weathered wood.

"What are we doing, master?" Remdig asked. "If you don't mind me asking, of course."

"Dispelling a bit of old magic."

"Old magic, you say?"

Remdig drew a deep breath next to Selene. She could not help but wish that everyone would stop sniffing her, as it was starting to become obnoxious.

"Ah, the catacombs."

"Yes, the catacombs," Warig repeated with a sigh. "Do try not to touch the rest of her magic."

A wisp of anxiety wriggled into Selene's stomach with the realization that whatever they were about to do might well affect her abilities.

"No problem at all," Remdig said with confidence. "I'm an expert in all types of magic, as you well know."

The stick of chalk gave off a faint green glow in the gnome's hand. He drew a little circle on the floor. "Have her stand over here, if you please, Mistress."

Aster directed Selene to stand at the center of the drawing.

Selene watched with interest as Remdig sketched a series of symbols, none of which she recognized, around the outside of the circle, and then another set of them within, surrounding her feet.

"You can't move from within the circle," Remdig warned her.

"She won't," Aster assured him.

The gnome set down the chalk and took up the staff. The crystal set into the top glowed with faint light as he touched it, echoing the color of the chalk below. He uttered no words of magic, yet the runes on the floor cooled so much that Selene could feel the chill of them through the oddly thin cloth of her boots. Remdig's eyes remained closed in concentration as he gripped the staff.

It was a lengthy process, so much so that even Naevus shifted impatiently. Several times during the spell Selene considered trying to sit, if only for a moment, though a glare from Datio warned her that it would not be wise.

Tendrils as clear as ice beneath the water drifted up from the runes on the floor. The chill of their magic caressed her skin. It moved to burrow through her flesh to her core. Her heart fluttered, constricting her chest and tearing her next breath from her lungs. The magic twisted through her. She struggled for breath, and just when she thought she might collapse, the air crackled like a summer storm and the magic was gone.

"Done," Remdig announced with glee. "And with all of her abilities fully intact. You see, Master Warig, this is a perfect example of how valuable I am."

"We'll see." Warig's eyes grew and shrunk within the warped blue glass as he adjusted the lenses of his goggles once more. "Looks like that's all of it. She's clean."

"She'll need help to walk for the rest of today at least," Remdig informed them. "I wouldn't recommend any usage of her abilities. She'll be as right as rain clouds by tomorrow, though. I guarantee it."

"Take her back to the carriage," Aster ordered.

Selene found that she could barely stand. Her legs attempted to crumple beneath her.

"I'll have Phaedrus bring that group of Rakaii to you this afternoon, will that do?"

"Indeed it will," Warig replied.

Datio and Naevus appeared at once by Selene's side. They took hold of her arms and helped steady her careful steps across the smooth cavern floor. In what seemed no more than a moment's time they arrived back in the carriage. She had barely touched the bench inside when the horses pulled forward.

The carriage made its way with haste through the winding streets to the compound. Each bump in the road caused Selene's stomach to turn, and at once she was thankful that Aster had not given her any breakfast.

"Do you think she'll give us something to eat when we return?" Datio asked his brother.

"If she thinks we've earned it, I suppose," Naevus answered glumly.

"What do they sell at a Gnomery?" Selene asked in a futile attempt to keep her mind off of the state of her stomach.

"You can't tell by the name of it?" Naevus replied.

"Well, it can't be Gnomes. The only one I saw there was Remdig."

"The only live one you saw there was Remdig," Datio corrected.

"The stone jars. They were filled with powdered gnomes?" Selene had not thought it possible for her stomach to feel worse than it did a moment ago.

"Not just gnomes," Datio said. "All sorts of magical creatures."

"Whatever for?"

"Humans are not born with much magical power, even those born as mages," Naevus explained. "Consuming the powder from magical creatures or using it in incantations boosts their power immeasurably, for a short time at least."

"And Warig makes a business of it? It's a shop for purchasing creatures that he's burned to ash?"

"*Master* Warig," Naevus replied shortly. "And yes, it's a shop. Perhaps Mistress Aster overestimated your intelligence."

"She does seem to be having a difficult time grasping the concept," Datio agreed. "Though in her defense, I doubt they have shops in the wilderness."

"Do they use Rakaii as well?" She already knew the answer, but for a reason known only to the Spirits themselves she wished to hear them admit it.

"Sometimes, if they're not worth anything at auction." Naevus offered her a pointed look. "Or if they can't be tamed."

"Oh, stop trying to scare her Naevus. They would never dream of rendering a female."

She wasn't frightened for herself, but rather for her companions. "What types of Rakaii aren't worth anything?"

"No more time for talk," Naevus said. "We're back."

The carriage pulled to a stop. Through the bubbled glass Selene could see Aster's compound, which had suddenly moved down the list to her second least favorite place.

"Yes," Datio agreed. "The mistress is rather cross with you after what you attempted earlier."

"But I didn't do anything," Selene protested as they stood and led her from the carriage.

"You were thinking up ways to kill our mistress," Naevus whispered angrily. "I feel like that's something."

"But I wasn't," Selene protested. "It was just a memory."

"Well, next time keep your memories in check," Datio chided.

"If you'd stay out of my mind then it wouldn't be a problem."

"I'm not the one who noticed it," Datio snapped. "Do you think the mistress never enters your mind? Just because she doesn't often do it doesn't mean she can't."

Datio and Naevus both dropped to their knees, clutching their heads as Aster strode towards them. Selene fell, for her legs alone could not hold her. Her hip collided painfully with the hard floor.

"Please, Mistress," Selene begged. "Don't harm them. It was my fault."

Datio and Naevus aided in keeping her in Aster's grasp, certainly, but could they truly be held accountable for the terrible things they were forced to do?

"Having a touch of regret for your actions, are you? Worry not. I'll see to you in a moment."

By the time it finally ended, Datio lay curled into a ball on the strangely smooth floor.

"Pick your brother up and take him to your enclosure," Aster ordered.

Naevus shook Datio lightly. The man groaned in agony.

"Now!" Aster screamed.

"Yes, Mistress." With the use of his latent ability Naevus lifted Datio and floated him silently through the hall. Selene watched them until they disappeared around a corner.

"Get up," Aster commanded.

"I can't," Selene replied, forgetting herself.

A dull ache spread through her body, coming to rest in her forehead. Aster grabbed hold of her wrist. Fingernails pierced Selene's flesh. With a strength Selene would not have thought Aster capable of, the woman pulled her across the floor and through the halls of the compound.

"Spirits keep you," Selene cursed.

She did not know if Aster understood the words as an insult, but she certainly caught their intention, for the pain in her forehead intensified, as did the woman's grip on her. Sharp nails bit further into her wrist as Aster walked. Selene's fingers began to tingle, and then to feel numb.

Naevus sat in the hall outside Selene's tiny cell, much to her surprise. He scrambled to stand as Aster approached.

"Throw her in," Aster commanded.

"Yes, Mistress,"

Selene's body lifted from the ground, and she was tossed into her enclosure, though not as heavily as she had expected, for she merely grazed the stones of the wall before landing on the pile of brightly colored pillows beneath it. The pain sloshed around in her head, worsening as she pulled herself to sit.

"For your indiscretion you can keep this pain until tomorrow's light."

With the last of her strength Selene took her stone cup and threw it at the woman. Apparently, Aster had not set the barrier to keep items from penetrating it, for it sailed through to strike the mage squarely in the center of her ribcage. Naevus jumped back in alarm as Aster clutched her chest in surprise. In other circumstances it might have harmed her, or at least left a bruise, but whatever magic the gnome had performed on Selene had drained her strength considerably.

Aster's face shaded a deep color of red. She pulled her sleeves back as if preparing a spell. Selene steeled herself for the pain that was to come. But then Phaedrus appeared. The man's face was creased with lines of worry and his breathing was elevated, as if he might have sprinted here from wherever he had been. He cautiously placed a hand upon his companion's shoulder.

"Aster, no. You must calm down."

The mage's expression softened in the slightest, and she lowered her hands.

"This one will be worth the aggravation."

"I'm beginning to think not," Aster replied through gritted teeth.

"Think of our new life," Phaedrus continued. "Of finally belonging to the upper caste. Every mark you make on her will lower her value."

Aster drew a deep breath.

"I'll bring you one of the worthless ones. You can do as you will."

"I promised that batch to Warig."

"But did you say how many?"

"No, I did not," Aster said with a smile that caused Selene to shudder.

"Then he will hardly notice one less."

Aster drew something from her pocket. She threw it at Selene's head. Selene moved aside just in time to watch it thud heavily against the wall behind her. She looked down at the item. To her surprise it was no magical thing meant to harm her, but rather a biscuit, similar to the type she had been given upon her arrival.

"That's only because I can't sell you if you're dead from starvation." The mage turned and kicked a nearby table which held a stone vase. Water and thick, white flowers cascaded through the air as the item thudded heavily to the floor.

Rage flowed thickly around Aster as she stormed away. Once the woman was out of sight Selene plucked the broken biscuit from the floor where it lay. It was thick, and so had only split into three pieces. She dusted them off. Her stomach had settled, but somehow she could not bring herself to eat. Instead, she took one of her pillows and set it next to the barrier. Atop it she set the pieces of biscuit. She knocked upon the wall. Naevus' face appeared, angry and ready to scold her, but then he followed her gaze. At first, he looked suspiciously from the biscuit to Selene, as if she had some plan to cause him further pain. When after several minutes she made no movement he sighed deeply, reached in to retrieve the offering, and retreated back to the other side of the wall.

"Thank you." The whispered words could barely be heard, even in the silence that now weighted the surrounding air.

Selene lay down upon her pillows and pressed her head to the wall, which was only slightly cooler than the room itself. She had to assume that Aster was finished with her for the day, which was well enough. She had certainly suffered enough of the mage for a time. Selene's stomach still rolled, and pain pulsed within her head. It would be a long wait until tomorrow's light.

# The Auction
## *Kerell – Capital City*

Selene issued silent thanks to the Spirits upon stepping out of the carriage. The green, cushioned seats were ever so comfortable, yet they did nothing to stop the rolling of her stomach during the hilly twists and turns of the city. Ahead lay a mercifully flat expanse of land which included the carriage drive upon which they stood and beyond that, a villa with finely manicured gardens. She followed about five paces behind Aster, as she had been trained. It had been little over a week since they had returned from Warig's shop. In order to avoid such punishment again, and also for lack of a better plan, she had decided to be as obedient as possible. It seemed that the better behaved she was, the more she was allowed to see and do. The more she learned of this place, the better her chance of escape. And as a more immediate benefit, Aster rarely listened in on her thoughts anymore, but rather chose to spy only on her feelings.

"Remember to level your chin," Naevus reminded her. "You're to look forward, but don't meet anyone's gaze unless it's another Rakaii."

"And don't hunch your shoulders," Datio added. "It'll give you bad posture."

Selene doubted that to be the truth. She squared her shoulders anyway.

The building was as open as most here, though Selene did note that unlike the other places she had visited since she had arrived, a handful of burly guards patrolled the grounds. These even wore a small amount of armor, which was highly unusual. It was made of leather, and only protected the chest and forearms. She supposed that nothing heavier could be used here without fear of perishing from the heat.

Above the main entry hung a large sign carved from stone. Gilded letters were rimmed in black paint.

*Lysander's Gallery*, she read silently. *Rakaii auction, preparation, and sales*, it announced beneath.

"That's Lysander," Datio whispered into Selene's ear as someone appeared from within. "It's an honor to be in his presence."

"Be on your best behavior," Naevus hissed.

Lysander's clothing was finely made, if perhaps a bit gaudy. Cloth dyed in the hues of newly sprung grass flowed down from beneath a white fur collar like a waterfall. The man greeted Aster with a kiss upon each cheek. His smooth, precise movements brought to mind the large cats that roamed the woods near Maresbane.

"Aster, darling," he said as he looked her over. "Such a pleasure to see you."

"I'm honored by your invitation, Lysander," Aster replied, tilting her head downward briefly.

"Please, call me Lysa," he insisted. "All of my friends do so, and we're of the same caste now, are we not?"

"Of course," Aster replied, though she looked somewhat in shock. "Thank you."

"Do come in," he said, gesturing to the inside of the building. The early light of day flashed across his well-oiled skin and fingernails, which were tinted gold to match the edges of his clothing.

Several of the villa's servants rushed to take Aster's shoes and set them in a little alcove decorated with fresh flowers. Selene started for her own, but Naevus took hold of her arm. He offered a look of warning while Datio removed her shoes for her. The brothers then tended to theirs before stepping inside.

Those with their freedom were sorted into castes in this land, yet there were levels of Rakaii as well, she had learned. It would seem that she ranked somewhere near the top. She had not yet decided whether this was of benefit or detriment.

The entryway was large enough to rival that of Evaria's castle, and upon the ceiling was painted an imitation of the sky, complete with clouds and several birds in flight. Farther inside they came to a room just the size of the common room at home. This had chairs and tables both, and behind that racks of clothing also lay in rows against the far wall. Closer still was a wall of mirrored glass. It was here that Lysander stopped. Behind him two servants hovered, invisible as shadeslight until summoned to a task.

"For any lesser capture I might have my underlings choose the theme." Lysander paused to take a glass jar containing a powdery substance from a nearby shelf. "But this deserves the most delicate touch, don't you agree?"

Aster nodded as she accepted a glass of wine offered by one of Lysander's servants.

"Naevus and Datio possess such skill that I would not dream of leaving my vision to any other." Lysander ran a slender hand over Datio's hair and down his cheek. The man leaned into the gesture, somewhat akin to a dog receiving praise from his master. "Have her stand over here," Lysander gestured to the center of a nearby rug.

Aster motioned Selene forward, and she obediently moved. The soft stripes of white and black fur were warm against the soles of her feet.

"More light, don't you think?"

Lysander did not wait for an answer, but rather whispered a few words, and glowing stones embedded in the walls brightened enough to match the sun at midday. The earth and sugar scent of coconut wafted around her as he moved closer. Only two days past she had learned that coconuts only looked to be inedible, for beneath a rock-like green exterior and then a layer of fur they actually contained white fleshy material fit to eat. Stranger yet, the middle was filled with water. When she finally found Felan she would tell him that they were indeed food, and that the smell was somewhat delightful. She smiled at the thought before remembering where she was.

"Very pretty," Lysander remarked. "You'll have her smile when we first bring her out."

Selene was growing accustomed to people speaking about her as if she was not there, though she still found it difficult not to grumble at the slight.

"Remove the garment," he ordered.

Naevus loosened the clasp at the top of Selene's dress and pulled the fabric from her. She took a deep breath in an attempt to hide her irritation, though she knew it would be clear to Aster. The warning glance and whisper of pain the woman sent her was enough to know that any less than complete obedience would not be tolerated on this day.

"Poor precious thing," Lysander cooed. "She looks mortified."

"She always does that when bare," Aster informed him with amusement. "They never appear nude in front of others where she comes from, apparently. It's quite a civilized society, the jungle."

"Your sense of humor is divine," Lysander laughed. "I cannot wait to introduce you to my friends. Let's finish this up with haste, shall we?"

"An excellent idea," Aster agreed.

"She is perhaps a bit muscular," Lysander commented after surveying Selene top to bottom, "Nothing that can't be remedied with time. A nice, angled nose and a round face. Lovely. And her skin is nearly spotless. You had her heal herself?"

"Ah, yes," Aster replied. "Ferals are simply covered with scars."

Selene scowled at the thought of it. She had not been well pleased to remove her pact scars. Particularly those she had made with her friends, for they represented what little she had left of her former life.

A servant appeared in the doorway, carrying a stone bowl and a cloth packet. Selene recognized the smell of the viscous substance within as he set it near her feet. It was the same honey and wax mixture that Datio and Naevus had used to forcibly strip the hair from her legs two days past. She could not fathom what they planned to do with it this time, for she had little hair left anywhere. Surely they did not intend to remove the hair from her head. The weather was hot here, yet she had only witnessed a rare few people with bald heads.

"A bit of shaping is fashionable," Lysander informed Aster as he waved the servant away. "I had mine done a few days ago and the response has been overwhelmingly positive."

Selene followed Aster's gaze, and she immediately wished that she hadn't. She discovered what hair Lysander was speaking of only as he pushed aside the wispy cloth that covered the space between his hips.

"The jungle must indeed be the most prudish place," he joked as he let the fabric fall back from whence it had come. He placed a hand upon Selene's cheek. "It's like the heat of a fire." He released her to turn to Naevus and Datio. "Put her hair up, with a small amount loose down one side. Get some morning star blossoms from the garden and use them in a cascade effect. For oils use jar eleven on the skin, number six for the hair, then the shimmer I've placed on the table for the finishing effect." He pulled a garment of white cloth from a nearby rack. Selene was pleased to see that it contained enough fabric to cover most of her body. "This dress will be perfect for the reveal," he said with delight. "White. It makes the buyers think of purity. It also plays nicely against her skin tone. Oh my, I nearly forgot to ask if you've had her certified."

Aster's smile faded. "No," she replied. "I hadn't thought of it. I've only ever owned male Rakaii until now."

"Not to worry. I'll have my telepath call for the Decuma."

"She'll come right away?" Aster asked in amazement.

"Yes, of course," Lysander replied. "We have somewhat of a standing agreement. She'll be here before Datio and Naevus are done preparing your Rakaii for the auction. I know that they're trained in waxing. Ideally this should have been done several days ago."

"Yes," Aster replied. "They're trained in several techniques. I simply wasn't aware of the trend."

"Not to worry. I have some oils to reduce the irritation. Open her manipulation ability in the slightest, and that should cover the rest. Come with me now and I'll introduce you to all of your new friends."

Selene scowled at Lysander and Aster's backs as they disappeared around the corner.

"I have this new wine that's made with honey from Zephyrus estate," he continued from the hall. "You simply must try it. And it comes with the most delightfully juicy bit of gossip. Apparently, the whole estate has recently been reclaimed…" Lysander's voice faded along with the tap of their bare feet against the tile.

"You'll behave, I assume?" Naevus asked the question as if he was in no mood to hear otherwise.

"I suppose," she replied as she lay cautiously on a settee upholstered in silk with stripes of white and pink. "Although the extent of my obedience depends on how many times you've done this before."

"Always have to be clever, don't you?" Naevus huffed. He plucked a pair of scissors from a nearby table.

"Well, it is a rather sensitive area," she countered.

"Many times, but not recently," Naevus admitted as he began to snip the hair in question. "It was in fashion some time ago, then it went back out, and now it's in again, apparently."

"I've the luck of the Tides," Selene quipped.

"Now hold still so I can finish this before the wax cools," he chided.

"Why is Lysander having you two do this, anyway?" she asked as Naevus applied the first layer of wax. "Doesn't he have any Rakaii of his own who prepare others for auction? He seems rich enough for them."

"We are his Rakaii," Naevus replied. "Sort of." He pressed the strip of cloth to her skin and then quickly ripped it away.

Selene bit the inside of her lip and narrowly resisted the urge to strike him in the face.

"He has a rental agreement with Aster," Datio explained. "She has us the first half of each month; the two weeks that hunting ferals is allowed. Master Lysander usually gets us the second half, though with you here the arrangement seems to have been altered a bit." He plucked a glass jar of oil from the shelf, swirled it around, and sniffed. "He has tried to buy us outright on several occasions, but Aster is reluctant to sell since we're so useful with new captures."

"Might change her mind, now that she's excelsus caste," Naevus said. "Master Lysander is probably oiling her up for it right now."

"Would be nice, living here full time," Datio mused. "Everything is so luxurious."

"You wouldn't miss Aster?" Selene asked, more as an attempt to ignore what was going on below than out of genuine curiosity.

"I'm not foolish enough to admit otherwise, that's for certain," Naevus replied as he ripped another strip of cloth away.

"That stings quite a bit, you know," Selene informed him through a clenched jaw.

"I've had it done several times." Naevus smiled. "But thank you ever so much for attempting to enlighten me."

"You look lovely." Datio handed her a cloth that had been dipped in cold water. "This should help with the sting."

"Thank you," she managed. She could not deny that the chill of the water was soothing, as was the herbal fragrance that emanated from the cloth. *Perhaps the worst of it is over with*, she hoped as she pulled at her healing ability to ease her inflamed skin. One miniscule thread was all that Aster would allow her to touch. Selene sighed. All that was left was to sit through some primping, which could not possibly be more embarrassing than what had just occurred. *And then the auction*, she reminded herself. She looked up to find Datio and Naevus both kneeling upon the floor with heads bowed.

"We are honored by your presence, Decuma," they said in unison.

The woman who entered was covered in tattoos; dark trails of ink that twisted into a forest of animals and plants hiding between the wrinkles of her skin. Ringlets of hair bounced against her head as she walked.

Selene removed the towel from between her legs and pulled herself into the most dignified pose that was possible while lying nude on a settee. This caused one corner of the old woman's lips to curve upward.

"You are Selene," she said.

"Yes, Mistress." By the grace of the Spirits, she remembered to add the title.

"My title is Decuma," the old woman said. "You may call me by such."

"Yes, Decuma," she echoed, remembering how much Aster hated it when she failed to form a reply.

"She was feral?" she asked Naevus.

"Yes, Decuma," he replied. "Mistress Aster captured her in the jungle."

The Decuma placed her hand on Selene's stomach beneath her navel. It was as warm as the pool that Datio and Naevus had bathed her in on her first day as Rakaii.

"When was your last cycle?"

Pride stopped her tongue. This place had stolen much of it from her, and she wanted desperately to keep hold of what little was left. Datio and Naevus were now standing and facing towards her, so she could clearly see their expressions. They were in awe of this woman. Upon looking into eyes with no more color than the night sky, she felt it too.

"Your last cycle, my dear?"

For reasons unknown, she told her.

"You've lain with another, but very few times."

It was a statement rather than a question.

"You have not borne any children, and you are not currently with child."

The myriad of rings upon the old woman's fingers clicked against each other rhythmically as she rubbed her hands together. The heat emanating from her palms grew until she felt they might burn her. The Decuma hummed as she pressed inward, as if feeling the secrets of her flesh.

"I see that you have never carried."

Selene did not speak, for the woman's eyes were as mesmerizing as deep-ocean waves at night.

"But I see that you can, and you will."

The thought of having a child in this place unnerved her, and the potential of having it forced upon her brought bile to her throat.

"You may continue your preparations," the Decuma said to Naevus. "I will find you for the confirmation after the auction is complete."

"We bend to your will, Decuma," Naevus replied most politely.

As the last slip of the Decuma's robe trailed like the fins of a golden koi into the hall they began to groom Selene. Datio applied shimmering oil to her skin. He then filed and oiled her nails as well, coloring the tips with a silver wash as Naevus put her hair up in the manner that Lysander had ordered. Her request to go along with Datio to the gardens to fetch the flowers for her hair was met with a disgruntled gaze.

"I thought as much," she replied as she plopped ungracefully onto the settee once more.

"Don't touch your face," Naevus warned. "You'll ruin all of my work. Stand up now so I can put your clothing on."

She wouldn't have ventured so far as to call it clothing, but she knew from experience that informing him of that would have little effect other than to cause mild annoyance. "I can't understand why you've bothered with all of the waxing and oiling when it's all going to be covered by a garment," she said instead.

"You won't have it on but for a moment," Naevus informed her.

"I've brought a few different sizes of blossoms," Datio announced as he popped back into the room. "And several unopened blooms for the bottom of the cascade effect." He placed the flowers gently upon the table, and then glanced up at Selene. "What's wrong with her now?"

"Only the same things as usual," Naevus said with a smirk.

Selene was not amused in the least. She watched passively as they dipped the flowers in oil, and then shook a small amount of clear powder onto each.

"To keep them fresh," Datio explained as Naevus arranged her hair, attaching each flower with a thin bit of wire to keep it in place.

"Don't touch it," Naevus warned as he finished.

"You say that about everything," Selene replied with a sigh.

"And I mean it."

"I'd say this is some of our best work," Datio chirped in excitement as he turned Selene around to face the mirror.

"No one would guess that she'd been feral," Naevus agreed. "Looks to rival the Goddess herself."

"Such blasphemy," Datio said with delight. "And such truth."

Selene had to admit, if only to herself, that their efforts had created an effect of ethereal beauty. No flaws could be detected beneath the luster of oil upon her skin. Her eyes seemed wider, her lips plump, and her hair did indeed cascade down one side as Lysander had requested, with flowers afloat in a stream of chestnut locks.

"Not so much as a word of thanks," Naevus muttered.

"Telepath says that they're nearly ready for us," Datio announced after a moment of silence. "Come along, then. We can't be late."

"It begins so soon?" Selene asked as fear constricted her chest. She had thought there would be more time.

"It's already begun," he replied as they led her into the hall. "Surely you didn't imagine that you're the only Rakaii to be sold today?"

She had indeed entertained the thought.

"Be certain not to step on your dress as you walk," Naevus chided. "And you could be a little more eager."

"Why should I?"

"Because you're to meet your new master or mistress tonight," Datio explained with a grin. "Females are rarely ever put up for sale after the initial purchase."

"They're not?"

"No, of course not. You're more than a possession. You're a symbol of wealth and status. You'll be passed down in the family, likely for generations since we live so much longer than the mages."

"Generations?" The word caught in her throat. She could not stand to stay in this place for a year, let alone a few hundred. It was unthinkable. She would find a way home or be sent to the Spirits while trying.

"Here we are," Datio announced cheerfully.

The curtain ahead of her ran the width of the door and was composed of a gray velvet fabric so thick that she imagined it was rarely seen in this sweltering land. Naevus pushed it aside and ushered her through. The glowing stones embedded in the corners of the floor emitted just enough light to navigate the length of the narrow room beyond. To her right was a solid wall, painted in a color as dark as a winter night. To her left hung another curtain of the same color as the last, or at least it looked to be so with as little as she could see. The murmur of many voices trickled through the waves of fabric, and above them a single tongue rose, uttering a series of numbers.

"What is that?" she asked.

"The auctioneer," Datio whispered. "Lysander likely put a couple of high-quality males up before you. It's common to warm the bidders up before presenting the most valuable Rakaii. Then, after you're sold, they'll let some of the lower castes in and continue with the rest of the auction."

"Are you coming out with me?" It seemed like a silly question when said aloud. She could find no logical reason for the quickening of her heart as she thought about venturing beyond the curtain.

"We'll be with you until you're sold," Datio assured her.

The auctioneer's voice, lilting and soft like the wings of a moth, floated down from somewhere above her. "And now we present the jewel of today's auction; captured and trained by Tenere Aster Thurii and her second, Phaedrus Nola. Our host would like us to officially welcome them to excelsus caste." Applause drifted through the curtain despite the thickness.

"Come on," Naevus ordered. "And don't forget to smile as you walk out."

With those words they stepped through the curtain. It was akin to stepping out of a cave into the light of day. Selene smiled as she had been ordered to but could not help but squint her eyes in protest against the strength of the light.

"Isn't she beautiful?" the auctioneer cooed. "The rarest of finds. This is not an escaped feral, but rather a wild-caught Rakaii trapped deep in the jungle outside the city."

The room slowly materialized as her vision adjusted. It was larger than she had expected, with many rows of seats leading up at an angle away from the stage upon which she stood.

"This Rakaii is a manipulator, so she is guaranteed to provide a return on your investment! Whether you own battle Rakaii or simply wish to entertain your companions, this one is not to be missed."

Perhaps one-third of the seats were occupied, although Selene could see in detail no farther than the first two rows. She scanned those she could while the auctioneer continued. Perhaps she would find Cael here, with Xaiden and Felan.

"Pay attention," Naevus snapped in whispered tones. He ushered her to the middle of the stage.

It seemed that the Tides were not with her this day. She could find no recognizable faces.

"She has been confirmed by incantation to be around twenty-five years of age," the auctioneer continued as Naevus motioned for her to turn to her left. "She has never carried, and so comes with a written guarantee signed by a Decuma that she is capable of bearing children, and with a complimentary witnessed confirmation."

Selene pondered what a witnessed confirmation could be. She decided that it was likely not anything she would enjoy.

"Turn to your right now," Naevus whispered.

Selene followed his instructions, remembering to do so as gracefully as possible. She did not move to cover herself as Datio and Naevus removed her robe, although the urge to do so was strong. *Nudity is common here*, she reminded herself. It did nothing to calm her rapidly beating heart, nor to cool the heat that rose up past her cheeks as the hushed words of the audience reached her. There were no mirrors here, yet she had no doubt that the tips of her ears were now the color of a ripe apple.

"We will begin at the amount listed in the program. Our host would like me to remind you that bids may only be placed in increments of ten thousand during this particular auction. Bidding is now open on this incredible investment for the future of your household."

Selene scanned the remaining rows of seats, for her sight had nearly returned to its natural state. None of her friends were there. Tears welled at the corners of her eyes. *My thoughts are pure serenity.* She repeated the words until her emotions obeyed her. Around the room hands were being raised, at which the auctioneer, whom she still had not located, would raise the cost. It seemed to work much like the auction of animals did back in Evaria.

"As you can see by her mark, this beautiful find has an animal form of raven, messenger of the Goddess and bearer of souls to the afterlife," the auctioneer said as the bidding slowed for a moment. "One could not ask for a more auspicious Rakaii."

The price continued to rise as Naevus walked her around the stage. She had no concept of what the coin of the realm was worth, though she imagined that the price had been high at the beginning, seeing as this was an invitation-only event.

The price had escalated to the point that only two bidders remained; a distinguished looking woman with a comb of precious gems in her upswept hair, and a well-groomed, portly man sitting between two lively male companions dressed in the gauze-like garb of the realm. Naevus and Datio continued to lead Selene around like prized livestock, turning her this way and that so that every inch of her flesh was visible.

"Such a high quality Rakaii is unlikely to be seen again in this lifetime," the auctioneer urged, as if to elicit further bids.

The woman with the comb of gems bid once more, while the man hesitated. He drew his brows into a scowl and shifted in his chair, then shook his head in the slightest.

"Congratulations to Pyra Leaena of excelsus caste on her newest acquisition." The auctioneer paused to wait for the applause to fade. "Complementary wine will now be served in the sitting room for all of our esteemed guests. The auction for battle Rakaii registered as rank seven and under will begin on the quarter hour, at which time those of lower castes will be admitted. We are honored by your attendance. Depart by the grace of the Goddess."

Quiet chatter began amongst those in attendance as they stood and made their way out of the room. Naevus ushered Selene along the back of the stage and wrapped her garment around her. He led her out through the curtain to a little room on the side. There were no windows, the realization of which forced a terrible feeling of confinement upon her. The room was lavishly decorated in tones of purple and gold. There was no furniture aside from a strange table with legs no longer than candlesticks. She began to sit, lured by a few plush cushions that lay upon the floor, but was immediately pulled up by Naevus as both Aster and the woman from the auction, who she assumed must be her new owner, entered the room. Lysander followed after, trailed only by the billowing fabric of his gaudy robe. In his hands he held a few slips of parchment, which he set upon the table beside a bottle of ink and a quill.

The three sat. They sipped at glasses of wine and spoke at length as the papers were signed, though Selene caught little of the conversation. She could do naught but think of how her freedom was being signed away. With an odd feeling, much like the flowing of a river within her mind, came the realization that her circlet had been transferred to her new owner.

"Obey your new mistress as you have obeyed me," Aster said. "I thank the Goddess every day that I found you. You have truly changed my life."

*You've changed mine as well*, Selene thought to herself. Though she could not honestly say that it was for the better. "Thank you, Mistress," was all that she dared to say aloud.

"Naevus and Datio, it turns out that Pyra is in need of an entourage for her newest acquisition. I have sold both of you to into her care with Lysander's blessing."

"Thank you, mistress," they said at once. Tears of joy formed in the corners of Datio's eyes.

Pyra must be an important woman indeed.

"It is truly an honor, Mistress." Even the stoic Naevus could not keep a smile from creeping onto his face.

"There is only one contract left to sign," Lysander announced. "Follow me, if you please."

Selene could not understand why they needed to travel to a different area of the building to sign yet another parchment. Her ankles ached from so much standing in one place, though the discomfort did naught to dissuade her from trying to come up with a solution to her current predicament. She could not spend eternity as a Rakaii, yet no matter how much she turned it over in her mind she could come up with no way out of this trap in which she had been ensnared.

Selene was lost in thought as they walked, and so was somewhat surprised when she rounded a corner to find herself outdoors. The area was sheltered from the sun, as were most places which were left open to the sky in the city, yet rather than being covered in cloth this one boasted latticework upon which a flowering vine grew. Its blossoms lay open in a blinding shade of pink and were surrounded by heart shaped leaves in various shades of green and white. Beneath lay a circle of fencing which looked as if it had grown where it stood rather than being built. At the center of the circle of fence stood a child.

"The Goddess has favored us this day, for the heir of Zephyrus estate has graciously loaned me his Axiom Rakaii for the remainder of this week," Lysander said.

Selene understood little of the sentence even though her circlet was supposed to be translating. Perhaps it wasn't working properly.

"The Decuma has brought her Keeper, by the grace of the Goddess." Lysander turned to the child at the center of the ring.

A shaved head and dark eyes peeked out from beneath a hooded robe of silver fabric that glittered like gemstones where the dappled sunlight struck it. Wind rattled across the leaves above, causing several flower petals to drift lazily to the ground. The child, who had been still thus far, caught one deftly between finger and thumb. They dropped the petal into the palm of their free hand, where it immediately disappeared. Selene's bewildered look was answered with a crooked grin.

Pyra laughed. The sound flowed softly, like the melody of a song. "That look may be all the answer we require."

"Perhaps so," Lysander replied in kind. "Still, we must follow procedure so that everything is in order."

Pyra nodded. "Of course. Continue."

Selene found it difficult to look away from the woman's fathomless eyes. Pyra put her in mind of a delicate heron or some resplendent creature of myth. Her dark curls had been trimmed close to the top of her head, and rather than detract from her beauty the cut served only to enhance the delicately formed angles of her face. Selene realized too late that she was staring and cast her gaze to the floor. She waited with clenched teeth, yet the stab of pain she had been expecting did not come. Rather, the woman lifted her chin and directed her face once more to the child at the center of the pen.

"Tell me what you see."

It was not the voice she had been expecting, for although it belonged to neither Pyra nor Lysander it was familiar all the same. She turned toward the source of it. Her heart quickened even before her mind retrieved a name to match the face.

*Xaiden.* She was elated to see him. Despite being clothed as ridiculously as everyone else here, he looked very well cared for. A shake of his head, barely perceptible, told her that she should not let on that she knew him. Still, joy threatened to bubble up from where it lay hidden. So long as one of her friends had survived then there was hope. But if Xaiden was now owned by the heir of Zephyrus, then what did that mean for Cael?

"The Axiom seems very much in favor of her," Lysander remarked.

"And she of him," Pyra replied with a grin.

"He is a bit older," Lysander informed her. "But he would make a fine match for her first breeding. I could contact Zephyrus estate on your behalf if you would like."

*First breeding?* Selene did not like the sound of that in the least.

"I would," Pyra replied. "Thank you, Lysa. You are so gracious, as always."

"Anything for you, my dear," Lysander replied. He then turned to Xaiden. "Try it once more. I believe she was too enamored with you to understand your words the first time around."

Selene fought the heat that rushed to her face, but to no avail.

"You did mention it earlier, though I must admit I was reluctant to believe such of a feral," Pyra said. "She is innocent to a fault. It is something to be admired in a Rakaii."

Selene could not recall the last time someone had referred to her as innocent before she came to the city of the Kerell.

"I'm rarely wrong about such things," Lysander replied.

"Look into the ring and tell me what you see," Xaiden said, pulling Selene's attention aside.

Selene could not see any point in the question, other than perhaps to cause her confusion.

"What do you see?" Xaiden asked again, adopting one of his more serious tones.

There was not much within the ring save for the child and a bed of wet sand which held their footprints, along with those of some cloven hooved creature which must have been kept within the space previously.

"I see a child in a silver robe," Selene replied.

"No other living thing?" Xaiden asked.

"No." As she replied she could not help but wonder what the point of this might be. "Just the child."

Xaiden turned to Lysander. "She speaks the truth, Master."

From behind Xaiden the Decuma materialized, her dark tattoos lifting from beneath a cover of shade like ripples of water. She must have been there since they had entered, although as hard as she tried Selene could not recall having seen her.

Lysander pulled both Pyra and Xaiden to where the Decuma stood, next to a table that held a quill, a jar of ink, and what Selene assumed must be the final parchment. The four of them signed.

"I've planned a soiree to celebrate my newest acquisition," Pyra said as she placed a hand on the small of Selene's back to guide her out the door.

Lysander laughed. "Only you would hold such certainty over a future purchase as to plan a celebration beforehand."

"Confidence is one of my better traits," Pyra replied. "And you know well that when I want something, I'm rarely denied it. I do hope you'll attend, Lysa."

"Of course," Lysander replied as he brushed his lips across each of her cheeks. "It will be my pleasure."

Selene scanned the room for Xaiden, but he was gone.

"Come along then, my darling," Pyra ushered Selene out of the courtyard with a wave of her hand.

The woman's essence was barely perceptible within Selene's mind. It was rose petals and thyme, so very unlike the feeling of stone and fire that Aster offered. The interior of Lysander's estate passed by unnoticed, and Selene was barely aware as they reached the front entrance, and Datio placed her slippers back onto her feet. Outside two carriages waited. They were larger than most, yet delicate and intricately adorned with tiny seahorses and urchins carved into wood painted white. Pyra entered the one at the front, escorted by what looked to be a footman and several guardsmen. Selene was ushered into the second one by Datio and Naevus. Inside, the ceiling was painted Evarian blue.

Selene brushed her thoughts away from home as she took a seat across from what was now apparently her permanent entourage. Both men seemed in so bright a mood as to rival the midday sun. During the long ride through town, and then a rambling woodland road, Datio and Naevus chatted about how fabulous their lives were to be now that they had been purchased by Leaena estate.

"You did so well," Datio chirped. "This is a dream. I know it is."

To Selene it seemed more a nightmare than a dream.

"You'll look back upon this day as the luckiest day of your life," he added. "It's a blessing from the Goddess, you'll see."

Selene leaned her head against the side of the carriage. She could not claim to know the future, but she doubted very much the truth of that statement. Her main priority now would be to somehow gain the chance to speak with Xaiden. Uncertainty constricted her chest at the thought. He was now owned as well, by Zephyrus estate. He could not help her any more than she could help herself.

Naevus pushed upon her shoulder, setting her upright. "You're disarranging your hair," he chided.

She had been given a few moments of reprieve before he had noticed, at least. Selene drew a deep breath and shifted positions. Her next days would seem very long indeed.

# The New Queen
## *Evaria - Capital City*

Viverr watched Cyanna through the partially open doors to the throne room. The girl rested her elbow on the throne with a sigh. She was clearly uncomfortable. He couldn't truthfully say that he envied her, yet it was also difficult to find any large amount of pity for someone who had so recently inherited an entire kingdom.

"This might be somewhat of a disaster," Viverr whispered to Islyr.

"I cannot fathom what gave you that impression," the man replied with what Viverr could only assume was an attempt at sarcasm.

"This could be worse than having the boy in charge," Viverr added. "Not that she isn't capable, mind you. She's my protégé, after all."

"She doesn't want the throne," Islyr said. "No amount of intelligence can raise one's enthusiasm for something they never wished to have."

"That's the Spirit's truth," Viverr agreed.

"The real question is, what might we do to change it. A kingdom without a sovereign is a mire of chaos. I cannot help but feel that our lives might depend on her acceptance of her new role."

"My life, perhaps," Viverr countered. "You haven't even been sworn into the Aranth, at least not officially. You can leave this place any time you like. Head out into the beyond without so much as a glance behind you."

"I do have morals." Islyr frowned.

"Yes, I've noticed."

"And a sense of responsibility that some others seem to lack."

"Let's focus on the girl," Viverr said, decidedly changing the subject. "I've been around her for quite a time now. You'd have to come up with an argument the strength of dragons' breath to change her mind on something she's decided."

"Is there another alternative?"

"We could fetch Devren back from Kerell, I suppose."

Islyr scowled but remained silent, which came as no surprise. Viverr was well aware of his feelings regarding the land of the Kerell.

"Let's go in," Islyr suggested.

Guardsmen snapped to attention around the room as Viverr and Islyr entered. There were easily two-fold the number that had been guarding Devren. How many would it take to stand up to a handful of mages? Likely more than the kingdom could afford to lose.

"We could have used Aurin these past few weeks." Viverr whispered as the soles of his boots slid across the pristine floors. How they had managed to scrub all of that blood off of white marble with no trace was beyond him. Perhaps the stone had been magically treated sometime in the distant past. "Aurin would have rendered those mages to no more than a pile of severed limbs," he added. "At least in his dragon form."

"True," Islyr replied. "And where is Aurin, again?"

"How am I to know?" Viverr could not keep the bite from his tone.

"He's your closest friend. Who would know better?"

"No one informs me of anything in this place," he huffed as he attempted to reign in his irritation.

"Your best companion has just disappeared. You have no idea where he went, and yet you're not concerned?"

"I never said I wasn't concerned," Viverr countered.

"But you haven't asked." It was a statement more than a question.

"I've asked plenty, in all of his usual haunts, though no one seems to have a proper answer for me."

"You're not asking the right people," Islyr informed him.

"Then perhaps you might assist me in figuring out who the right people are." He could not help but be irritated at this particular puzzle, for despite his skill the answer refused to be found. That and the fact that his best friend in the world had left him without so much as a word of warning.

"I would start there," Islyr said, gesturing to the pouting queen.

Spirits knew it was worth a try. Viverr could not help but feel as if he had suffered enough on account of the man, regardless of the caliber of their friendship. "Oy, Mouse," he said as they drew close to the throne. "Do you have any idea where Aurin has gone?"

This elicited a slip of a grin from the girl, which had not been his intention but was gratifying, nonetheless. It also caused several of the guardsmen to shift uncomfortably, which he considered to be a bonus. It was doubtful that they had ever heard anyone refer to a queen in such a manner.

"All guards will wait outside the throne room," Cyanna ordered.

The guardsmen filed silently out of the room. Viverr approved of their strength of will, for he certainly would have issued at least one whispered remark. Perhaps it was for the best that he had never applied to be a member of the standard guard.

"That's Queen Mouse to you, sir," Cyanna said in a falsely haughty tone once the last of them had gone.

"Sincere apologies, my queen," Viverr replied with a mockingly deep bow.

"Your apologies are accepted. Though I don't know exactly where Aurin has gone. Devren mentioned that he sent him off somewhere, though he never told me where."

Potato let out a little squeal. Viverr reached into his belt pouch and ran his fingers along the ridge of fur upon his back to quiet him.

"I thought you were going to set that scrub pig back into the courtyard with his companions," Islyr said.

"I nearly did," Viverr replied. "But then I realized that he makes quite a valuable addition to my dwindling crew."

"I might be a fool to ask this, but how so?"

"In so many ways," Viverr informed him. "He notices those few things that escape my highly trained senses, for one."

"Their hearing is much better than ours," Cyanna agreed.

"And he shares many of my dislikes, such as boats, mages, and more recently, unicorns."

"Ah, is that all?" Islyr asked. "It seemed that he was more in favor of the unicorn than not, if you ask me."

"Fine that I didn't ask, in that case," Viverr replied.

"So, it isn't at all because you've grown attached to him?"

"Obviously not," Viverr lied. "I simply thought he might prove useful, what with so much danger lurking about these days." He could not help but feel that the man was mocking him. "Unless you want him back of course, Mouse. He does belong to you, after all."

"You can keep him," Cyanna replied. "He says the courtyard is boring, and he'd rather adventure with you."

Potato chattered as if in agreement.

"See, there you have it." Viverr crushed down the bit of pride that had formed upon hearing the statement.

"And he said that Aurin is in the Barren Lands," Cyanna added.

"The Barren Lands? What in the name of the Spirits is he doing there?"

"Should we not be more concerned about how the scrub pig knows he's there?" Islyr asked.

"They communicate with each other by sounds, but also within their thoughts," Cyanna explained. "They can pick up images in people's thoughts too when they've a mind to. Perhaps he saw something that Aurin was thinking before he departed."

"And now, seeing as he is burrowing into everyone's thoughts, will you agree to put him back with the other scrub pigs?" Islyr asked.

"Certainly not," Viverr replied. "It's not any worse than having Felan around. You're only jealous because I've got an official animal companion, like a proper Aranth."

"No Aranth has ever had an animal companion," Islyr corrected. "They've all been other marked ones."

"Yes, but no one knows that except for other Aranth, for the most part. The magic of the city sees to it. And setting that fact aside would only mean that I have the first actual animal companion, which makes me all the more exceptional."

"Your belt pouch is not the safest place for a small creature," Islyr informed him.

"He's sturdier than he looks," Viverr countered. "And he's intelligent too. He figured out where Aurin is, which is better than I managed."

"How does the pig know of the Barren Lands at all?" Islyr asked.

"Scrub pigs are native to the northern part of the Barren Lands," Cyanna explained. "It's so different from the rest of the Barren Lands that some call it the Northlands, as if it's a whole separate region. The vendor I bought him from must have captured him from there."

"Aurin is from the Northlands as well," Viverr mused. "The landscape is unique there. Weird, pointy rock formations, vibrantly colored plants, and quite a bit of snow. Potato must have recognized it from his thoughts. But that still doesn't answer the question of what Aurin is doing there."

"It does not," Islyr agreed.

A commotion of raised voices sounded through the small door closest to the throne. Viverr grabbed his latent ability, holding it at the ready. He was just close enough to make it to the passage beneath the throne if needed. No mage would get the better of him today.

"It's only one of our men," Cyanna said.

Despite her words, Viverr did not drop his guard. He locked his gaze on the man, who seemed to be struggling for air.

"I think he's been hit by a spell," said a lanky guardsman who rushed in behind the first. "It's taken his speech!"

"Don't be daft," Viverr replied. "There's no magic upon him. He's only out of breath."

The palace was practically drowning in anxiety these days. The Viverr of old would have fled to a place of better fortune, or at least one with a better guarantee of safety. *Spirits curse my newfound morals*, he thought as he watched the man huff and struggle to form a coherent word or two.

"Breathe first, then speak," Islyr instructed.

"There is someone…" the man began, as if attempting to take Islyr's advice to heart.

"Someone where?" Islyr urged.

"Sometime before tomorrow's light, if it's alright with you?" Viverr added. The comment earned him a scowl from Cyanna.

"In the Lady Selene's room," the man finished, seemingly ages after he had begun.

"We'll see to it," Islyr said. "You should stay here, my Queen," he added when the girl began to rise.

"And if it's an attempt to get us away from Cyanna so that they can take her?" Viverr asked.

"And if it's not?" Islyr replied. "If it's something dangerous?"

Viverr was torn. "Hide, Mouse," he instructed, though he truly had no business giving orders to a queen. "Not in this form, in your other."

Bones cracked as the girl transformed. From beneath a crumpled pile of clothing emerged a little brown tabby cat.

"In the usual place," he instructed. "I'll find you when I'm ready."

The cat nodded. She ran to the far side of the room and disappeared through a small hole in the wall.

The guardsmen's eyes widened as they witnessed the transformation, but their faces relaxed as the magic of the palace wormed its way into their memories.

Islyr wasted no time in leaving the throne room. Viverr reluctantly followed. He could not help but sympathize with the out-of-breath guardsman upon reaching Selene's room, for it happened to be up several flights of stairs, and he was not overly fond of running.

"Do you need a moment?" Islyr asked in a whisper.

He did, though he loathed to admit it. Perhaps there was some reason for the absurd amount of exercise the Aranth tried to force upon him after all. The sound of shattering glass emanated from inside the room. It was followed by the clattering of objects, and then a round of stomping, which sounded more animal than human.

"I'm fine," Viverr replied flatly. He did not want to give the man the satisfaction of knowing that he had drawn his ire. "Do we simply go in?"

Islyr tightened the grip on his staff. "Perhaps," he pondered. "But it doesn't sound like mages."

"Agreed. They're nearly as quiet as thieves, and usually not so destructive as whatever is ransacking the place." Viverr turned the door handle ever so slightly. It was locked.

"Give me a moment." He pulled his lock pick set from his pocket and set to work. It was not a complicated lock by far, and happily no spells had been set upon it. In a few brief seconds it was done.

"They could be in a rush and looking for something in particular," Islyr suggested. "Perhaps keep your latent ability up, just in case it is mages after all."

Little did the man know that he'd had it up since they'd approached the door.

"On three then?"

Viverr nodded his head in consent.

"One," Islyr began.

The rogue held his latent ability at the ready.

"Two."

He gripped the hilt of his knife.

"Three."

Viverr threw open the door with just enough force so that it would stop before hitting the wall. Before him lay nothing, aside from a terrible mess. Selene had a penchant for cleanliness more so than most, but at the moment her room resembled a midden heap, though the smell was slightly better. It was dark, though oddly he could see no source of the destruction within. He crept into the oddly silent room at Islyr's heels, stepping deftly between shards of glass and splinters of broken furniture.

*Where did they go?* Viverr signed in the language of thieves. *Bedroom?*

*Balcony,* Islyr replied in kind.

The man's ability to sign was becoming decent, he had to admit.

Viverr glanced at the partially open balcony doors. The curtains were drawn, and thus nothing outside could be seen. An odd scratching sound snuck through the space between the two doors, one of which was blocked by a fallen wardrobe. Islyr grabbed the handle of the free door with one hand while keeping his staff at the ready with the other.

Viverr could feel Potato shaking through the leather of his pouch. Whoever was out there, the pig did not approve. The door swung open on silent hinges. At first the balcony seemed to be empty as well.

*Perhaps they fled?* Viverr signed. It was then that he spotted something odd; a neatly set row of bones clinging to the edge of the balcony beneath the railing.

"What in the name of the Goddess?" Islyr pondered aloud as he levered his chest over the top of the railing to get a better look.

Viverr mimicked the man's movements. Below him, hanging from the balcony by the tips of its bony fingers, was a bloodsoul. Selene's bloodsoul, to be precise, for at some point before leaving she had drawn its number onto the bone of its forehead with a piece of charcoal so that the staff of the castle could easily tell it from any others.

"Forty-Two," Viverr said, calling the skeletal creature by name, though in truth it did not deserve one. The monster tilted its empty skull ever so slightly towards him at the sound. Or could it be his imagination? He shuddered along with the scrub pig.

"This is the one she's been training," Islyr said.

There was no way to tell how much Islyr knew of Selene training the bloodsoul, or of her keeping it as one would a pet. As for how the man felt about bloodsoul in general, only the Spirits knew the truth. Best to speak cautiously.

"Perhaps we should return it to wherever it came from?" It was the least offensive thing Viverr could think of to say in the moment.

"I believe it was locked in the wardrobe," Islyr replied. "Which is now broken."

Viverr had meant putting it back into a grave, or some especially thick-walled mausoleum, which was where the monster most obviously belonged. "Why is it hanging from the balcony?" he asked instead of correcting the man.

The bloodsoul issued a rattling growl.

"How should I know?" Islyr replied. "I cannot control them. I can only create them."

"I was rather hoping you could," Viverr said. "Control them, I mean. It would help us out quite a bit."

"We'll need to capture it somehow. But getting it off of the balcony will be difficult."

Viverr realized that he had never taken the time to look at one of the creatures closely, mostly for the fear of being killed, which he felt was a valid excuse. For some reason, the monster felt much less fearsome clinging to a balcony than it had under Selene's control. She had chosen an older one at least. Rotting flesh no longer hung from its yellowed bones. It was no less disgusting in his mind, despite that fact.

The bloodsoul had been a living human once, but was now unnatural in nature, held together with some rare and troublesome magic that his latent ability could not touch. He could think of few things he hated more than a bloodsoul, mages and unicorns included.

"Is there a way to capture it without putting hands upon it?" Viverr asked, for the thought of its bones upon his flesh made the bile of his stomach churn like stormwater.

"Not unless you've suddenly gained the power of levitation."

Sadly, he had not. The bloodsoul released one hand to swipe at Islyr's foot, but he sidestepped the gesture with ease. The creature was not attempting to pull itself up or drop itself to the ground, oddly. It merely hung and grumbled, as if displeased by its fate.

"It would be foolish to pull the beast up here with us," Viverr said, hoping that Islyr would agree. He really did not want to be any closer to it than was absolutely necessary.

"It's a fair way down. Perhaps it will break apart if we push it from the balcony?"

Viverr sighed with relief. "Yes, but then what will we do with it?"

"We tie it up." Islyr stepped inside briefly and pulled the ropes from Selene's curtains. He handed one to Viverr. "You take one part and I'll take the other. That way we keep it from pulling itself back together."

"Assuming that it splits into at least two portions."

"It should, I hope. But we'll have to get down there quickly."

"Should we warn someone of our plan?"

"And leave it here unattended?" Islyr asked. "It could drop and run off to slay what few guardsmen the mages left behind."

"Alright then." Viverr drew a deep breath as he reached for the creature. The bones of its fingers were smooth and unnaturally cold. "Are you going to help me?" he snapped.

"After I take a moment to enjoy the look of disgust on your face," Islyr replied. "I wasn't aware that you had such an aversion to bloodsoul."

"They're perversions of nature." The words spilled from his mouth before he could stop them.

Islyr was silent for a few seconds. "That we can agree on," he replied at last. He levered his staff beneath the creature's other hand.

Viverr pushed, yet the creature's grip was like forged iron. With a second attempt, which included all of the force he could muster, the finger bones moved at a slug's pace towards the edge.

"As soon as it drops, we run downstairs," Islyr reminded him unnecessarily.

"Yes," Viverr replied shortly. He would soon be out from under Islyr's control, and in charge of this newly formed branch of the Aranth. Cyanna assured him that his dragon's egg was soon to hatch. Islyr placed a high value on honor, and so would abide by the rules of their bet without fail.

Finally, the bloodsoul's fingers could hold no longer. It dropped from sight.

"No time to watch," Islyr said as he sprinted away.

Viverr found his feet keeping time with Islyr's as they crossed the room and ran down the hall. The man apparently had a mind like a cartographer, for he navigated the castle as if he had lived in it for years. In the shortest amount of time that Viverr had ever taken to get down so many flights of stairs he found himself outside, rope still in hand. Unfortunately, the bloodsoul was nowhere to be seen.

"It drew together faster than expected." Islyr knelt down to examine its tracks, which led across the soft dirt. "This way," he continued before sprinting away once again.

"It's gone back inside," Viverr said upon noting the splintered door at the far side of the courtyard. It was his best attempt not to sound as if he was out of breath, though poorly accomplished.

Screams of terror travelled easily through the hole in the splintered door. They reached it in good time, though it took some force to pull it open, damaged as it was. More screams followed the first, interwoven with a symphony of clattering and smashing sounds, as the door moved slowly outward in concert with their efforts. After several minutes, the opening was large enough to fit through.

Once inside they tracked the bloodsoul, which was a simple affair as the creature had left a trail of destruction in passing. Viverr noted no bodies nor blood amongst the wreckage, oddly, for such things were often to be found where bloodsoul and living creatures mixed. The trail led to one of the castle's smaller kitchens, which serviced the highest ranking members of the standard guard. It was mostly empty, though cutlery lay scattered upon the floor amongst broken earthenware plates.

"This is odd," Islyr noted.

Viverr followed his gaze. The far side of the long wooden table that split the room in two was still set with carefully placed cutlery and plates intact, while the other side had been destroyed.

"Look there." Viverr rushed around the table to find the lower kitchen's cook, Maglin, laid out upon the floor. He held the flat of his knife near the man's open mouth. His breath fogged the blade. "He lives."

"Perhaps passed out?" Islyr suggested.

"After throwing most of the kitchenware at the bloodsoul, by the looks of it," Viverr mused. "Maglin is known for being faint of heart. Whispers around the castle say that he does so for attention. Took a liking to one of the healer's assistants and realized that passing out was the fastest way to the infirmary."

"Perhaps the rumors are wrong," Islyr said. "In this case I'd call the affliction legitimate."

"He's incapacitated, yet the bloodsoul didn't take so much as a bite of him," Viverr noted.

"It is unusual," Islyr agreed. "What bloodsoul leaves a victim alive?"

"None that I've encountered."

"It went out the window." Islyr vaulted easily through the opening.

Despite being thoroughly sick of both running and climbing, Viverr followed.

The bloodsoul was quick on its bony feet, as most of the more weathered creatures tended to be, and they soon fell behind as it led them through the city of Evaria. By the Luck of the Tides, it stuck to the side roads and alleys rather than traversing the main thoroughfare.

"What's wrong with this Spirits-forsaken thing?" Viverr asked through labored breaths as they reached the edge of Evaria's fishing docks.

A fisherman with a long, graying beard rushed past with as much speed as his old legs could manage.

"Thank the Spirits you're here, Aranth." His accent was a thick mix of all places. "You'll find the monster just there at the end of dock one." The old man's eyes conveyed fear that remained hidden in his words.

"I don't think there's anything wrong with it," Islyr said as the fisherman hobbled onward to safety.

"Is that so?" Viverr countered. "What's it doing, then?" He gestured towards the creature, who swayed at the edge of the aforementioned dock like seaweed caught in the waves.

The bloodsoul turned towards them. Its rattling screech drowned out Islyr's reply.

"Get the legs." It was all the man said before rushing the monster.

Viverr sighed and vaulted towards it, reaching for the creature's legs. It dodged him easily. As he reached in for a second try Islyr dropped his length of rope on the dock and swung at the bloodsoul with his staff. The monster woke unexpectedly from its daze. Islyr was fast, even amongst the Aranth, but he was not as fast as the creature. It snapped towards them, twisting to grab the staff with both hands. Islyr did not let go. He kept a grip on his weapon with one hand and smashed his free hand against the creature's wrist, separating it from the rest of the arm. Islyr quickly repeated the feat with the bloodsoul's other hand, freeing his staff. He whipped the weapon around from one end, causing both of the creature's bony hands to fly off of his staff and into a nearby pile of crates. It might have been comical, had the situation been less dire.

"Viverr, the legs!" he yelled.

Viverr huffed. It wasn't as if a bloodsoul in the midst of battle was an easy target. He looked in vain for an opening to allow him to grab the legs, but between the shifting of its feet and the strikes of Islyr's staff there was none to be had.

A terrible scraping noise emanated from somewhere behind him. Viverr looked to see both skeletal hands pulling back towards the rest of the monster, which was deftly blocking Islyr's strikes with the bones of its wrists. Islyr drew his staff back. He swung it at the creature's head like a club. To Viverr's surprise, it connected quite soundly. The bloodsoul's skull shot from its body and flew over the water. It struck between waves and disappeared beneath the sea.

Viverr took the chance he had been afforded and dived at the bloodsoul. He wrapped his arms around the creature's legs. It wobbled, pressing frigid bone against his face before tipping sideways onto the dock. Viverr twisted his rope around the creature's legs several times while the bloodsoul writhed in a violent attempt to free itself.

Viverr felt the pressure of some small thing upon his leg. He knew what it must be, and resisted the urge to look upon it, though barely. He focused on knotting the rope several times to be certain it wouldn't come apart. Meanwhile, Islyr wrapped the second rope around the bloodsoul's chest, binding its arms to its ribcage.

The pressure moved across Viverr's back. Islyr reached and plucked it from him as he stood, holding it aloft as if it was a prized fisherman's catch. The hand of bone ripped itself from Islyr's grasp and found its home upon the bloodsoul's wrist.

"A good amount of pull on that, is there?" Viverr could not manage to keep the disgust from his voice.

"More than expected," Islyr replied.

They paused to watch the creature's skull jump from the waves like a fish and roll to attach to its neck. It screeched and rattled with anger.

"We'll need to take him back to the castle and contain him somehow," Islyr said.

"As long as you're getting the front end." Viverr struggled to make himself heard above the creature's cries of fury.

The noise was soon combined with the muttering of people returning to the docks. No doubt they were angling to catch a glimpse of the deadly monster now that it was properly contained.

"Here." Viverr ripped a length of cloth from a portion of old sail that lay nearby and handed it to Islyr. After several attempts he was able to tie it around the bloodsoul's snapping jaw and then the top of its head, which served to hold the mouth in place and reduce the chance of being bitten.

"It looks as if we're about to gift it to someone," Viverr quipped.

One corner of Islyr's mouth twisted up to form half a smile. "That wasn't my intention."

"It does look much less imposing with a bow atop its head, so thank you for that, I suppose."

"You're welcome," Islyr replied over the continued rattling cries of rage.

"I've been thinking," Viverr began as they made their way through the gathering crowd. "The creature is clearly angry, yet on the dock it did no more than block your blows."

"It swiped at you on the balcony, but other than that has shown little sign of aggression," Islyr agreed. "Even when it had ample opportunity to kill the cook, it chose to flee instead."

"Perhaps some instruction Selene gave it before leaving is still in effect?"

"Could be so," Islyr mused. "Is your pig still intact?"

"What's that now?" Viverr asked, caught off guard.

"Your scrub pig," Islyr explained. "He hasn't been crushed in the battle with the bloodsoul?"

"Ah, no worries there," Viverr replied. "I bought a special pouch for him at the market a few days back. It's enchanted, from the land of the Kerell."

"Is that so?" Islyr asked.

He figured that would get the man's attention.

"What magic does it possess?"

"It guards whatever is within against damage," Viverr explained.

"What types of damage?"

"Crushing, water, fire, all types. I had Cyanna check it to make sure that the magic's legitimate. Not that many would dare sell fake magical items to an Aranth. Bought two pouches, as a matter of fact. Can't risk any of my perfectly legally obtained goods being destroyed, eh?"

"Or your new favorite companion?" Islyr said with a knowing half-grin.

"What's that supposed to mean?"

"Seems odd that you bought the pouch before you knew for certain that you'd be able to keep the pig."

"Not at all," Viverr countered. "I was going to use both pouches for loot, but now that Potato's with me for good I found a better use for one of them, that's all."

"That makes perfect sense," Islyr replied in the most infuriating manner possible.

By the luck of the Tides, they had just then reached the castle's front steps. "Why is this Spirits-forsaken thing so heavy?" Viverr complained in a bid to change the subject. "It's only bones, after all. You spent many years in the land of mages. Is it possible for magic to have physical weight to it?"

"Not unless it is specifically constructed to do so," Islyr informed him. "Though the magic which holds bloodsoul together is somehow different from other magic."

"How can that be?" Viverr asked as he hoisted his end of the bloodsoul up the first step. It was irritating at best that his latent ability could not strip the magic from them as it could everything else in the known world. "Your latent ability creates these Spirits-forsaken things. That must be magic of the regular sort. The same type as the rest of us have."

"My latent ability helps me pull a soul back from its time with the Spirits and bind it into a body," Islyr corrected. "But when the body is too damaged or has been left to rot something else occurs. An ancient magic lies in wait. It binds to both my ability and the soul like a leech to flesh and spreads corruption."

"For the record, I'd rather stay dead."

"I shall take that into consideration." Islyr nodded to the guards who stood outside the castle's main doorway. The closest one pulled open a single door to allow them easier passage.

"Where should we keep it?" Islyr asked. "On a regular occasion I would suggest the Mages' Wing, but they have yet to repair it."

Viverr rolled the situation over in his head. "I have an idea," he said at last. "But we'll need to take it up to my room."

"I must be honest," Islyr replied. "That's the last place I expected you to recommend."

Viverr could not help but wish that this might be the last time he would traverse a set of stairs on this day. The muscles of his legs protested with every step.

"Let's put it down for a moment," he suggested when they finally reached their destination.

They set the bloodsoul carefully upon the floor at the center of the sitting room, and Viverr hurried to his bedroom. The servants had already been in to make the bed and tidy his belongings. *Unfortunate,* he thought as he pulled the top sheet from beneath the quilt, creating an avalanche of useless decorative pillows. He brought the sheet out into the living area.

"Hmm, it's a bit big." Viverr pulled his knife from its sheath and sliced the sheet into a very crooked square, perhaps just big enough to cover the top of a bathing tub.

"Help me lay this out flat." He and Islyr spread the sheet out in the middle of the floor and set the bloodsoul upon it. "Alright, now just watch him for a moment."

The suggestion helped him twofold. For one, Islyr would be keeping an eye on the dreaded creature in case the knots came loose, and secondly Islyr would not see the method by which Viverr gained access to the wall behind his wardrobe, where he stored his most treasured possessions.

Viverr entered the bedroom once again and closed the door behind him. He removed his belt pouch and placed it carefully upon the floor. His muscles already ached, which made the transformation to his ferret form more painful than usual. Tomorrow would be a day of rest if he had his way of things. He slipped from beneath the darkness of his discarded clothing and squeezed underneath the decorative wooden carving at the bottom of the wardrobe. Behind it was a hole just big enough for a ferret, and beyond that, in the space within the wall, lay a carefully arranged pile of loot.

Viverr scampered over bags of coins smelling of precious metals and pilfered pieces of jewelry laid out in a row against the back side of the wall. He came at last to a line of potions held in tiny, corked glass vials. There were so few magical concoctions within his possession that he knew them all by name. He moved forward carefully, sniffing as he went. *Create rain, invisibility, poison element, heat to fire,* he recited each within his mind as the smell came to him. *Healing, there you are my beauty.* He grabbed the string that he had tied to it for easy transport, then pulled it out of the wall and back beneath the wardrobe. He transformed and dressed quickly, so that Islyr would not wonder and come looking for him, then made his way back out to the bloodsoul.

"Hold this, but don't use it yet," he instructed. "Back in a moment."

Before Islyr could protest, he sprinted out the door, ignoring the pain in his legs and spine, and headed down the hall past the first three doors to an unoccupied Aranth bedroom. The door was unlocked. He stepped inside. The furniture was covered in sheets to protect it from dust. The light breeze from opening the door caused it to look much like a family of oddly shaped Spirits had moved in to possess the room. He still could not fathom why Spirits in stories so often hid beneath sheets. Why would one want to ruin the gift of being invisible?

Viverr entered the bedroom. Beneath this bed was an opening in the wall similar to the one in his room, yet slightly larger in size. He had discovered it one day while exploring, and had taken note, as he often did when something seemed like it might be of use. In this case it had turned out to be the luck of the Tides, for the hole was decidedly cat sized. Viverr knocked three times just above the headboard. After a moment Cyanna appeared from beneath, still in cat form.

"All is well," he explained as the cat jumped up on the bed. "It was only Selene's bloodsoul.

Viverr threw open the doors of the wardrobe, within which they had stored a few extra pieces of Cyanna's clothing for just such an occasion. "Get changed and meet me in my room. We're going to need your help."

The cat nodded, and Viverr left to return to Islyr. The man was only slightly disgruntled by his disappearance. Once back inside his room Viverr stepped over to the small cabinet that sat next to his chair. From within he grabbed the stone jar that he had pilfered from the mage's belongings aboard the Misty Maiden.

"You took that from the ship," Islyr said upon noticing it.

"I did," Viverr admitted.

Islyr's brow knotted, likely with disapproval.

"It doesn't count as stealing when it belongs to an enemy."

"I'm not certain that's true," Islyr replied. "But I don't care that you stole it."

"Looks otherwise from that expression you're giving me."

"I'm not giving you any particular expression," Islyr insisted.

"You definitely are. But that aside, I thought we could use this to keep the bloodsoul in. That's after we get the monster into the proper shape, mind you. This jar should be able to hold it. The thing is simply dripping with magic. Strong stuff."

Islyr looked from the bottle of potion, which was still in his hand, to the jar in Viverr's. "Ah, I see. I suppose we could. May I study it more closely?"

Viverr reluctantly handed over the jar. Islyr squinted at the unreadable words upon it. "I believe most of the magic resides with what's within the jar," he said cryptically.

"And what might that be?" Viverr asked.

Islyr scrutinized him for a moment. "I don't think you want to know."

"Well, you've thought wrong," Viverr replied. All he wanted at the moment was to be rid of the bloodsoul, and perhaps to drink enough ale to dull his aching muscles. "I haven't yet found a fact in this world that I don't want to know. And speaking of facts, my least favorite thing is not knowing something that someone else knows. So, tell me. What's in the jar?"

"Powdered gnome," Islyr said flatly.

Viverr paused. Perhaps there was one thing in this world he could have gone without knowing. The truth of it settled over him heavily, like drenched clothing. "Samuel," he muttered.

"Perhaps you know of another gnome who resides nearby?"

"Unfortunately, no." Viverr drew a deep breath and tried to push thoughts of Samuel aside. Was it better or worse than not knowing where he was? He found that he could not decide.

"A friend of a friend, you said?" Islyr asked through the brief silence that followed.

"Yes. We weren't intimately acquainted. Not so much as to be true friends, but he was a valued member of the Thieves Guild, and a good man." Viverr wiped at the corner of his eyes as tears began to form.

"No need to continue. I understand."

Viverr pulled a deep breath to steady himself. "And what do they use that for, then?"

"The mages consume it," Islyr replied. "To strengthen their magical abilities. Or mix it into alchemy potions. Rumor amongst the Kerell says that the empress uses it to extend her life. Gnomes have some of the most powerful magic of all creatures."

"They're not creatures," Viverr corrected. "They're people."

"To the Kerell we're all creatures."

It was then that Cyanna entered the room.

"Spirits keep every mage that exists," Viverr cursed. "Let's get this over with."

"Agreed," Islyr said.

"Are you all right?" the girl asked.

He'd hoped that she would fail to notice his reddened eyes. "I've been better," he replied. "But I'll certainly survive."

Cyanna nodded. She had the courtesy not to ask anything more.

"Can you tell me what kind of magic is on this jar, Mouse?"

"It's a tracking spell."

Fear trickled icily through Viverr's veins.

"And one of containment. They're tied together. If you remove one, you'll remove the other."

"Why in the name of the Spirits must mages be so irritating?" Viverr fumed. "And why would you need a containment spell on a jar with something dead in it?"

"In case he decided to put something else in there instead, I'd imagine," Islyr replied. "He likely prepared the container, along with others, before leaving Kerell."

"What's inside the jar is quite strong," Cyanna noted. "I've never felt such strong magic, but for some reason I can't tell what it does."

"That's because it has the potential to do many things," Islyr explained.

"It's powdered gnome," Viverr said bitterly.

Cyanna wrinkled her nose with distaste. "Oh, that's a terrible thing to do."

"Never mind that for the moment," Viverr said quickly. "We'd better hurry. I've had this thing for far too long already."

He plucked a miniscule wooden chest from a nearby table and poured the few contents onto the floor, mostly coins, mixed with a few peppermint sweets he had pilfered from the Royal's kitchen. "My apologies, friend." He poured what remained of Samuel into the chest and set it back upon the table. "May the Spirits protect and guide you on this day and thereafter."

Cyanna and Islyr bowed their heads respectfully. "May the Spirits protect and guide your soul," they echoed, nearly in unison.

"We should send him off properly when we're through," Cyanna suggested.

"Good idea, Mouse," Viverr replied. "He deserves better than what the mages had planned for him."

"We had better finish this quickly," Islyr reminded him. "If other mages sense the tracking spell they will surely come for the jar. There are few things of more value to the Kerell."

"You're right," Viverr agreed. "Drop some of that potion on the bloodsoul if you're ready. Might want to stand back a bit, Mouse. I've seen Selene do this a few times, with her ability rather than a potion mind you, but either way it'll be a mess."

Cyanna stepped back a few paces as Islyr stepped forward, glass vial of potion in hand. He pulled the cork.

"How much?" he asked.

Viverr loathed to lose any of his potions, for they had all been costly in one way or another, but he supposed this was worth it.

"Just a drop. I heard Selene say once that it only took the slightest touch."

The liquid contents of the bottle shimmered in the meager light. A single drop clung to the lip of the vial. Islyr tapped the glass to release it. It pattered against the bloodsoul's skull like a wayward droplet of rain. The creature grumbled with irritation.

Islyr stepped forward to look. "Should I use anoth-"

The man's last word was cut short as the creature exploded. Powder cascaded, settling upon everything in the room like a dusting of flour upon a cake pan.

"That was unpleasant," Islyr commented as he pulled a hand across his mouth.

"It's much worse when they've got rotting flesh clinging to them," Viverr replied.

A few piles in the shape of bones, which looked much like they were composed of grains of oddly colored sand, were all that remained of the bloodsoul. They began to move, and with it Viverr's skin began to itch as if maggots were crawling upon it. The powdered bloodsoul shifted across the surface of his skin. It dropped to the floor and pooled, melting together like candle wax.

"It's pulling together already," Islyr said with confusion. "I've never seen one reassemble so quickly."

'We've got to get it into the jar." Viverr did not like the thought of being covered in bloodsoul powder a second time.

They each grabbed a side of the piece of bedsheet and pulled them all together. Viverr gathered the ends. He shoved the bloodsoul into the jar, sheet and all, and returned the lid to the top. The powder continued to shift. It clung angrily to the sides of the jar, coating it in writhing white. Once all of it seemed to be upon the sides of the jar Viverr opened the lid briefly once again. He pressed it firmly in place once the grains slipped inside.

"It's contained," Cyanna said. "But now what shall we do with it?"

"We certainly can't keep it here with a tracking spell upon it."

"Hand it here," Islyr said. "I have an excellent idea."

Viverr offered him the jar. He did not care much where the creature went, so long as it ended up as far from him as possible.

# A Cherished Pet
## *Kerell – Capital City*

Selene gazed out the window as the carriage maneuvered the twisted streets of Kerell city. She ran her fingers along the plush rose-colored velvet of the seat beneath her. From what she had learned from Datio and Naevus, her new mistress was one of the wealthiest women to be found in the city, the empress aside. It showed in not only her belongings, but the way she treated her Rakaii. Selene's stomach was full for the first time in weeks, and she had not been punished with pain since being turned over to Pyra's care. Perhaps her luck had changed for the better in recent days. *A kind mistress is still a mistress*, she reminded herself as the carriage rolled smoothly along a sand-strewn road which ran parallel to the beach.

Pyra had informed them this morning that they were on their way to the tailor's shop. The excitement that emanated from Datio and Naevus upon hearing the news was so thick that she expected to see it hanging in the air like a giddy fog.

"I would look grand in mauve, don't you think?" Datio said.

Naevus smiled, which until recently was a rare occurrence. "You would," he agreed.

"And breakfast today was fit for the empress herself," Datio continued. "Those pastries were divine, weren't they, Selene?"

Selene looked up, startled away from the push of waves which lapped against the shore outside her window with a mesmerizing rhythm. The one good thing to come of this was that Pyra had allowed her to keep her own name. "I did enjoy the icing," she admitted. It had been flavored of oranges; a fruit that was common here but only appeared in the far south at home. She turned her thoughts quickly away from food. In truth, riding in the carriage made her stomach turn, and she would much rather be left alone with her thoughts because of it.

They arrived at the tailor's shop before she lost her breakfast, by the luck of the Tides. Selene took a moment to examine the front window of the shop, which oddly contained no clothing that she could see. Datio escorted her from the carriage. She politely followed, keeping several steps behind Pyra as Aster had taught her.

Selene traversed the smoothly tiled steps to the building's interior as gracefully as she could manage through her fatigue. She had not slept well despite the comfort of the overly large bed that Pyra had provided for her. Datio and Naevus trailed closely behind, shadowing her every movement. They seemed ever more eager to attend her since the auction. The brothers now served as more of an entourage than guards, for Pyra had half a dozen actual guards in attendance whenever she left the estate. Selene found that she did not mind the brothers' presence overly much, aside from the fact that it caused escape to be nigh impossible.

The door to the shop swung open, perhaps by some spell, as Pyra drew close. It was much cooler within than it had been outside, thank the Spirits. This tailors' shop was not at all like those she had encountered at home. The chaotically piled rolls of fabric most usually found in these places were nowhere to be seen. In fact, not one mound of cloth, nor pile of clutter or indeed one speck of dirt could be found. Absurdly clean, brightly colored tiles coated the floor in a mosaic pattern. She realized too late that one wall of the place was coated from top to bottom in the most pristine mirrors she had ever seen. The reflection was so exact that she jumped when it moved in time with her. Pyra grinned with amusement. Her fingers were warm against Selene's cheek.

"Calm, my darling," she said. "It's only your reflection."

Selene shoved her irritation aside. "Thank you, Mistress," she replied politely. It was embarrassing, to say the least. The expression upon Naevus' face informed her that he would surely bring it up later.

A man with skin as pristine as the shop entered the room. His flowing robe was finely made; a subtle cascade of color that put her in mind of a sunset. It flowed expertly around his generous form, ending just above his ankles. He was familiar to her in some manner, though her mind stubbornly refused to place him. He greeted Pyra with a light kiss upon each cheek.

"Pyra, my darling," the man said. "You eclipse the dazzling light of the moon, as is usual."

"The moon can never hope to outshine the sun, Varro, my friend," Pyra replied. "Most especially when he appears in a freshly made robe."

"You speak of this?" Varro gestured to his clothing. "It may as well be as old as the colosseum. I designed it so long ago. Several days at least."

"Ah, but it is beautiful still. And I have not seen you in several days, to be fair."

Varro's laugh was dainty and quick, like a bouncing hare. "While we are speaking of things that hold beauty, your latest acquisition is even finer than I recall."

Selene stiffened as she realized that the man spoke of her.

"She is a prize to be certain," Pyra replied. "The bidding was evenly matched. You hold no ill will, I assume?"

"How could I do so against my closest companion?" Varro took Pyra's hands and grasped them gently before releasing her. "There will be another in good time."

"So true," Pyra agreed. "And for now, I have need of your expertise in dressing her."

Varro's eyes lit with glee. "I have been anxiously awaiting those very words."

"I have several galas planned for the coming weeks."

"To find her a match, I assume?"

"Indeed," Pyra replied.

With a twist of Varro's fingers, a Rakaii appeared from the depths of the shop carrying bolts of fabric in a myriad of colors.

"Perhaps one of these." He held the varied shades fabric up to the skin of Selene's arms and face and frowned thoughtfully at each one.

Selene turned her attention to the road beyond the tailor's shop window. It had a beautiful view of the ocean, as did many of the shops in this area. She would know, as she had been forced to visit far too many of them in her brief time with Pyra. Before coming to this place, she would never have imagined that there could be so many types of tea, or candied fruit, or any of the myriad of items they sold in Kerell city. The sheer number of them was overwhelming.

*"Pay attention,"* Datio chided. His words echoed through her head, which brought Felan briefly to mind.

*"To what?"* Selene replied in kind, though in truth she knew quite well what he meant.

"The blue, perhaps?" Varro pondered. "For the first?"

"Yes, it's perfect," Pyra replied.

*"To your fitting,"* Datio snapped.

A slim but well cared for Rakaii with a swirl of white ink above his left eye angled a measuring tape against Selene's torso, pulling it as taut as her patience.

"*I can't focus,*" she said.

"*Why in the name of the empress not?*"

Selene resisted the urge to sigh. "*I need to use the privy,*" she lied.

"*No, you don't,*" Datio replied.

"*You can't possibly know that.*"

"I'll need matching attire for Datio and Naevus," Pyra said, oblivious to the altercation.

"Of course," Varro replied.

"*Once the measurements are complete, then we'll take you,*" Datio said.

"*I don't think I can wait.*"

She could feel the man's frustration as clearly as if it was her own. Rising above it was her anxiety, and the need to get out of this room. The Aranth had at least afforded her some freedom. Perhaps she was more like a wild animal in nature than she had been willing to admit, for the frustration of being restricted ran as deep as the Crimson Abyss.

"*The Aranth?*" Datio pondered. "*Was that the name of your people, in the jungle?*"

How foolish she was to have thought of it. "*Unless you want a terrible mess, I suggest you take me to the privy within the next few minutes,*" she snapped. "*I guarantee that I won't be the one to clean it up.*"

"I beg your pardon, Mistress," Datio said at last. "Selene has an urgent need for the washroom."

Selene had yet to figure out why they called it such in this place, for little to no washing ever occurred there from what she had seen.

"Yes, go ahead and take her," Pyra replied absently.

Selene had assumed correctly that Pyra would not mind her temporary absence. This seemed to be more social visit than transaction, as her conversation with Varro had already strayed far from the topic at hand.

"End of the corridor," Varro added.

Selene breathed a sigh of relief as Pyra's laugh faded into the relative silence of the hall.

"I'll be fine on my own," she said as they reached the door in question.

"Not a chance," Naevus replied.

She pushed the door open perhaps a bit too hard in her frustration. It struck the wall behind it with a satisfying thump.

"Could you at least attempt not to destroy everything you touch?" Naevus hissed.

Datio was silent for a few seconds, as if listening to words unsaid.

"I told the mistress that Selene is fine. That it was an accident."

"And?" Naevus prompted.

"She doesn't seem angry, yet."

Selene glanced about the room. Luckily there was no one within. It was a communal privy, as she had feared. The Kerell seemed to put no value on bodily privacy. She scowled at the row of rounded holes. They had been cut at even intervals into a slab of polished stone, though much too close together, if anyone should ask her opinion on the matter.

"Why in the name of the Goddess would you need one all to yourself?" Naevus asked.

"If you have to ask, then I won't be able to explain it to you," she snapped.

"No need to be rude," Naevus replied.

"You wouldn't ever be in here with intact male Rakaii," Datio explained in one of his usual, ill-conceived attempts to calm her.

"Thank the Goddess for that."

"No need for sarcasm either," Naevus chided.

The room was well lit, though sadly no windows lay within, and thus no hope of escape. An intricate pattern of lighted stones lay upon the ceiling instead. Together they equaled the brightness of several dozen candles. These particular stones didn't seem to produce any heat. She reached up to touch one, from boredom more than curiosity.

Datio caught her hand. "Stop it," he demanded. The typically deep well of his patience was quickly running dry.

"Use the facilities now, or we're leaving," Naevus warned.

The door swung gently open, which startled both men to silence.

"Why hello, Selene. Fancy meeting you here. You're looking very well."

"Remdig," Naevus muttered unhappily.

"It's fabulous to see you, Naevus," Remdig said without so much as a hint of sarcasm. "Seems like things are looking up for you these days." The gnome was dressed in the brightest clothing imaginable, this time in shades of yellow and blue. In his right hand he carried what looked to be a lantern. Inside was not a candle, nor one of the glowing stones, but rather a tiny, winged creature, vaguely human-like in appearance.

"It's wonderful to see you as well, Remdig," Selene replied brightly, for the man's presence seemed as good a distraction as any.

"Now she finds her manners," Naevus grumbled.

The gnome posed no threat to her, apparently, at least nothing like that of the male Rakaii, for the brothers did not seem to fear his presence as they had with others who had approached her. In fact, he was the first person she had been allowed to speak with outside of Pyra's presence in any manner.

"What are you doing here?" Selene asked.

"The same thing you are, I suppose," the gnome replied. "Nature does take hold at the most inopportune times."

Selene remembered at once exactly where she was. "I meant at the tailors," she clarified quickly. "Not in the privy."

"Mistress Pyra wants us back," Datio announced worriedly.

"Simply running a few errands for Master Warig," Remdig said. "The good master doesn't like to be out in crowds. It puts him in a nasty mood. Nobody wants that. Well, me, mostly, if we're being honest. I'm the one who doesn't want it. He's quite the horse's ass when he's angry." The gnome either did an excellent job of ignoring Naevus' irritation, or perhaps he simply didn't care. Selene hoped it was the latter.

"Selene, we must go now," Naevus demanded.

The creature in the lantern folded its tiny hands into fists and pounded them against the glass.

"What's that you have?" she asked.

"A faerie-pixie hybrid," Remdig explained proudly. "Fascinating, isn't it? I'm calling it a Fixie."

"Ridiculous," Naevus huffed. "Come Selene, let's go."

"I rather thought pixies and faeries despised each other," Selene continued, ignoring him.

"Ha!" Remdig exclaimed. "Well, two of them got along for at least for a few minutes, by the looks of it."

Naevus took Selene's wrist. "I knew she was just trying to get away from the mistress," he said to Datio.

"Seems angry," Selene said as she struggled free. She pressed her face close to the lantern in order to see the creature better through the dirty glass. It looked ill-fed. Tiny, needle-like teeth shone metallically as it opened its mouth. A rough patch of hair like scrub grass had been slicked back with some dark liquid to show the gaunt angles of its face. One sunset-colored wing remained, the shape of which put her in mind of the petals of a rose. The other seemed to be missing.

"She insisted it was urgent," Datio defended. "How was I to know? She's barely tame. What would mistress Pyra have said if she'd messed on the floor."

"I wasn't specifically asked to purchase any Fixies while I was out," Remdig continued. "But, you see, I was at the Shoreline Market perusing the new goods, as Master Warig asked me to do, and there were so many things that just arrived from Evaria."

"From Evaria?" she echoed.

"I beg your pardon, from the Wildlands, I mean." He offered her a slow wink.

"We're leaving now," Naevus interrupted.

Remdig continued, heedless of the brothers' complaints. "And so, I saw this little snippet of a thing and it was so oddly interesting that I knew I had to purchase it. It's my hope that Master Warig might let me keep it. Like a familiar, of sorts. Ancient mages used to keep them, or so I've read. Though it seems like they were mostly cats. Isn't that odd?"

"Yes, I suppose it is." Selene's feet lifted from the floor, and she knew her time was up. "Apparently I must go," she said as gracefully as she could manage while being dragged by Naevus' latent ability.

"Very well then," Remdig replied. "Down to business, I suppose. Perhaps we'll meet again sometime."

"Good day," Selene replied.

Happily, the door closed just in time.

Naevus set her upon the floor just before they reached the fitting area.

"You must behave now," he whispered.

"Offer me a reason to," she replied.

"Because if you do, then we can go to the Shoreline Market."

She lowered her brows into a scowl.

"Don't pretend you aren't interested," Naevus said.

"That's right," Datio agreed. "Because we know that you are."

Selene sighed and nodded. It was a small price to pay for a bit of freedom.

The fitting dragged slowly on. When it ended, five new dresses had been ordered. With each came matching robes for Datio and Naevus. As promised, Datio mentioned the market to Pyra and, it being a market, she happily agreed that it was a splendid idea to go. Better yet, she invited Varro along, which served Selene quite well as it kept the woman's attention from straying to her.

Pyra and Varro decided that they should walk to the market, as it was reasonably nearby, and they were in a mood for such. Naevus and Datio did not seem thrilled by the idea, but it did not matter overly much to Selene how they got there. She had no desire to get back into the carriage, in any event. It was stuffy, and the movement turned her stomach. It also gave her an opportunity to further irritate Naevus, who had been tasked with trying to keep her beneath the shade of a parasol and thus out of the rays of the unrelenting sun.

The Shoreline Market had been built upon a pier that stretched out into the gentle waves. The water beneath was shallow and more turquoise than blue, a color which one would never expect to see at home. Selene watched as fish in rainbow hues brighter than Remdig's clothing circled little forests of coral. She looked up just in time to avoid running into a stately looking woman holding a purple parasol ringed with delicate, white ribbons.

"Eyes ahead," Naevus chided.

"They're only fish," Datio added. "Not of as much interest as you're making them out to be."

"I like them," Selene replied. "Don't you ever just stop to watch them swim?"

"Certainly not," Naevus replied. "We have much more important things to accomplish with our time."

"What sort of things do they sell here?" Selene asked in an attempt to hide her irritation.

"All manner of things from abroad," Datio replied. "From those lands the empress has taken for her own."

"And there are things here from the Wildlands? Remdig said that it was so."

"No more than a small amount, I'm certain," Datio said. "The Wildlands have yet to be completely conquered."

Naevus waved a hand to quiet his brother. "That's blasphemy," he whispered. "The Goddess is owner of all lands in existence by divine will. Even those which are not yet officially under her rule."

"So right," Datio replied. "Let us not speak of it again."

Datio's eyes had become distant at the mention of those other conquered lands. Was it possible that he had not been born a Rakaii?

*That's none of your concern*, Datio snapped. A stab of anger traveled through her mind with the words.

"Apologies," Selene replied aloud.

Antagonizing the man would do her no favors, and it was comforting to be near the ocean despite the heat. She had no desire to misbehave to the extent that Pyra would take her home.

Selene pulled her eyes from the water as instructed and turned her focus to the crowd. Many of the mages here kept animals. A spotted cat, whose shoulders easily reached its owner's waist, wore a gilded collar to match its patterned fur. All manner of colorful birds perched upon mages' shoulders, along with a menagerie of smaller creatures.

"What type of birds are those?" she asked. They were just as bright as the fish, and nearly as large as a chicken in size.

"Parrots of some kind," Naevus huffed. "May the Goddess save me from your constant queries."

An alligator of more than sufficient size to eat her glanced up to meet her gaze as it brushed against her leg. Her mark did not burn at the touch, which was greatly disconcerting, though likely due to the circlet.

"Are these all Rakaii?" she asked.

"Yes, of course," Naevus replied. "No mage of any worth would keep a real animal at their side."

Farther into the market there were cages which held creatures for sale. Of these she recognized quite a few. Some of them had come from Evaria.

"Are some Rakaii not sent to auction?" she asked as she looked them over.

"Not all of them," Datio replied. "It depends on the type of Rakaii, and the seller."

"Exotic creatures, straight from the mysterious Wildlands," announced a man with thick, muscular arms. His head had been shaved into an intricate pattern of swirling lines much like a mark.

"Look at that one," Datio said to his brother. "How odd."

*Red Tufted Tree Rat*, Selene read upon a little sign that was tied to the cage in question. Happily, the words did not dance within her vision as some others had. Selene squinted at the creature. It was most certainly a squirrel.

Datio furrowed his brow at her.

Pyra approached the vendor. "Welcome." The man dipped his head downward politely. "What an honor to be in such esteemed company. "We have all manner of Rakaii from the Wildlands available, as well as goods from the conquered coast."

"It is pleasant to hear that the invasion has been swift," Pyra commented as she looked over his wares.

Selene tried to keep her breathing even, though her heart could not help but quicken at the words.

"Of course," the vendor said. "All lands bend to the will of the empress."

"May she brighten the realm for eternity," Varro added.

"How much of our new land have we officially occupied?" Pyra asked. "I have not heard the most recent news."

"It is an expansive realm," the man replied. "Only a portion of one coastline, but it was most easily taken."

"That bodes well," Varro mused.

"Perhaps you would consider taking one small piece of the Wildlands for yourself, in the form of this most unusual, masked cat Rakaii." The vendor pointed to a caged raccoon. "They have excellent vision at night and are quite agile in nature. Stories say that they have a penchant for collecting items which reflect the sun."

"That is most interesting," Pyra replied. "But not today, thank you."

"Too much training required," Varro agreed with a dismissive wave of his hand.

"Perhaps a plant, then?" the vendor attempted. "This mint bears beautiful purple flowers, and the leaves can be used to make a delightful tea. The scent is pleasant, yet quite unusual."

"May I, Mistress Pyra?" Selene glanced towards the mint, which had been planted in a little glazed pot.

"Of course, dearest," Pyra replied.

The vendor held the plant up to Selene. She drew the familiar scent deep into her lungs, then immediately dispelled the memories that attempted to follow it.

Datio cautiously sniffed the plant and wrinkled his nose in distaste.

"Oh, what a lovely scent," Selene said, projecting her voice so that Pyra would be sure to hear her through her conversation with Varro. "You say it can be made into tea?"

Pyra gave the plant a delicate sniff. "Rather unusual," she said.

"Not unpleasant," Varro added after doing the same.

"Could I have it, Mistress?" Selene asked. "I would very much like to try the tea."

"I suppose it could be interesting," Pyra agreed. "Yes, we'll take it."

They left the market with a handful of colorful glass beads, like the kind that were commonly woven into women's braids in Evaria, and the little plant of mint. Pyra allowed her to hold the plant as they walked, which was surprising given that she had not yet allowed her to carry anything at all. Selene desperately wanted to find out which portion of Evaria had been conquered. Near the end of the pier, she finally summoned the courage to ask Pyra of it.

"I beg your pardon, Mistress. How long do you think it might take for the Goddess to conquer the Wildlands?"

Datio and Naevus visibly stiffened beside her.

"What a curious mind." Pyra ran a single finger along the curve of Selene's jaw. "Why would you think to ask such a thing?"

"There were such wondrous things from that realm at the market," Selene said. "I am simply curious as to when I might see more of them, Mistress."

"You mustn't worry yourself over such complicated matters," Pyra replied. "The Goddess rules all the lands by divine will. The Book of Life tells us so. We'll visit again next week, shall we? Perhaps there will be a few more precious things to purchase."

"Yes, Mistress. I am quite thankful for your generosity." Selene pressed her nose to the mint leaves and allowed the scent of home to fill her as they made their way back to the carriage.

"Smells quite terrible, if you ask me," Naevus whispered when Pyra was out of earshot. "Oddly pungent."

"Might I plant this at home, Mistress?" Selene asked. "The vendor mentioned that it has some lovely flowers."

"Yes, my darling," Pyra replied absently. "Give it to the garden Rakaii when we arrive at the estate, and we'll have it planted."

She offered Naevus a knowing grin. The more mint the better, in her estimation.

"She doesn't call many of her Rakaii by name," Selene noted as Pyra turned back to her conversation with Varro.

"I won't have you question the Mistress," Naevus replied. "She'll call us what she pleases."

"I meant no offense," Selene replied. Having a regular conversation in this place was like trying to crawl through a stretch of brambles without getting scratched.

"Brambles?" Datio asked.

"Vines with thorns on them," Selene replied. The man was only slightly more curious than Naevus. Neither of them seemed prone to asking questions of any kind if it could be avoided.

Naevus nudged his brother. "Forget that nonsense. Look."

Selene followed his gaze down the street to find Xaiden.

"He shows up frequently these days," Datio noted.

"Don't pretend as if you mind it," Naevus replied.

"Greetings, Mistress," Xaiden offered politely as he caught up with the group. "And please accept greetings from my master as well." With him he carried both the raccoon and the red squirrel, in what looked to be bird cages.

"I see that you've made some purchases for your master," Pyra said, eyeing the animals. "Perhaps I misjudged their usefulness after all."

"You have excellent judgment, Mistress," Xaiden said. "Though unusual, these Rakaii are not of the highest caliber, and are thoroughly feral. Master Zephyrus delights in training wild caught Rakaii as a hobby."

"What an intriguing pastime," Varro noted. "Perhaps we shall ask him of it when at last we meet."

"By the grace of the Goddess it will be soon, Master Varro."

"You may go," Pyra allowed. "And offer your master our respectful greetings in return."

"I will do so," Xaiden replied. "Good day Mistress." He leaned into a graceful bow. "Master."

With that he turned away. Selene lamented that she could not speak with him.

Datio and Naevus offered her an odd look.

"What are your thoughts concerning Mr. Zephyrus?" Varro asked as they continued to walk. "I have heard little of him thus far, aside from the fact that he has purchased a large number of Rakaii since reclaiming his family estate."

"He is of our caste," Pyra replied. "Perhaps he has discerning tastes, and the Rakaii at Zephyrus Estate were not to his liking."

"That holds to reason," Varro agreed.

"I have heard that he is most finely formed," Pyra noted. "Perhaps I should attempt to arrange a private meeting."

"Ah, but then you might attempt to keep him to yourself," Varro quipped.

"I always share," Pyra replied. "You know this well."

Varro laughed. "Most obviously I do."

Selene could not help but wonder, who was this man who now owned Xaiden, and why was he collecting so many Rakaii?

# The Colosseum
## *Kerell - Captial City*

They had left early from the estate. Morning light gleamed from buildings of polished, sand-colored stone as the carriage rolled smoothly by. Pyra's lands were large enough to rival the grounds of Evaria's castle, yet Selene longed to be somewhere less confining. She was happy to finally have a bit of freedom, however small.

"Bring your head back through the window," Naevus chided. "You're making us look uncultured."

It was not the first time he had said it, nor even the second.

"There's not much else to do while riding in a carriage," Selene countered as buildings gave way to airy shops which lived beneath colored swaths of fabric.

"You promised to behave yourself," Naevus reminded her with a scowl.

Selene reluctantly pulled her head back into the carriage. It was no longer worth the battle, as they would likely reach their destination soon. She could see a little through the window, at least. At the center of what looked to be a circle of shops lay a fountain of impressive size. It was a magnificent thing. At its summit water poured from a massive ball composed of white stone as smooth as freshly fallen snow. The thought of snow brought with it thoughts of Evaria. She quickly shoved them to the back of her consciousness. The carriage followed a road which curved around the fountain, then finally stopped beside several other carriages in a place which seemed designed to park them neatly in rows.

A footman opened the door to release them. He was dressed in a flowing robe which draped elegantly against his skin, rather than the vest and breeches Selene had come to expect from his Evarian counterparts.

"Thank you," she said as the man helped her down. This earned her a stern look from Naevus and Datio both. She was now above thanking servants for anything, apparently, due to her station. It was an odd rule by her estimation.

Pyra had already exited the carriage at the font of the procession and was waiting. She did not seem to notice Selene's words, or perhaps she did not care. Either way served in Selene's favor.

"Breakfast first," Pyra announced. "Come along."

Selene resisted the urge to huff in annoyance and dutifully followed Pyra towards a little shop with low wooden tables encircled with embroidered pillows. She would have liked to explore the city and had never been one to eat much in the morning. She waited obediently and looked over a few nearby murals, which had been expertly painted onto the walls of the eatery. The closest was that of a fishing boat, beneath which a tentacled monster lurked. Several men in the boat held spears, and one seemed to be casting a spell; his hands held high as if in motion. *I wish you the luck of the Tides with that*, she thought. If the monster was anything like the kraken she had encountered on her way to this Spirits-forsaken place, then it was doubtful that any type of spell would stop it. Beneath the painted ship swam creatures which looked very similar to the one that had pulled her through the water.

"What are those?" she whispered to Datio as he came to stand beside her. "The ones with the top half of a human and the bottom of a sea creature."

"Sirens," Datio replied quietly after checking Pyra's location. The woman had drifted to a nearby table and was occupied speaking with another patron. Datio pointed to the kraken. "It is said that Sirens command these monsters of the deep ocean as masters command their Rakaii. In this way they pull sailors into the sea to drown them and eat their corpses."

"But they don't eat Rakaii?"

"They don't eat creatures of magic. Only mages and humans. It is said that they feel some kinship with Rakaii."

Perhaps the Siren had been attempting to save her after all.

"It's all stories, of course," Datio continued. "No such creatures exist."

"Be quiet, the both of you," Naevus snapped. "The mistress is returning."

"I was teaching her our lore," Datio replied. "I doubt the mistress would mind me providing her with a bit of culture. Goddess knows she could use it."

Naevus waved a hand to silence him.

They sat beneath the kraken, and tea was poured for them. Selene plucked the tiny porcelain cup from the table and breathed in the spice-laden steam. Hot tea was fine at home, but here, where the heat of the day was unyielding, it made no sense whatsoever. She took a tea biscuit when Datio handed it to her and chewed while she surveyed her surroundings. It was pleasant enough. A view of the waves beyond the beach provided some amusement. Closer by, strange plants with leaves pointed like knives had been artfully arranged in a cascade. Everything was so clean and tidy here, and all of it was placed with such care, unlike the chaos that reigned in the cities back home.

Those serving did not hurry in this place, but rather moved with the smooth grace of a drifting spirit. *Perhaps this is the land of the dead*, she mused, *where souls go to spend their time with the Spirits*. The billowing white robes so often seen here did nothing to dissuade her of the notion.

"Not quite so," Pyra replied. "Though the Empress strives to make the city as beautiful as the world beyond our knowledge is thought to be."

Beside her Naevus stiffened. She still found it difficult to remember that both of the men and Pyra were connected to her thoughts by circlet. She could not sense them, and the Mistress rarely listened to her thoughts directly.

"I meant no disrespect, Mistress Pyra," Selene said. She waited for the stabbing pain to pierce her, but then remembered that Aster was no longer her mistress. "This place is more beautiful than any other I've seen." It was true, after all, though she would go home in a shadow's breath should the opportunity arise.

"Not to worry," Pyra replied delicately. Her voice was melodic in nature, as if every word was the start of a song. "Now, tell the girl what you'd like to eat."

Selene had lost track of how many days she'd been here, but not in all of that time had she actually been asked what she'd preferred in any manner, including food, so when the beautiful woman with the intricately braided hair turned, ready to take her order, she found that she had no answer.

"Don't be shy," Datio urged in a whisper. "Speak up and tell her what you want."

"I'm not very hungry," she lied. It was as if the bite of biscuit had reminded her stomach that it required food.

"You must eat something," Pyra insisted.

Selene glanced beyond the next table at the stone oven which sat in the corner. "I'll have some of that flat bread with the soup," she said. It looked ready-made and it smelled good enough.

The server offered her a strange grin, then nodded before turning to see to the others.

"It's dipping sauce for the bread, not soup," Datio informed her while Pyra was busy giving the woman her order.

"Well, how was I to know?" she asked.

"Because everyone knows," he informed her.

"I've planned some splendid things for today," Pyra announced, seemingly oblivious to the altercation.

Selene made her best attempt at suppressing her thoughts on the matter, for she had found that most of the activities Pyra preferred were a potent recipe for boredom.

"What sort of things, Mistress?" she asked in as neutral a tone as was possible.

"I do admire your curiosity," Pyra said between sips of tea.

Naevus released a nearly imperceptible sigh.

"Mr. Zephyrus has extended us an invitation for a tour of the colosseum. We are to attend the first two matches of the day."

The woman at once had Selene's full attention.

"After we attend the bout, we'll take you all to get new clothing. I've several important events coming up in the next few days."

"The dresses you've given me already are so splendid," Selene said as thoughts of untold hours spent at the clothier's ran through her head. "Surely I could wear one of those."

Naevus' hand, which now clutched her left wrist, tightened around it beneath the table. She slipped from his grasp under the guise of taking a second biscuit from the fresh basket that had just been delivered.

"Those will never do," Pyra informed her. "You can't possibly wear anything that you've already been seen in. It's simply not acceptable."

"Yes, of course," Selene replied, though she did not truly understand at all. "My apologies, Mistress."

"Not to worry," Pyra said, patting Selene's free hand. "The rules of civilized life will be second nature to you, soon enough."

"We all appreciate your generosity, Mistress," Naevus said.

"I realize that you must not have been exposed to such luxury in the past," Pyra continued. "But you belong to Leaena estate now, and you must look and behave as such."

"Of course," Selene replied before Naevus or Datio could scold her. "I'm honored to have you as my mistress."

"Ah, he has arrived at last," Pyra exclaimed.

Selene noticed for the first time that there were six pillows at the table rather than the four that were needed. She looked up to find the clothing designer, Varro. At his heels was a strapping young Rakaii that Selene did not recognize. It seemed that Varro must be Pyra's most favored companion, as he was so frequently in her presence.

Pyra stood upon noticing them. "Such a pleasure to see you this morning, Varro," she said as she placed a light kiss upon each of his cheeks.

"And you as well," he replied. "I was so pleased to accept your invitation to breakfast, and to the colosseum, of course."

"I could hardly attend without you," Pyra replied graciously. "Please, sit."

Varro lowered himself onto an empty pillow with much more grace than Selene had expected him to be capable of. He began to talk with Pyra of everyday things, beginning with tomorrow's predicted weather. Selene had learned long before coming here that such pointless chatter was expected in polite society. It still managed to irritate her, somehow.

Upon noting that everyone's attention was turned elsewhere, she let her gaze wander to the small creatures that slipped up and down a nearby garden wall, defying the pull of the earth with their movements. They were slender, and no more than the length of her fingernail, yet were quicker than a shadow fleeing from torchlight. Long, delicate legs, more than she had ever seen on a creature, splayed out in all directions giving them a feather-like appearance. A shadow crept across their territory, which ignited a volley of hissing and posturing amongst them. She looked up to find its source and was met with a familiar face.

"My apologies for interrupting, Mistress Pyra," Xaiden said. "My master bid me to tell you that his viewing box is ready at your leisure." He looked at home in the clothing of the realm, with its delicate fabric to mimic the fins of a fish from the ocean's shallow waters.

"Give Mr. Zephyrus our thanks," Pyra replied. "And tell him that we shall arrive within the hour."

"He also sends his apologies, for he will not be able to attend today's bout."

"That is regrettable," Pyra said. "I was so looking forward to his company."

"But he gives his word that he will attend your gala on the eve of the ninth."

"Of course, he is forgiven. Tell him so for me."

"I will, Mistress," Xaiden replied with a bend of his waist.

Selene strained to catch Xaiden's gaze without being noticed but received no reward for her efforts. He was gone just as suddenly as he had appeared and did not so much as look at her before turning away.

"She's fond of him," Varro noted.

"I have noticed," Pyra agreed between sips of tea. "Each time she sees him her face shows colors to rival that of a ripe pomegranate, yet she didn't spare a look for the young Rakaii you brought with you today."

Selene had no idea what a pomegranate was, but she had to assume it was red, given that the heat of her face certainly echoed that of the late morning sun.

"Ian is beautiful and he's a highly talented pleasure Rakaii," Varro replied. "But he's not suitable for breeding. His animal form is mundane at best, and his ability is utterly useless, unless you've any desire to change the color of your belongings at random."

"I do not." Pyra sipped at her tea. "Though I've had the thought that it could make for an interesting afternoon event."

"What a splendid idea. This is but one of the many reasons why I so adore your company."

"I do try," Pyra replied with a delicate smile.

"That Rakaii belonging to Mr. Zephyrus would be an excellent match for her first, would he not? You'll be hard-pressed to find a mark of higher value."

"Assuming that he still has enough youth about him to breed."

"There is no set age for such a thing," Varro said with a wink. "Any old man you ask would be sure to agree."

"Have you asked very many?"

"Not in so many words," Varro replied. "It is a pity that I don't have any viable options for her. Mine are all castrated, save for those useful in pleasure, and none of those marks are top grade."

"Lysander did offer to put in a good word with Mr. Zephyrus for me."

"Not an offer to be taken lightly," Varro said after emptying his cup in a final, dainty sip. "Shall we make our way to the colosseum?"

"We should walk, yes?" Pyra suggested. "The day is cool yet."

It was not at all cool by Selene's estimation, but going by carriage was not likely to be any better.

"You have little choice in the matter," Naevus reminded her in whispered tones.

Worse than simply hearing her thoughts alone, Datio opened them up for his brother as well, she had recently learned. Now they were both able to catch anything that entered her mind if so inclined.

"I would prefer it if you would stay out of my thoughts," she whispered back as politely as her ire would allow.

"There's one thing you'll learn about life," Naevus informed her. "It doesn't often turn out how you'd prefer."

"Come along," Datio added as Pyra and Varro argued politely over who would pay for breakfast.

The walk was pleasant enough despite the heat, and soon rows of arched doorways loomed before them.

"The colosseum," Datio squeaked excitedly. "I've never seen a match from the boxes."

"You've been inside?" Selene asked.

"A few times," Naevus said.

"Mistress Aster would deliver Rakaii here on occasion," Datio explained. "Sometimes she'd stay to watch a few matches."

Marbled stone brushed like silk beneath Selene's fingers as she passed into the cool shadows of the structure. Around and up a flight of stairs they walked, and the city outside grew smaller with each step.

Selene pulled a breath of awe as they entered the belly of the colosseum. Twenty carriages could easily have fit across the rounded structure, were they arranged end to end. Rows of seating were set throughout each level, and down below was a layer of sand much like that of the sparring pit at home. At its center two men practiced with long wooden staves similar to the one her brother Islyr preferred to use. She banished the thought before Datio could pick up on it and occupied her mind by looking upward beyond the railing. It seemed that they had traveled up so many stairs, yet still two more levels towered above them. Beyond the top row of seating, stretches of gauzy white fabric partially obscured a cloudless sky.

"Isn't it the grandest thing you've ever seen?" Datio whispered as they followed Pyra into a private viewing box.

There was enough room within it for perhaps a dozen others. Facing the center of the arena, near the railing, were two rows of seats. At the back a table had been set with little square cakes and various pitchers of drink.

"Yes," Selene replied honestly. "It's quite impressive. There's nothing to rival this at home."

"Are there many buildings in the jungle?" Naevus quipped.

"How many people does this place hold?" Selene asked in place of the reply soaked in sarcasm that her mind had quickly prepared for him.

"Several thousand at least," Datio replied as he ushered her towards the seats.

Naevus gestured to the second row. Selene sat obediently. The heat of this place was exhausting. The stone was cold against her backside, at least, though it brought with it an uncomfortable reminder of how little she was wearing. She shifted in her seat, turning back to look at the pitchers of drink. Perhaps Pyra would let her have some.

"Quit fidgeting like a child," Naevus ordered. He caught Selene's hand as it reached up to scratch her nose. "And don't touch your face. You'll ruin all the effort I put into your makeup."

Why was she the only one with sweat dripping down her neck?

"The heat isn't so bad today," Datio informed her.

"And we're in the shade, for the Goddess' sake," Naevus added as he sat beside her. "I've never seen a person sweat so much."

"Where is everyone, then?" she asked. It seemed a safe enough question. Pyra and Varro were too deep in discussion about the competitors who were slated to fight in the upcoming match to notice anything she said.

"Mistress Pyra has privileged access," Naevus explained proudly. "As do a few select others. Those in the lower classes will be allowed in later."

"But this isn't her viewing box," Selene noted.

"No," Naevus replied. "Hers is on the other side of the arena."

"Then what are we doing here?"

"We're being polite," Naevus replied. "Which is something I know you're not familiar with."

"We're accepting Mr. Zephyrus' gift in order to gain favor with him," Datio explained quietly.

"If we're trying to gain his favor then why are we accepting a gift from him? Shouldn't we be the ones offering him gifts?"

"That's not how it works," Naevus snapped. "Now quit chattering, the both of you. The loudest pigeon is the eagle's breakfast."

Selene pondered for a moment whether eagles even ate pigeons. She eventually moved on to watching the seemingly endless lines competitors practicing their sparring, one group following the next.

The row of seats she was in was set slightly higher than the one in front, so she had a perfect view of the arena despite being behind Pyra and Varro. Shade covered one half of the arena floor, yet many of the competitors fought in the heat of the sun. *I'd rather die of heat down there than of boredom up here*, she thought.

"That seems a bit extreme," Datio said. "You certainly do bore easily."

"Perhaps you don't bore easily enough," she replied.

Eventually groups of people began to trickle into the seats on the opposite side of the colosseum, filling the rows of white stone with dazzling swaths of color. The voices of the crowd grew; from a din like a few sea-birds squabbling over a clam to the sound of a dozen, then to a flock of hundreds as the seats filled with spectators.

"It's about to start," Datio exclaimed.

The outburst, though quiet in Selene's estimation, earned him a stern look from his brother.

The competitors for today's matches had arranged themselves into several rows near the center of the arena. They stood as her bloodsoul had at home, just as silent, though perhaps sturdier in appearance. At once they began to march, forming twisting lines in the sand. She noticed as they turned that little flags of various colors had been attached to their staves.

"Are those the colors of the estates they belong to?" she asked.

"Yes." Datio pointed to one on the left. "Look, there's the empress' turquoise and gold."

They warriors stopped abruptly. They waved their staves once in unison before filing out of the arena through a narrow doorway. Selene strained but could see little of their faces, encased in helmets and armor as they were.

"On the search already, are you?" Datio said. "You may want to wait until the finals to look them over. Pyra won't match you with any less than a champion."

"We're only watching two matches," Naevus reminded him. "Then we're going down below."

"Below?" she asked. "What's below?"

His answer was drowned out by hundreds of voices chanting with such force as to cause a ringing in her ears, and hundreds of feet stomping with such eagerness that the colosseum rumbled with them. Two of the many gates that surrounded the sparring pit lifted, and the first competitors stepped into the arena. They wore bright colors, much like the crowd, yet their metal helmets had been painted to match the fabric of the flags; blue for one and red for the other. Aside from the helmets they wore little armor over their clothing, only a chest plate above and a codpiece below.

"I've heard that some of the upper tiers fight in the nude," Datio remarked to his brother. "I wonder if we'll get to see one of those matches?"

"That certainly would be a sight," Naevus replied. "We're high enough class for it now, so I suppose anything is possible."

Mr. Zephyrus' viewing box was by far one of the best seats in the arena. It was close enough to the arena floor to see the combatants well, but not so close that there was any danger of weapons or spray of sand flying up to greet them.

The competitors began circling each other with staves in hand. The first bout lasted only a few minutes. The shorter of the two men had terrible form and was easily defeated. His limp, unconscious body was dragged from the arena by two burly women, while the winner raised his hands to the cheers of the crowd. Selene longed to be down in the ring. Then, perhaps she could feel as if she was fighting for something, rather than wasting her life functioning as no better than a prized breeding mare.

"Little chance of that," Naevus said. "They don't allow females in the ring."

"What of those two?" Selene countered. She gestured below, to the women who had dragged the unconscious competitor away.

"He was speaking of female Rakaii," Datio clarified. "Too rare. If you were a mage, it would be a different matter altogether."

"You should at least try to appreciate what you've been given," Naevus chided in a whisper. "Just the thought that you'd rather be down there with those ruffians, getting beaten half to death for entertainment, is an insult to our mistress and all that she has done for you."

Selene looked towards Pyra to see if she had been paying attention. Thankfully, the woman was too engrossed with cheering to notice the slight. All was well, then. Selene said nothing by way of apology, for she had not been forced to. She hoped that Naevus would take her silence as shame and turned to face the ring as the next set of fighters entered. It was with only mild interest that she watched them, for neither seemed able to land a blow upon the other. They were more evenly matched than the first pair. The two men danced around each other like animals competing for a mate, resplendent, one in gold and the other in deep purple.

Just as the competitor in purple finally landed a blow, a man entered the far side of their viewing box. He had a narrow face, but thick arms that looked as if they had once carried a large amount of muscle. A little crown of leaves and gold wire surrounded his otherwise bald head. His eyes carried with them a sense of unease as he looked Selene over before bending low at the waist and saying something to Pyra which Selene could not quite hear. The intent was clear, however, as Pyra stood and he led her away.

Selene had learned upon her first day here that wherever her mistress went she was to follow, so follow she did. Down a different set of stairs from those upon which they'd entered, and then down another to the underground. They moved along a narrow passage until they reached the area beneath the arena. It was dark while her eyes adjusted, and the noise of the match above was drowned out by sand and stone. She could smell that animals were kept here, though they were kept well. The scent of hay mingled with only a mild odor of urine and droppings. The place put her in mind of a dungeon, and although she could not see them, she could hear the scratching of what she imagined to be those many-legged creatures she had seen at the café this morning. The thought of them caused her to step away from the wall, more instinct than rational thought, and that was when something cold dropped from the ceiling and wrapped itself around her arm. She batted at it with her free hand. It tightened, creating an impenetrable circle, a hundred legs tucked beneath it to impede removal, and pain like the stabbing of a blade pierced Selene's flesh. Panic found her then, as memories of her days in the cave returned to constrict her lungs with fear. Naught but the shadow of a scream emanated from her as she pulled at her latent abilities in vain.

No sooner did her eyes land on the creature, its spots glowing in waves in the darkness and its mandibles piercing her skin, than it was ripped by something invisible from her arm to land on the stone floor below. Datio's foot came down so hard upon it that a crunching noise could be heard.

The man with the leafy crown turned suddenly, a look of shock upon his face. Pyra turned with him. She frowned at the growing welt on Selene's arm.

"Are you alright, darling?" she asked.

"Fine, Mistress," Selene replied.

Her body shook with each breath. She shoved away the hatred she felt for allowing herself to be afraid of something no larger than a garden snake.

"I appreciate your concern for my welfare," she added.

What she actually appreciated was the little bit of her healing ability that Pyra had opened, momentary though it was likely to be. She healed the swollen bite. Her ability spread like drink through her veins, making her pleasantly dizzy. *Or perhaps it is the bite of the creature,* her mind countered. Could they be poisonous? No one else seemed concerned enough for it to be so.

"They're not poisonous," Datio assured her.

"I only have fifteen available this month," Pyra said to the man, apparently satisfied that Selene would be fine. "There are several other buildings with whom I have already signed a contract."

"Only fifteen?" A worried look tightened the man's brows. "The colosseum is revered by the city entire, as surely you know. We can pay well. Perhaps more than most others."

"It isn't a matter of coin. The transition brought more rain than is typical, and thus the infestations are more burdensome this year than the last. The palace has rented more than expected. The empress' requests come above all others."

The man stiffened. "Yes, of course. We'll make do with fifteen."

"It will be enough," Pyra assured him. "I do realize how important the colosseum is to the people. I'll send some larger ones with the group."

"That would be much appreciated," the man replied.

"Do take her outside," Pyra demanded with a little wave of her hand. "She looks pale. Perhaps a bit of fresh air is in order. I won't be more than a few moments. Take her up to the viewing and have her sit in one of the alcoves."

"Yes, Mistress," the brothers said nearly in unison.

"It's quicker to go out this way," the bald man informed them. He pointed in the opposite direction from which they had come and handed Pyra a key, which she then passed to Naevus.

The room swayed drunkenly around Selene. Naevus and Datio grasped her, one upon each arm.

"I don't want to go," she protested. "I want to see the rest." There was only a small chance that one of her friends had ended up in this place, but small chances were all she had left.

"I'm sorry, my darling." Pyra patted one of Selene's cheeks as she passed. "We'll come back another time. Perhaps next month, after it's been thoroughly cleaned."

A month was far too long in Selene's estimation. But she knew better than to argue with Pyra.

"Yes Mistress. Thank you," she managed.

The hall was better lit at the far end, and as Selene had guessed there were people kept here as well as animals. Most seemed in fairly good shape, though only a few buckets and a bed of clean straw graced most of the cell floors.

"Not people," Datio corrected. "Rakaii, like us."

"We're people," Selene countered.

"Mages are people," Naevus said. "And these Rakaii are in such good shape because this is where they keep the ones who have yet to fight this week."

They came to a hefty door composed of metal. Naevus unlocked it, and they ascended a wide set of stairs to a clean open area with mosaic tiles upon the floor. The scenes were of arena battles against all manner of creatures, most of which she struggled to put names to.

"Excellent job in removing that disgusting creature," Datio said to his brother.

"And you, in killing it," Naevus replied.

"I'm certain that Mistress Pyra was pleased by the swiftness of your reaction."

"She did seem appreciative," Naevus agreed. "Despite the fact that some others did not."

"Thank you," Selene muttered, for she knew she would not hear the end of it otherwise.

There were more dungeon-like cells in this section of the arena, although these were larger, and no metal bars crossed the front of them. Instead, the openings rippled like water in the wind;

like the invisible barricade that stretched across her tiny room on Aster and Phaedrus' compound.

Naevus and Datio led her to a rounded alcove, within which was a little bench, and there they sat. Portraits covered the walls here; one between each doorway. Selene focused on the painting that lay directly across from where she sat. Shock jolted her chest as she recognized it. She could not help but stare, though her mind did nothing but warn her to turn away. It was of someone she knew well. A decorative flag had been painted above his portrait. *Ferir*, she read to herself. It was Islyr.

"You do know some history after all," Naevus said proudly, as if he had taught it to her himself. "That is indeed Ferir the Champion. Few people know the hidden name of one of the best fighting Rakaii in the history of the arena."

"Hidden name?"

"Feral Rakaii often have a name that they use before being integrated into true society," Datio explained. "That's their hidden name. But many times, our masters or mistresses give us a new name. That's considered your proper name. Mistress Pyra allowed you to keep your name, so your hidden and proper names are one and the same."

"Oh," she replied vacantly.

"We could see some of the other paintings," he offered. "I'm certain the Mistress would approve."

"I'd like that." Keeping memories of Islyr from her mind was taking much of her concentration, and she badly needed something more to occupy her thoughts.

"Why are all of these paintings here?" she asked.

"This is the viewing," Datio replied. "The combatants for the death matches are kept here. It's decorated with the portraits of those who are most celebrated."

Islyr had said little about his time in this place, and then often only if prompted by a question from another. It was a rare person who did not have memories that were happier left buried, and so with respect she did not ask.

The cells in which these Rakaii were contained were much nicer than those below the arena. The hall was wide. It hosted a fair breeze and had been decorated with colorful flowering plants in glazed pots. Inside the cells was a living space to rival the nicest rooms in Pyra's estate, complete with plates of fresh fruit and lengths of vibrant fabric draped from the ceiling.

"They seem well kept," she noted.

"Selene?"

Hearing the name caught her off guard. It had not come from Naevus or Datio, but rather from within the cell. She scanned the interior, and a familiar face appeared from behind the draped fabric.

"Felan?" The word came in a whisper though she had not bid it to do so.

Dark tendrils of ink swirled down from beneath Felan's blonde hair to snake around his left eye. It was perhaps more subtle that Islyr's inking, yet shocking to see, all the same. He was not only alive but seemed well; perhaps in better health than he had been since before the events with Perfidia.

"Back away," Naevus warned, tugging on Selene's arm.

"There's a barrier between us, in case you hadn't noticed," she said as she writhed from his grasp. "Even if there wasn't, he would never harm me."

"He's in the viewing," Datio pointed out. "That means he's killed many other Rakaii in the ring."

"Only the most violent survive here," Naevus added, as if she was having trouble understanding. "They can't be trusted around other Rakaii."

There were a great many words Selene would use to describe Felan. Violent was certainly not the first that came to mind.

"And there are a few things he could do to you aside from kill you, which would in turn get both Naevus and myself killed by Mistress Pyra."

"I want you to know that I don't blame you for any of this," Felan said, ignoring the brothers altogether.

"You followed me into the cave," Selene said. "It was a mistake to go in there."

"That's right," he said. "I followed you. I chose to follow you. I was wrong, anyway."

"Wrong? About what?"

"About my being worth no more than a cur. My skills are of better use in this place than I expected. I'm more of a prized war hound."

"I believe you've got the better end of the deal," she replied. "I'm apparently of most use for purposes of being an accessory and breeding."

"Breeding?" Felan said the word as if it made him feel ill. "Please say that they haven't -"

"No," she interrupted. "Not yet."

"She's coming," Datio warned.

"Alright," Naevus said. "There's been enough chatter. Mistress Pyra is on her way up the stairs at this moment, and if she sees you this close to him, let alone having a conversation, then we'll all be harshly punished."

"Wait," Felan begged.

"Time is up," Naevus said firmly as he dragged Selene away with a combination of physical strength and his latent ability.

"I'll come back," Selene said, although she had no idea if she would be able to, in truth.

"My next match is in a few days," Felan replied.

It was not an invitation. It was a warning that he might not be here when she returned. At the words Mistress Pyra rounded the corner into the hall. By the luck of the Tides, it was just as Selene's bottom landed on the bench in the alcove where she was supposed to have stayed.

"We have an agreement, then," Pyra said as she crested the last step. "I shall have the parchment drawn up and delivered to you here tomorrow morning."

"Yes, that would be wonderful," the man replied. "It has been a pleasure to speak with you."

"And you as well," Pyra replied politely.

The little man bowed his head before heading away.

"Well," Pyra said to Selene. "What do you think of the viewing?"

"It is unexpectedly extravagant, Mistress," Selene replied truthfully.

Pyra laughed. "I suppose it is." She moved to leave. As Selene followed, she could not help but look back to see if she could catch one last glimpse of Felan. Unfortunately, Pyra noticed her interest.

"Have you seen something you like, or are you just curious?"

Selene remained quiet, as she was uncertain of how to best respond.

"*Ferum*," Pyra read the title that had been painted above Felan's enclosure. "Sounds a bit ominous. Strange are the ones that manage to capture your attention. Let's take a look, shall we, my darling?" Pyra took Selene's hand. "Not to worry," she added when she encountered resistance. "A barrier of magic lies between us." She flicked her hand towards it, and the barrier showed itself, like ripples across calm water. "Do you see that we are safe?"

"Yes, Mistress."

"Come out, so that we may see you," Pyra called into the seemingly empty cell. "And do behave yourself."

To Selene's surprise Felan did make an appearance, slipping between the swaths of hanging fabric to stand just in front of the barrier.

"My, but you do have exotic tastes," Pyra murmured. "Hair like the sun and eyes of the deep ocean." The woman glanced at the lines of letters upon the wall to her right. Selene attempted to read them, but unlike the name they danced annoyingly within her gaze. "He has won four matches," Pyra said, reading aloud. "Not high enough rank as it stands. Perhaps if he survives long enough for your next breeding, I might consider it."

Selene tired her best to keep her emotions from reaching her face, but to no avail. Was breeding all the woman ever thought of?

"Oh, not to worry, dearest," Pyra said upon noting Selene's expression. "Mating involving death match Rakaii is always highly supervised."

She imagined that the only thing more awkward than attempting to do such a thing with Felan would be attempting it in front of a crowd of people.

"How long have you served in the arena?" Pyra asked Felan.

"Apologies, Mistress, but it is difficult to say."

"He is well behaved for a Death Rakaii," Pyra noted, seemingly to no one in particular. "So many are no more than wild animals."

Felan lowered his head submissively.

"Which estate holds your title?"

"No estate, Mistress," Felan replied softly. "I am owned by the empress herself."

"Interesting. You may go."

Felan bent at the waist before backing into the shadows of his enclosure.

"Let us not linger here," Pyra said decidedly. "We have much to do. The mysterious Mr. Zephyrus has promised to attend my gala, and all must be perfect. Datio, Naevus, you must help me prepare Selene. This next week will be solely for you to ready her while I coordinate events for the party."

"Of course, Mistress," Naevus replied.

"We would be honored, Mistress," Datio added.

"Back to the viewing box, then. I must consult with Varro."

Selene looked back once again as she was ushered away, but Felan was gone; lost to the depths of his enclosure. She followed obediently, though as she did so her heart sank to the depths. Felan was owned by the empress. It would take more than the luck of the Tides to find a way to set him free.

# An Infestation
## *Evaria – Capital City*

Islyr crept around the numerous stacks of crates that filled Evaria's docks, following a few steps behind Viverr. The rogue had thought of the perfect place to set their trap, or so he had said. Islyr had chosen to trust him. Whether or not it was a fool's choice remained to be seen.

*Almost there*, the rogue signed.

They were near dock six. It usually held larger ships from overseas, and thus was likely to contain some with mages from Kerell. They came to a stop in a narrow, alley-like strip of dock between crates which were large enough to hold several barrels of ale apiece. Viverr set the jar containing the bloodsoul on the ground between them. They then retreated several stacks away, to lie in wait. It would not do for some unsuspecting fisherman to stumble upon the jar and retrieve it in hopes of making some coin.

The rogue turned out to be correct. This was the perfect spot, for within a few moments three mages squeezed between the crates, headed towards the prize.

Viverr held out a hand to still him. *No killing,* he warned with his other.

*Why not?* Islyr signed back.

*Because they'll see us,* the rogue insisted.

*Not if they're dead.*

*You can't kill them all. Then who will take the jar?*

*I could kill just one,* Islyr suggested.

Viverr rolled his eyes.

Islyr could not see how killing one mage would make a difference to their plan, so long as no one saw the deed and there were enough of them left to take the bait. He tightened his fingers around his staff as he waited, running his thumb over the smooth indents created by repeated use, both in practice and in combat.

"*I felt something,*" the first mage said in the language of the Kerell. "*Didn't I tell you so?*"

There were two males and one female in the group. They were dressed in Evarian clothing, most likely in an attempt to remain hidden, though each still sported two rings upon their index fingers. The first ring at the base of each mage's finger, he noted, was a plainly carved band of onyx. For the second ring each wore a band of a different color. Purple for the first mage, blue for the female, and green for the last. These mages were in the empress' upper ranks. How many of them had she sent to this place? Even those of the lower castes were dangerous enough to warrant concern.

"*But how did it come to be here?*" Purple pondered.

"*Does it matter?*" Green snapped.

"*This is Marcellus' work.*" Blue pushed forward through the group to pluck the jar from where it sat. "*He was forever tying spells together unnecessarily and acting as if it made him a master of his craft.*"

"*I wouldn't call it unnecessary,*" Purple chided. "*Blending spells can be useful at times.*"

"*Not useful enough, it seems,*" she replied. "*He was killed by the most basic of creatures. Unicorns are prone to violence, yet not once have I heard of an experienced mage meeting his end by one.*"

*How do they know of that?* Viverr signed.

Islyr shrugged. Perhaps the few surviving sailors had passed the tale along, or the mages had been able to retrieve the ship before it drifted too far into the open ocean.

*"This is because a mage with any intelligence would not attempt to trap one without a handler at the ready,"* Green said.

*"I might have described Marcellus as ambitious, but never as intelligent,"* Purple agreed.

The others laughed.

*"All the better for us,"* Blue declared. *"He tried to leave without our knowledge, and now we three shall claim glory from his effort."*

Green shifted, pulling at his breeches. *"How they suffer through this clothing is beyond me. It constricts my every part like an angry snake. Let us take the jar and go back to the ship. With this last offering of gnome, we have enough to please the Empress. We could leave at first light tomorrow."*

*"Little is left for us here,"* Purple agreed. *"Their leader has been taken. That event alone will gain the empress' favor. If only we had accomplished it ourselves."*

*"Those who dwell in the past will soon drown in it,"* Green said.

Islyr recognized it as a quote from the Book of Life. The only thing Mages valued more than that tome was chatting incessantly, at least by his estimation. He resisted the urge to shift in place, for it might draw their attention. Oh, how easy it would be to rid the world of just one of them.

*"I do tire of the Wildlands,"* Blue agreed. *"This cold and dreary land disgusts the Goddess so that the sun dares not shine upon it for fear of shame."*

*"I would offer a vat of gnome powder to be last on the list when this place has been conquered and the Empress searches for those willing to settle it,"* Green said.

*"If the offer of Rakaii and land was great enough I might consider it."* Purple held out a hand. *"And on the subject of riches; because we are all to share in the glory of this find you will not mind that I carry it to the ship, I suppose?"*

*"I am the strongest of the three of us,"* Blue informed him. She held her free hand at the ready. *"Would it not be safer in my care?"*

The mages stilled; muscles tensed.

*"Perhaps so,"* Purple conceded at last.

*Their alliance is more of a slender thread than a length of rope,* Islyr thought. He glanced at Viverr. The man shook his head slowly, as if knowing his plan. The rogue held a fear of mages that matched the strength of Islyr's hatred for them.

The mages began to make their way back out to the open dock, with Blue at the head of the line. Green lingered as his companions squeezed their way out of the maze of crates. He waited until they had disappeared well beyond view before muttering a few words of magic. The mage pulled what looked to be a miniature rounded stone from his pocket and swallowed it with an audible gulp. It was the compressed remains of some unfortunate magical creature, no doubt. Green then waved a hand over the sealed crates, searching. He wished to see if there might be something more of value that he could bring to the empress to gain her favor. He would not find it here.

Islyr could wait no longer, lest the chance escape him. He crept from his hiding place and positioned himself behind the mage. The space was far too narrow to gain proper leverage. After taking a few precious seconds to level his staff with the mage he struck, punching one end at the man's spine. Just as it was about to connect, the staff jolted back against him. His hand smashed painfully against a nearby crate. He fumbled and his weapon clattered to the ground nearby. Green turned on him. His expression held as much shock as Islyr's hands had felt upon striking him. *Magic of protection.* Islyr realized. He scrambled for his staff, which had fallen between two nearby stacks of crates.

With a twist of the mage's hand sparks surrounded Islyr. They landed upon his clothing and quickly caught to flame. Islyr ignored them and rushed towards the mage, wrapping his arms around him. As expected, the mage had prepared for him to move backward rather than forward. Flames licked Islyr's face as the heat strengthened, but he would not let go. The mage cried out beneath him. Islyr pulled back. His fist struck the mage's face. Bone splintered beneath the force of it. The mage dropped between the crates, cradling his head in pain. Islyr's fingers reached his staff. He struck again. His weapon connected with the mage's temple. The crunching sound told him it was a killing blow, but he had no will to stop. His staff jolted and bloodied with each strike.

It came without warning, the rush of cold engulfing him. He pulled back from what was left of the mage's face and looked up to see Viverr holding an empty bucket.

"You were on fire," the rogue explained as he tossed it aside.

"I know that."

"You didn't act as if you knew." He gestured to the mage's ruined face. "Feel better, do you?"

"For what they did to me," Islyr replied. "This is not enough."

"I know that, friend. But it must be enough for now."

Only as Viverr brushed a hand against his shoulder did Islyr realize that some of the flames still burned upon his now soaked clothing. They disappeared with a sound like a storm wave against the cliffs, though the pain remained. It slid across his burned skin as the hatred within him faded. The salt of the water only served to enhance the discomfort.

"Part magic and part real flame," Viverr's face twitched with distaste. "They're nearly as clever as I am."

"Nearly," Islyr agreed. His mind drifted like fog.

"You're a mess, my friend," the rogue noted. "Lucky for you I found that bucket. We should head to the infirmary."

"I'm not badly injured," Islyr countered.

"You smell like an overcooked roast," Viverr said. "And we've created quite a lot of noise here. Aranth or no, I don't think we want anyone to find this, most especially the other mages."

"Are you saying we should do something with him?" Islyr asked as he rubbed his injured hand.

"Is he still breathing?"

Islyr glanced at the mage, who was now half engulfed in his own flames. "No," he replied simply.

Viverr touched the tip of the man's boot. The flames retreated to leave no more than a few wisps of smoke. "No need to set the whole dock on fire," Viverr explained.

Islyr searched the man's pockets. He came up with two stone-like capsules of powdered magical creature, and a slip of parchment, which was far too burnt to read.

"Job done then, let's say," Viverr announced. "There's no need for anyone to know the details."

"Agreed." Islyr slipped out from the maze of crates.

"What's your plan for those?" The rogue eyed the stones of compressed powder in Islyr's hand.

Islyr pressed them, closed within his fist, to his forehead. "May the Spirits protect and guide you on this day and thereafter." He stepped to the side of the dock and tossed them into the sea.

The rogue said nothing, but rather nodded in respect.

"It's unusual for mages to have protection magic up permanently, as it requires a large amount of power to keep in place," Islyr noted.

"Perhaps they don't feel as secure as we thought," Viverr suggested.

"Or perhaps they fear each other more than us."

"That would make more sense," Viverr agreed. "They don't seem particularly concerned by our defenses."

"This place is primitive to them," Islyr said. "They have no need for fear."

"Ah, but perhaps they do with the two of us."

Islyr raised a brow at the rogue.

"The mere mention of our names must cause the mages of Kerell to tremble."

A wisp of a grin crept across Islyr's face despite the pain of the burns. Viverr quickly returned it. "You've become accustomed to my antics," the rogue said. "Might as well admit it now."

"Not at all," Islyr replied. "You've simply grown less irritating than you once were."

Viverr offered no more than a snort of amusement in reply. "I've been thinking," he said after a moment. "Although I detest mages, I can't deny that it would be of benefit to have one on our side."

"It would," Islyr admitted. "Though most of them cannot be trusted. Mages are rare in Evaria. The chance of finding one who would aid us is not high."

A single standard guardsman caught Islyr's attention. He marched from the castle grounds with purpose.

"Perhaps word has spread of our adventure already," Viverr whispered.

"It would be faster than expected."

The guardsman headed straight towards them. Viverr's scrub pig squealed in excitement. The creature made so little noise that at times he struggled to recall its presence.

"Ah," Viverr said. "That'll be Erud, Cyanna's companion."

"Her mate?" Islyr asked.

"I prefer to stay out of such things as they're no business of mine," Viverr replied. "But it would be an accurate title, technically."

The lad was fit enough from training as a guardsman, but he had barely outgrown his youth. He might survive a few rounds in the colosseum, but not many.

"Cyanna bid me to find you, sir," Erud said to Viverr. "It's about the egg."

The rogue stilled. "Where is she?" he asked.

"Her room, sir."

The last word had barely left the lad's mouth as Viverr sprinted away.

"Thank you," Islyr said, remembering his graces.

The rogue could move with speed when he was of a mind to. By the time Islyr reached Cyanna's room Viverr was already within. The man held a mottled piece of eggshell in one hand. A few more broken pieces lay in the bowl of water that sat upon the Queen's writing desk. The creature that had emerged from the egg was draped contently around Cyanna's neck like a scarf the color of crimson sea glass.

"Isn't she beautiful?" Cyanna exclaimed.

"She is," Islyr replied.

"Look," Cyanna said proudly. "Page eighty-seven in my tome of foreign animals. She comes from the land of the Kerell."

"A dragon of the Kerell?" Viverr said hopefully.

"Well, no," Cyanna admitted. "Though the paragraph says that they are very distantly related to dragons."

The creature hissed as it positioned itself more firmly around Cyanna's neck. Its knife-shaped body was edged in dark, delicate fins which flared out now and again as it considered its new surroundings.

"She is a volantes," Islyr informed them.

"But not a dragon?" The rogue looked as disheartened as Islyr had ever seen him.

"They are highly prized in the land of the Kerell," Islyr said in an attempt to cheer the man. "The red ones are exceedingly rare. And females of this species are not often hatched, much like female Rakaii. This one has the worth of a half-fleet of sailing ships, at least."

For once the Rogue fell to silence.

"What do they eat?" Cyanna asked curiously. "It explained in the passage that their favorite food was vehementis, but I don't know what that is."

"An insect creature native to Kerell," Islyr explained. "They feed upon magical energy but require a warm atmosphere. I doubt they would survive in the climate here."

"I don't wish for her to starve," Cyanna said.

"Take her outside," Islyr suggested. "They will consume all types of insects and are self-sufficient from birth. She will find something to eat on her own."

"That's a splendid idea," she said. "You don't mind if I borrow her, do you Viverr?"

"Of course not," the rogue replied. "Just keep a good eye on her, will you?"

Cyanna smiled and bounded out the door. It was an unsettling reminder of just how young she still was.

Viverr looked pointedly in Islyr's direction. "Not a word," the rogue said.

In fact, Islyr had no need to say anything. It was clear that he had won their bet, for the volantes was certainly not a dragon. He was now the leader of this new, albeit tiny, faction of the Aranth.

The rogue had lost his leadership and his dragon all at once. Good graces said that Islyr should offer something to appease him. The solution came to him easily.

"Would you like to go down to the kitchens with me?" he asked.

"I'm not much in the mood to eat," the rogue grumbled.

"That's unfortunate," Islyr said as he headed for the door. "I overheard one of the chambermaids say that the Mistress of Kitchens ordered several batches of ginger cookies made for today."

Viverr's eyes narrowed in the slightest. "I know what you're trying to do," he informed Islyr as he kept pace beside him.

"Do you?"

"Yes, and it might work."

"What do you mean by that?" Islyr asked with false curiosity.

"It might work, depending on just how many ginger cookies we can get our hands on."

"As many as we like, I would assume."

"How do you figure?" the rogue asked with confusion. "Mistress of kitchens never gives up her baked goods to any but the royal family. It's like pulling spines from a venomvine. You're likely to get yourself killed."

"We'll just explain that the Queen is your protégé."

"Will we, now?"

"Yes, and we are the most important branch of the Aranth, after all."

"Fair enough," Viverr replied.

"Or I could cause a distraction while you pilfer them."

"A much better plan, I think," the rogue laughed. "I am at your command, great leader."

# Volantes
## *Kerell – Capital City*

Selene's patience was fading more quickly than the chill of night at the touch of the rising sun.

"I don't want to sit down," she insisted. "I've had enough."

"That's not for you to decide," Naevus countered.

"The only way you're going to get that scent onto my body is if my spirit is no longer in it!"

Naevus' face began to redden. "I picked this out specifically for you to wear to the gala, and you'll do so even if I have to hold you down while I apply it."

"You won't do that," Selene said knowingly. "You might disarrange my hair, or worse, ruin my makeup."

Naevus huffed.

"Or what if my dress became torn during the struggle? Pyra might never forgive you."

"Sit down right now, or I'll have Datio call the mistress herself and we'll see what she has to say about all of this."

"Pyra is quite engaged at the moment. If you call her then she'll assume that you don't know how to do your job. You'll be punished, while I'll get only a slight reprimand."

Selene hoped that she was not bluffing. Pyra was rather busy making certain that everything was prepared for the gala, as it was beginning in little less than half an hour. She would be angry at any delay in getting Selene ready, but as to who would be punished, it was uncertain.

"What about if we take a brief respite?" Datio suggested. "How about a walk?"

"We don't have time for a walk," Naevus snapped.

"I might like a walk," Selene admitted. She did not know how long they had been preening her for the gala, but at that moment it seemed no less than a century.

"Fine," Naevus agreed. "But if we take you for a walk, then you must promise that you'll allow me to apply the oil when we return."

Selene sighed. "I will," she agreed. The scent was far too strong. It managed to invade her nostrils with cloves and various other spices even from within the sealed bottle. "But only a small amount," she added at the thought.

Naevus opened his mouth to disagree.

"We should wait to discuss it until after our walk," Datio interrupted.

And with that each man looped his arm through one of hers. They led her from the room and out into the nearest courtyard. The light scent of flowers lingered from the blooms of the day. Those of the night, which were much more beautiful in Selene's estimation, had spread out to take their place. Of the four courtyards in Pyra's estate this was Selene's favorite. The small pond at one side hosted a fountain shaped like the head of some cat-like creature, and below it lay a grouping of lily pads reminiscent of those which grew wild in the ponds at home.

"It's called a lion," Datio informed her as she watched the water spring from the fountain's mouth to land in the pool below.

"A lion." The word lay strangely upon her tongue.

"That's a male," he said knowingly.

"Why do you say that?" The statue was only of the head, which was mounted upon the wall. No body, and thus no parts by which to identify it as either male or female, were present. Though she had never seen the other side of this particular wall. Perhaps the rest of the statue's body was there. She rounded a nearby doorway to check and was followed by Datio's laughter.

"It's just a head. I know it's male because only the males have that mane of hair surrounding their face."

"Are these lions native to here?" she asked.

"No," he replied. "But they bring them in to fight in the arena, on occasion."

"Actual lions, or Rakaii?"

"Both," he said. "But you might never see one. Lions are difficult to come by, Rakaii or otherwise."

As Datio spoke, a flash of silver caught Selene's attention, like a coin glinting in the sunlight, though there was no light left to speak of. Her eyes were drawn to it, and she could do naught but follow where they strayed. The glint of light led her down a henceforth unfamiliar hallway.

"We haven't the time for wandering about, following your every fancy," Naevus complained. He followed her all the same, though a few steps behind as if in protest.

The sky was mostly dark. The glowing stones that mages were so fond of had brightened to counter it, perhaps in response to whatever spell had been set upon them. They created a row of light along each side of the floor, illuminating a stairwell leading downward.

It flashed again; a pinpoint of light that left spots in her vision.

"What is that?" she asked as she moved closer to investigate.

"Ah, there he is," Datio said. "Pyra will be pleased."

"What is it?" Selene ventured closer, her bare feet patting gently against the cool stone of the steps as they led her downward. The fact that her uninvited entourage let her anywhere near whatever it was meant that it could not possibly pose any danger.

"We're not your entourage," Datio said. "We're bodyguards for the Mistress' most valued possession."

Why couldn't the man stay out of her head?

"Because you can't be trusted to behave in a civilized manner."

Selene suppressed a sigh borne of pure aggravation.

"I told you he'd show up here eventually," Datio said as Naevus, who still lagged a few paces behind, rounded the corner above.

"Yes, you just know everything there is to know," Naevus huffed. "Let's scoop him up and take him back where he belongs, shall we?"

Selene was happy to participate in anything that didn't have to do with clothing or makeup. She neared the creature.

"It's a volantes," Datio explained, as if the name should mean something to her.

Its shape was akin to the blade of a kitchen knife, though it was several times larger in size. It undulated as a silk flag would in the wind and moved through the air much like a fish did through water. A flexible barb protruded from the end of the creature's lip, and at the end of this was the spot of light she had seen from the top of the stairwell. The volantes floated upward so that one eye was level with her own. The sheen of its scales was like that of polished silver.

"How do I get it to come with me?" Selene asked as it looked her over.

Before Datio could answer, the creature flowed around the back of her neck to rest there like a scarf. It felt as much like silk against her skin as its movement suggested.

"They're very tame," Naevus said. "Now let's go, shall we? The mistress might thank us for finding him, but it won't be enough to counter her displeasure if we're late to the gala."

"True," Datio agreed.

It was then that Selene noticed the large door of steel and bolts that blocked the end of the stairwell. "What's in there?" she asked. "More volantes?"

"Nothing of interest in there," Naevus said much too quickly.

"If you wish to see more of them, I'll show you where he lives," Datio offered, gesturing away from the door and into the hall that led away from it. "Their enclosure isn't too far from the courtyard."

Selene nodded in compliance and managed to leave with no more than a single parting glance at the most interesting of doors. She followed Datio around several corners before arriving in a section of the estate that she did not find familiar. She had come to accept that this would be a common occurrence due to its sprawling nature.

She followed Datio through the next doorway and found herself in a place that was unlike any other room she had seen here. It was much larger, to begin, and the ceiling was composed of glass panes held together by metal bars, much like the sky-room at home. The air was heavy with moisture. Her mind wandered back to the cave in which she had found herself after the shipwreck. Datio offered her an odd expression. She immediately banished the thought from her mind.

Above were a great number of glass orbs much like fishing floats, and by some spell they hovered in the air as the floats would in water. In each was a volantes. They varied in size and color, as did the orbs which contained them. Most of the creatures seemed to be sleeping.

"There are so many," she said in awe as she gazed upward.

"Mistress Pyra has nearly one hundred of them," Datio informed her. "This is but one of several rooms which house them."

"Are they pets?" Selene asked.

"No, of course not," Naevus said. "They're working animals."

"They eat insects, most especially vehementis."

"Vehementis?"

"Like the hideous creature that landed on you beneath the colosseum," Datio explained.

"They're disgusting parasites," Naevus huffed. "Devourers of magical energy."

"The little ones aren't very dangerous," Datio assured her, as if it was needed. "Though they leave these terrible welts on your skin. It can last several weeks without a healer." He shuddered, as if recalling something he would rather have left buried.

"How big do vehementis get?" she asked warily. "The one that had encircled her arm was already larger than she would have preferred.

The volantes slipped from her shoulders. It flared its fins and hissed at a nearby companion before settling like a snake on some sizable white mushrooms which grew from the trunk of a little tree.

"Your ceaseless questions are making my head ache," Naevus announced. "Job done. We'd better go."

"Shouldn't we put him back into his orb?" Selene protested. She had no desire to see the poor creature contained, but also wanted to keep from going to the gala for as long as possible.

"The silver one is the dominant male of this group," Datio explained. "He chooses to sleep in the tree to keep watch. The rest will emerge from their orbs tomorrow, within a few hours of daybreak. They are by no means held prisoner in them."

*Unlike myself,* she thought irately.

"Your walk is over now." Naevus headed for the door. "Let's go."

"Fine," she reluctantly agreed. That made two things of interest he had torn her away from this evening.

Naevus had not forgotten her promise to him, unfortunately, so after a brief stop in the dressing room to apply the dreaded scent Selene found herself in the main courtyard. The day had cooled significantly, and the sun had completely set. Torches of actual flame replaced the more commonly used magical sources of light. The scent of burning wood and flickering light set her immediately at ease, for it reminded her of nights at home.

"I said you'd like it, didn't I?" Datio whispered.

"You did," she replied.

He had attempted to convince her of such for most of the time they were preparing her, but she had been reluctant to believe him.

A glance around the area revealed that quite a few people had already arrived, dressed in their best robes in all colors of silken fabric. She did not recognize any of them, nor did she recognize any of the Rakaii, despite the fact that a large number of them were present.

"The gala is just warming up," Datio assured her. "There will be many more guests arriving over the next few hours."

"The next few hours?" she asked in dismay. "How long do these parties last?" Would she be expected to stay here all night?

"For the Goddess' sake." Naevus rolled his eyes. "Go and get her a drink, will you, Datio?"

"I'm not thirsty," Selene countered.

"Something strong, if you will," he continued, ignoring her. "I have no desire to hear her complain all night."

Datio grinned. "My pleasure," he said before heading off towards the bar.

While Datio was procuring Selene's unwanted drink Pyra found them. Her hair had been swept upward and was held with a cluster of crystal pins. Her dress was composed of many shades of pink which, despite being lovely on their own, were not best put together.

"Your hair is simply beautiful, Mistress," Selene said, tactfully avoiding any further thoughts on the woman's dress.

"Why thank you, darling," Pyra replied. "She's always such a sweet thing, isn't she, Naevus?"

"She's like a seraph of the Goddess, Mistress," the man replied.

Selene was impressed that he was able to say so with a straight face.

"And so beautiful," Pyra continued. "You and Datio did an excellent job getting her ready."

"Our deepest gratitude, Mistress. It was our honor." This time the grin on his face was genuine.

"Let's go and meet a few of our guests, shall we?"

"I would be pleased to do so," Selene lied.

It quickly became evident that Pyra meant to introduce her to all of the guests rather than just a few of them, and each guest was accompanied by a strapping male Rakaii. As the party progressed it became ever more difficult to focus, and after only a few hours she was mentally exhausted.

The man Pyra was currently speaking to was in the business of mining for precious gems. In fact, he had been describing the profession in excruciating detail for what seemed like a lifetime. She imagined that Pyra must only be mildly entertained. Though if it was true, she feigned interest with a level of skill that Selene had yet to achieve. As Selene's attention drifted here and there the man's Rakaii, whose muscled torso had been oiled to such a ridiculous sheen that the light of the torches glinted from it, slipped glances at her whenever his master was not looking. If only she could scrub away the feeling that came over her as his eyes wandered up and down her torso.

"He is very fine in appearance," Pyra said, indicating a change of subject that Selene had missed.

"He is a confirmed stud," the man said proudly. "He has consistently produced high quality Rakaii, and he has never lost a match at the colosseum. One mating even produced twins."

"He is impressive," Pyra mused. "I shall certainly keep him in consideration."

The guests parted, creating a path which heralded Lysander's arrival. His entrance was a grand affair, which Selene could only assume must be typical. Two young men tossed sparkling powder that hung in the air in Lysander's path as he walked, and an entourage of finely groomed Rakaii followed behind. The man was dressed in a gown of silver which perfectly accented his form. A few jewels, which had been tastefully woven into his hair, flashed in the torchlight as he made his way towards Pyra with a grace that few of the mortal realm could hope to achieve. With

Pyra temporarily distracted, Selene could not help but consider ways she might escape her mistress' side and perhaps the whole event itself.

"Not another thought on that subject," Naevus warned her in the most severe tone one could manage while whispering.

*"You don't have to tell him my every thought,"* she chided.

*"Reprimanding you is an exercise best done by two,"* Datio's voice echoed in her mind. *"I might perish from exhaustion otherwise."*

Some relief came as Varro appeared by Pyra's side. "By the Goddess, he does put the rest of us to shame," the man said as he gazed at Lysander.

"Certainly," Pyra replied. "Who could do less in a robe you conceived?"

One corner of Varro's mouth twisted into a grin.

"We shall greet him together," Pyra said. "Come, friend."

"I would love nothing more."

"Find Selene another drink, and meet me when you've finished," Pyra instructed.

"Yes, Mistress," Datio replied.

"Do you find it odd that she didn't want me to follow her?" Selene asked as Datio handed her what would be her fourth drink, had she not covertly poured as much of the others as was possible into the shrubbery when his attention was elsewhere.

"Not at all," Datio replied. "Master Lysander doesn't own any breeding Rakaii, they're all for pleasure. He is unlikely to have brought along a potential mate for you."

"But if he doesn't breed his Rakaii then where does he get them all?"

"Some are imported or wild caught. Many are from the culling."

"What's the culling?" she asked. The name was both curious and ominous at once.

"You may be surprised to learn this, having been wild-caught," Datio said. "But not every child born of a mage will be another mage. Some few are Rakaii."

"Oh," she replied. She had not given it much thought, in truth. "They can tell as soon as the child is born?"

"No, of course not," Naevus said. "It's impossible to tell until the child is older, most usually around twelve years of age. Older for some. It is then that they either develop the ability to control magic, or their mark appears."

"And if they're Rakaii then these families willingly give up their children to slavery after raising them for so many years?"

"Yes, of course," Naevus replied. "If the child is Rakaii then it becomes property of the empress. The Rakaii is sold at auction and the family receives compensation, most usually two thirds of the selling price."

"And what if they want to keep the child?"

"It's not really a child." Naevus punctuated the words with a roll of his eyes, as if she was missing something plainly obvious. "It's a Rakaii."

"Why would they want to keep a child that's not human?" Datio added.

"I suppose I don't know." Selene fought down the rage that was building in her chest.

"What of Lysander?" she asked, for she was eager to change the subject while her temper remained in check.

"What of him?" Naevus asked.

"Why did he bring so many Rakaii if none of them are potential mates?"

"They are likely a gift for Pyra," Datio said.

"He's giving her Rakaii?" She could not imagine how many Rakaii the man must have if he gave them away at every party he attended.

"Don't be ridiculous," Naevus chided. "He's not giving them to her, he's lending them to her for the duration of the gala."

"I don't understand."

"For the activities later in the evening," Naevus explained.

"The highly anticipated end to every great soiree," Datio said with a sweeping gesture.

"Perhaps she's more pristine than we assumed," Naevus added upon noting Selene's expression.

"I am not," Selene snapped as the realization of what was to occur formed in her mind and heat rushed to her face. "I simply would rather not think of it, as I am obviously not to be invited."

Her words brought Naevus to laughter. "You do say some odd things."

"Let's go find the Mistress, shall we?" Datio suggested.

"I'd rather not," she replied.

"I don't think you want to make a scene at the gala that Pyra so carefully arranged," Naevus cautioned, returning quickly from his mirth.

"She went to great lengths to plan it," Datio added. "All so that you could find a suitable mate."

"I suppose so," Selene replied carefully. It was far less satisfying than telling the insufferable man that she did not want a mate. She would have screamed it loud enough to draw the party to silence, if only the imagined punishment was not so severe. Instead, she drew a deep breath. *I will not let anger control my actions. My thoughts are pure serenity.* While reciting the mantra a second time something cool and soft slithered around her neck. She jumped back, knocking her cup of drink from the table as she did so.

It was the silver volantes.

"How did you get out here?" she asked it as her heart slowed.

The creature twisted around to look up at her but offered no reply.

"Fabulous," Naevus said with a scowl. "We can't very well leave the gala to put him back."

"Do you suppose he matches well enough with her dress that we can wait and return him later?" Datio asked, looking her over.

"He matches," Selene said, although she could not fathom why it should matter. Never had she met two people more obsessed with fashion. She felt secure with the volantes around her shoulders, and so wanted to keep him. With the luck of the Tides, he would bite the first person who attempted to mate with her. So pleased was she by her newest companion that she was startled to find Xaiden standing directly next to her.

"A pleasure to see you again," he said as he replaced the cup she had knocked from the table, empty though it now was.

Both Datio and Naevus stiffened beside her. "Where is your master?" Naevus asked as he stepped in front of Selene to shield Xaiden from her.

"He is currently entertaining your mistress, who has given me permission to speak with Selene."

"And you are appropriately contained?" Datio's tone was one of suspicion.

"Of course." Xaiden replied. He shifted his robe near where the folds came together at the hip to reveal a portion of a strange metal undergarment.

"It is the truth," Datio announced as Xaiden straightened his robe. "Pyra gives her permission."

"I am an axiom Rakaii," Xaiden said. "I only speak the truth. Would you be so kind as to give us a moment?" he posed it as a question, although it clearly was not.

Much to Selene's surprise, both Naevus and his brother not only agreed to leave her but headed towards Pyra, who was several feet away in a group of guests which oddly no longer included Lysander or Varro.

"It is a pleasure to finally make your acquaintance properly."

The phrase served as a reminder that others were listening. Selene resolved to watch her tongue however difficult it might be. "And yours as well," she replied. A bend of her waist served to add formality. Xaiden looked well kept, at least. This was as close as she had come to him since the disaster on the ship.

"I feel you should know that my master is in negotiations with your mistress at this moment."

"Is he?"

Try as she might, Selene could not manage to catch a glimpse of the mysterious Mr. Zephyrus. Too many other guests hovered near Pyra, perhaps hoping to eavesdrop on whatever conversation played out between the two.

"And what would these negotiations be concerning?"

"Nothing to be stated in polite company."

It was far from bright where they stood, yet she could have sworn that she could see color rise to Xaiden's cheeks.

"No need to explain any further," she said.

"Excellent." He smiled. "Master Zephyrus is most anxious for us to come to an agreement after what he has heard of you, but your mistress believes that you must be amenable to the match for it to be blessed by our empress, the Goddess."

"Of that I am well aware," Selene said with a sigh.

It had been a long night, and her patience was nearing its end. "I'm just not certain how my approval of this match will benefit either of us." It would not get her home in any way that she could fathom. It was nice to see Xaiden, but he was in no better position than she was. At the moment getting home was one of the few things that mattered to her.

"Well, if you agree to it then you will be given leave to come to my master's estate, and you will be transferred to his circlet, for however long it takes." Xaiden paused and cleared his throat. "However long it takes for us to conclude our business, that is. You do see what I am attempting to convey?"

He seemed to find the situation equally uncomfortable, at least.

"I might," she replied.

"This will greatly benefit us both," Xaiden said. He leveled his gaze with hers. "You must trust me."

She did, no matter how foolish it might be.

"I agree," she said.

She was about to ask if she should let Pyra know of it when the woman made her way over to them. Her excited movements were like those of a little bird flitting about.

"Is my makeup still in place?" Pyra whispered to Datio, who stood by her side.

"Yes Mistress," he replied with a genuine smile. "You look stunning, as usual."

"You're such a dear," the woman replied. She pressed a hand to his cheek, then turned to Selene. "This is a momentous occasion," she continued, perhaps louder than needed.

As silence crept across the courtyard Selene realized that Pyra was in fact addressing the entire gala.

"I must first thank you all for attending," Pyra began. "Tonight, I have seen many fine Rakaii worthy of mating with my beautiful Selene. From them I have chosen the one most fitting for the match. Mr. Zephyrus and I have come to an agreement for his Axiom Rakaii, Xaiden." Pyra paused as the expected clapping and murmuring occurred. "Do not fret, for although your Rakaii were not chosen tonight, there is still hope. I plan on breeding her every alternating year, as the law allows."

Selene's stomach twisted into an uncomfortable knot, which tightened as Pyra continued speaking. The heat of the night seemed thicker than it had been a moment ago. The volantes hissed and slithered from her shoulders as the world tilted dangerously beneath her. Xaiden caught her before she could touch the floor.

"My darling," Pyra exclaimed. She seemed genuinely concerned. "Are you ill?"

Selene could feel the woman in her head, rummaging around. It caused her stomach to roll once again.

"I'm fine, Mistress," she managed as Xaiden helped steady her. "A bit too much excitement, perhaps. Or a bit too much drink."

"Take her for a few moments of quiet," she ordered. "I'll call you when I've finished addressing everyone."

"As you will, Mistress Pyra." To Selene's surprise it was neither Datio nor Naevus that replied, but rather Xaiden.

Her mark burned as Xaiden took her hand and led her out to sit on a bench in a quiet alcove near the corner of the courtyard. Laughter and the occasional clink of glass upon glass could still be heard from beyond the wall.

"Are you truly fine?" he asked once they were alone.

"As much as can be expected, I suppose."

The room had ceased spinning, at least.

"You can speak with a fair amount of candor," he said. "Pyra will be concentrating on her speech, for the next few moments, at least."

"What of Datio and Naevus?"

"You are no longer connected to either of them."

The fact came as somewhat of a shock.

"But why not?"

"Tradition," he replied. "You and I are to be given every opportunity to bond with each other. They are likely to leave us alone, aside from a light connection with Pyra, and later myself and my master. They expect that I will defend you from all others with my life now that mating rights are officially mine."

"That might be used to our advantage," Selene said. "How long will it last?"

"For now, overnight. There is generally a celebration of some sort between the two parties owning the Rakaii to be bred."

"Another gathering?" Selene could not help but frown.

"Yes, another. After the celebration we will remain connected until you are with child, so that we are able to engage in certain activities privately. It is said to bring good fortune."

"Just so you are aware, you and I are not going to engage in any type of such activity, privately or otherwise," Selene snapped.

"Obviously not. And frankly it pains me that you would assume such a thing."

There was a bite to Xaiden's tone that was difficult to ignore. Selene rubbed her hands across her face, heedless of the fact that she might ruin her makeup. Datio and Naevus could be kept by the Spirits for all she cared.

"I'm sorry, Xaiden. I know I should believe better of you. I've been through many ordeals in my short life, but this place…" She considered words that would not be terrible should they be overheard. "It's overwhelming in a way I've never before encountered."

"That is a fair description."

"I'm happy that you're alive."

He offered her a brief smile. "I am pleased that you survived as well. I may not have forgiven myself otherwise."

"Have you thought of any way that we might get home?"

His smile faded. "I am making progress, I assure you. Although tonight I am here simply in an attempt to buy you some time."

"And because Pyra wishes to build an alliance with your master."

"You are perceptive, as usual." He offered his hand to help her from the bench.

"Your attempts to ensure my safety are appreciated, don't misunderstand me, but won't they expect me to carry a child? What will happen when I remain barren?"

"I do not know. We shall figure out the details at a later point."

"That's more than a detail."

"You are out of danger for a time. That is of the most importance."

"You're right," she admitted. "That's well enough. Thank you for attempting to help me."

"Has Pyra been kind to you?"

"More than I expected. She cares for me, albeit like a beloved riding horse, or perhaps one of those tiny dogs that the ladies of Evaria are so fond of carrying about. What of your master?"

"His wealth is on par with that of your mistress. He is one of the few that can claim such. That is why an allegiance between us holds such importance. He is from one of the oldest families in this place."

"I've heard that much from Pyra. What is he like in truth?"

"While you are in his care, he will not let you come to any harm. That much you can be assured of."

Selene had vast experience with Xaiden's penchant for sidestepping important facts when he wished to.

"That part is given," she said. "It would not be prudent to allow Pyra's favorite Rakaii to come to harm if he wishes to form an alliance with her."

He was holding back something of importance, she would bet her freedom on it.

"Xaiden, please. If I'm to stay in your master's care, then it would help me to learn as much about him as possible."

Xaiden seemed deep in thought for several seconds. "Pyra has finished with her speech," he said.

"How could you know that?" Selene replied.

"Because my master told me. Come, she wishes to see you."

Selene grudgingly followed. There were still just as many people milling about the courtyard, much to her dismay, though the air felt nowhere as suffocating as it had those few moments ago.

"Intemperantia," Xaiden said.

"I beg your pardon?"

"It is what the wealthy call these galas they are so fond of," he explained. "They're celebrations of excess."

"Like one of Kyrros' parties?"

"Very much so," he replied.

Datio and Naevus had said as much, earlier in the night. Selene could not help but surmise, upon noting the current level of inebriation, that the gala would indeed soon dissolve into something to match the end of one of Kyrros' infamous parties. With what she had learned of this place so far, she was astonished that such an event had not started as the guests arrived.

"Are you feeling better, my darling?" Pyra asked as they approached.

"Yes, Mistress," Selene replied. "I appreciate your concern."

"And you approve of him still?"

"Yes, very much, Mistress." She tried to think of something more to say to convince Pyra to let her stay with Xaiden but could not find any suitable words.

"Excellent." Pyra stroked Selene's hair as one would the fur of a beloved dog, though being careful not to push so much as a strand out of place. "Come along now and meet Mr. Zephyrus."

Selene followed obediently, in part because she wanted nothing more than to have this particular day come to an end, but also because she was curious about what Xaiden's master was like. Xaiden did not seem to have any strong feelings about the man, so far as she could tell, yet as Pyra ushered Selene along he hesitated and lingered a few steps behind. She had barely the time to notice the concern that shadowed his face before it was gone.

"What's wrong?" she whispered, dropping back to match pace with him. "You must tell me."

Xaiden merely shook his head.

"You two will have plenty of time to spend alone later tonight," Pyra chirped. "Be obedient now and follow."

Selene was in no way willing to disabuse Pyra of the thought that she merely wanted to spend more time alone with Xaiden.

"Let's go." She offered her hand to him. The burn that rushed over her as he took it was accompanied by a strong sigh.

They lagged behind Pyra only in the slightest, and Xaiden drew close enough to whisper in Selene's ear. "Remain calm, or it will be the end of us."

"Be quiet and respectful now despite your excitement," Pyra interrupted. "Rumor has it that Lysander's Rakaii are the best trained in the city and beyond. It is an impressive achievement. You would not want to disprove that notion."

"My deepest apologies, Mistress," Xaiden said with a dip of his head. "It will not happen again."

"For your sake I should hope not." Pyra stepped around a group of her guests with a nod of greeting. "Ah, there he is."

The man stood politely at their approach. Selene could say nothing as the flickering torchlight moved across a face that often visited her dreams. The reason for Xaiden's reluctance to speak of his master was made most suddenly clear.

Pyra spoke where Selene could not. "Selene, this is Master Logan Zephyrus. His estate produces the finest wine and honey on the continent."

"You honor me by saying so," Cael replied smoothly.

Selene was dumbfounded. It made no sense. How had Cael convinced the upper caste that he was a member of one of the oldest families in the land of the Kerell?

A little spike of pain startled her from her daze.

"Greet him properly, Selene." Pyra's tone furthered the thought that nonsense of any kind would not be tolerated.

Pyra had never hurt her so before. It served to ground her somewhat.

"It is an honor to meet you, Master Logan," she managed.

Cael himself seemed unphased and very much at home. "She is as beautiful as you described," he said.

Pyra smiled. "I knew you would agree. The moment I saw her I knew that she should be mine."

Selene had truly believed him to be dead. The realization came only now as she saw that he was not. She did not want to cry, for fear that Pyra would ask what was wrong, but this was more than she could bear. A little gasp of air threatened to turn to tears.

"She has been very emotional these past few days," Pyra remarked. She caught the first tear with her kerchief before it could ruin Selene's makeup.

"Perhaps the night wears on her," Cael replied. "Excitement at the prospect of mating has been known to trigger such things."

"Indeed, that must be the cause," Pyra said. "My poor darling thing," she added to Selene.

"No doubt this day has been most exhausting for her," Cael suggested. "Perhaps a bit of respite is in order."

"Ah yes," Pyra agreed as she leaned much closer to Cael than was necessary. "I'll send them to her room and have Datio bring some tea."

"An excellent plan."

"Xaiden, take Selene to her room," Pyra ordered. "She can show you the way."

"Yes, Mistress Pyra," he replied.

"One moment," Cael said. He waved his hand towards Xaiden's hip. The metal belt that hung at his waist dropped to thump against the grass beneath.

"I'd nearly forgotten," Pyra said with far too much excitement. "Now you may go."

It was difficult for Selene to take her eyes from Cael. Seeing him was to see an earthbound spirit. He had been nothing more than a spark of hope to her for so long. She clung to Xaiden's arm as they wove their way through the many watchful eyes of the crowd.

Walking became much easier once she managed to calm herself, and it was only when Xaiden spoke that she realized they had been travelling for several minutes in silence.

"You truly care for him." It was a realization rather than a question.

"I never said that," she replied stubbornly.

"I see," he said in a thoughtful tone that Selene did not much appreciate. "Isn't that your friend from earlier tonight?"

It took her a moment to realize that he was speaking of the silver volantes. It hovered at the end of the hall; its sinuous body reflecting flashes of light from the stones on the floor. The volantes turned an eye upon Selene before disappearing around the corner.

"We should fetch him back," Selene said decidedly.

"Your mistress will not mind?" came Xaiden's cautious reply.

"He has a penchant for escaping."

She knew that it did not answer Xaiden's question, and she did not much care. The creature led her around several corners and down a now familiar set of stairs, at the bottom of which was the curiously locked door.

"Why do you keep coming here?" she asked the creature.

It offered no more than a hiss in reply as it wove through the air near the door, eyeing it with interest.

"Are you certain we should be here?" Xaiden asked with a frown. "I seem to recall that Mistress Pyra asked me to take you to your room. It would not be wise to anger her so early in this process."

"Pyra doesn't become angry easily," she replied. "Irate, perhaps, but you must do something spectacularly aggravating to make her angry."

"How lucky for you. Regardless of that fact, I believe we should head to your room."

"I want to see what's in here first."

She had suffered enough galas and dress shops to fill a lifetime, and simply wanted a bit of adventure.

"Fine," he agreed. "Go ahead then."

It took a few seconds to realize that he had agreed with her, for the ease of it was unexpected.

"I am a bit curious myself," he explained. "And Mistress Pyra will become thoroughly occupied at any time now, given that the end of these parties are much like those Kyrros throws."

*Occupied, indeed.* She chose not to think on it any further since Cael was attending.

The volantes moved away from the door as Selene approached it. Upon testing it, she found that the lever upon the front of it was no longer locked as it had been previously. She shifted it to the opposite side, and by the luck of the Tides the door simply swung open. The volantes slipped through the space between and disappeared into the darkness beyond. Selene followed.

Inside was not what she had expected. She stepped forward into a cavern, damp though oddly warm at the same time, and complete with pointed stalactites, which clung to the ceiling. The rest was a vision of smooth, white stone, like the fountain at the market. Spheres of light set against the floor activated as they entered.

"The color of new snow," Xaiden remarked as he followed her in.

The walls felt soft and oily beneath her palms; like the bit of soapstone her father had bought her from the market as a child, long before his disappearance. *It hails from overseas*, he had said. The thought had driven her young mind wild, fueling imagined expeditions to the land of silken stone with her brother Islyr. Even still, the places she had dreamed of were nowhere as fascinating as this.

Down the stairs she crept. The beauty of this place caused them both to fall naturally to silence. At the bottom of the space the stairs ended. There the walls widened into a room with a strangely rounded floor, much the shape of the little cups used to hold tea in this place. Water dripped slowly from the ceiling to form a shallow pool around a clutch of perfectly rounded, melon-sized stones in mottled shades of white and gray.

"This place seems familiar to me," she said.

"Have you been here before?" Xaiden asked.

"No," she replied. "But I've been somewhere like this, and I feel as if there should be something more here." The silver volantes slithered around her neck once again. It was then that she saw it; a glint of light which reflected strangely from the water that clung to the walls and floor of the cavern like dew on grass in the morning.

*The cave*, her mind echoed.

A creature emerged from what Selene had previously considered to be a solid section of wall. Its sinuous body was as long as several horses. The creature's flesh was transparent enough that you could see entirely through it, past the pale white organs of its interior to the wall beyond. Selene found it difficult to track against the walls of stone surrounding.

"We must go," Xaiden whispered.

Selene was barely aware of the burn that washed over her mark, or of the pull of Xaiden's hand against her wrist as he spoke.

It was so beautiful; like the silver volantes, but magnificently grand in size; perhaps double that of the volantes she had met in her escape from the ocean cave. The creature opened its mouth. Its growl of warning rumbled through Selene's chest. Two long tendrils, stiff yet as soft as rabbit's fur, brushed first over her face and then over the body of the male volantes, which had come back to hang as a scarf would around Selene's neck. The massive creature had just levered one dark eye towards Selene when it disappeared from view; like a river of invisibility which flowed from its head backward until nothing more could be seen.

"It is a female," Xaiden said, pulling her with more effort.

Breath as cold the depths of the sea washed against Selene's face.

"They are most dangerous when guarding a clutch of eggs. We should go."

"Naevus told me that they're tame," she said as she backed away carefully.

"The males are tame," he clarified as the back of Selene's foot touched the beginning of the stairs. "Females will become attached to one master but are aggressive with most others. That is likely why the door was locked."

The silver volantes left Selene's neck suddenly to float sideways towards the female. Its fins flared in and out as it paraded through the seemingly empty space before them in an odd, floating dance. Selene could no longer feel the female's breath brush against her. It was not as comforting an idea as she had expected, for now the creature could be anywhere in the room.

"Do not move too quickly," Xaiden warned.

The volantes growled once again. Droplets of water shook from the ceiling to splash to the floor beneath.

"What in the name of the Goddess are you two doing down here?" Pyra's voice echoed from the stairwell. The woman's tone was severe, which made Selene feel as if she should turn her head towards her. Still, she feared to turn away from where the female volantes lurked.

"Isis, come here," Pyra commanded as she strode to the edge of the creature's nest.

A low hiss emanated from the massive volantes as it revealed itself. Pyra raised a hand, palm flat, and the volantes slithered over to press her side against it. With a few words of magic, what looked to be a dried worm appeared in Pyra's hand. Isis circled around eagerly to accept it.

"Now, go and lie down," Pyra ordered with a wave of her hand.

Isis issued a growl, but slipped through the cave to hover, curled like a snake, just above her clutch of eggs.

Cael appeared at the top of the staircase. "Ah, there they are," he said.

"I've told the Rakaii that cares for Isis not to leave this door unlocked," Pyra hissed as Cael descended the stairs. "Perhaps he'll require a more straightforward lesson in obedience."

"It seems as if no harm was done," Cael replied smoothly.

"I simply loathe to think that your Axiom Rakaii could have been injured," Pyra sighed. "Not to mention my beautiful Selene."

"I'm certain that such punishment could wait for tomorrow." Cael reached out to touch Pyra's shoulder. "Should we not return to the celebration?"

Pyra leaned into his touch far too easily. "We should indeed. You must accept my apologies for the distraction."

"No apologies necessary." Cael ran his fingers along Pyra's neck before releasing her.

"Come along now." Pyra wobbled in the slightest as she ascended the stairs. "You as well." The mage snapped her fingers at the male volantes. "Isis is not impressed by your mating dance."

Selene flinched as something cold touched her neck, but relaxed as she realized it was the smaller of the volantes.

"I am in a fair mood this evening." Pyra's words were mildly slurred. "Luckily for the three of you."

Selene was not pleased to be grouped in the same mental capacity as a volantes, but in order to avoid punishment she chose not to voice her thoughts on the subject.

"But that shall certainly change for the worse should your antics interrupt my festivities once again." The woman's breath was scented heavily of spices and liquor. "Now go to bed, all of you!"

"Yes, Mistress," Selene answered nearly in time with Xaiden.

She counted herself lucky that Pyra did not become more violent with drink as Aster had tended to do.

The sounds of chatter, interrupted by the occasional squeal of joy, followed Selene down the hall. As they walked and the noise faded, the volantes released from her neck once more. Perhaps it would return to its nest by the same route it had used to escape in the first place.

They reached Selen's room, and she ushered Xaiden inside. The room felt oddly empty without Datio and Naevus, as both of their narrow beds lay empty.

"You can have either bed, I suppose," she offered, for she assumed that the brothers would sleep elsewhere tonight.

Xaiden drew a deep breath. "This will undoubtedly be awkward," he said. "But we must both sleep in the same bed. They must assume that we-"

"I see," Selene interrupted. She rolled the thought around in her mind for a moment. "No more awkward than the ship, I suppose."

"There is that," he agreed. "But I am not so tired, as of yet. Would you care for some tea?"

He gestured to the pot of tea sitting between two rounded cups of precious stone, which Datio had undoubtedly left for them.

Selene sighed. Datio must have been the one who had told Pyra that they'd failed to arrive at her room, and thus the woman had come looking for them. Even when not present, the man somehow managed to aggravate her.

"That sounds fine," she agreed.

She was not much for idle chatter on any normal occasion, but she was curious to learn what had happened to them after the shipwreck. The tea had been placed, as usual, on the short table at the center of her room. Two pillows surrounded it for seating. She poured two cups, offered him one, and sat. The tea was still hot. It tasted first of cinnamon and had a pleasantly sweet aftertaste that she could not quite identify.

"Will you tell me of your journey so far?" she asked.

"With pleasure," Xaiden replied.

With the luck of the Tides, he would have enough tales to last the night.

# The Invitation
## *Kerell – Capital City*

Selene woke early. She ate breakfast despite the fact that she was not hungry, dressed with Datio and Naevus' unwanted assistance, then traveled by carriage once again to the colosseum. On this particular day, prized Rakaii and masters alike traveled together, which did not please Selene at all. This was mostly due to the fact that the seating was arranged with she and Xaiden on one side, and Cael and Pyra on the other. She struggled to keep her mind off of what had likely occurred between the two after she and Xaiden had left the party. The one grace that the Spirits offered to her this day was that Datio and Naevus had been assigned to ride in a separate carriage, which followed behind them.

"You look exhausted, my dear," Pyra noted upon surveying Selene's face.

"Sleep did not come easily, Mistress," she replied cautiously.

The answer caused Pyra to smile. "It seems that your Rakaii is as virile as you've said, Logan."

And in one night he had gone from Mr. Zephyrus to Logan. She was not certain what else to have expected, in truth, given the way Cael ingratiated himself with others so easily.

"My word is always true," Cael replied. His reddened eyes conveyed that he might have had too much to drink over the course of the previous evening and was now suffering for it.

The day was already too warm for Selene's liking, and as usual a few beads of sweat began to snake their way down her neck as they pulled through the crowds that milled beneath the columns at the entranceway. The ascent to the viewing box was brief, and by the Tides it was mildly cooler within the colosseum than it had been in the carriage.

"I'll send for some drinks," Cael offered as they reached their destination.

"Thank you," Pyra replied politely.

The drinks arrived quickly. The frigid breath of winter met Selene's fingertips as she took the glass from the attendant. She retracted her hand in surprise, nearly spilling the contents onto the tray as she did so.

"Some silly bit of magic they use to chill things," Xaiden explained in a whisper. "Have you not encountered it before?"

Selene offered her mistress a glance before speaking. Pyra was seated next to Cael at the center of the viewing box and was laughing over something he had said.

"Pyra doesn't practice a large amount of magic," she explained. "She would rather leave that to her Rakaii."

"Cael practices perhaps more than is necessary," Xaiden replied.

Selene plucked the cup from the tray once again. She swirled the cold, red liquid before taking a sip. It was nearly too saccharine and had a strong essence of mangoes. She could not taste any alcohol in this particular drink, which was surprising given the fact that a large portion of the drinks Pyra had offered her before this day contained it in some manner.

"They are unlikely to give you alcohol at this point," Xaiden explained. "Perhaps for quite some time, in fact."

She swallowed some more, enjoying the chill as it traveled down her throat, and sat at the end of the front row, a few seats down from Cael.

"Although they do lace the drinks of Rakaii with many things other than alcohol in this place," he continued as he sat beside her. "Some have little to no taste at all, so you should be cautious."

Selene set the drink carefully on a nearby table as a line of warriors bearing flags appeared in the ring below. They marched in unison, flooding the sand in the empress' colors of turquoise and gold.

"You must remember to act in an appropriate manner," Xaiden warned.

"I always do."

Xaiden's brows creased into a scowl.

"You don't trust me?"

Xaiden placed his hand upon Selene's. Her heart slowed as the calming burn of his mark ran through her. "I would not think to do otherwise."

Selene was confused at first, but then realized that Pyra's attention was upon them.

"They get along well," Pyra noted. "I would say that they were acquainted with each other previously if I didn't know the truth of it."

Selene's could not help but draw a nervous breath.

"Xaiden has always done well with other Rakaii," Cael replied with a well-crafted grin. "Give him a moment and it's as if he's known them for ages."

"Varro mentioned that you have a similar gift," Pyra said. "Though it lies with mages rather than Rakaii."

"How kind," Cael replied. "I believe I shall come to enjoy his company."

The first competitor stepped out into the ring. He wore light armor and a matching helmet, both crafted of metal and leather. With a grand gesture he swung one end of a silver post into the air. The tip of it erupted into a white flag bearing a turquoise wave with gold edges. This he placed snugly into a setting near the entrance of the arena that looked made for the purpose.

"The symbol of the empress," Xaiden whispered. "And when I speak of acting appropriately, I do mean in this particular situation."

Selene was poised to ask what he meant when the competitor removed his helmet. They were a fair distance above the sand of the arena, but not so far up as to render her unable to recognize a familiar face. It was Felan.

"Not a word," Xaiden warned.

"Such an exotically beautiful Rakaii," Pyra purred. "He may have some talent for the arena, but were he mine I would send him to Varro for training."

"A pleasure Rakaii is more than beauty," Cael replied.

"True, yet Varro can mold any Rakaii into pleasure."

"So I have heard it told," he said.

From a little box on the other side of the arena a man's voice sounded. "Greetings, to all," he shouted with glee. "And welcome to the fifth death match of our reigning champion, Ferum!" The crowd roared with approval, but quickly quieted as he continued. "Owned by our beautiful Goddess, the benevolent empress herself, he certainly is a sight to behold."

Selene looked to Xaiden, but he refused to meet her gaze. He had known about this and had chosen not to inform her of it before it began.

"And today this treasure of the empress will face the most challenging of opponents," the man continued. "One who has defeated nearly every challenger he has faced thus far."

"How is it possible to defeat *nearly* every challenger in the death matches and still continue?" Selene whispered irately.

Xaiden sighed, which was in no way a satisfactory reply and served only to deepen her displeasure.

"Xaiden?"

A horn sounded to signify the beginning of the match.

"Xaiden, who is the other competitor?"

"I'm sorry, Selene," he whispered as a massive gate on the other side of the arena rattled open.

At first there was nothing, just a void where the metal spikes of the door had once been. Then at once it thundered into the arena, spraying sand in a wave as it slid to a halt. The roar of excitement from the crowd was not loud enough to drown out its rattling screech. It was a bloodsoul, certainly, but she struggled to identify what type of animal it had been while it lived. The creature was so large that it its skull scraped against the top of the gate as it passed through, leaving bits of rotted flesh hanging from the metal tines. Its feet were thick and flat at the bottom, at least the three that still had flesh upon them, somewhat akin to trees that had been chopped at their base. Thick skin the color of a stormy sky hung in clumps from its bones, though bits of it fell free to the sand as it moved. Long, yellowed tusks protruded from the front of its head near where the mouth likely lay.

Selene stiffened. "He's to fight a bloodsoul," she said through clenched teeth. "We can't allow this to happen."

"We will allow it to happen," Xaiden whispered into her ear. "Because anything you do to stop it could well be the end of us. Now smile as if I've paid you a compliment."

Selene put on her best false smile as the creature stormed towards Felan, stopping short in an attempt to stomp him with one of its great feet. He managed to roll aside, though barely.

"Is that an elephant?" she asked through a nauseating mix of awe and horror. She had only ever seen them in paintings and tapestries.

"It is." Xaiden's eyes remained fixed on the arena below. "They're from neither here nor Evaria. I find its presence surprising, for I thought them to be extinct years past."

"I would say its presence is more horrifying than surprising," Selene countered. "And they may well be extinct. This one isn't particularly alive."

The creature charged again. It swung its tusks at Felan in an attempt to gore him, much to the delight of the crowd. Felan ducked beneath it with only a second to spare, and then crawled between the creature's feet and out the other side.

Selene failed to realize that she was leaning forward until Xaiden gently pushed her back into her seat.

"I've never seen my Selene show such interest in a match," Pyra commented to Cael. "Although, she did seem to have a strong attraction to that particular death match Rakaii when we visited last."

"Did she?" Cael raised a brow. "Yet she also seems taken with Xaiden, as you mentioned. Perhaps her interest today lies with the novelty of seeing an elephant. They are as rare as female Rakaii, from what I've heard."

Felan swept his sword through the bloodsoul's back leg at the knee. With a swing of his foot, he separated the bottom of the leg from the rest of the creature. It flew to land on the ground nearby. Felan sprinted as the creature tumbled, but he was not fast enough to avoid its full girth. The bloodsoul landed on top of him. Silence blanketed the arena as Selene watched the fallen creature struggle to rise.

Cheers erupted from the crowd once again as Felan crawled from a hole on the creature's side. He struggled, climbing out from within its chest. With a final push he tumbled to the sand below.

Selene exhaled a breath of relief, though it lasted for only a moment. The foot of the creature scraped through the sand. It reattached itself to the rest of the beast with a snapping sound much like that of a breaking tree branch. Felan, still much too close to the bloodsoul, struggled to catch his breath.

The creature stood. Its shriek of rage rattled the stands. Felan sprinted towards the opposite side of the arena. Bits of flesh splattered against the stone of the arena walls as the bloodsoul tossed its head angrily about. It found Felan's position. He could do no more than continue to run as it galloped towards him. He attempted to jump from its path, but the creature was faster. It reached his position and reared, coming down where Felan stood. He disappeared in a cloud of dust beneath its massive feet.

Selene's stomach clenched. "Where is he?" she whispered.

Xaiden's hand tightened around hers. Seconds stretched to pass as hours.

"There," Xaiden said at last.

Felan appeared from the settling dust to a rush of applause. It came too soon, for the creature was close behind him. With a toss of its massive head the bloodsoul rushed at him. One of its tusks caught Felan's side, lifting him and tossing him to strike a nearby wall with a sickening thump. He fell to the sand and did not move.

Selene leaned forward to get a better view. This time Xaiden did not restrict her.

"Xaiden," she whispered.

Felan struggled to stand. The bloodsoul pawed at the ground, sending out a spray of sand as it readied itself for a final charge.

An odd feeling caused Selene to turn. Cael's eyes met hers for no more than a second. Her heart quickened as the rush of her latent ability swept across her flesh. It was a miniscule amount, like a drop of water from a leaf after a rainstorm. Pyra must have transferred her circlet to Cael sometime last night, though she had not felt it.

Xaiden tightened his grip upon her hand until it was painful. They were connected, so he must have felt the release as she did. "No," he said through a clenched jaw.

The bloodsoul charged as Felan rose slowly to his feet. Felan grabbed his sword and held it at the ready as best he could, though Selene could see even at this distance that he was at the end of his endurance. He did not bother to flee, for perhaps he knew that he could no longer outrun it, but rather readied himself for one last stand. It was then that Selene took her chance, pulling her latent ability as the creature uttered another rumbling screech. *Falter*, she commanded it. One of the creature's front feet folded beneath it as it ran. Selene's latent ability snapped away as the bloodsoul tumbled forward, leaving a terrible, empty feeling in its wake. Felan jumped from the creature's path with no time to spare. He twisted his sword around to one side, catching it on the bloodsoul's bony neck. The creature's head split away from its body. The head struck the sand, landing upright, steadied by its giant, yellowed tusks. Felan climbed atop the skull. He thrust his sword through it, pinning the head of the creature to the floor of the arena.

Selene startled as the horn sounded to signify the end of the match. She drew a ragged breath of relief. Felan had won.

Xaiden said something as he released her hand, though his words were lost to the noise of the audience. The walk back down the steps and out to the carriage was mostly lost to her as well, for the stress of the battle combined with the sudden rush and subsequent loss of her latent ability had made focusing difficult. Xaiden's posture alone told her that he was displeased with her. She found that she did not much care. She had not been discovered, and the match would have ended much differently without her interference.

"That was by far the most exciting match I have witnessed in quite some time," Pyra remarked as she settled herself next to Cael in the carriage.

"Agreed," Cael replied. "One can never predict how a death match will end."

"Did you find it odd, how the creature stumbled?" she added as the carriage pulled forward.

"Not in the least," Cael replied. "From what I hear tell, that creature has been falling apart since they obtained it. It is only by some odd bit of magic that it keeps what little flesh it has left on its bones."

"True," Pyra laughed. "Well, I must say that I am eager to see your estate. I've been told that it is one of the finest in the city.

"I believe I shall leave you to judge that for yourself," Cael replied with a slip of a grin. "To praise what is under my ownership would be highly impolite."

They arrived at the estate in little time. It was just long enough that perhaps Xaiden had forgiven her, for the burn of his mark calmed her as his hand once again found hers. The twists of the road allowed Selene a view of the entrance gate, and there she glimpsed statues of what she had learned with Datio's assistance to be male lions. They were of such a height that she could only glimpse the bottom of their massive jaws as the carriage rolled through a gateway large enough for two of the creatures to lay end to end. The wall of stone that ran behind them was thick enough that it would surely keep the beasts out, had they been real. Beyond the wall was a jungle to rival the one she had raced through on the day of her capture. Four guardsmen pulled closed a set of tall, iron gates with aid of magic as they passed.

"Your grounds are perfectly manicured," Pyra noted as they passed a small waterfall with a pond beneath.

Selene realized upon hearing the words, and with another look through the expertly polished window, that the jungle outside was not wild as it appeared, but rather expertly crafted to mimic the wilds. Each plant had been placed artistically for best composure amongst its brethren with ample space for growth between, and very few dead leaves lay within her sight.

"You are most kind," Cael replied.

"Do you have a Rakaii in your employ with an ability to grow plants?"

"I have heard that my family did, long ago," Cael replied. "But the success of my garden today can only be attributed to my groundskeeper and his many apprentices."

"And you have animals," Pyra added. "They're delightful. Are they Rakaii as well?"

Several lanky gray creatures with odd yellow eyes regarded them from the branch of a nearby tree.

"Lemurs," Cael replied. "Not Rakaii. They are not captive, but free to come and go as they please. The wall is no obstacle for them."

"What an interesting concept," Pyra mused. "But allowing for free will can be most dangerous in lesser animals. Do you not worry that they will leave for the wilds and never return?"

"I have found the opposite to be true," Cael replied. "All you must do is provide them with an incentive to return. In this instance, many of the trees my ancestors planted here bear fruit, and the wall provides protection from predators. Not only do the lemurs return, but they have done so for many generations."

"How clever," Pyra replied. "Incentive sways animals and humans alike, it seems." She placed a hand on Cael's thigh.

Cael did not recoil from the gesture, as Selene so wished he would, but rather placed his hand atop Pyra's. Selene had little time to become irritated with the situation, as they had arrived at the front of the manor. Several well-groomed servants rushed out to stand at attendance as the carriage slowed. The entrance was a rounded building which was open to the air. Cleanly swept ground turned into a flat expanse of mosaic floor patterned with lily pads and colorful fish. The mosaic floor dropped off abruptly to become a true pond accented with live water lilies in bloom.

Cael raised a hand, and with a twitch of his fingers a servant appeared with a tray, atop which sat a decanter of spirits and four delicately blown glass cups. Selene looked up from the tray as the man drew close. She was startled by the familiarity of the face. It was Jevelir. He smiled and bowed his head politely, then filled the cups one at a time, handing them out in the proper order according to importance; Cael, Pyra, Selene, and lastly Xaiden. Naevus and Datio, who stood at Pyra's side, received nothing, though if they were displeased by the fact then it did not show upon their faces. Jevelir then bowed once again and left the room.

"A toast to new beginnings," Cael announced over the trickle of water from a central fountain.

"To new beginnings, indeed," Pyra echoed.

The ping of glass against glass rang in Selene's ears as Cael's glass touched Pyra's.

"Selene?" Xaiden was staring at her with his glass and one eyebrow raised.

She tapped her glass to his and drank. The spirits were cold and bitter upon her tongue. Upon remembering what Xaiden had said she then downed the rest of the glass. This might be the last time that she was offered a true drink for quite some time, and her nerves were still somewhat in a knot from the events of the colosseum.

Selene's attention was drawn to a nearby doorway as Jevelir reappeared. The man glanced at Cael cautiously, as if afraid to speak.

"I assume you have something to tell me," Cael said between sips of drink.

"A most important visitor has arrived, Master Logan," Jevelir answered. His voice was laced with trepidation. "I have been told she passes through the gate at this moment and will soon grace us with her presence."

"He is suddenly quite nervous," Pyra remarked. "Why does he not speak plainly?"

"I indulge in a great many hobbies," Cael explained. "As you may have heard, one such diversion is the acquisition of labor, Rakaii and mages alike who, having failed under their previous masters, thus require additional training."

"Yes, I have heard something to that effect," Pyra mused. "You are a champion of those who are lost and require direction. An admirable trait. I would not have the patience for such."

"My belief is that no being exists who cannot be trained. One must only find the appropriate method to do so."

"You have so many ideas of great interest. But perhaps we should speak on this later. I'm greatly intrigued by whom this visitor might be."

"Jevelir," Cael said, turning his attention to the man. "A name?"

"The Goddess." Jevelir's voice shook in the slightest as the words left his lips.

Cael and Pyra stood almost as one.

"Show her in the instant she arrives at the door," Cael commanded. "It would not do for her to deem us uncourteous."

Datio rushed to check Pyra's makeup and hair, while Naevus smoothed her robe. It was just in time, for Jevelir returned to them in no more than a few short moments. He was followed by six mages draped in fine clothing the turquoise color of warm ocean waters. Strands of gold had been braided through their hair and twisted around their arms in spiraled bands. They parted, three upon each side of the room, to allow the empress entrance. She was a vision as ethereal as the realm she commanded. Her fine skin held the sheen of a pearl beneath the dappled light of the room. The cloth of her resplendent attire was so light as to seem intangible. It contoured her form as she walked, and portions of it floated behind her as a spirit would move through the night.

Selene was the last to bend to knee, and it was Xaiden who pulled her to the floor. They were there for only a few seconds before the empress bid them to rise. She then prompted Cael to speak.

"I am honored that you would choose to grace us with your presence, Empress," he said with lowered eyes. Selene had heard that looking directly into the empress' eyes without being asked to do so was considered an offense which could cause one a great amount of pain, depending on the woman's mood. She had also heard that the empress rarely gave permission for such.

"You do not ask why I am here?"

"If you find me worthy of knowing the answer then you will surely provide it," Cael said smoothly.

"A silver tongue can be an admirable trait," she remarked. "So long as it is combined with loyalty to one's empress."

"You shall have my loyalty always, my Goddess."

"Look upon me," she commanded. "I would see for myself if the tales of the mysterious Mr. Zephyrus are truth or fallacy."

Cael lifted his gaze to meet that of the empress, as commanded. Selene took the chance to get a better look at the woman without fear of accidentally drawing her wrath. The empress' narrow face was accented by a sloping nose, much like a bird of prey. Selene imagined that she was one of many things of nature which were both exquisite and dangerous at once, such as the mottled scales of a saltsnake, or the delicate feathery appendages of the creatures that had poisoned her in the caves beneath the shoreline what seemed like so many moons ago. She could tell that the empress saw beauty in Cael as well, for the corner of her mouth twitched into a momentary smile as she pulled from his gaze.

Selene dipped her eyes to the floor as the empress turned her way. She shifted her gaze to one side as the woman placed a finger beneath her chin and lifted it upward.

"And what are my thoughts on you?" the empress asked.

Selene knew that she was not meant to reply, but still found it challenging to keep silent.

"She was difficult to train?"

Selene risked a glance at her mistress. Pyra's posture was stiff, and although her face was still pointed towards the floor it was clear that the woman had not expected to have been called upon to speak.

"I have heard that it is so, my Goddess. She was trained before I obtained her."

"Her soul is strong." The woman brushed her fingers against Selene's cheek. Her skin was surprisingly warm. "And ravens are an omen of luck," she added upon glancing over Selene's shoulder at her mark.

With a twist of her fingers the empress motioned for one of her guards to come forward. Selene thanked the Spirits that there was finally something new to keep the woman's attention. The mage produced several cards of parchment and a quill from somewhere beneath her robes. She wrote something on one of the cards and handed it to Cael. The writing upon it twisted in Selene's gaze, refusing to be read. She then wrote out a second card and handed it to Pyra.

"You will come to my bath house today, after the sun has fallen," the empress informed them. "And you will bring your Rakaii, the stallion and the raven both, for it will please me."

Cael and Pyra bowed deeply in place of a reply.

Selene moved her gaze back to the floor. Fabric from the empress' robe trailed past her, floating as if swept by a breeze that did not exist. And then she was gone, leaving as suddenly as she had arrived. Moments passed in silence before anyone dared to speak.

"I had planned on spending the night here," Pyra chirped. "But I beg your forgiveness Logan, for I must go. I have so much to prepare in the few hours left to me. Surely you understand?"

"I do," Cael replied. "Think no more of it, for you have caused me no insult. I'll have one of my Rakaii send up a carriage to deliver you back to your estate."

"What they say of your manners; it is surely true." Pyra kissed him once upon each cheek. "Be well then. I shall see you tonight."

"I look forward to it."

Pyra took only a few steps down the hall, with Datio and Naevus trailing behind her, before pausing. "An invitation to the baths of the empress, and within such a short time of knowing you. Surely it is a blessing from the Goddess herself that we've become acquainted." She then made an agile turn, continuing down the hall and out the door.

All was quiet between them until it was certain that Pyra was truly away. It was then Jevelir who spoke first.

"A champion of those who are lost?" He erupted with a snort of laughter.

"Pyra's words, not mine," Cael replied. He topped his cup with spirits and handed it to Jevelir.

"It is so very lovely to make your acquaintance, oh savior of poorly trained Rakaii."

"She does seem rather attached to me," Cael admitted.

"Savior, my balls," Jevelir swore as he downed the contents of the cup in a single gulp.

"You're lucky I purchased you from that auction house before anyone else could, my friend, or you might no longer have them," Cael quipped.

Jevelir laughed and clapped Cael on the shoulder. "Should I take that to mean you don't think me handsome enough for a pleasure Rakaii?"

"Near enough," Cael replied with a wry smile.

"Hand me the rest of the spirits, will you? Today has been enough for me already, despite the fact that it is still young. I thought we were done for when the empress arrived."

"As did I," Cael admitted. "There's more of that in the larder, if you have want of it later," he offered as Jevelir started away with the bottle. "I imagine we might not be back here tonight."

"I must agree. I assume you'll want something to present to her. It's unwise to appear without a gift or several."

"You assume correctly. Leave it by the entryway, will you? And construct it before the drink takes hold, if you please."

"Of course, Master Zephyrus." The statement was accompanied by a mockingly clipped bow. "It has been lovely to see you again, lady Selene," he added before turning on heel and departing.

"What does he mean by that?" Cael asked as Jevelir disappeared around a corner. "Have you met before?"

"Yes," Selene replied. "He helped me a great deal when I first arrived in this Spirits-forsaken place. Did he not mention it to you?"

"No," Cael replied. "Although I suppose it doesn't matter. I'm simply pleased that you're here, and that Pyra has finally gone so that we might speak openly."

"Yes, we must thank the Spirits for Pyra's vanity," Xaiden said.

"Indeed," Cael agreed. "Otherwise, we'd never be rid of her."

"But there is no clothing permitted in the empress' bath house," Selene said. "At least if what Datio and Naevus have told me is true. I cannot imagine what she might need to prepare without need of getting dressed."

"Much plucking of stray hairs and oiling of skin, I'd imagine," Cael said.

Selene would rather that he did not imagine, in truth.

"An invitation to bathe with the empress is not to be taken lightly," Xaiden informed them. "I shall give you a moment, for surely you have much to discuss. After that you should prepare to depart." And with that he walked away, leaving them truly alone.

She should have had many things to say to Cael, but yet the words lay trapped and refused to leave her tongue. Would she tell him the tales of her mistreatment by Aster, or of her hope all the while that he was not truly dead despite the odds against such. Would it matter to him at all if she did?

"This place has not changed him," she said instead, referring to Xaiden, as it seemed the safest topic of conversation.

"No, it wouldn't," Cael said. He ran one hand through his hair. It was shorter than she had remembered ever seeing it.

The silence that followed was too much to bear, and she decided at once that asking directly was the best route to follow for the sake of her sanity. "You weren't at my auction," she said flatly. "Surely you knew of it, for you sent Xaiden there afterward, and you must have purchased Jevelir there as well."

"There were circumstances beyond my control," he replied.

"What play of circumstance could possibly be of more importance than saving me from an eternity of slavery?" She could feel the weight of anger pressing against her chest. She struggled to smother it.

"I wanted to. You must believe it to be so. I simply could not afford you."

"Truly?" Selene could not keep the heat from her voice. "Do the other mages lie when they say that you're one of the wealthiest and most influential mages in this realm?"

"No." Cael bit down upon his lower lip. "They do not lie."

"Did you not just a moment ago receive an invitation to bathe with the empress herself?"

"Selene, I wanted to come for you."

"That is to say nothing of the fine clothes, the private viewing box at the arena, and so many staff and Rakaii. Yet you say that you could not afford me. Are we not standing upon the vast acreage of your magnificent estate? How did you obtain all of this, yet somehow you cannot afford the one thing that should mean the most?"

"I did not purchase most of these things," he insisted.

"Then how did you come by all of this finery? Did the benevolent Spirit of exquisite things drop it at your feet while you slept?"

"No need for sarcasm."

Selene heaved a sigh. "I need you to explain."

"Your anger is justified."

"That was never in question. And it is not an explanation."

"I assure you that I did not purchase any of the things I own here. They were given to me. The circumstances surrounding the acquisition are rather unusual however, and thus my liquid assets were rather in short supply for some time."

"So you say," she huffed.

Had he used his latent ability to achieve this? It would make sense, though it would be a great risk to do so in this place.

"Finding a way to get to you has been foremost in my thoughts since we arrived here. Ask Xaiden if you like. I never meant to abandon you."

"But yet you did."

"What can I do to appease you?" he asked. "There must be something I can give in apology that you'll accept."

"Not that I can think of, aside from my freedom."

"It is too great a risk," he said. "But I'll give you this as a show of good faith."

Selene gasped as the full force of her latent abilities returned to her. She had been without them for so long that the flood of it warmed her veins more so than the strongest of spirits. It both calmed and elated her at once. With the return of her power, her anger pulled away like waves receding near low tide.

"You did warn me of the danger," she admitted. "I agreed to come to this place."

"Yes, but I would never have asked you to join me if I'd dreamed of this turn of events. It was meant to be the three of us together."

"You'll swear to me that's the truth of it?"

"I swear it. I read the notice of auction and knew it could be no one else but you. I couldn't bring myself to attend when I knew that I didn't have the funds to purchase you."

"You could have rescued me. Stolen me away."

"You've seen much of this place and its people. Enough to know that I could not have traveled far with a stolen Rakaii of your value. I offered Xaiden's services to Pyra because I wanted him to tell me that you were well."

"As well as one can be while enslaved."

"Have faith that we'll find a way to free you."

"How simple for you to say so as you walk free. Does the plan to win my freedom begin before or after I'm offered up for breeding like a mare in heat?"

"I became close with Pyra and offered Xaiden for your first breeding. All of that was done only to give us time to come up with a viable plan. You're safe for now. It's the best I can do."

"And when my imaginary union with Xaiden fails to produce a child?"

"These things can take time in some instances. We have perhaps a few months before she begins to think anything of it."

"I suppose."

"For now, we should prepare. The empress will expect nothing less than our finest, therefore some grooming will be required. Walk with me and I'll show you to your room."

The trickling water faded as she followed him, leaving only the tapping of their bare feet against the tiles of the floor.

"Pyra sent over enough clothing for ten Rakaii while we were out. Jevelir told me it required several carriages."

"She does have some strange love of dressing me in ridiculous things," Selene noted. "Though with as little as the people here care for clothing it's a wonder anyone bothers."

"The main concerns in this place are status and fashion."

"I feel as if I'm properly clothed, yet I'm barely wearing anything at the moment."

"I had noticed that, yes," Cael replied distantly as they stopped within a doorway.

Selene entered the room. It was easily half again as large as her room at Pyra's estate.

"This is a bedroom?" she asked in jest. "Shouldn't it have a bed?"

Cael led her to a smaller, connected room. Within, beneath an arched window, lay a bedframe with a plush looking mattress bearing sheets in tones of orange and gold.

"Tell me," she began as she pressed a hand to the fabric. "What shall I wear for the Empress' party?"

"Would you like me to choose something for you?"

"I've not been given a great many choices these past few months. Perhaps I'm no longer able to make decisions for myself."

Cael furrowed his brow. "Surely you can't believe that."

"Of course not, but you wouldn't know what it's like to never be given a choice, would you?"

"In fact, I would," he countered. "My life was not my own for some great length, in a time before you were so much as a wisp of thought."

"You've never told me of such."

"Because I do not like to speak of it," he said. "Surely you are in a position to understand. Many of our kind have suffered at the hands of the Kerell." His eyes traveled the length of her.

She looked down at the dress she currently wore, which as usual was no more than a few strips of fabric. "Back home I'd be flogged for appearing in public dressed in so little."

He lifted a strip of her dress between his fingertips. "My first thought upon seeing you in this was certainly not to flog you."

"Is that so?" Selene closed the distance between them.

She gave in then, and pressed her body close to him, burying her face in his neck. The scent of him was somewhat different, hidden amongst spices that she would have once considered exotic, but beneath it was what she searched for. She dragged it into her lungs. It was the scent of home, comforting and familiar. She pressed her lips gently to his neck. The rushing burn of his mark did not come forth to greet her as expected.

"I cannot feel you," she gasped.

"I encounter Rakaii far too often in this place," he replied. "It would betray me."

"But how did you accomplish it?"

"The silver liquid that Damaeus discovered. It seems that he shipped quite a large amount of it here before his demise, as it is commonly available. I can still practice the magic of the mages, but the feeling of my mark remains hidden to others. A few drops in my tea each morning is enough."

"They used it in my capture," Selene said distantly.

She buried the thought and pressed her lips to his.

"I have missed you, in truth," she said as they parted.

"There are a few details I feel you should know before you continue with what you are currently planning," he said in a whisper.

Selene pressed herself more firmly against him. "Do you not approve of my plan?"

"You can tell that I do."

She certainly could, for his body betrayed him.

"Perhaps the details could wait," she suggested. "If only for a short time."

"I don't know that they should." Cael's voice trembled in the slightest. She would never have noticed, had she not been so close to him. "What I must tell you; it should have been said long before we left."

"If that's so, then it cannot matter overly much," she insisted as she bit lightly upon his ear.

"But it can. It could change many things."

Selene pulled away from him just far enough to meet his gaze. "This place seems created of differences. Nothing here is at all like Evaria and that, I must believe, is of the Goddess' design. No words can change this place for better or, by the Spirits, cause it to be worse."

"I must disagree."

She pressed a finger to his lips. "Listen to me now," she ordered in whispering tones. "Neither fate nor the mages have allowed me a decision of my own since I arrived in this Spirits-forsaken land. Might I be allowed at least a single choice before I return to an eternity of being Rakaii once again?"

He pushed her hand aside in order to speak. "Is this really what you want?"

"We are connected by a circlet. Can you not tell that I do?"

He released the clasp that held the fabric of her dress. It made no sound as it slithered to the floor.

"You do realize that mages are not permitted to lay with female Rakaii," he said as his hands ran smoothly across her bare skin.

"Obviously I do," she replied as her fingers strayed below the small of his back.

"I could be put to death for this."

"Then why haven't you stopped?"

"I'm afraid it's far too late for that," he said with a laugh. "Not without causing myself a great deal of discomfort, anyway."

"In that case, just listen and do as I say." Selene pushed him over and pinned him atop the mattress.

Time lingered perfectly, and they had just enough of it to be ready to depart before Xaiden came to find them.

"You were supposed to be getting ready for our audience with the empress," he informed them upon surveying the somewhat disheveled room.

"We are ready," Selene replied as she tossed a stray pillow back onto the bed.

"Apart for so many days, and this is how you choose to spend your time together?"

"You can think of some way better?" Selene asked, knowing that he likely could not come up with any.

"She began it," Cael said. "I am guilty only of compliance."

"And if someone should bear witness?"

"Then I would first ask what they are doing in my house uninvited," Cael snapped. "Let's go. We mustn't be late for our audience with the Goddess. Although it will likely be nowhere near as pleasant as what recently occurred, it could also end with me being put to death."

# The Past
## *Kerell – Capital City*

The empress' bath house was simultaneously roughly hewn and more luxurious than anything Selene could have brought forth from her imagination. It was built upon a hot spring within a cave created by nature. Portions of rough stone between the stalactites which hung from the ceiling had been smoothed in order to bear painted histories. The scenes' gilded edges reflected the rippling of the water beneath. The stone was cold, yet the water, as it had been for her very first bath at Aster's home upon arriving here, was warm enough that she felt it might sear her flesh.

The empress herself was already within, her nudity barely concealed beneath the ripples that crossed the surface of the water. Flanking her on the left was a female Rakaii who was wearing no more than a tiny circlet of blue crystal and gold above one ear.

Circling the outside of the pool, lingering stoically upon the sand-colored stone, were six of the empress' mages. Selene recognized their robes of turquoise and gold from their visit to Cael's estate.

"I have brought an offering," Cael said.

He handed a package wrapped in white silken fabric to the nearest mage. The woman waved a hand over the item, then nodded to her peers before passing it on to the empress.

"May it please the Goddess." Cael bent low at the waist.

The empress rested the gift on the ledge that surrounded the pool and pulled the silver bow which held it. The fabric fell away to reveal a rounded gemstone whose swirling colors of yellow and white put Selene in mind of the sun at mid-day. Bright wisps of color erupted into the air above it like fireworks in miniature. The colors turned to a flock of birds and then to a school of tiny fish with flowing fins before disappearing in a burst of sparkling light. Jevelir had done well in creating the gift. It was beautiful.

"This pleases me." The empress raised a hand from the water to beckon them. "Come."

They shed their robes, placing them neatly upon a nearby bench. Selene allowed Xaiden to take hers, as it seemed that it was expected. The urge to cover her more sensitive parts in a room full of strangers was still quite strong, even after being in this place for such a time. How long had it been? The days had begun to blend with each other like one of Pyra's saccharine drinks.

The clothing of Kerell at least offered the feeling of being covered, which turned out to matter much more than it should. Cael and Xaiden seemed to have no more issue with nudity than those who had been born here. Perhaps they simply hid it well, for Xaiden had acted differently at home.

The calm of Xaiden's mark washed over Selene as he took her hand to escort her into the bath. She reminded herself once again that the water would not burn her as she gingerly set one foot and then the other onto the top step. At the bottom of the pool a colorful mosaic of tiles had been set, the theme of which was difficult to make out due to the movement of the water. This bath was different from the others Selene had experienced in that only one side of it held stairs. The other sides had benches of carved stone, which were set at just the right height so that most of the occupants would be up to their shoulders in water when seated upon them. Pyra and Cael took a place to the empress' right, and Xaiden and Selene to her left, near the female Rakaii. The heat of the pool quickly seeped into Selene's bones as she sat, dissolving her anxiety. Perhaps this would not be so trying an event as she had assumed.

"How do you find my bath house, Logan?" the empress asked.

"It is more elegant than any I have seen, my Goddess." Cael kept his eyes to the water as he replied.

"I intend to learn much about you this evening," the empress informed him. "Therefore, I give you permission to return my gaze for the remainder of your time in my palace. What say you to this?"

"I would say that I am honored by such a permission, Goddess."

"As it should be. Sit closer, for I find your form more pleasing than most."

The empress waved away her Rakaii who, much to Selene's irritation, came to sit directly at her side. Warmth rushed through her mark, causing the heat of the pool to seem as nothing, as the woman ran a finger along her arm. Seldom had she seen anyone with finer features. Dark eyes met Selene's with curiosity from beneath the short curls that graced the woman's head.

Cael swam expertly across the middle of the pool, temporarily obscuring the lighted stones that had been spaced throughout the bottom. He settled himself directly next to the empress at her urging and angled himself so that he was facing her.

"Logan Zephyrus," the empress began. "Named after your grandfather. I pride myself in knowing all of the upper caste in my city, as well as the lands beyond. And so, you might imagine my interest upon hearing tales of your sudden appearance. Wherever have you been hiding?"

"During the time when my mother still lived, we traveled seeking new lands. After her passing I attempted to stake my claim in the Wildlands, having been raised there for a portion of my young life. It is as untamed as one would expect."

"The Wildlands?" the empress mused. "What a wonder that you are so cultured. The tales of your return are grandly told amongst those in my city, though perhaps they are exaggerated, as stories tend to be." The empress turned her attention to Pyra. "Tell me, what have you heard amongst the upper caste of Logan's journey?"

"It is said that he encountered a group of sirens and their kraken on the return to his ancestral home, my Goddess. They say that only by Ethereal Grace did he and one of his Rakaii survive the attack."

"Like a history of old. But is it the truth?"

"It is the truth, my Goddess," Cael answered. "Sadly, the wealth that I had collected during my time in the Wildlands now belongs to the sea, as does my ship and its crew."

"What luck that your estate had not been sold during your absence," the empress mused. "It was widely thought that the last of your direct family line had crossed to the thereafter. If you had sent word, indeed if anyone in the city had known of your existence, certainly you would have been summoned and your lands would have been held for your return."

Selene resisted the urge to shift on her rocky seat. The conversation was crossing into dangerous ground, and she could do nothing but hope that Cael could turn it back to his favor.

"I did send regular correspondence in the form of monthly letters to my late cousin's wife, who until recently held the title to the estate."

"Ah, yes, Thera," the empress replied. "Barren and unwilling to take an outside heir. Her death was unexpected. May she be renowned in the thereafter despite her faults."

"I appreciate your gracious thoughts," Cael replied formally with a nod of his head. "Though you might imagine why I was never mentioned, considering what effect it would have on her claim to the estate."

"I might," the empress mused. "You should know that your grandfather was a favorite of mine in his youth. His soul held great strength. His mark bloomed much later than others, but it is well known that the most beautiful flowers open at night, after all others are spent. When it was found that he was Rakaii I was elated, for I could at last have the chance to own him. His mother accepted my generous offer of compensation with pride, but it was not to be."

"Ah yes," Cael said. "I was told that the blaze consumed all who dwelt within the estate."

"It was my greatest disappointment when I was told that he passed into the thereafter. I still think on it to this day. I suppose it is good fortune for us both that your grandfather spread his seed widely before his passing, for if there is one family line that the sky would weep to see the end of, it is that of Zephyrus."

"I am honored by your words, my Goddess."

"You bear more than a passing resemblance to him."

"So I have been told."

Selene looked to the water just in time, for the empress' gaze turned suddenly upon her. The warmth of the female Rakaii's mark trickled up her arm once again as the girl's fingers encompassed her wrist.

"You must follow me," the Rakaii said. She swam gracefully, as would one who is born to the water, and stopped upon reaching the steps of the pool. Once there she motioned for Selene and Xaiden to follow.

"Eva will take care of your Rakaii while we entertain ourselves," the empress announced.

A male Rakaii appeared, carrying a tray containing a bottle of cut crystal filled with clear liquid, along with three matching cups.

"You may look upon me as well, Pyra," the empress informed her. "Only for tonight."

"I cannot express my thanks, Goddess." Pyra's voice trembled with excitement.

The warmth of the water lingered oddly on Selene's body after she left it, and the linens that Eva handed her to dry her skin were as soft as rabbit's fur. The woman pulled several silken robes from where they hung in an alcove cut into the cavern wall. She handed one each to Selene and Xaiden before donning one herself. The fabric was nearly as warm as the water of the pool. Selene resisted the urge to look back at Cael as she left, difficult though it was.

Eva escorted them up a set of stairs. They soon arrived in what appeared to be a dining hall, which was open to the night on one side. A long table was set with bowls of dried fruit, flat bread, and cured meats. Attached to the room was a balcony that looked out upon the lights of the city below. Selene stepped to the railing. She rested her arms against it, leaning out into the cool air. In the distance lay the edge of Kerell, and beyond that, the ocean. Its dark waves reflected a crescent moon and a layer of stars that lay scattered throughout the clear night sky. Pyra was reluctant to allow her to use her animal form. How long had it been since she'd flown? Perhaps with Cael she might meet the sky once again.

Eva's hands found Selene's shoulders, working away what little tension was left there after the heat of the water had subsided. She pressed her lips to Selene's neck. Selene slipped from her grasp and turned to face her. The heat of the woman's lips lingered, running pleasantly down her spine.

"Do not worry," Eva said. "The empress allows me to engage in whatever pleasures I find." Her lips then found Selene's, and Selene found that she had no desire to deny her. She drifted in the pleasant warmth of Eva's mark and the touch of her flesh for a tantalizing moment. The sound of Xaiden clearing his throat jolted her back to her senses.

"I should not," Selene said as she stepped back.

"Your mate could join us if you wish," Eva offered. "The empress has no need to find a particular match for me, as her caste is already higher than any other in the realm. If I should come by a child from the union, then all the better, for Xaiden is of strikingly high quality."

Xaiden looked uncomfortable, at best, though whether due to the offer or the compliment she could not be certain. Perhaps it was both.

"The issue isn't whether or not Xaiden should join us," Selene began, for in truth she was uncertain of what she should say.

"Are you not fond of other females?" Eva asked. "I have heard that there are female Rakaii who prefer only males for pleasure, though I have yet to meet one."

"I am fond of both males and females," Selene assured her. Thoughts of Kalia slipped briefly from the archives of her memory despite her best effort to contain them.

"Am I not pleasing to look upon?"

Selene's mind struggled to find a reply that didn't involve her allegiance to Cael.

"You are very beautiful," she said at last.

"Then why?" The woman seemed greatly confused by the situation, as if she had never encountered such a thing in her time and was uncertain of what to do next. "The Empress has given me orders to entertain you."

"Do not worry upon it," Xaiden said, placing a hand on the girl's shoulder. "Selene is quite devoted and so prefers to keep to only one mate while breeding."

"Surely there are other activities with which you could keep us entertained," Selene suggested.

"Perhaps you could show us some of the palace," Xaiden offered. "I would be greatly interested to view the opulence of this place firsthand."

"The grounds are vast, and I am allowed to wander freely through most of them," Eva informed them proudly. "What would you like to see?"

"Is there a garden?" Selene asked as she followed Eva away from the balcony and out of the room.

"Yes, of course," Eva replied.

"Of what kind?" Selene inquired, for she wished to keep the girl talking.

"There are so many. One has been planted with fruit trees, and there is a butterfly garden. The empress' favorite is one which is filled exclusively with exotic flowers."

"Perhaps one with water?"

"I do love the ones with water best," Eva said excitedly. "My mark is of water, do you see?" She proudly displayed the swirling shape that graced her back near her right shoulder. It was a mark that Selene had not previously seen, though in truth she had witnessed few of the great many types that seemed to exist.

"Mark of an otter," Xaiden said.

"Yes." Eva smiled. "I've been told that the animals themselves are common in the cold water of the Wildlands. None live here, sadly, or else I might ask the empress if I could have one."

"She would simply give it to you?" Selene asked in wonder.

"Of course," Eva replied. "The empress is most kind. Every second week I am allowed a single item of my choosing. She gives me most anything I ask for."

Pyra often gave Selene things, but rarely had the woman actually asked what she might like to have. It was perplexing, to say the least, that the empress would do so.

Eva eagerly described each portion of the grounds as they passed through it. Selene feigned interest, nodding eagerly as areas from aviaries to dining halls were described in great detail, until at once something odd caught her attention.

"What is this place?" Selene asked, levering her gaze around a partially closed set of doors.

"That room is… not my favorite," Eva replied cryptically.

"May I see it, just for a moment?"

"Yes, of course. It is not restricted." Eva pushed the door aside with a sniff of distaste.

Inside was one of the strangest sights Selene had witnessed since coming to this place. She first focused upon what had caught her interest through the door. It was much like a horse in shape and size, yet its fur was patterned in stripes of black and white. As her eyes adjusted, she realized that it was just one of many animals in the room. All had been prepared, stuffed and preserved like a deer's head in a tavern. Yet these animals were whole and had been arranged in poses as if still alive.

Behind the oddly colored horse she recognized a male lion. A thick mane of fur surrounded the creature's face. It had been set in the air next to the horse as if pouncing upon it and was held up by thin posts of metal. Its mouth was open, exposing teeth large enough to lance a man's head. Its knife-like claws protruded as if ready to tear into the horse's flesh. The creature was a great deal larger than what she had imagined.

Similar scenes were fixed in time throughout the room, which itself was easily four times longer than the dining hall at home. The extent of the space had been decorated as if it was outdoors, complete with sand upon the ground, live trees and twisting vines which hung from the ceiling. Each section was made to represent a different environment, perhaps where the creatures naturally lived. Upon the walls each scene was extended by magic, so that there seemed to be no walls at all but rather an open, outdoor space to match the decoration.

"This is the trophy room," Eva said with none of the enthusiasm that she had offered for the previous rooms.

Selene wandered down the path of flat stones that split the room into two sides. Some animals, like a fox and a rabbit sporting white winter fur, she recognized at once. Others, like the gryphon, she knew only from books or tapestries. There was even an elephant, which looked much kinder than the bloodsoul version, with its full coating of gray skin. She marveled at its absurdly long nose, which the decayed one in the arena had lacked. At the end of the room a waterfall in miniature cascaded into a shallow pool lined with stones.

"These animals are all male," Xaiden noted.

It was true. Selene realized at once why Eva had such a strong dislike of this room.

"These were all Rakaii," she murmured.

"Yes," Eva replied. "It is difficult to get them to stay in animal form after death, so a mix of magic and common taxidermy is used."

Selene's breath did not come as easily as it had a moment ago. "I believe I've seen enough. Perhaps we should move on to something else."

She spied a small door to the side.

"What does that room hold?"

"I would be happy to show you." Eva rushed past Selene. Her quickened movements were so unlike anything she had seen from the woman thus far. "This door leads to the portrait room."

It sounded safe enough, leastways, and likely to be free of stuffed Rakaii. Selene followed Eva and Xaiden inside. The sound of falling water faded as she pulled the door closed behind her.

The portrait room was, as named, a room full of painted portraits. It was larger than the size of the door had conveyed, and thankfully included a door at the other end, so that they would not have to go back through the trophy room to get to the hall.

So eager was Selene to get away from the room of stuffed marked ones that she did not notice that Xaiden had stopped walking. She might have bumped against him had he not put out a hand to stop her.

"Is something wrong?" Eva's hand was already poised to open the door upon the far side of the room.

"No," Xaiden replied. "Whom did you say these portraits depict?"

"I had not been given the opportunity," Eva informed him. "Our benevolent empress commissions portraits of her most beloved marked ones and subjects of the upper caste. They are all kept in this room."

Xaiden turned quickly and kept walking, motioning for Selene to follow. It was then that a particular portrait stood out amongst the others.

"Ah, yes," Eva said, following Selene's gaze. "This is your master's grandfather. As you likely heard earlier, he was a favorite."

"I thought the empress said that he passed to the thereafter before she could own him."

"He was a member of the upper caste when this was commissioned, or so I have been told. His family had not yet discovered that he was truly a Rakaii."

"We should move on," Xaiden suggested.

"They greatly resemble each other," Eva said. "I hadn't realized how much so until seeing this. It is no wonder that the Goddess is so taken with Master Logan."

They didn't merely resemble each other. The portrait was of Cael, much younger, yet otherwise exact down to the rogue wave of hair that always fell across his face. Cael had not lied his way into taking someone else's estate. It had belonged to him all along. The man was posing as his own grandson, and by the longevity of a marked one he looked the part. Selene's stomach twisted uncomfortably as her mind turned over the unspoken portion of Cael's plan. It was a part he had neglected to share with her when asking her to come to this place.

"Xaiden?" she muttered. "Were you aware of this?"

Xaiden sighed deeply. "Yes, I have long been aware that master Zephyrus' grandfather was a favorite of the empress."

The meaning was clear enough to her. He had known that Cael was from this place, though it would be foolish to state it plainly within Eva's hearing. Words strong enough to convey how angry she was at this moment did not exist in either the tongue of Evaria or that of the Kerell.

"Is the quality of the portrait not pleasing to you?" Eva asked in confusion.

"The butterfly garden," Xaiden said suddenly. "Perhaps we could see it."

"Yes," Eva replied, brightening. "By the grace of the Goddess it is nearby. It is beautiful and will please you."

Selene might have been pleased by the butterfly garden, had anger not so consumed her thoughts. Flurries of white butterflies with a coating of rainbow iridescence fluttered through it, like drifting snow that defied the heat of Kerell as if by magic.

"Stay here," Eva instructed, gesturing to a wooden bench beneath a tree. "I'll only be a moment."

Selene sat, and Xaiden took a place next to her. She knew well that she should not say too much while in the palace, yet so many questions begged to pass her lips.

"He was born here," she whispered.

"Yes," Xaiden replied in kind.

"And you were as well?"

"Yes, though so long ago that none should remember me."

"I assume that he was the cause of the blaze at his estate, after which he fled, for they thought him deceased."

"I do not know," Xaiden admitted. "I have not asked him."

"If you were to guess?"

"I would assume so as well, yes."

It explained so many things that she should never have dismissed as trivial. Least of all, both Cael and Xaiden's ease of being in this place and their expertise at speaking the language.

And to think that as they studied Kerell together on the boat she had thought herself slow at learning.

"Why would he bother to take us back home? His home is here."

"Now suddenly he loses your trust?"

"When I find that I've been lied to, yes."

"An omission of the truth, at best."

"Strange words coming from your lips." Selene kept one eye on Eva as she spoke. The woman was searching the trees for something, and luckily was still a decent distance away.

"Perhaps you do not know me as well as you assume," Xaiden said evenly.

It was not simply anger that filled her, she realized at once. Rising to match it was despair.

"He has everything he once lost. His estate, his caste. He no longer lives under the rule of the Aranth. Perhaps he'll choose to stay here; to leave us enslaved as Rakaii. There will be nothing we can do to stop him."

"Do you truly believe him to be capable of such a betrayal?"

She didn't want to, but fear poisoned all reason. She could not bear to live in this place for eternity, but Pyra would never give her up. And if, as had been her only hope, somehow Cael managed to purchase her, would she fare any better?

"Here is the perfect one," Eva called out as she plucked a rounded, yellow fruit from a nearby tree. She split it into three by pressing her thumb into its soft center, then handed one piece each to Xaiden and Selene, and kept the last for herself.

"You hold it out." She demonstrated with an outstretched arm. "Like this."

Selene copied the woman's actions. Butterflies came eagerly from all directions to land upon her hand and the fruit within it. Their delicate legs and rolled tongues were soft upon the skin of her arm. If only they could lick away at anger as they did the fruit and the salt of her sweat.

"You will stay until tomorrow," Eva said suddenly. "The empress has extended an invitation." The woman was an odd sight, as a multitude of butterflies had perched upon her arms and head. They lifted in a cloud as she began to walk. "It is late. I should show you where we will sleep."

"What do you mean?" Selene asked.

"Just as I said," Eva replied, as if that qualified as an answer. "Your master and mistress will stay with the empress tonight at her request, and thus you shall stay here as well."

This made Selene's anger rise all the more, though for a reason far different that of the previous betrayal.

"There is no acceptable reason to refuse an invitation from the Goddess." Xaiden placed a hand on Selene's shoulder. "We would be honored to stay with you."

"As I knew you would be," Eva exclaimed. "Do you have any desire for food? We could take some with us to my quarters."

"Yes, that would be delightful," Xaiden replied.

Selene could not find anything delightful about this situation, no matter how hard she tried. Eva led them once again to the room they had started in, where enough food for at least thirty people still stood prepared. She handed them each a finely made bowl, the stone of which was smooth and oddly cold to touch. Selene filled hers with a few pieces of cheese and dried fruit in an attempt to be polite, though in truth she was not hungry in the least.

"It is tiresome sleeping alone," Eva informed them. "It will be pleasant to have companions for a night."

"Are there no other female Rakaii here?" Selene asked to distract herself from her irritation.

"I am the only one residing here at the moment," the girl replied. "The empress has declared it a time of breeding."

"I see," Xaiden said. "They have been sent to the estates where their current mates reside."

"Yes," Eva said. "It is an important tradition. The empress offers them up for breeding when the mood strikes her, as a gift to her favorites of the upper caste so that the lines of their favorite Rakaii might continue. The offspring of a female Rakaii is nearly guaranteed to be another Rakaii, unlike when a male Rakaii breeds with a mage."

"But she did not send you for breeding?" Selene realized that the question might be considered impolite, but only too late.

"No, because I am most favored," Eva replied proudly. "Come, I have all manner of drinks in my quarters."

Upon arriving at Eva's bedroom, it proved to be true. A little table was filled with bottles of drink in all colors. Selene cordially accepted the tiny glass she was handed.

"You are breeding," Eva reminded her unnecessarily. "So, I'll give you one without liquor."

The liquid within the cup was sweet and far too thick. Selene drank it anyway, as she did not wish to insult the girl. The room had a proper bed, though only one, along with several mounds of pillows spaced out upon patterned rugs. It must be true that Eva was a favorite of the empress, for everything in the room was of quality and intricately crafted.

"This is quite good." Eva held out a piece of flat bread coated in honey. "It always raises my spirits to eat it. Would you like some?"

Selene politely declined the bread. The scent was far too familiar, and she could see within it a peppering of tiny seeds to match those that Aster had once tricked her into eating to pacify her.

"Just the dried fruit will be fine, thank you," she replied. It was somewhat worrisome that Eva had noticed her mood.

After far too many drinks and a feast fit for ten, both Eva and Xaiden slipped from the waking land into that of slumber. Selene watched the two lay peacefully upon the massive bed, Eva with her head upon Xaiden's chest. Perhaps she did not know enough of the man to judge him after all. When she was certain that they were soundly asleep Selene took her chance and slipped from the room, placing her bare feet carefully upon the floor so as not to make any more noise than was necessary. She remembered the way back to the dining area, happily, and once there she poured herself a glass of water, which seemed to be the only type of liquid Eva did not keep on hand in her room. She pulled her legs up onto a chair and sat quietly upon the balcony, watching the glow of lamplight in the city below. It was there that Cael found her. He said nothing at first, but rather pulled up a chair beside her and watched the city in silence.

"I owe you an apology," he attempted after so many minutes of silence.

"You do say that quite a bit these days. Should I assume that you were listening to my conversation with Xaiden through the circlet?"

"I'm sorry about that too. I only wanted to make sure you were safe."

"I'm enslaved in a land full of Mages. I'm as far from safety as I am from Evaria at the moment."

"A fair statement," he replied quietly.

"You should have told me," she said, looking not at him but at the lights below. "Back before the circlet, before we left for this place."

"You're right," he admitted.

"It wasn't fair to ask me to do this when you neglected to tell me the whole of your plan."

"I didn't think I could do it without you."

"You already have," she replied bitterly. "You have your estate, your wealth, a life of freedom. All you had to do was return to your homeland and ask for it. Evaria is a wilderness compared to this place. You don't need to go back, and you don't need me."

"But I do." He placed his hand upon hers. The continued lack of burn from his mark put her ill at ease.

She reluctantly met his gaze. For all of her anger, she could still see what might well be regret reflected in his dark eyes.

She noticed that he was dressed in a robe of white silk and nothing more. He had not bothered to tie it together at the front.

"And what activities did you and the empress engage in during my absence?" She could not keep the bite from her tone.

"Whatever she asked of me." Cael scowled. "As I have no desire to forfeit my life unnecessarily. I will happily tell you in great detail, if you so desire."

"No," she replied firmly. "I believe I would rather not hear of it."

"Nor would I ask what you, Eva and Xaiden did on your own, for you couldn't be held accountable for it."

"It was not of as much interest as it could have been."

"I see," Cael said.

"I could tell them your secret." The thought had come to her, appearing for just a moment through her rage. "Then our circumstances would align."

"You won't." He sounded far more certain than she felt. "I've left your abilities open, and I am unshielded from Rakaii magic. If I had truly broken your trust, then I would be long dead."

"That might be true." She could not bear the thought of killing him, despite her anger. "I might kill you still, given time."

"If you feel that you must, then I will not fight against it."

"I shall reserve the right to make that judgment at a later date."

"Fair enough, but you must believe that I will find a way to remedy this."

"I can't see how," Selene said. "I'll die here after bearing so many children, all of them destined to be sold into slavery. My heart breaks at the thought of it."

"I won't allow it," Cael said.

"This place of horrors cares little for what you might allow, Cael." She studied him for a moment. "Apologies, for I only recently learned of your true identity Mr. Zephyrus. Do you have a few other names that you might like to add for the sake of fostering confusion? Are you named Cael? Is it Logan? Or Lord Altair? What should I call you?"

"Call me whatever you like."

"For the sake of being courteous I don't believe I should."

"Logan Zephyrus is my true name. I traded the surname Zephyrus for that of Altair upon reaching the shores of the Wildlands, and then became Cael when I joined the Aranth. I assumed I was being hunted. The length of the ocean between here and Evaria would not have stopped the empress if she'd known that I lived. I was being cautious, as we definitely are not being at this moment. We shouldn't even be speaking of such things within the palace walls."

"Then why are you here?"

"Because I felt the need to clarify my intentions and did not wish to wait until tomorrow's light. I attempted to explain all of this to you earlier tonight, before we came to the palace, in my defense."

"True, but still far too late." She pulled her hand from his.

"And is it too late for you to offer me forgiveness as well?"

"Perhaps," she replied.

Someone entered the room behind them. They turned to find one of the empress' Rakaii.

"Apologies for the intrusion, Master Zephyrus," the man said. "The Goddess requests your presence." He was well built and fine of form, as the empress seemed to prefer, yet she struggled to see his face, for he looked neither at Cael nor Selene, but at the floor as he spoke. It seemed that all of the Rakaii in this place had been trained to do so.

"She is awake at this hour?" Cael questioned.

"She wakes whenever she pleases," the man replied. "I beg that you follow me, Master Zephyrus. Your Rakaii is invited as well, for the empress is pleased by her."

"Fine," Cael said. "Lead the way."

After several minutes of walking, the length of the night finally began to wear on Selene. The entirety of the day had been trying, and although she could not be certain what hour it was, it was certainly late. At last, they arrived outdoors in an octagonal garden area with what looked to be cells on all sides. It put Selene in mind of a decorated version of the training area where Aster had placed her circlet upon her arrival. There was some commotion at the center, where two mages held down a young man whose face was covered by a burlap hood. Beside them stood the empress. She wore a silk robe, much like Cael's but rose in color, with expertly embroidered birds flying down one side.

"I have learned that there is much truth in the tales of what bounty the Wildlands hold," the Empress said as they drew close. "In the past I have obtained many Rakaii by trade with foreign lands. But why should I pay for something which I can take at no cost? The people of the Wildlands, even those who are not Rakaii, are little better than animals. Do you not agree?"

"Of course, I agree, my Goddess," Cael said. "It is a savage place that cannot be tamed. Thus, I decided to return to civilization, for there is only so much time one can spend in such a place and remain cultured."

"An intelligent choice," the empress replied. "Much like my decision to send mages to collect Rakaii from the Wildlands. The result, and the quality of Rakaii, has been much better than I had expected."

Selene kept her eyes away from the empress. She focused instead upon the Rakaii. He was young, or perhaps merely small in stature. His clothes were in tatters. Little else could be determined due to the fabric covering his head.

"This one arrived on the hour," the empress explained. "He is unique, but merely a consolation. Several of my mages fell in an attempt to acquire the true prize."

"They came upon a female Rakaii?" Cael said as if guessing.

"You may not have noticed during your time in the Wildlands, for they keep their secrets well hidden, but several of those who are considered royalty are truly Rakaii. They reside in a city which the beasts have named Evaria."

"Rakaii in power?" Cael sniffed. "Deplorable."

"Indeed," the empress replied. "A situation which will soon be remedied."

"I trust in your wisdom, my Goddess."

"As you should."

The empress approached the hooded Rakaii, gliding across sand raked into a series of circles as delicately as a shadeslight would move through the mists of the Crimson Abyss.

"This acquisition might be of particular interest to you," she said.

The empress motioned for her guards to remove the Rakaii's hood. Selene's thoughts stilled as her mind recognized him. Devren's face and body were swollen and coated in bruises. The boy must have put up a struggle.

"He does have a unique look about him," Cael replied with unfounded calm.

"I have been told that it was quite a feat to remove him from his castle. The mages I employ are not only talented magically, but they are also wise and well versed in battle strategy. This, I insist upon."

Selene's heart pounded with such ferocity that she was certain the empress must be able to hear it.

"It is a pity that I was not able to procure him for myself," Cael noted.

"He is one of the rarest types of Rakaii," the empress explained. "His mark is of a wisp of a creature native to only the darkest of places."

"You would not think it to look upon him," Cael said smoothly. "He is but a wisp of a man as well."

A slight laugh, a sound as haunting as the growl of a venomvine, escaped the empress' lips. "He was the reigning sovereign of the realm; I have been told. I find it amusing that they would trust a kingdom, if it can be called such, to one of so few years."

"It is truly an uncivilized place, as I have said."

"He is young, which is well, and has a look about him that he may be considered well-formed given time."

"A spectacular trophy indeed," Cael replied.

Devren's eyes met Selene's. They widened as he recognized her. Selene's breath and heartbeat quickened as one. She begged the Spirits that he would not speak out and betray them. The boy found Cael then. His mouth opened as if to call to him. Selene prepared herself to flee, though she could not fathom where she might go. She watched Devren's mouth open and close. No speech came from his lips.

"Can he not speak?" Cael asked.

"My mages have a standing order to place a spell of silence upon all of my Rakaii until they are properly trained," the empress explained. "This one in particular offered a wide variety of insults when he was first captured, or so I have been told. You must know that such insolence is not acceptable."

Selene exhaled silently, though her heart still refused to slow.

"Then you will listen to his thoughts?" Cael asked.

"And find myself inside his vulgar mind? I think not. Andromidus will question him in my stead. She will relay to me any information which might be of value."

"Let us hope that she finds what you require," Cael said.

"I am pleased by this acquisition," the empress announced, addressing the mages. "You will both be allowed one favor of your choosing. I am finished with this Rakaii for the moment. Find him a cage and summon a trainer for him."

Both mages, who Selene noted were now down upon one knee, bowed their heads while keeping a tight hold on Devren.

"Come," the empress ordered. "We should not waste this perfect night with sleep. Bring your Rakaii, and we shall see what other favors tonight has to offer."

Selene followed with as much enthusiasm as she could manage, though fatigue dragged against her feet like mud on a riverbank in spring. She wanted nothing more than to sleep. As Cael gestured for her to pick up speed, she could not help but think that she should have stayed and slept with Eva and Xaiden. She did not wish to discover what horrors the evening might yet bring.

# The Conquered Coast
## *Evaria – City of Coastwood*

Islyr inched forward. He and Viverr had settled themselves on a rocky outcropping at the edge of the little town of Coastwood, which was nestled within a great forest by the Ocean of Tides. The mages sat a horse's length below them; a group of five clustered around a bonfire. Perhaps he could take them all. It would soon be dark, and he did still command the element of surprise.

*No,* Viverr signed, as if reading his thoughts. *Danger. Too many.*

There was little light by which to see the swift movement of the rogue's fingers.

*You say that no matter how many there are,* Islyr signed back. *We move closer.*

The rogue scowled and shook his head, but it was too late. Islyr was already headed forward through a group of ferns. The foliage was thick here, though not too dry. They would not hear his movement over the crackling of the fire so long as he was careful.

As he drew closer to the bonfire there was better light by which to see the movements of the rogue's hands. He was still signing, though Islyr was not of a mind to pay him any further heed. The heat of the flames washed across his flesh in bursts as the ocean breeze caught it. It rolled the scents of burning hair and seaweed through the air. This was the third town they had come to, and the only one to contain any life aside from a few loose chickens and one ram turned feral who had not been appreciative of their company. Mages cared not for living things, Rakaii and other mages aside, and there were few of either to be found on Evarian soil.

Islyr stopped behind a tangle of vines and grass that would easily conceal his form. Once settled, he surveyed the fireside. The leader of the mages pulled a cork from a glass bottle and drank. The liquid within looked to be heavy spirits, likely plundered from the village. They had no notion yet of his presence.

Viverr crouched silently next to him. *Too many*, he signed again.

This was a much better spot for purposes of eavesdropping. After all, why were they here if not to learn of the mages' plans? Another mage emerged from the patch of darkness that dwelt at the edge of the firelight. The body of a villager floated behind him, limbs hanging, as if held aloft by a Spirit. With a flick of the mage's hand, the body swung forward. It landed at the center of the bonfire. Sparks erupted, fluttering briefly through the air like faerie light before being swallowed by the night. With luck the villager had been fully deceased when he reached the flames.

A thin man on the opposite side of the fire looked up from where he sat. He balanced an orb of magic, no larger than a child's marble in size, in one hand. *"Did you find them all?"* He spoke in Kerell and had a strong accent. From the west, perhaps? The mage twisted the white, glowing form between his fingers briefly before rendering it to nothing. It was a show of power; a sign to his brethren that he had enough magic to spare on such foolishness.

*"Yes."* The newly arrived mage pushed back the hood of his cloak to reveal an angular, beardless face. *"The village is empty, Orven. There were no mages here, and we found only one Rakaii."*

*"Only one?"*

*"This place is not as ripe with feral Rakaii as we were told."*

Orven was on his feet in a no more than a shadow's breath. The spark that pulsed from his fingers crossed the open air with remarkable velocity. *"We do not question the will of the Goddess."*

*"I understand. Please accept my apologies."* The lowly mage did not show any visible reaction to the burn that now marred his skin. It was not surprising, for to do so would have lowered his status in the eyes of his peers.

Islyr turned to catch Viverr's attention. The rogue shook his head slowly, adding a roll of his eyes for good measure. He knew what must come next on their journey. He should, at least, for they had travelled together long enough for it.

*You say that everything is too dangerous*, Islyr held back the urge to sigh.

*Not everything*, the rogue countered. *Only things that will get us killed.*

*"Who holds him?"* Orven asked from his seat by the fire.

*"I do,"* the lowly mage replied.

*"My patience wanes, Erik, Bring him forward."*

Rings of precious stone glinted against the firelight as Erik raised his hand and crooked his index finger. A weathered Rakaii stumbled into the ring of light provided by the flames.

"Where are your kin?" Evarian lay strangely on Orven's tongue.

"Dead, by your hand." The man spat in the Mage's direction. By the Tides, he missed, for the mage would not have taken the insult well had it landed.

*Usual technique*, Islyr signed as he crept ever so carefully past Viverr.

The rogue nodded reluctantly and then transformed, disappearing into the brush.

*"Dead?"* Orven asked with an angry scowl at the lesser mage.

*"Neither his wife nor his son were Rakaii,"* Erik explained with haste. *"I tested them myself. They were of no value."*

"Not dead by my hand," Orven informed the Rakaii.

"By your decree then, which is no better," the man countered.

Glass shattered somewhere beyond the reach of the firelight. The mages turned at once in the direction of the sound, though surely no source could be seen in the meager light. The leader twitched his head towards it. The underling mages moved into the shadows at the gesture, leaving only one.

As his brethren disappeared from the light, Orven stood. He pushed the captured Rakaii to his knees with a trace of magic.

"Let us see what you are worth," he said in Evarian.

He ripped open the back of the man's shirt to search for the mark that lay beneath.

*"House cat."* He reverted to his native tongue, perhaps from sheer disgust.

*"At least we have one,"* the remaining underling offered.

*"One of poor value. Better to have none."*

With a twist of magic, the mage flung the bottle of spirits into the flames. It burst with a flash of light, sending shards of glass cascading from the fire.

*"Cannot the light of the Goddess breach this forsaken place?"* he questioned. *"Can she not lend her aid to my endeavor?"*

*"His ability could be rare,"* the underling offered.

*"With a mark of cat? Unlikely."*

*"We should test him, to be certain."*

Orven's eyes narrowed.

The man dropped his gaze. *"I meant no disrespect,"* he offered.

*"The best way to avoid showing disrespect to your betters is not to speak at all. It is not worth the effort to bring this Rakaii back. It will cost more to feed him on the journey home than he is worth."*

Islyr could wait no longer. The life of the Rakaii lay in the balance. He stepped into view.

Orven straightened slowly upon noticing him. "You have entered the wrong place, my friend," he warned.

*"You asked for aid,"* Islyr said in Kerell. *"So perhaps I am in the right place after all, assuming that I have better luck than those you tossed upon the fire."*

*"You do not look like the Goddess, and it is she from whom I requested aid."* The mage paused to consider. *"The lines of ink on your face do pull at my memory. Have we met?"*

It was a play for time, for the mage backed away as he spoke. Perhaps he was not as confident in his magic as he led his underlings to believe.

The Rakaii still knelt where the mage had left him. With a sudden movement he clutched his head in agony. Firelight flashed against the metal of the circlet as it fell from his ear. It landed silently on the ground beneath him. The Rakaii fell to one side. His body pulled into a ball of agony. It was the sign that Islyr had been waiting for. The mage Erik, to whom the man's circlet was bound, was dead.

Islyr closed the space between himself and the underling mage at a sprint. He spun as fire magic singed his breeches. The end of his staff met the mage's stomach. The man folded in pain, clutching the site of the strike. Islyr rolled to the ground to extinguish the growing flame at his hip, then stood in one smooth movement. His staff swept up and to the side. It cracked the mage's temple with a sharp thud.

He turned in time to see that Viverr had found Orven. The mage did not lose consciousness as Viverr severed his magic, which was unusual for his breed. It did seem to cause him some confusion, however. Islyr swung his staff back in preparation to land a fatal strike.

The newly freed Rakaii moved with more speed than expected. He pulled an angular item from the shadows at the edge of the fire, sprung to his feet, and shoved it through the Orven's throat. Islyr watched the mage clutch his neck in a futile attempt to cease the rivulet of blood that flowed from it.

Silence fell as Orven landed upon the soil. The whisper of flames from the bonfire moved to fill it.

Viverr bounded into view. He snapped into human form with ease. "That didn't go as badly as I anticipated," he admitted as he grabbed Orven's feet and dragged him away from the fire. The man was still breathing, though only a small amount.

"You took your time," Islyr chided. "And you missed one."

"There were eight of them, not counting the leader," Viverr snapped. "Eight! That's far too many. Which is what I tried to tell you just before you barged ahead."

"There were nine underlings," Islyr corrected. "One stayed here by the fire. And how was I to know how many lay hidden in the village?"

"Much like rats, you should always assume that there are at least twice as many as you can see." Viverr rummaged through the mage's robes. He pulled a tiny glass bottle from the mage's pocket. The contents shimmered in the light of the flames.

Islyr grinned and shook his head. It was true enough. "Put on some clothing, Viverr." He had spent enough time in Kerell that nudity did not concern him, but their new friend might not feel the same way.

"I suppose I might need my pockets for all of this loot," the rogue agreed as he wandered off in search of his clothes.

The Rakaii had made no attempt to speak during the exchange, but rather stared distantly into the flames of the bonfire. The curved triangle of glass he had pulled from the ground still lay embedded in Orven's neck.

"Thank you for your assistance," Islyr began politely.

"My family burns in this pyre."

It was something, though not technically a reply. The man clenched one hand as he spoke, partially obscuring the burn that lay upon his palm. The shard of glass must have seared his flesh as he had pulled it from near the fire.

"When the sun rises, we should find some herbs for your hand," Islyr offered.

The Rakaii made no reply.

Islyr tensed as something rustled through the nearby vines. He reached for his staff in preparation to strike but stumbled. The Rakaii faded from view like an object thrown into the depths of the sea. As he disappeared, Viverr emerged from the forest, now fully clothed.

"Where's our new friend?" the rogue asked.

"I am still here." The Rakaii's voice emanated from nothing.

Viverr jumped as if stung. "Spirits' sake, are you trying to make me wet my breeches?"

Islyr could not help but smile.

"I'm happy you can find this situation amusing, given that everything dear to me has been destroyed by the mages," the Rakaii chided. "My house might still stand, but my family," the man choked on the word.

"I mean no disrespect," Islyr replied. "It's simply the irony."

"What irony?" the man asked. "I see nothing but loss."

"Orven planned to have you killed. He assumed that since your affinity was of low value your latent ability would be as well."

"I must admit, I'm not seeing this irony either," Viverr said as he pulled a handful of jewelry from the dead mage's robes.

"Your ability is to fade," Islyr explained. "Light bends around you, and you can step through materials that others would consider to be solid. Am I correct?"

The man nodded, though he did not turn his eyes from the fire.

"Rakaii who can fade are of high value to the Empress. She trains them as assassins. The mage lost both a valuable Rakaii, and his life."

"I only wish I could have made him suffer for longer," the man said.

"I offer my sympathy for the loss of your family." Islyr bent at the waist in respect. "A mage took my father from me, when I was but a child." It was still a difficult thing for him to say aloud.

"Thank you for your help." The man wiped at a tear that lingered on his cheek.

"The Kerell imprisoned me for many years," Islyr replied. "I am happy to keep others from that fate."

In truth, it seemed like centuries had passed.

"May the Spirits keep all mages," Viverr agreed. He examined some small item he had pulled from the underling mage's clothing, then scowled and tossed it into the woods. "What should we call you, friend?"

"My name is Kith."

"Kith," the rogue repeated. "I like it. Rolls well on the tongue. My name is Viverr, and this is Islyr."

"I would like to repay you, but I cannot bear to go back into my home," Kith said. "I hope you understand."

"No payment is needed," Islyr replied.

Kith nodded. "You shouldn't feel obligated to stay here. I can manage on my own."

"We've done what we came for," Viverr said. "We don't have anywhere else to go at the moment."

"You came here for the mages?"

"Yes," Islyr replied. "We've been hired by the crown to hunt mages as they arrive on Evarian shores."

"But you're marked. I heard tell that the boy king had no hatred for marked ones, but to employ them is far beyond anything I had imagined."

Islyr shot a wary glance at Viverr. It seemed that word of Cyanna's ascension had not yet travelled this far. Perhaps it would be better if Devren's fate did not become common knowledge.

"He certainly is a good bit more relaxed in his views than his father," the rogue replied with a grin.

"I know of something that might aid you in your hunt for mages," Kith said. "An odd, flat stone piece by which they came here. There were more in the group."

"More?" Islyr echoed with interest.

"Spirits' sake," Viverr swore. "You can't tell him things like that."

"The others used the stone to travel away."

"Could you take us to its location?" Islyr asked. "Perhaps we could use it to follow them."

"Of course," Kith replied. "It's by the roadside, just past the edge of the village."

Darkness now thoroughly blanketed both the village and the woods surrounding it.

"Likely could have found it on our own," Viverr noted as they approached.

It was true, for the stone gave off enough light to rival that of a small torch, though blue rather than any regular color of fire. The mages had not been discreet. Upon closer inspection it was flat, like a paving stone, and about the size of a baking tray.

"Do you think it leads to their ship?" Viverr asked.

"Maybe," Islyr replied thoughtfully. How many mages would be on such a ship? It might be more than they could handle, though he would never admit the fact aloud.

"Will it even work for us?" Viverr approached the stone with gentle steps, as if it might suddenly jump up to bite him. "Voyage rings need a word to activate them. I have no desire to be burned to ash."

"You can't be burned to ash by magic if your ability is active."

"Yes, but I also can't use the stone to travel if my ability is active," the rogue huffed.

"I have seen these stones a few rare times in Kerell," Islyr informed him. "They don't need any words of activation. They simply lay open, like a passage."

"A magical passage," Viverr mused. "That sounds just terrible."

Islyr could not help but sigh.

"We probably shouldn't use it," the rogue continued. "Too risky. And how would we even know what place to think of? We might end up somewhere we don't want to be."

"We won't need to think of a place," Islyr assured him. "With a voyage ring you can connect many together and choose which one you travel to. That's why you need to think of a specific place when stepping onto it. With these there is only a single passage, so there is no need to know where you're going before you get there."

"That also sounds terrible," Viverr complained.

Islyr was no longer in a mood for the rogue's antics.

"Come along, Viverr. We've mages to slay."

"I'll go with you," Kith offered. "It will be many hours before the fire dies down, and it would do my heart well to make sure that these mages don't cause any further suffering."

"We gratefully accept your offer." Islyr stepped closer to the stone. "I'll go first," he added for Viverr. "That way you'll know it's safe."

"I won't be able to tell that you made it safely to the other side, now will I?" the rogue complained.

Islyr chose not to reply, but instead gripped his staff tightly and stepped onto the center of the stone. Frigid air engulfed him. His vision faded for only seconds before returning. He stepped off of the stone. It was not the deck of a ship that lay before him, but rather a courtyard. *Perhaps it used to be a courtyard, in the distant past,* his mind corrected. Vines as thick as his arms covered every available surface. They must have taken years to grow.

A breath of cold air hit his back. He turned to find Kith.

"Is he coming?" Islyr asked.

"He insisted on going last," Kith replied. "Are you certain there are mages here? It looks abandoned."

"That would please Viverr far too much," Islyr said in place of a reply.

The rogue appeared as if summoned by his name. He jumped away from the stone and pulled his arms to his chest. "Terrifying," he grumbled.

"And yet by the grace of the Goddess, you still live," Islyr noted.

"I don't see any mages," Viverr said.

"Yes," Islyr replied. "We were just discussing that."

Viverr pressed a finger to his temple. "This place looks familiar."

"It does to me as well," Islyr admitted.

"What's that?" Viverr pointed to a recessed area of vines that was oddly rounded at the top.

"A doorway, I think." Islyr moved closer to investigate.

"Not the doorway," Viverr said. "That red bit near the middle there."

A crimson rose poked out from between the vines. It was surprising that the rogue had been able to spot it in the darkness. Beneath its silken petals lay a slip of wrinkled, green fabric.

"There's something else here." Islyr levered his staff between vines and pushed. Some long, pale thing dropped out from within. It landed with a thump on the ground beneath.

"Congratulations, you've found a mage," Viverr quipped as he approached.

It was indeed a mage's severed arm, complete with stone rings on its index finger, which now lay at Islyr's feet.

"The rest of the group could be dead as well," Kith surmised.

"Likely so." The rogue wrinkled his nose as he inspected the arm. "Well, that's our job done, then. Better go, eh?"

"No." Islyr grabbed the rogue by his shoulder. "We must make sure they're all dead."

"Can you hear that?" Kith injected. "It sounds like voices."

Islyr listened. The sound was too soft to identify.

"I don't hear anything." Viverr reached out to touch the rose, which had suddenly opened to bloom. His tone at once switched from trepidation to excitement. "I know where we are."

With a rushing sound like a wave against the shore, the vines above them receded to reveal a balcony.

"Identify yourself," A voice called from above. "Unless you wish to be crushed to death."

"Kyrros, you great idiot, it's Viverr."

"I beg your pardon?" the voice replied with confusion.

"It's Viverr," the rogue repeated much too slowly. "And Islyr, of Evaria city."

"I know who you are."

"And this is our new friend, Kith," Viverr continued. "Also, not a mage."

"Fair enough," Kyrros said. "But how did you get in here?"

"By murdering some mages and using their travel-stone… thing. Look, does it truly matter? Spirits' sake, let us in before more of them arrive."

"And this isn't some mage's trick?"

"It's really me," the rogue insisted. "I owe you two silver candle sticks and a necklace with a sizeable moonstone from the last time I was here."

"That necklace was going to be a gift, before it disappeared," Kyrros growled.

"Perhaps we could discuss restitution inside?" Viverr suggested. "Over some food?"

"We've done away with the rest of the mages," Islyr added. "Or so we believe."

"Hello to you too, Islyr," Kyrros replied. "Yes, you might come in, I suppose."

The vines across the doorway pulled back to reveal an entryway. As it did so, three bodies thumped to the ground. All were mangled, which gave them an oddly inhuman look. It seemed fitting, for most mages did not have many human qualities in Islyr's estimation. Above them, an arched trellis of roses remained.

"Found the owner of that arm," Viverr quipped. "I might feel bad if I wasn't so sure he would've killed me. You lived amongst mages for some time, Islyr. What causes them to be so terrible?"

"How should I know?" Islyr stepped carefully around the dead mage. "Perhaps it's their unfounded hatred of any living being that differs from them?"

Beyond the shadows of the archway, two great wooden doors carved with roses drew open. Kyrros stood in the passage behind them. On any regular occasion, the man's countenance would be immaculate down to the finest detail; a level of personal grooming which always brought members of the Kerell upper caste to Islyr's mind. On this day he would say the man seemed disheveled, at best. In one hand Kyrros held a torch, which he used to light the sconces upon the wall.

"You're looking a bit rough, my friend," Viverr noted as light slipped across the features of Kyrros' face.

"It does tend to happen when one is battling mages." Kyrros carefully brushed the dust from the left sleeve of his shirt before starting on the right.

"Were you having one of your parties before the mages arrived?" Viverr asked.

"Sadly, no," the man replied. "I fear it will be quite some time before that becomes a possibility."

*What does that mean?* Viverr signed when Kyrros' back was turned.

Islyr shook his head in the slightest. As personalities went, he and Kyrros were as far from each other as Evaria was from Kerell. How was he to know what the man was thinking?

Kyrros led them through several lavishly decorated halls to a sitting room. Islyr stared down at the plush chair that he was offered. Highly polished mahogany wood had been offset with a seat upholstered in gold colored velvet. He sat upon it gingerly. It was a futile attempt to keep the soil on his clothes from ruining what was surely expensive fabric. He had no wish to offend Kyrros.

The rogue, it seemed, had no such reservations.

"A few snacks would be nice," Viverr announced to no one in particular as he dropped into a chair similar to Islyr's. "You can't ruin anything here," he added, perhaps upon noting Islyr's expression. "It's all been enchanted to keep the dirt off. It's ridiculous."

"Enchanted?" Islyr echoed in confusion.

"Of course, if I wanted to ruin the furniture, I could just use my ability to remove the magic," the rogue continued.

"Don't you dare," Kyrros warned. "I've had enough of my things ruined of late."

"Do you have a mage here?" Islyr asked cautiously.

"Only one," Kyrros replied easily, as if having a mage on the premises was of no consequence at all.

"And you trust them?"

"He has been under my employment for many years."

Kyrros offered Islyr a tray with tiny sandwiches. They had been cut into triangular shapes and looked to contain some sort of vegetables in white paste. He was not particularly hungry but took one anyway, as he felt it was expected.

"He's got to be at least eighty." Viverr grabbed a handful of sandwiches.

"Who?" Islyr asked as he took a bite. The bread was sweet enough to make his stomach turn.

"The mage," Viverr replied through a mouthful of sandwich. "I'm not usually one to trust mages, as you know, but Gilam is no threat."

Islyr would keep his guard up, all the same. As he put the last of the sandwich into his mouth, he caught movement in the shadows of the hall.

"You may come in," Kyrros called out before Islyr could reach for his staff. "We don't lurk in the hall in polite society, Thomas."

A boy just beyond childhood entered the room. Islyr recognized him after a moment as one of the Aranth younglings in training.

"Xaiden may have taught them battle skills, but they could certainly use some additional training in manners," Kyrros said. "That aside, I did ask you to stay hidden, did I not?"

"I'm sorry, Sir Kyrros," Thomas said.

"Apology accepted," Kyrros replied. "I assume that you'll use more discretion in the future."

"Well, it was Oliver's idea."

"It was not!" a second child countered from somewhere out in the hall.

"So, this is where Devren sent them all," Viverr said with a laugh. "How in the name of the Spirits did he convince you to take them?"

Kyrros sighed. "It wasn't a choice so much as an obligation. And it's only temporary. I do owe the kingdom a few favors, after all."

"Devren knew they would be safe here," Islyr guessed.

"It's well-fortified," Viverr agreed.

"Apparently not well enough." Kyrros scowled at Viverr, who was helping himself to a nearby bottle of spirits.

"You invited us in," Viverr countered as he took a sip.

"Viverr?" a small voice called out.

The rogue stood as yet another child entered the room.

Just how many young marked ones had the Aranth found? This one Islyr recognized after a moment as Barrik, Devren's and Cyanna's youngest brother.

"I thought you'd been captured," Viverr said in confusion. "How did you get all the way out here?"

The boy shrugged. He had never been much for words as far as Islyr had seen. It was not surprising, given what he had been through in his young life.

"Only the Spirits know," Kyrros said. "He just appeared recently. I assumed you'd ordered him to come here, otherwise I would have sent word of his presence."

"I used my latent ability to escape the mages," Barrik said proudly. "Nobody sent me."

Viverr checked the boy's shoulder. "No mark," he said in confusion.

"Marked ones can develop their latent abilities before their marks appear," Islyr said. "It's rare, but not impossible."

"I am marked," the boy snapped.

"Nobody said you weren't," Viverr began.

Before the rogue could say another word, Barrik vanished from sight.

"Lovely," Kyrros huffed.

"Where's he gone?" Viverr asked.

"Couldn't say." Kyrros snatched the bottle of wine from Viverr and poured himself a glass. "I'm hardly equipped to watch children with common latent abilities, let alone one that can travel at will."

"Consider it experience," Viverr suggested. "You know, for when little Flynn starts using his abilities."

Kyrros waved the rogue's words aside. "He's merely an infant. Spends most of his time with the wet nurse. I've many years before that time comes." He held his wine glass aloft, at which one of the children stepped over and pressed their palm to it. Ice spread across the glass, chilling the drink within. "And he'll be using his middle name, Noctis. It's much more fitting for someone of his station."

"You'd better not let Selene catch wind of that," Viverr warned.

"It doesn't infringe upon the terms of our agreement," Kyrros informed the rogue before turning to the boy. "Thank you, Kade. It seems that the danger has passed. Please make sure that everyone gets back to their rooms."

"You've trained them a little," Islyr noted as the children filed towards the door.

"We're not trained like animals," Thomas countered. "Just helping Uncle Kyrros in exchange for staying here."

"Uncle Kyrros, is it?" Viverr echoed with a laugh. "Never thought I'd see the day."

"Some of them might have grown attached to me," Kyrros admitted. "I suppose it's to be expected."

Kade hung back as the other children disappeared into the hall. "What about Barrik, sir?" he asked.

"If you find him, ask him to go to his room," Kyrros replied.

Kade nodded and followed the others.

"You don't seem concerned about Barrik's whereabouts," Islyr said after the last of the younglings had left the room.

"Can't make him stay anywhere he doesn't want to," Kyrros replied easily. "And I'd say he can keep himself safe, wouldn't you?"

Islyr had seen younger Rakaii left to fight for themselves in the ring. Those who survived became emotionally unstable adults, at best. Then again, he knew very little about raising children.

"I don't suppose he can take others with him when he travels?" Viverr asked.

"Not that I've seen." Kyrros poured himself more wine. "And he's not likely to return tonight, from my experience. If you're looking for a quick way back to Evaria, I doubt you'll find it there."

"We should go," Islyr informed him.

The night was wearing on, and he was eager to return to the hunt.

"We could stay the night," Viverr suggested. "No need to rush."

"Polite society would dictate that you don't simply invite yourself to stay at someone's estate," Kyrros informed him. "But yes, I suppose you're welcome to stay if you'd like."

"I appreciate your hospitality," Kith announced from the shadows in the corner of the room.

The man had been so silent that Islyr had nearly forgotten he was there.

"I'd like some more time before going back to my village," he continued.

"I understand," Islyr said. Upon consideration, staying until morning's light would not set them back too far. "Tomorrow we will go back with you. Viverr can remove the magic from the stone once we pass through it, then we'll help you provide proper interment for the remains of your family."

"I would like that, but we've only just met. What would you ask in return?"

"Join us," Islyr offered. "A tide of Kerell washes onto our shores like debris from a storm. We shall end it together."

Kith cleared his throat. "There is nothing for me at home. Not anymore." His voice cracked as he spoke. "I'll go with you, to find revenge."

"Revenge is slippery," Viverr informed him. "It's something you can never catch, from what I've seen."

"Justice then," Kith replied. "And perhaps a new purpose."

"Well said, my new friend." Islyr rose to shake Kith's hand. A light, airy heat passed over his skin from the man's mark. "Welcome to the Aranth."

# The Unicorn
## *Kerell – Capital City*

Selene slipped from beneath Cael's arm and out of his bed with the stealth of a shadeslight. The sun had just crested the walls of the estate, sending scattered beams of light through the open halls to bathe every surface in her path. Her bare feet patted gently against the smooth mosaic tiles that graced the floor as she made her way to the kitchen. Nearly a month had passed since Pyra had handed her over to Cael's care. The days had slipped away like a mouse in a hawk's shadow. She feared the end of her reprieve more than she could form into words.

The nearest kitchen, which was her preferred of the few scattered throughout the estate, was already occupied upon her arrival. Xaiden and Jevelir looked up from their tea as she rounded the doorway. Jevelir most especially was not known for his silence, and a sense of unease grew as he gestured for her to sit. Their mood relayed as somber, at best.

"Good morning," she offered as she settled herself on a silken cushion, which sat amongst a few of its brethren along the low, wooden table.

"Hello Selene," Jevelir replied.

None of the levity he usually displayed was present, which served to amplify her anxiety tenfold.

"I made something for you," he said.

"Oh? What is it?"

He opened one hand to reveal a portion of blue crystal, which he set gently upon the table. Upon closer inspection, it had been carved into the shape of an elephant.

She marveled at the beauty of it.

"Touch it," he urged.

She pressed a fingertip to the center of the carving's head. The stone grew warm, and blue light swirled within it. A flurry of butterflies in miniature erupted from the carving. They fluttered briefly, filling the room with a shower of iridescence the color of warm seas before landing on the table and erupting into bursts of starlight. Selene could not help but smile.

"It can be used indefinitely," Jevelir said. "The crystal was made to reabsorb the magic each time it's activated."

"Thank you," Selene said. "Though I don't know what I've done to earn such a gift."

"Ah, well," the man paused. "Nothing in particular. I only thought it might bring you some joy."

"It's beautiful," she remarked. "It certainly will."

"I must be off then," he said as he stood. "May the Spirits protect and guide you, Selene."

"And you as well," she replied.

"He acts as if he might never see me again," she noted as Jevelir disappeared. "Is he going somewhere?"

Xaiden said nothing, but rather pushed a cup of tea in her direction. She inhaled the steam briefly before taking a sip. It was peppermint, which was her favorite. It was also difficult to come by in this place. It could only be obtained from Evaria, aside from the small section that had been planted in Pyra's garden.

"You're about to tell me something that I do not wish to hear," she guessed before taking another sip. It tasted of home.

"I am not," he replied. "For I do not feel it is my place to do so."

A vexing answer. "Can it be so terrible?"

"Perhaps," he replied. "All the more so if you have yet to realize it on your own."

"Speak plainly," she chided. "You know I don't care for riddles."

"Nor do I," he replied.

The calming warmth of his mark washed over her hand as he placed his fingers gently upon it. It was then that Datio and Naevus appeared in the doorway.

"What are you two doing here?" she snapped.

"Good day to you as well, Selene," Datio replied with all of his usual sarcasm.

"Just as testy as ever, I see," Naevus added. "I consider it a miracle of the Goddess herself that Master Zephyrus didn't call us to retrieve you for ill behavior the moment you arrived at his estate."

"I shall have you know that I've been perfectly behaved since my first day here."

"I find that unlikely," Naevus sniffed.

"Master Zephyrus is known for his talent in training difficult Rakaii," Datio said. "Perhaps she shall return better trained than when she left."

"I am not a difficult Rakaii," Selene replied, straining to keep the indignant tone from her voice. "It hurts me that you should say such a thing."

In truth it did, though she could not fathom why it should.

"Did Pyra send you to check on my progress?"

"They have come to ready you to travel to the Decuma," Xaiden said.

"But why?" Fear slithered into her belly, turning it against her despite the soothing effects of the tea.

"So many questions," Naevus said. "Come along now. Mistress Pyra will be angry if we're late."

"She never truly angers," Selene replied. "Not as Aster did."

"This situation has nothing to do with the manner of discipline our previous mistress employed," Naevus informed her. The calm of Xaiden's mark slid from her grasp as he pulled her away.

"Show us to your room," Datio said.

It was not truly a request.

"Can I bring my tea?" she asked. "My stomach has turned in the past moment, and there is still a carriage ride ahead."

"Yes, I suppose it will have," Naevus said.

"Whatever do you mean by that?"

"Yes, you can bring the tea," Datio said, ignoring her question.

Selene tried desperately to still her mind as they walked, but to no avail. She stopped at the door to her quarters.

"What will we do when we get to the Decuma?"

"Whatever the Decuma asks of us, as per usual," Naevus replied quite unhelpfully.

"Your room is so tidy," Datio remarked as they entered.

It was only so due to the fact that she rarely slept in it.

"Have you slept in Xaiden's bed every night since you've been here?" Datio asked with a smirk. "Virile indeed."

"That's no business of yours," she huffed.

She had forgotten how he circled within her mind like a vulture.

"Your manners don't seem to have improved in the least." Naevus scowled as he gestured for her to sit upon a nearby chair.

She realized that she had not missed having to sit for untold hours while they fussed over her hair and makeup each morning.

"Let's see," Datio muttered as he rifled through the clothes in her wardrobe. He pulled out a flowing turquoise robe the color of warm seas. "The empress' favorite color," he said as he held it against her skin. "For luck."

"Luck of the Tides," she murmured.

"What a strange turn of phrase," Datio said as he pulled off her night shirt. "It runs through your head so often, but I've never heard you say it aloud."

"The tides have nothing to do with luck." Naevus poured a few drops of oily serum into his hands and briefly rubbed them together. "They're a steady and dependable force of nature."

The scent of coconut found her as he smoothed his hands against her face.

"If you say so." She brushed thoughts of home from her head.

Datio sighed. "Your hair is a mess. Have you so much as brushed it today? Who cares for your appearance in this place?"

Both Datio and Naevus at once ceased their tasks and lowered themselves to one knee. Selene looked up to find that Cael had entered the room. He was dressed and well-groomed despite the early hour. He must have risen shortly after she had.

"I care for her in this place." Cael did not look pleased.

"My deepest apologies, Master Zephyrus." Datio's words trembled with him. "Selene has been cared for exceedingly well. I meant no insult."

It was both gratifying and sad at once to have Cael put the man in his place.

"You should take care with your words lest they cause insult," Cael said.

"Yes, Master Zephyrus."

"Rise and continue your work with greater speed," he said. "It would be of great disrespect to the Decuma if we arrived late."

"Yes, Master," Datio and Naevus said, their words nearly in unison.

No emotion came through the circlet, yet Cael briefly caught Selene's eyes before turning to leave. She was not pleased by what she witnessed there.

"I do wish you would learn to keep your mouth shut," Naevus chided while he applied color to Selene's lips.

"How was I to know he was there?" Datio smoothed a light, herbal oil through Selene's hair, then wove it deftly into a complicated braid.

"If you refrained from saying anything at all then it wouldn't be of concern."

"And you say I'm the one with poor manners," Selene injected.

Both men stopped for a second to scowl at her before hurriedly continuing. They were finished in little time at all, and she was herded into one of Cael's excessively decorated carriages.

"I hardly think it's excessive," Datio said as he settled himself onto the pillowed fabric of the bench, which happened to be deep orange with colorful birds set between jungle leaves.

"Is Xaiden not coming?" she asked.

"You've certainly become attached to him," Datio said.

"Perhaps too much," Naevus added.

She had to assume that meant Xaiden would not be accompanying them. Her fear was confirmed as the carriage pulled away from the estate without him.

"No need for fear," Naevus said in a rare moment of kindness. "We can protect you as well as he can."

"She's formed a bond with him," Datio noted. "I've heard that happens sometimes with a first breeding."

"My, that is strong indeed," Naevus exclaimed.

"What did you just do?" Selene asked irately.

"I projected your emotions to Naevus," Datio replied, as if it was of no consequence.

"Please refrain from doing so in the future."

She received not a promise, but rather a laugh from Datio and a smirk from Naevus.

The brothers talked quietly of frivolous things as the carriage moved through the streets. The city was mostly empty at such an early hour. Selene's stomach was more disgruntled by the bumping of the carriage than usual. She attempted to settle it by looking out the window rather than at the gaudy interior, but to no avail. By the time they arrived at the Decuma's residence she felt as if she might lose its contents entirely. As Naevus escorted her down the steps, the feeling disappeared with such speed that the world swung around her, leaving her stomach hollow with a touch of hunger.

Cael was stepping out of the carriage ahead. He looked away as soon as she caught his eye, and then turned to help Pyra down the steps and onto the mosaic of tiles that formed the entrance to the Decuma's residence. It was a richly elegant version of a healer's abode. Many herbs and flowers grew outside, though in neat circular patterns arranged by type rather than the usual chaotic mix. Rows of polished rocks snaked between them in a rainbow of colors. Each section of plants was marked by a little wooden sign, the letters of which danced within her vision.

They entered a door carved with patterns of swirling lines much like those of a mark. Beyond it she found herself wading through a sea of drying herbs, which hung from the ceiling like growths of seaweed spied from beneath the waves. The smell was strong enough that it should have turned her stomach once again, and she could not help but wonder at the fact that it did not. Was this some miracle of the circlet? If so, why had Pyra not used it upon her in the past, during one of their many rides through the rolling hills into town?

Selene followed Cael and Pyra through what looked to be a kitchen, with shelves of pots organized neatly along the walls. The sheen of their metal put her in mind of silvered glass, and indeed she could see her warped reflection within each as they passed. Around one last corner an inner courtyard lay before them, open to the sky, and within it a rounded portion of fencing could be seen. Several massive trees grew within the large space, and jungle ferns were scattered upon the mossy ground beneath. It was a captive piece of the wilds, cut from the whole and cultured until no true wilderness remained. A vision of false freedom.

Cael and Pyra stood back from her as if expecting something, though she could not fathom what they might wish for her to do.

The question had nearly released from her lips when the Decuma appeared. Her dark eyes scanned Selene as Cael and Pyra offered reverent greetings.

"Tradition first," the Decuma rasped. She extended a hand. Rings adorned every finger, and swirling lines of ink wove in and out of wrinkles as deep as the crimson abyss.

Selene accepted the woman's hand, for it was clear that she should. The Decuma escorted her to the side of the circle of woods. Delicate shards of sunlight breached the shadows of the captive forest. It was within one of these that Selene spotted the child she had seen at the auction so long ago, enrobed still in a silver cloak that caught the light and released a subtle shine. The child stepped towards her, and from around the trunk of the nearest tree trotted a creature she had seen before only in sketches and tapestries. Her mind struggled to believe the truth of it.

"What is it?" she asked, though she already knew.

The creature was somewhere near a young deer in size, with similarly cloven hooves, though unlike a deer each of them held a tuft of fur where the hoof joined the leg. Its coat was composed of patches of black and white, and its tail put her in mind of a lion, complete with a tuft to match its hooves at the end. Upon its horse-like head was a spiraled horn the color of bone porcelain.

The creature sniffed the air. It approached her, picking its way cautiously between ferns and tree roots. It drew close. The heat of its breath brushed her skin as it considered her. The animal's horn was as sharp as the point of a blade. Her heart quickened, and she dared not move. It was beautiful, but like many things of beauty it could still be the end of her.

"You will not come to harm," the Decuma said. "He listens to your soul."

The animal regarded her curiously, as if considering. She held out a hand. He pressed his muzzle into her palm like a horse expecting a morsel of food. With that he turned and trotted back into the forest, disappearing in a wave as she had seen with the female volantes. Selene found that she could do naught but stare.

"He gives his blessing," the Decuma announced.

"A blessing," Pyra exclaimed. "It's more than I hoped for." The woman looked ready to burst with excitement.

Cael, by contrast, seemed fully unwell.

Metal clicked upon metal as the Decuma rubbed her hands together. She deftly moved Selene's robe aside. The woman's hands were warm against her belly. The heat grew briefly before subsiding.

The Decuma drew back before nodding to Pyra and Cael. "Come," she said. "The parchment is ready. You will sign that the contract is complete."

Selene moved to go with them, but Naevus caught her arm. "Not you," he said. "We are to wait in the carriage. Pyra's orders."

She followed them in a daze back through the Decuma's home and out onto the street. The light seemed far too bright, and the world began to swing as she walked despite the fact that true heat had not yet touched the day.

"Too much excitement," Naevus chided. "Come and sit."

"We'll be off in but a moment," Datio said, as if to comfort her.

"Back to Xaiden?" she asked.

"For one more night, yes," Naevus replied. "There are many traditions which must be upheld within the next few days. We would not wish to bring ill luck."

A footman came to close the carriage door. Selene focused on the clattering of the horses' hooves as they pulled away and rolled smoothly along the road.

"Can you tell me how it looked?" Datio asked.

"How what looked?"

"The unicorn, of course," he replied eagerly. "I've always wanted to see one."

"Whatever do you mean?" she replied. "You were there."

Selene took a deep breath as the carriage twisted around a particularly terrible bend which marked the turn onto the central road of the city, but the nausea did not return.

"They have a special sort of magic," Datio continued. "A unicorn could be in a room full of people, but only those it has chosen would be able to see it; those it feels are not a threat, which excludes most mages and Rakaii."

"Why should I be the only one who could see it?" she asked stubbornly.

"Not the only one," Naevus corrected. "The Keeper can see it too."

"Because they are so young," she murmured.

"Yes, and you can see it because you are with child."

Selene supposed she had known it from the time Naevus and Datio had appeared in the kitchen, so early this morning. But to say it aloud was a different matter entirely. She drew a deep breath in an effort to stave off the fear which threatened to devour her. It had crept, unnoticed, like a shadeslight in the dark of night to make a home within her chest.

"Don't be frightened," Datio cooed. "We'll be here with you, to care for you both until the birth and well after."

Naevus nodded. "We scold you only for your safety. We would never let any harm come to you. It's our responsibility."

"Only because it's your task, then?" she asked bitterly.

She should not care what they thought of her in any respect. Yet the thought of living the rest of her life solely amongst those who perceived her as a treasured pet, or worse yet, a piece of property, was beyond what she could bear.

"Of course not," Datio consoled.

"We may have come to enjoy your company as well," Naevus added reluctantly.

Datio reached up to brush a tear that had slipped onto her cheek.

"Wouldn't want to ruin your makeup," he said with a grin.

"Thank you," she replied numbly, though in truth she did not care an ounce for the state of her makeup.

"Pull your thoughts together," Naevus instructed. "We're nearly home."

Upon looking out the window she found that they were not approaching Cael's estate, but rather Pyra's.

"Who is Cael?" Datio asked curiously.

She had forgotten herself after so long at Zephyrus estate. "It is what the staff call Master Zephyrus," she lied. "Not within his hearing, of course."

"Ah, I do love a bit of gossip."

"Yes, you certainly do." Naevus rolled his eyes, making certain that his brother would see.

"You like it too, you simply won't admit it," Datio countered. "You must tell us everything."

"There is nothing to tell."

"Even those of the upper caste know so little about the mysterious Mr. Zephyrus. You must have at least one tale to tell us."

"Little occurred that would be of note. He is a very wealthy, well-connected mage who happens to be forgiving with his Rakaii."

"Forgiving." Naevus uttered the word as if tasting it. "Sounds as if there might be a story behind that."

"I thought you weren't interested," Selene said.

"I'm not," Naevus shot back. "I'm simply looking out for the interests of my dearest brother."

The conversation ceased as the carriage pulled to a stop. Selene navigated the steps without waiting for Datio or Naevus. Climbing vines with delicate white flowers arched across every corner of the estate, perpetually in bloom. The scent was familiar to her now, though it was less than comforting. She would never call this place home, no matter how many years she spent here.

"You're rather dramatic today," Datio remarked.

She started through the hall, hoping to leave him behind. They both followed, much to her dismay, though by the grace of the Spirits they kept a few paces behind her. The other house Rakaii offered her curious glances when they thought her eyes were elsewhere. She attempted in vain not to care what they might think of her.

"I thought we were going back to Master Zephyrus' estate," she said as she stopped in a shaded courtyard. "You said that I was to have one more night with Xaiden."

"You are," Datio replied. "Xaiden and Master Zephyrus are to be Pyra's guests tonight."

"Why not simply have me stay there for one more night? I can't see what it would matter after so much time."

"Tradition," Naevus explained. "Everything must be arranged with the utmost care to ensure luck with the breeding."

"I suppose we wouldn't want to have any ill luck befall me."

It was difficult to fathom how her luck could become any worse, in truth.

"And there is the matter of payment."

"Payment for what?"

"Xaiden's stud fee."

"They're to pay him for that?"

"A ridiculous thought," Naevus said. "Master Zephyrus shall receive the stud fee, of course."

"How fitting," Selene snapped.

Naevus raised a brow in her direction. "I can see that you're in a fine mood. I must say that I'm very much looking forward to eight more months of this nonsense."

"Eight and a quarter," Datio corrected.

"Is that how far along I am?" Selene asked. "Several weeks already?"

"So we've been told," Naevus replied.

"They're here," Datio announced. "I'll go and fetch Xaiden. Perhaps that will raise her spirits."

"Doubtful," Naevus muttered.

In truth it did raise her spirits in the slightest as he entered the courtyard, though she had doubted that anything could. His presence was calming, as always, and it was painful to think that this might be the last day she would be able to speak freely with him.

"Could we have a few moments alone?" she asked.

"The whole night is yours," Datio replied.

"I look forward to continuing to serve you tomorrow." Naevus' voice dripped with sarcasm.

With that both men started away, and she and Xaiden walked in silence to her room. Once there she closed the door and sat down upon the bed. He remained standing; arms crossed. There was no way to tell whether Datio was still in her head, but she would take the risk.

"So, when do we make our escape?" she asked.

Xaiden's eyes met hers. In that moment the candle's flame of hope she had held died, leaving not so much as a wisp of smoke in its wake.

"I cannot save you," he said. "Though I wish by the Spirits that I could."

"Then what am I to do?"

Xaiden looked away. She could not recall ever seeing him so conflicted.

Selene pulled a deep breath. "You must leave," she said.

"Travel back to Evaria without you?"

Selene nodded. "There is a female volantes, deep in a cave by the shore." She described the location as well as she could with the cliff as her bearing. "I am told they are worth a large amount of coin."

"A female volantes?" Her words had stirred Xaiden's interest. "Of what color?"

"Silver."

Xaiden sighed. "She will not be worth as much as a female Rakaii."

"I'm not telling you this for my welfare, but for that of Evaria. Capture the volantes and use the funds to purchase more Rakaii. Take them, along with those Cael already owns, and make your way home. You will have more than enough to begin rebuilding the Aranth."

"Cael will never agree to it," he said. "He will never leave you here."

"Is it me, or the child that he will not leave? I must assume that he knows."

"He has known since it began," Xaiden said. "The circlet can tell such things."

"Then why bother with a trip to the Decuma?"

"Rituals are of great importance. Many unnecessary things are done in the name of tradition, not only here but in Evaria as well."

Selene struggled to keep her anger from rising, for there was some small chance that Datio might check in on her emotions.

"I suppose Cael told you of my condition the moment he found out?" she asked.

"He did not tell me until two days' past."

"And neither of you thought that I might like to know?"

"I told you that it is not my place."

"And what of Cael? It would be his place above any other."

"Perhaps he wanted to be sure it would take. The matter is delicate this early on, as you may know."

"Tell him that I do not wish to see him. I do not care for him. He must leave and not spare me another thought."

"Selene," he began.

"Promise me you'll relay to him exactly what I've said."

"It is not the truth."

"But it is true that I said it."

"I promise," Xaiden said reluctantly. "Though I have known Cael for many years, and I highly doubt that anything I impart to him will change his mind on the matter."

"You'll help him change his mind." The words held much more confidence than she felt. "For Evaria."

Xaiden embraced her then, and tears began their escape despite her best effort. He held her for a brief moment, and when she pulled back, she looked up to find that his eyes brimmed with them as well.

"You have become family to me," he said.

"I feel the same." She pulled a hand across her face to dry it. "I will miss you so."

"I hope we shall meet again, in time."

"We will," she promised. "It will be when you come back to burn this city to ash with the full strength of the Aranth behind you."

# The Last Day
## *Kerell – Capital City*

Selene sighed and rested her chin upon one hand. She focused on the sound of rushing water, which echoed from a central fountain beside which she had chosen to sit. She had hoped above all else never to return to Cael's estate, but either the Tides of fate, or perhaps Cael himself, had quite another plan. They had been here many more hours than she would like to count, and the moon was now high, nearing the center of the sky. Perhaps her luck would turn for the better, and she would not see him at all for the duration of the event.

"Are you ready to return?" Datio asked impatiently.

"No," she replied stubbornly. "I am still feeling rather fatigued."

Spirits keep the Kerell and their love of ridiculous galas.

"We'll give you five more minutes," Naevus snapped.

Little, yellow fish nipped at Selene's fingertips as she swirled her free hand in the water.

"You'll give me as long as I need."

The one grace the Spirits had provided for her was that Cael was not one of the great many people Pyra had paraded her past at the gala, despite the fact that it was thrown at his estate. She could not help but find his absence puzzling. It had been nearly two weeks since her abrupt return to Pyra's side, and she had not seen nor heard from the man since. Perhaps Xaiden had relayed her message, and Cael had taken it to heart.

"You think of Master Zephyrus far more than you do of Xaiden," Datio said with a scowl.

"He was kind to me."

In truth she had been attempting not to think of him at all, but that had turned out to be easier said than accomplished.

"As is Mistress Pyra," Naevus reminded her. "You shouldn't so much as think such things. What if she was to take insult?"

"If you refrain from relaying my thoughts to her then it will cease to be an issue." She made a show of pulling her hand from the water and wiping it upon her gown.

"Stop that at once." Datio grabbed her wrist. "And Mistress Pyra can listen in whenever she so chooses, just so you're aware."

"I am well aware," Selene countered. "But she won't. It is considered uncivilized to rummage around in the mind of a Rakaii. We are such lowly creatures."

"That's enough now," Naevus demanded. "Come along, we're going back to the gala. We've been away far too long as it stands."

"I'm not going back."

"Yes, you are," he insisted. "Either you can walk back on your own, or I'll carry you back with my levitation. It's your choice."

Selene stood and twisted her wrist from Datio's grip. She crossed her arms in defiance.

"I've had enough galas to last a lifetime. I won't go." A pull for her latent abilities left her with nothing. Pyra made certain that they were locked away on most occasions, but somehow she still felt the need to attempt it from time to time.

"Put me down, Naevus," she demanded as her feet rose ever so slightly from the ground and she began to move forward.

"I warned you, didn't I?" he chided.

"It doesn't always have to come to this," Datio added. "You could simply do as we ask."

"I'm not feeling well," she lied. "I need to sit, just for a few more minutes."

"There's nothing wrong with you," Datio informed her. "Attitude aside."

She drifted across the courtyard, hovering like a Spirit.

"Stop it," Selene huffed. Her anger was growing with each passing second.

"Will you walk?" Naevus asked.

"I've already told you that I won't." She would have slapped both men if she could have reached them.

Selene's feet hit the ground so abruptly that she struggled to keep her balance.

"Was that so difficult?" she snapped as she righted herself.

Both men stared at her, eyes wide.

Naevus brought a hand to his chest. "I've lost control of my ability," he said.

"I can't feel her, can you?" Datio rasped.

"No," Naevus replied.

Selene gasped as her latent abilities returned to her in a wave. She pulled a ragged breath. Her head spun as if she'd had too much ale.

"We must find Mistress Pyra. Come, Selene." Naevus snatched at her arm.

Selene summoned her levitation ability and shoved him. It came with more force than she intended. Naevus' legs struck the side of the fountain. He tumbled backwards into the water.

"I don't want to hurt you," she said as Datio approached her.

Naevus scrambled to get out of the water. He was thoroughly soaked and far angrier than she had ever seen him. He levered one foot over the side of the fountain as she backed towards the entryway to the courtyard. She would be in raven form and out of this place in a shadow's breath.

Selene willed herself to turn. Her mark would not obey. She was severed from it, as she had been from her abilities mere moments ago. Her mind could make no sense of it. Why could she reach one and not the other?

Naevus and Datio crept towards her slowly, as one would when approaching an escaped animal. She turned. If she could not fly, then she would run. She would be free of this place at any cost. Selene sprinted down the hall, caring only to get away, no matter the direction.

"Selene."

She stopped short at the sound of the voice and turned to find Cael. There was no time for words, as Naevus and Datio lagged only a few steps behind. They slowed upon noticing him. The men bowed in unison.

"Master Zephyrus," Naevus said between labored breaths. The man had no great love of running, nor of exercise in general.

Cael glanced from one man to the other. He scowled at Naevus' robe, which was so thoroughly soaked that it clung to his skin.

"It is far from courteous to track water across my entire estate."

Naevus' mouth gaped in the slightest. He bent to one knee and lowered his head, nearly to the floor as if in the presence of the empress herself. Selene could only imagine how mortified the man must be. It would be a lie to say it did not give her some measure of satisfaction to see it.

"I must humbly beg for your forgiveness, Master," Naevus panted.

"Remove that immediately and procure yourself a change of clothing," Cael ordered.

"Yes, Master Zephyrus," the man stammered. He pulled the soaked robe over his head with no small amount of difficulty.

"Third door on the right." Cael pointed down the hall. "There is a wardrobe in what will be your room for the night. You may take whatever clothing you deem suitable."

"You are very gracious, Master." Naevus bundled his wet robe between his hands and took a breath as if to continue.

"I will take Selene with me," Cael interrupted before Naevus could utter another word. "Your mistress will call for you in the morning when she is ready to depart."

The two men stared at him. Water dripped from the robe in Naevus' hands to the floor in a steady rhythm.

"Was I not clear?" Cael snapped. "Leave us."

The brothers bowed briefly with as much grace as they could manage. Selene averted her eyes from Naevus' bare bottom as the men walked briskly away. Once enough distance lay between them Cael started to walk, heading in the opposite direction. He turned back when Selene did not follow.

"Are you taking me back to Pyra?" Selene asked.

"No," he replied. "I am not."

A delicate tendril of hope twisted within her belly. "Then where?"

"I cannot tell you within these walls."

"You cannot steal me," Selene whispered as she caught up to him. "You said that it would only be the end of us."

"We have very little time," Cael warned. "The empress is on her way to the estate. If we are not gone from this place before her arrival, then we are done."

Cael took her arm then and they walked, slowing only when approaching footsteps could be heard. Selene thought briefly to ask where they were going, but decided that it did not matter overly much as long as it was away from Naevus and Datio.

After traversing several unfamiliar halls, they reached a modestly sized courtyard which was open to the night sky. Selene caught only a brief glimpse of starlight before Cael ushered them beneath a vine-covered arbor and onto a thin road carved from the jungle. Before them, a carriage stood ready. It was dark in color, as were the horses, and its lamps remained cold. It refused to remain in focus, as if some spell of concealment had been placed upon it. He ushered her inside. Within lay a familiar, yet unexpected face.

"Lady Selene," Remdig exclaimed enthusiastically, "It is ever so splendid to see you again." He looked better rested than when she had last seen him. "I do hope you hold no ill will about what occurred at Master Warig's establishment. The magic of the catacombs is a nasty business indeed. You could never have been placed on the market with it hanging about."

Selene stumbled into her seat as the carriage pulled roughly along the narrow road through the jungle. She could not imagine how Cael had managed to convince Warig to give the gnome up, nor what he planned to do with him now that he had claimed ownership.

"I was as eager to be rid of the magic of the caves as my former mistress," Selene replied. "You've done me a great favor."

In truth she had not been aware of it until after Aster had requested its removal, yet beyond that point the mere thought of it clinging to her skin like a coating of barnacles had turned her stomach.

"All is well, in that event," Remdig announced happily. "And I look forward to many years of valued service upon our return to my homeland."

"Your homeland?"

"Yes, indeed. I'm Evarian born, just as you are. I was captured by Evarian mages and sold to the Kerell long ago. I'm lucky that Master Warig saw my potential. Most of us just end up rendered to dust. The empress must have her precious tablets, you see. Wouldn't want a rogue blemish popping up to ruin that youthful face."

"We're actually going home?" Selene steadied herself as the carriage pulled from dirt to cobbled city road.

"If all goes as planned," Cael replied with a sigh.

"Did Xaiden not relay to you what I said?" she asked.

"He did."

"Yet you came for me anyway?" She edged towards the door. "Stop the carriage and leave me here."

"Why would I do such a thing?"

"Pyra will not cease until she finds me. I can't imagine what spell you cast to free me from the effects of my circlet, but I can only assume that it's temporary and will dissipate with time." She turned to Remdig. "Are you responsible for this?"

Remdig drew a deep breath. "It certainly isn't beyond my abilities to do so." He puffed his chest with pride. "But I assure you that I cast no such spell upon you. That would be unnecessary."

"What in the name of the Spirits do you mean by that?" She looked to Cael. "You said that you couldn't afford to purchase me. I can only assume that my value has risen since I am with child."

"You're with child?" Remdig echoed. "In that case I must extend my hearty congratulations, Lady Selene. Who sired the child, if I might ask? The talk in town was that you were to be mated with Xaiden, but having known him for better than a hundred years I can't imagine that he would do so without your permission, circlet notwithstanding."

"Perhaps that's enough, Remdig," Cael suggested. It was a struggle to see his expression, for little moonlight penetrated the windows and there were no lamps within.

"Will you at least tell me now where we're going?" Selene asked after a moment of awkward silence, within which Remdig hummed quietly to himself.

"To the colosseum," Cael said.

"Whatever for?"

"I cannot say just yet. If we're captured while traveling and you know nothing, then you'll be in no worse a position than before."

"And what of you?" she asked, for she could think of naught else to say to which he might offer a reply.

"If my plan doesn't work, and they take us, then it will be best if you don't think on what happens to me."

Selene asked no more questions as they rode, but rather gazed out the window in thought. She preferred the city at night, when glowing stones lit the empty streets with ethereal light. She often gazed upon them when returning from one of Pyra's beloved parties, and welcomed the silence as Datio and Naevus dozed on the seat across from her. It suddenly occurred to her that she would not set eyes upon the two brothers again in her lifetime, if the Spirits were with her.

The colosseum was dark upon their approach. The carriage pulled to a side entrance, which held a narrow door. Cael exited hurriedly and Selene followed, with Remdig close behind. It was a rare night, at least by Kerell standards, for a few scattered clouds crossed the usually clear sky. One of the larger ones had obscured the moon, blocking its light. It was ideal for staying hidden, yet not so much for being able to see.

"You remember what I said?" Cael reached up to retrieve some small item from the driver, who remained invisible in the darkness.

"Yeah, you've only repeated it five or six times now," the man replied.

"Jevelir?" Selene whispered.

"Hello Selene." The man tipped his hat. "Luck of the Tides in there."

"Thank you," Selene replied, for she knew not what else to say.

They left Jevelir and slipped beneath an awning of cloth. There they stopped at the narrow door, which upon closer inspection was composed of iron and heavily bolted. Remdig pressed his hand against the metal. The bolt hissed as it retracted. It swung open upon silent hinges. Cael motioned for them to follow and stepped into the darkness beyond.

Selene ventured cautiously into the shadows. Cael's outstretched hand caught her just in time, as her second step met only air. Her eyes adjusted slowly. It was not a room which they had entered after all, but rather a descending staircase. Remdig eased the door closed behind him, and at a muttered word the steps emitted a faint glow.

At the bottom of the staircase lay an open area. The rattling of chains could be heard as if something large moved within. The familiar scent of decay slithered into Selene's lungs, and with it her latent ability begged for release. She could feel his anger, the bloodsoul elephant, and in that moment one small part of Cael's plan became clear to her. Several rows of glowing stones brought the creature to light. It was much bigger, and much closer than she had anticipated.

"Hmmm." Remdig considered the creature as if it was some small curiosity.

Selene's head barely reached the bottom of one of the creature's massive tusks. It had not been clear from the seats of the arena just how large the monstrosity was. It swung its head from one side to the other and stomped its feet in irritation. Her latent ability touched upon the hunger of a bloodsoul, this was familiar, but there was something else here as well.

"My, but this is a magnificent creature," the gnome muttered, perhaps more to himself than anyone else. "These bones, they hold magic with so little effort. What wonderful things I could make of them."

The bloodsoul issued a rumbling growl and bent its head down towards Remdig.

"Ooh," he exclaimed, still foolishly unafraid. "Why, look at that. I've never witnessed the skull of an elephant before. The hole makes it seem as if it should have just one large eye. How odd."

"Focus," Cael demanded. "Can you remove the magic that binds it, or not?"

"Yes, easily. This magic is nothing. Poorly woven. Of course, a mage could never achieve the level of magic of a gnome. Not even close. That's why they grind us into little tablets of pressed powder. Pure jealousy."

Cael turned to Selene. "You must order it to stay on the lift until it reaches the arena. We'll climb the stairs to meet it. From there we set it free, with orders to destroy as much of the city as possible. It should cause enough distraction for us to escape this place without notice. Remdig will free Felan while you and I handle the bloodsoul."

"We are to free Felan, then?" she confirmed.

"I thought we might," Cael replied. "Although if you would prefer not to, we could just set the bloodsoul loose and go."

It might not have been a jest, by the expression upon his face.

"What of the other battle Rakaii?" she asked.

"I could free a few of them on my way by," Remdig offered with excitement.

"Fine," Cael agreed. "But battle Rakaii only. None from the death match wing aside from Felan."

"The more chaos the better, I say."

"Are you trying to get us killed?"

"Obviously not," the gnome replied. "That would be rude, seeing as you freed me."

"Get on with it, then," Cael ordered. "We haven't much time."

"Yes, yes." Remdig rubbed his hands together briefly. "You might give it an order first."

Selene's ability rose to the surface at the words. The bloodsoul held as much anger as any of the human variety, though the feeling of connection was altogether different.

"*Stay where you stand,*" she uttered in the rumbling language of bloodsoul.

The elephant planted its feet firmly on the ground. Its head continued to shift from side to side.

"I have the lever at the ready," Cael called from the other side of the room.

Selene did not feel anywhere near as ready as Cael sounded. "I fear it might not understand me well." She had never attempted to command an animal bloodsoul, due to the fact that she had not previously encountered one.

"Let us hope that it does," Remdig replied. "Well, no time to wonder. One, two, and go!" The man clapped his hands. A snapping sound rung out as the magic holding the bloodsoul dissipated. The iron clasp that had tethered the great beast's leg split in two. With a clattering noise it dropped to the floor.

Selene drew an even breath as the elephant swung its head to face her. She focused on the steady beat of her heart, and the command she had given the bloodsoul.

"*Stay,*" she repeated.

"She's ready," Remdig said. "Raise the lift."

Well-oiled gears moved smoothly together. What had seemed to be a solid floor shifted apart and began to rise, taking the bloodsoul with it.

Selene's ability urged her forward. "I'll meet you in the arena." She clambered onto the platform.

"Selene, wait."

It rose more quickly than anticipated. Cael slipped from view, and she found herself in a closed room behind an iron gate. The platform had stopped a few inches below ground.

The bloodsoul's anxiety grew. Its low growl vibrated the floor beneath her feet. Sand spilled onto the platform from the arena, which lay just beyond the gate.

Selene placed a hand gingerly upon the bones of the bloodsoul's leg. *"Calm,"* she whispered.

The creature did not wish to be calmed. An oddly familiar feeling slithered into her, twisting through her connection with the beast. *Revenge*. The word entered her mind as she identified the comfortingly familiar emotion.

*"We shall have it, my friend,"* she whispered.

"Got it." Remdig's voice rang out over the rattling of the gate as it pulled open.

"Can you not do anything quietly?" Cael chided as he appeared.

"There are no mages close enough to hear us," Remdig countered. "They would have already arrived. We're also about to blast a massive hole in the wall of the arena, might I add. Thus, I feel that sounds must not be as much of an issue as you're making them out to be."

"I haven't missed you overly much," Cael replied.

"You're the damned fool who purchased me from Warig," Remdig countered. "So, I have to assume that's a lie."

"I'll admit nothing," Cael informed him.

*"Follow,"* Selene ordered. She led the bloodsoul out into the arena. The area was larger than it had looked from above. The sand remained warm beneath her bare feet despite the dark of night.

"You should give it some instructions before we set it to roam the city," Cael said.

"How did the mages get it in here?" Selene asked. There was no door large enough to fit the bloodsoul, at least not that she could see.

"They brought it in piece by piece, or so I have been told. But I have a better idea for its release." Cael opened his palm to reveal a stone no bigger than a songbird's egg. "This was made by Jevelir. It is set to explode upon striking any surface with force."

Selene placed a hand upon the bloodsoul. The creature's rage fed through her, fueled by her own. *"Destroy everything in your path upon leaving the arena,"* she commanded. *"Make your way to the center of the city, and then to the top of the hill."* Selene visualized the road to the empress' palace in her mind. *"Spare no Mage nor any Rakaii who attempts to harm you."*

"It's done," Selene said, returning to the common tongue.

"In that event, I'm off to free some battle Rakaii," Remdig announced happily.

"Wait for the signal, if you please," Cael requested.

"Yes, yes," the gnome replied with a wave of dismissal.

"And don't forget about Felan," Cael added.

"I never forget anything," Remdig informed him. "Well, nothing of importance, at least."

"The spell?" Cael gestured towards the bloodsoul.

"Ah, yes." Remdig waved his hand over the bloodsoul's hind leg. Its bones, and what little flesh was left upon the creature, glowed briefly with violet light.

The bloodsoul's rage snapped abruptly from Selene's grasp. "What did you do?" she asked.

"Shielded him from incoming magic," Remdig replied. "Can't leave our distraction vulnerable, can we?"

"Can mages cast healing spells?" Selene asked. She could not help but think of how her healing ability shattered bloodsoul to dust.

"Some few can," Remdig replied. "It's a terrible drain on their magic. Not sure how that would matter, mind you. Unless you're planning on slicing through a few mages on your way out of the city? I'm not against the idea, so we're clear."

"I was simply curious about their magic," Selene replied, mostly to keep Remdig from continuing. "If they seek to harm me, I'll certainly return the favor, but I believe I shall leave most of the destruction to our bloodsoul, as it seems they are made for the task."

"Suit yourself," Remdig replied. "Though a bit of retribution never hurt anyone who didn't deserve it."

With that the gnome ran off. A flash of light pierced the shadows of the arena as he made his way through a previously hidden door.

"He's an odd one," she noted.

"Always has been," Cael replied. "At least as long as I've known him." He clutched the stone that Jevelir had given him. "Shall we?"

Selene nodded. Cael approached the wall of the arena until he was nearly ten feet away. There he drew his arm back and released the stone. She could not see its flight, but within a few seconds the air before her burst with flame, and the ground shook enough to knock her from her feet.

The bloodsoul surged forward before the dust could settle. Selene rolled to one side as it thundered past her. The massive bones of the creature's feet struck where she had lain only seconds ago. It had missed her chest by no more than a shadow's breath.

Cael's hand found hers. The curiously strong burn of his mark flashed through her as he helped her to stand.

"I can feel you," she said.

"It's no longer of any consequence," he replied. "We must go."

Selene ran with him, trusting that he could see his way through the dust better than she. She had thought they would follow the bloodsoul's path, but instead she found herself at the door through which Remdig had made his escape. Cool air, heavy with the scent of animals and the straw upon which they were kept, rushed to surround her as she followed Cael through it. This was not a set of stairs, as she had assumed, but rather a short hall. It led to a rounded alcove which contained the now-empty cages of the higher rank Battle Rakaii.

Further along, the ceiling disappeared. The décor became considerably more ornate, and she soon came upon an area she recognized. The portrait of Islyr glared down from the wall above her. They were now in the holding area for the death match Rakaii. Selene glanced into the cell where Felan had been kept as they rushed past. It was empty, so with luck Remdig had done as he had promised.

"Spirits keep him," Cael swore.

She at first thought he was speaking of Felan, but as they moved forward an overturned chair caught her eye. It lay directly across the line where the barrier for the next cage should be. Felan's cell was not the only one that had been opened. Remdig had taken all of the death match barriers down despite Cael's warning.

The rattling groan of the elephant bloodsoul reached her. By the volume of its cry there was now some distance between them, but its voice shook the walls in the slightest all the same. Selene spotted movement ahead as the sound ceased. A burly Rakaii emerged from the shadows in front of them, blocking their path.

"Should we assume that Remdig blocked their circlets from control?" Selene asked.

The question had barely left her lips when she was wrenched from Cael's grasp. She attempted to twist free, but whoever held her was much stronger. Her back and head slammed against unforgiving stone. She struck out with her levitation ability but missed. The air was heavy with dust and the world refused to still, making it impossible to find her attacker. Nearby someone cried out in pain. A heavy thud sounded. A body dropped to the floor. Had it been Cael?

Thick hands closed tight around her throat. Above her a strange, wide face loomed, resting on muscular shoulders. The man growled as some wild creature would. She summoned her latent ability, but before she could use it Cael appeared. With a touch of his hand the man collapsed. Cael pushed him aside. Selene took the hand he offered and struggled to her feet. The feel of his mark was different. It came with more strength.

"You claimed them with your ability?" she asked, though in truth she knew the answer.

"I did," he admitted.

"And their energy? Their souls?"

"Fractured," Cael replied as he picked up speed. "Don't mention this to Xaiden."

They found their way at last to a little door which led out into the night. The silence that met them was quickly dispelled by scattered screams and the distant crash of falling rubble. They ran not towards the carriage, as she had expected, but rather down a narrow alley that loomed nearby.

"Will you tell me now where we're headed?" she whispered between ragged breaths. Months of being forbidden to exercise had withered her endurance.

Cael hesitated.

"When, if not now?" she urged.

A clattering noise erupted from the alley ahead. Voices argued loudly in Kerell. Behind them a carriage sped by. It stopped abruptly, blocking their escape.

Cael gripped her shoulders. His panic carried plainly through the bond of the circlet.

"Can you fly?"

She nodded, though in truth she had not left the ground in so many days that it seemed an eternity. Shadowed figures rounded the corner at the end of the alley. The hands of the closest lit with magic, casting Cael's face with an auburn glow.

"To the east," he whispered. "The low caste docks."

"You're coming?"

He shook his head. "Look for a green light at the helm."

She opened her mouth to protest.

"Please go," he begged. "Promise me that you will."

Never before had she felt such fear from him.

"I promise."

Selene took a deep breath and summoned her affinity. Her circlet dropped to the cobbles below. She had no time to think on it. The mages had already spotted them. She ignored the pain that encompassed her as muscle and bone rearranged themselves. Her body remembered. She reached her raven form easily, as if no time had passed since her last transformation.

Selene took to the sky. A burst of flame licked the feathers of her left wing. The heat of it forced her aside. She struggled to right herself and pushed higher, hoping for the shadows of night to hide her. Flashes of light emanated from the alley. She desperately wanted to go back to help him. Her promise alone kept her from doing so. She flew east, as he had said. The city below was in chaos. The bloodsoul was carving a path of destruction towards the palace, though it was visible only in scattered sections of light.

The docks were dark when she reached the air above them. She circled once but failed to find the green light he had spoken of, nor indeed any light at all. Perhaps it had not yet been lit? *Or they have been found*, her mind echoed. She circled again. Was she in the wrong place? There was no way to know. Neither Pyra nor even Aster would dare to be seen at the docks of the lower caste, and thus she had never been there. She circled a third time. In the waters far from the shore she spotted it, a faint green light. She turned, coasting on the currents high above the water. The ship was fast, but she drew closer ever so slowly.

Selene struggled to fly in her final descent to the ship and landed hard upon the deck. She re-formed and was at once surrounded by shadowed faces. A hand was offered. She accepted. The calming rush of Xaiden's mark greeted her. With it came relief.

"What of Cael?" he asked.

She shook her head. "I don't know."

He had not made it yet, but perhaps he would still.

"Back to work," Xaiden ordered the others. The group parted at his urging and began hauling items from the deck to within the hull. It seemed that they had not had time to finish loading before they set sail.

"Come," he said gently. "Let us find you some clothing."

She could not make out any faces through the darkness. Xaiden guided her to a nearby chest which sat against the railing. Beyond it the city of Kerell was dwindling from sight. Light flickered in odd places, as if consumed by flame. She would have wished it all to be consumed by fire, if not for the fact that Cael still likely walked within it.

Selene pulled some thick piece of clothing over her head at Xaiden's urging. Only then did she realize that she had been shivering with cold.

"You should rest," he said.

"No." She leaned against the railing, as she had so many times during their voyage to this place. "He might yet come."

Xaiden sighed.

"Tell me how he managed to free me," she demanded. "He did not steal me from Pyra, that much I've learned. But I know that he could not afford to purchase me."

"Does it matter?" Fatigue clawed at Xaiden's voice.

"It does. There are so many men here. I assume that they're all Rakaii?"

"They are, yes."

"And he purchased them all?"

"If I explain, will you rest? Your condition is delicate."

"The only delicate condition you should be concerned with is the state of my temper," Selene snapped.

Xaiden drew a deep breath and turned away. She could only imagine the scowl that must currently encompass his face.

"Yes, I promise to rest if only you will explain," she consented at last when the silence became too much to bear.

He ushered her into the depths of the ship, down a narrow hall and into a small room with several cloth hammocks strung across its length.

"He purchased most of the Rakaii over time," Xaiden explained as he pulled open a nearby cabinet. "Remdig, he traded for. We visited the cave and captured the female volantes you told us of."

"Warig won't render it to powder?"

The creature had attempted to kill her, but only to defend its clutch of eggs.

"He will not." Xaiden handed her a blanket and pillow. "Volantes are far too valuable for such. I have no doubt that he will sell her for breeding."

It came as somewhat of a relief.

Selene turned to face him. "Tell me plainly, is there hope for Cael yet?"

"He demanded that we set sail as soon as Remdig and Felan reached us," Xaiden said in place of a reply.

"He wanted to be certain the ship could leave before it was discovered," Selene realized as she clutched the blanket to her chest. "We were to fly to reach it."

It would have worked, had they not encountered the mages. Who would think to look for birds in the sky at night?

"You should not have doubted his intentions," Xaiden said. "He gave up everything he gained in this place. He sold his entire estate to Pyra. That, along with a touch of his latent ability, was enough to buy your freedom."

"I believe I do want to rest now," Selene's voice trembled.

"As you wish." Xaiden reached for the door.

She took hold of his arm. "You'll wake me when he arrives?"

Xaiden offered her a somber grin. He said nothing as he closed the door behind him.

# A Ship of Mages
## *Evaria – Capital City*

Islyr scanned the horizon. It was empty, mostly. A single ship approached through an expansive stretch of deep, Evarian blue. By its speed it would be close enough to dock in little time.

"You think this is the one?" Viverr asked. The rogue pulled a spyglass from his belt pouch and lifted it up to one eye.

"Do you not trust your source?"

"The whole of the Thieves' Guild is trustworthy. Every last one."

Islyr could not tell if the words were meant as a jest.

"You look, then." The rogue handed him the spyglass.

Islyr accepted it. "The flag is of teal and gold," he noted upon scanning the vessel.

"So?"

"It's certainly a Kerell vessel."

"How many mages do you think could be on it?" The rogue shifted a silver coin nervously through his fingers as he spoke.

"No more than a few, if the Tides are with us."

"And what are we to do once they disembark?"

"In truth, I don't know. That depends on the number."

"Couldn't we just borrow a couple of the kingdom's cannons and blow them from the water?" Viverr suggested. "It would be easier. And less likely to result in our deaths."

"Though perhaps they will have constructed some magic to protect against the attack of cannons," Islyr replied.

"Perhaps," the rogue agreed. "But that's not the whole reason for your reluctance. I'd bet a few silver on it."

"I would prefer it if they were disposed of by my own hand," Islyr admitted.

"I'm sure you would," Viverr replied.

"How else could I be certain that they're truly dead?"

The coin stopped, trapped between his finger and thumb. "I can't imagine."

"Every success in hunting marked ones and magical creatures will result in the empress sending more mages to Evaria," Islyr said. "The Goddess will not be denied."

"Sometimes an empress and sometimes a Goddess," Viverr mused. "Is this a person or a deity?"

"Both," Islyr replied. "If the Book of Life is to be believed."

"And what do you believe?"

"She is a mage, albeit a powerful one who has lived far longer than she should."

"Sounds dangerous," the rogue remarked.

"She is," Islyr agreed.

They fell temporarily to silence as the ship pulled up to the dock.

"Should we kill them outright?" Viverr asked. "I could fetch Kith."

"It would be safer," Islyr replied. "Though not as entertaining. No, I think not."

"You have an odd idea of entertainment," Viverr said. "But you're in charge."

"Yes, I am," Islyr confirmed. "For now, we wait until they disembark. Try to look inconspicuous."

Viverr rolled his eyes.

"And keep the pig quiet."

"I'll try," the rogue informed him. "Potato is not fond of mages."

"A sentiment we share," Islyr said. He watched with feigned patience as the plank was lowered and passengers funneled onto the dock. It was only as the first of them drew close that he noted the strangeness of the crew.

"What's this then?" Viverr wondered aloud. "Those are no mages."

It was true. The members of the ragged looking group were no more likely to be in the employ of the empress than Viverr's scrub pig.

Islyr squinted towards the end of the dock. The one in the lead had a familiar look about him.

The rogue squinted along with him. "Is that Xaiden?"

# Return
## *Evaria – Capital City*

Selene stared in disbelief at the row of shops that lined Evaria's docks. "How can it have changed so little in the time we've been away?" A flutter of excitement reached her at the sight of the city despite the sadness that lingered just beneath.

"It seems as if a lifetime has passed," Felan agreed.

He had changed more over time than Evaria had, though perhaps not as much as she would have expected from his days in the colosseum. It was difficult to perceive, caught only in the odd, quiet moments now and again.

"How do you think I feel, then?" Remdig asked as he pushed his way to Selene's side.

In one hand he carried a glass lantern. Within it was the one-winged pixie hybrid he had purchased at the market in Kerell. Spirits knew how or why he had brought the creature with him. Perhaps Warig had not wanted it.

"No matter though. We're home now, aren't we Miranda?" Remdig said.

"When did you learn her name?" Selene asked.

"Ah, well," Remdig said. "I decided to make up a name for her. She still refuses to speak with me."

"Are you certain she can speak?"

"Both pixies and faeries can speak," Remdig reasoned. "It would be odd if she couldn't."

Miranda hissed at him as he held her enclosure aloft.

"It's been several lifetimes since I've seen this place." Remdig grinned. "Several human lifetimes, I mean. They're so terribly short. It's a shame, really."

Selene had been attempting to distract herself from Cael's absence in the long weeks since leaving Kerell. Remdig's antics had helped somewhat, though they were far from enough to keep her mind from him completely.

Remdig wrinkled his nose. "This place is abhorrent."

Selene glanced over Evaria's docks as she walked. Stacks of crates were scattered across it, with nets and fishing equipment strewn in piles between. Nothing out of the ordinary for a port.

"Perhaps it's not as clean as Kerell," she admitted.

Felan surveyed the dock. "Doesn't look terrible to me."

"Not the physical aspect," Remdig corrected.

"What other aspect is there?" Selene asked.

"The magic." The gnome gestured grandly with his free hand, as if they could see magic clinging to the city like ice in winter. "My beautiful spells. They're just falling apart."

Selene offered Remdig an amused look.

"Not figuratively," he added, as if to hammer the point home. "Literally. What sort of half-rate mage did you hire to look after things while I was gone?"

"The most recent one was named Damaeus," Felan informed him.

"Is he around somewhere?" Remdig asked.

"He's dead," Selene replied shortly. The mage's name still caused her stomach to twist uncomfortably.

"That's a shame," the gnome muttered. "I would have liked to smack him directly across his incompetent face."

Selene could not help but laugh.

"That would be right after I ask him which refuse pile he shoveled his magic skills out of." Remdig paused and squinted towards the end of the dock. "Now there's a familiar face. And famous, I might add."

Selene followed the gnome's gaze to find Islyr. He returned the smile she offered and accepted her embrace as they met.

"I've missed you," she said as she released him.

"I was concerned when I heard you'd been sent to Kerell," Islyr replied. "I would have given my life to stop it, had I the chance."

"All did not turn out as we had hoped," Selene admitted. The thought of it nearly brought fresh tears.

"Well, I'm happy to see you safely on Evarian shores."

"There were times when I thought I might not be able to return. It seems that nothing went as planned."

"Nothing ever goes as planned when mages are involved," Islyr informed her.

"It's a pleasure to see you again, Ferir," Remdig said. "Though surprising. Word is that you're dead."

"Islyr," he corrected. "Never call me by my Kerell name. They speak the truth when they say Ferir is dead."

"I understand," Remdig replied evenly. The gnome never seemed to take offense to words of any kind, no matter what was said. "I also wish to rid myself of the memory of that place."

"You're acquainted with each other?" Selene asked.

"Yes," Islyr replied. "We met on several occasions while enslaved by the Kerell."

"I find it more interesting that the two of you have met, in fact," the gnome said.

"We're siblings," Islyr explained.

"Yes, it certainly does look like it," Remdig said. "And your personalities are very similar. I'm hardly surprised."

"We became reunited by a few twists of fate long after my escape from Kerell," Islyr informed him.

"Why hello Viverr, it's so wonderful to see you," the rogue announced to himself as he reached them. "Thank you ever so much for watching the castle while we were gone."

"Hello Viverr," Selene offered. It was good to see the rogue, despite how trying his personality could be. It was nothing compared to the annoyance that Datio and Naevus had provided her.

"I would thank you much more if you hadn't lost the king," Xaiden said.

It was the first thing the man had said for several days. She could not help but be thankful, for his near silence had unnerved her somewhat.

"How'd you know about that?" Viverr asked, bewildered.

"Because the Empress is training him as her personal Rakaii," Selene replied. "I saw Devren there, in the palace."

"The palace is a dangerous place." Islyr's voice grew distant. "Perhaps worse than the colosseum."

"I can't imagine anything worse than the colosseum," Felan muttered from behind her.

"There was no way to free Devren," Selene admitted. "The security of the palace was too much to even consider it."

"It is impossible to enter the palace without permission," Islyr agreed knowingly. "The magic there holds too much strength."

"I could get through it," Remdig announced. "Like a knife through cream."

"I believe you mean butter," Selene corrected.

"Whichever." Remdig shooed the correction aside with a wave of his hand.

"Then why didn't you?" Felan asked.

"Have you lost your senses?" the gnome replied. "Only a complete fool would take on the empress without an army behind them. I said I could get through the magic. Her Rakaii and guardsmen are quite another matter."

"She has sent a great number of mages to Evaria already," Islyr said. "And she will no doubt send a great many more. I believe we are now firmly at war with Kerell."

Xaiden sighed. "Indeed. We will begin to discuss a plan for defense at tomorrow's first light. Today, we must rest."

"Of course." Islyr looked over the line of bewildered marked ones who trailed with varying degrees of speed behind them. "It seems that you returned with a great many despite the odds. What number of them did you manage to save?"

"Eighty-seven, in all," Xaiden informed him.

"An impressive rescue," Islyr said.

One corner of Xaiden's mouth twisted downward. "It was Cael who accomplished the feat."

"I see," Islyr said. "It was a valiant sacrifice."

"It is possible that he could still live," Selene added. She was not yet ready to believe otherwise, for it would bring far too much pain.

Islyr gazed thoughtfully upon her. "Come, sister," he said as he wrapped an arm about her shoulders. "I'll take you to your room. I'll send for mint tea, from the kitchens."

Selene nodded in consent and allowed Islyr to lead her. Now that freedom stretched beyond her with the length of the world, she had little idea what to do with it.

"I'll take some of that tea as well," Remdig announced. "Black tea though. Herbal types belong right in the midden heap if you ask me. And I'll need someone to show me to the alchemy lab of the worst mage in Evarian history. I assume that he had one?"

"Yes," Selene said. "We did take a few things from the room, but it remains mostly intact."

"Can't say I'm disappointed that he's dead," Remdig said. "I assume he must have done himself in with one of his own spells, poor thing."

"Not exactly," she replied.

"I find that extremely surprising. Though I suppose it's of little consequence either way. I'll need additional supplies. I'm assuming the room will be poorly stocked. It will take quite a large amount of magic to defeat the mages of Kerell, even for one with so much talent as myself."

"I suppose I could show you where it is," Viverr offered.

Selene had to assume that the rogue intended to pilfer some things while inside. Cael had forbidden him from doing so, but it seemed that the room now belonged to Remdig.

"Ah, a volunteer," the gnome said. "You and I shall become the greatest of friends."

"I don't recall saying anything of the sort," Viverr replied.

"Nonsense." Remdig held Miranda up so that her lantern was level with Viverr's face. "First, you'll show me to this Damaeus fellow's lair, then Islyr will order us one regular sized cup of black tea and one miniature one from the kitchens."

"For the pixie?" Viverr asked. "Where's my tea?"

"She's not a pixie," Remdig corrected. "She's something entirely new. Isn't that amazing? I've decided to call them fixies. Selene can fill you in on the rest."

Viverr offered her a confused look.

"That's really the whole of it, as far as I'm aware," she informed him.

"That's all of it?" Remdig echoed. "I discover a new species, and that's the only thing you have to say?"

Selene drew a deep breath. "Congratulations on your discovery, Remdig," she said evenly.

"It's hardly a new species when there's only one of them," Felan piped in from somewhere behind them.

"That's true," Viverr agreed. "If you want to hear something really amazing, listen up. I recently encountered a unicorn."

"I don't perceive you as someone who can see unicorns," Remdig noted.

"How dare you?" Viverr replied with mock indignation. "I'll have you know that I'm as meek as can be. And I didn't say that I saw one, I only said that I encountered one."

Evaria's castle stood as steady as time, resting high above the city. The longer Selene was away from the land of Kerell, the more her experiences there seemed like a nightmare rather than reality. *Perhaps not all of it was terrible.* She rested a hand gently upon her belly as she walked. *Might it be all I have left of him?* She had to believe that it was not.

"Is it tame?" Viverr leaned down to inspect the inside of Remdig's lantern.

"By the Goddess, I should hope not," Remdig replied. "Wouldn't want her to lose her spirit, would we?"

"The most dangerous thing in this world is hope," Viverr quipped. "The second most dangerous is pixies, or hybrids thereof."

"Hope is all I have left," Selene said.

Both rogue and gnome paused to look at her.

"What are you thinking?" Islyr asked.

"I'm thinking that we must go back to Kerell," Selene said.

# Forever
## *Kerell – Capital City*

Cael kept his eyes on the intricate pattern of glazed tiles beneath him. He had come to know the palace by its floors. Tan and black in the kitchens, mauve and gray in the empress' bedroom, and here, in the throne room, turquoise and white. His knees ached. They had for the past few hours. He had lost track of how many days had passed. Had it been six weeks? Perhaps not. Perchance it had been far more. The powder she mixed with each of his meals had thieved all sense of time. It scattered his thoughts and stole all reasoning from him.

The empress stroked his hair thoughtfully as one would some small, treasured pet. Her perfectly polished nails ran down his back. Shivers crossed his flesh in a wave. She stood, and so Cael stood with her. He risked a glance at Devren, who had been placed on the opposite side of the throne. The boy didn't look up from the floor. Two sets of bare feet tread softly against the tile to approach the empress.

"If you are wise, then you have come to tell me that all is prepared," she said.

The mages' footsteps ceased. They bent to one knee.

"All is nearly ready, Goddess," the mage closest to him said.

It was a grave mistake, at least on this day. The empress was in a foul mood, and they should not have approached her until the task was complete. She raised a single finger. Cael moved swiftly forward and pressed his hand against the man's forehead. The mage's eyes grew wide, and he had time to utter no more than a breath as Cael ripped his soul from his body. The mage crumpled to the floor. Cael closed his eyes briefly as the pleasure of it cascaded through him. He could not touch the empress' thoughts through his circlet, but a subtle gasp told him that the feeling had reached her.

The empress circled her finger gently inward. With a groan of agony Devren's bones cracked. He melted into his shadeslight form. A creature of night, it was pale and faded even in the meager light of the throne room. The empress flicked her hand outward. Devren slipped like an oily shadow across the floor and onto the mage. A sound like boiling water reached Cael's ears as Devren consumed the man, melting the flesh from his bones like ice from a branch in the heat of spring.

"Beautiful," the empress exclaimed with glee. "I shall never tire of it."

"Tidy that up and place it in the cabinet," she ordered as Devren returned to his human form.

The boy looked as if he might soon vomit.

Cael could not have protested Devren's treatment, even if he had wished to. Some trick of the circlet had rendered him unable to utter so much as a word. He plucked an empty tray from a nearby table and began to pile the mage's bones upon it. They were clean, as smooth as fine silk, and sickeningly warm to the touch.

"Now, you may speak."

"Yes, my Goddess," the remaining mage replied. The shaking motion of his smallest finger, nearly imperceptible, remained the only visible tell to portray his fear. "Your warships are prepared. They are ready to sail at your word."

Cael took the tray of bones to a small cabinet behind the throne. It opened silently at his approach. Inside was the source of the empress' power; a collection of rendered magical creatures. The bones would be taken down to ash, and then compressed into pills small enough to easily swallow. Who could know how much magic the mage held in his bones at the moment he died? The Empress would claim the whole of it, however insignificant.

"Send them out at first light. The trinkets that have been bestowed upon me thus far are not enough to satisfy your Goddess. You will bring me the bounty of the Wildlands."

Cael hurriedly placed the bones in an empty spot on the shelf. He paused as movement caught in his sight. A stone jar sat to one side. It was different from the others; larger and marked with gold lettering. The jar rattled, knocking against the smaller one next to it, which tipped from the shelf. He grabbed for it. The drugs slowed his responses, both mental and physical. He managed to catch it before it could tumble to the floor, though just barely.

The empress snapped her fingers. She did not look at him, but there was no need for her to do so. Cael set the jar carefully onto the shelf and closed the doors. He returned the tray and took his place at the empress' side.

"Yes, Goddess," the mage assured her. "The Wildlands are yours by divine will."

The empress crooked a finger. Cael took a capsule from a small, gilded bowl and placed it upon her waiting tongue. He then handed her a goblet of honey wine. She tipped it to her mouth and swallowed delicately. The woman moved like a shadeslight. Perhaps that was why she enjoyed Devren so much.

Pain, like the point of a knife against flesh, pierced Cael's mind. It was not due to anything he had thought. Much like those of her upper caste, the empress would never be so base as to listen to the thoughts of a Rakaii. She sent these small jolts of pain several times per day, to serve as a reminder that he was her property and would be so forever. Most of all it, was a reminder that he must obey. It didn't matter. She could have him, but she would never have Selene.

# A Note from the Author

Thank you so much for taking the time to read my work. It means everything to me that someone might love the stories I create as much as I do! If this story has inspired you, please consider leaving a review on your favorite bookseller's website – that kind of support goes a long way to help independent authors!

# About the Author

Originally from Canada, Angèle has lived in many different states and provinces over the years. When she's not writing novels you can usually find her spending time with her family and menagerie of animals or helping pets and their people at her "real" job at an emergency veterinary hospital. She enjoys both fantasy and science fiction, and is an avid aquarist and gamer.

www.ingramcontent.com/pod-product-compliance
Lightning Source LLC
Chambersburg PA
CBHW070734120726
47910CB00001B/94